Praise for Phillipa Ashley

About the Author

Phillipa Ashley is a *Sunday Times*, Amazon and Audible bestselling author of uplifting romantic fiction. After studying English at Oxford University, she worked as a copywriter and journalist before turning her hand to writing. Since then, her novels have sold well over a million copies and have been translated into numerous languages. Phillipa lives in an English village with her husband, has a grown-up daughter and loves nothing better than walking the Lake District hills and swimming in Cornish coves.

Phillipa Ashley

All We Want For Christmas

PENGUIN BOOKS

PENGUIN BOOKS

UK | USA | Canada | Ireland | Australia
India | New Zealand | South Africa

Penguin Books is part of the Penguin Random House group
of companies whose addresses can be found at
global.penguinrandomhouse.com

Penguin Random House UK,
One Embassy Gardens, 8 Viaduct Gardens,
London S W 11 7B W

penguin.co.uk
global.penguinrandomhouse.com

Published in Penguin Books 2025
001

Set in 10.4/15pt Palatino LT Pro
Typeset by Six Red Marbles UK, Thetford, Norfolk

Printed and bound in Great Britain by Clays Ltd, Elcograf S.p.A.

The authorised representative in the EEA is Penguin Random House Ireland,
Morrison Chambers, 32 Nassau Street, Dublin D02 Y H68

A CIP catalogue record for this book is available from the British Library

I S B N : 978–1–804–94558–2

For Joy Skeels,

Happy Birthday

xxx

Chapter One

Lara gazed up at the fells in sheer amazement. The first snow of the Lakeland winter had arrived at Ravendale Castle, dusting the trees with icing sugar and adding snowy hats to the statues in the gardens.

She crunched across the cobbled courtyard that led to the front of the castle. Here the view was even more spectacular, with white-robed mountain peaks soaring into a sky of washed-out winter blue.

It was a scene of perfection, and, if Lara had her way, snow would always fall exactly like this: just enough to look pretty without causing any disruption. However, as she was painfully aware, the weather in this remote part of the Lakes had never run to plan – rather like her life.

At least today the snow had made its entrance with perfect timing for the Christmas at the Castle tour that would mark the start of the festive events programme at Ravendale. The previous autumn, Lara had landed her dream job as manager of this medieval castle tucked away in a remote corner of the Lake District, and it had been her idea to run the tours, offer festive afternoon teas, and create a Christmas-tree tour through the castle's principal rooms. The highlight of the events programme would be the Winter Spectacular, a fantastic light trail that would illuminate the grounds and hopefully draw in thousands of visitors.

Her fingers were firmly crossed, however, because the previous month a major glitch had threatened to derail their plans. Gerald, the well-loved castle maintenance manager, had gone on long-term sick leave and there was no sign of him returning – in fact, rumours had started to circulate that he might retire, though nothing official had been announced yet.

His absence had been sorely felt and meant that Lara had taken on the job of liaising with the illuminations contractors directly. On top of all her other duties as curator and events manager, it had been a big strain. Her history degree hardly qualified her as an electrical expert.

With a deep breath, she let her eyes rest on the snowy fells again, the view calming her as always, just as it had when she'd first arrived at Ravendale a year ago, nursing a broken heart and a loss that had been hard to bear.

She reminded herself that the light trail *would* happen, even if she had to give up sleep or meals for the next two weeks. And she wasn't totally alone: Ravendale had a team of enthusiastic staff and dedicated volunteers who had become her friends.

As the working day swung into action, they began to appear, pushing trolleys of supplies and equipment from the car park into the grounds.

Dull clangs rang out from the rear of the castle where the contractors had arrived to start installing the lighting infrastructure. A laundry van arrived with linen for the banqueting hall and café, and the local postie jogged up the stone steps to the oak door and handed over several parcels to the housekeeper.

Lara felt an electric thrill of hope and excitement run through her: Christmas had finally started at Ravendale. Surely this one – her second in the job – had to be a huge improvement on the last, which she'd spent hiding her sorrows behind a professional smile.

She was about to walk up the steps to the castle when she became aware of a new sound, one that sent a different kind of thrill through her, far more powerful than anything that work could inspire.

It was the distant roar of a motorbike. Nothing unusual there: the twisting road that hugged the Cumbrian coast was a magnet for bikers looking for a spectacular route. However, this was a working winter morning in November, and no summer bank holiday. It must be someone on their way to work . . . Even so, Lara found her feet rooted to the spot as the whine of the bike changed tone. It had become louder and lower, indicating that the bike had slowed to negotiate the sharp steep bend that led down to the entrance to the castle.

Then the engine sputtered and the motorbike came into view, gliding down the gravel driveway, leaving a trail in the snow. And somehow she knew, even though he was the last person she'd ever expected to see again, that its rider was Flynn Cafferty.

He killed the engine, kicked the stand down and lifted his long leather-clad limbs off the Harley.

3

Her pulse rate galloped like a runaway stallion. Surely he wouldn't look like she remembered? Not the man who'd filled her dreams and fantasies for the past two weeks before riding off into a dark November morning.

He took off his helmet and pushed his thick black hair off his forehead. His smile was warm enough to thaw an icy lake and turn her limbs to butter. In answer to her own question, he was even better than she remembered. She shivered, though Flynn seemed unruffled.

'Morning,' he said, looking her up and down in amusement. 'I must say this is rather nice. I hadn't expected a personal welcome party.'

Still stunned by his appearing out of the blue, it took Lara a few seconds to reply. 'This isn't a welcome party,' she squeaked. 'I mean – um, of course you *are* welcome, but I – um – wasn't expecting you. Are you visiting in the area?' she managed, remembering that he had once been a guest at the castle, even if that one night had turned him into more in some of her wilder dreams.

He'd booked into the Haunted Halloween Sleepover and they'd ended up working together to deal with a power cut – and got trapped in the castle dungeons together for a while. Nothing physical had actually happened – although she'd wanted it to – and being stuck in close proximity to Flynn wasn't something you forgot in a hurry – or ever.

His handsome brow creased. 'In the area? No . . . Hasn't anyone told you?'

'Told me what?' she asked, her confusion growing.

'That I've accepted a job here. I'm your new technical manager.'

'You? Our new technical manager? That's not possible,' she said, her shock and disbelief overriding her politeness. 'I mean, I don't see how it *can* be possible. Fiona and Henry haven't said a word about a new person being appointed yet,' she added. The aristocratic couple whose ancestors had owned Ravendale for centuries usually kept her well informed about anything that affected her role.

'Ouch. That's awkward. Fiona and Henry assured me that they'd warn you before I arrived. Gerald has decided to retire and I've been asked to take over as head of the maintenance team and I'm going to be in charge of the light trail.' He softened his tone. 'Fiona did say you were desperate for the help . . .'

'I – I mean, we, are – but everything's happened so fast. I didn't know you were even looking for a job. I thought you were going biking across Asia.' The last time she'd seen him, Flynn had told her his plans once he was finished with his work contract at the Cornish theme park.

'I was . . .' His dark blue eyes sparkled and Lara's stomach did a double flip. 'But this opportunity was too good to resist.'

Under that enigmatic gaze, Lara found it difficult to frame a coherent reply. Flynn had once again ruffled her outwardly calm and collected persona. 'I . . . I must speak to Fiona and Henry. I'm sure they meant to tell me, but everyone's been rushed off their feet with the light trail and the new events programme starting.' She needed to get hold of her employers at the first opportunity.

'I'm sorry, I've rocked up with no warning. No wonder you look so shocked.'

'No. No, don't worry . . .' Lara smiled, recalling that Flynn was now her colleague and she had to be professional. She was determined to regain control of the situation. After all, she was the one who'd been castle manager for the past year. Flynn was the new boy, even though he seemed perfectly at home already. 'I'm sure it's just an oversight.'

'Lara!'

One of the castle guides jogged across the gravel towards them. The tip of her nose was bright red and she was out of breath. 'Y-your t-tour party has started to arrive. I said you'd m-meet them in the great hall in a moment.'

'Thanks,' Lara said, recovering herself. 'Please tell them I'm on my way.' She left Flynn to unload his bike, hurrying through the melting snow and into the castle, trying to tame a maelstrom of emotions.

It had been barely two weeks since Halloween, when Flynn had made a dramatic entrance in a storm, arriving late and walking into the banqueting hall in his leathers. Sparks had flown between them that had nothing to do with the power failure that had plunged them into darkness. However, despite their instant connection, Flynn had ridden off back to his home in Cornwall the following day and Lara had expected to never see him again.

Since that chilly morning, she'd convinced herself it was for the best. Even so, Flynn was the only man she'd imagined falling for since the break-up that had led to her own move to Ravendale.

After the heartbreak of the split, she'd vowed to never get involved in a workplace romance again. Now, Flynn's reappearance – and as a colleague who she'd be living and working alongside at that – had threatened to derail her all over again.

Chapter Two

'And this, everyone, is the famous Lucky Chalice of Ravendale. It was given to the owners' ancestor by King Henry after he took shelter here on Christmas Day on his way to London. The Lake District was a wild and dangerous place in the fifteenth century and the king was grateful for the Penhaligons' hospitality. He told them that the castle would never fall and the Penhaligons would always prosper as long as the chalice remained intact.'

Having temporarily banished Flynn from her mind, Lara swept up the tour party with a winning smile. 'As you can imagine, we look after the chalice very carefully indeed.'

Every eye was on the simple glass goblet in the display cabinet. A velvet rope kept visitors at a safe distance and – just in case anyone decided to do something weird – the glass was bulletproof and built to withstand a sledgehammer.

'Bet it's worth a bomb, eh, love?' A man in a Santa hat smirked. Even though there was still over a month to Christmas, Lara didn't blame him for getting into the festive spirit early. Besides, the castle was chilly at this time of year. However, her heart sank at his comment about the value of the chalice.

'It's priceless to everyone at Ravendale,' she replied diplomatically.

'And has it ever been damaged?' barked a woman from the rear.

Lara smiled. 'Not as far as I know. Not bad when you think it's been here for almost six centuries. Shall we move on to the haunted tower and then to the banqueting hall for mulled wine and warm mince pies?'

She led her tour party down the stairs, savouring the tang of wood smoke and pine wafting up from the banqueting hall where the refreshments had been laid out on the oak table by Ravendale's catering team.

There were gasps as the guests gazed up at the vaulted ceiling with its coats of arms and floor-to-ceiling tapestries of medieval hunting scenes. The mullioned windows were filled with vases of holly and fir collected from the estate, but it was the tree that drew the biggest 'wows' of admiration. A twelve-foot spruce, it stood in the corner of the hall, its twinkling baubles and bows in shades of amber, red and gold. Lara allowed herself a quiet glow of pride, having supervised its decoration herself.

Everyone gathered around the fire, enjoying the refreshments and chattering about the castle. Lara answered countless questions about the legends and ghosts associated with the place, feeling the tension ebb from her body at last, relieved that the first festive tour of the season had been such a hit. She still hadn't worked out how she felt about Flynn returning. They desperately needed a technical manager, with Gerald now off the scene, and she had no doubt

Flynn would do a great job, but working so closely with him every day? How would she cope with that when her every cell zinged whenever she looked at him?

With a professional smile still in place, Lara said her farewells to the tour party, several of whom had booked for the Winter Spectacular on the spot. The catering staff collected the empty glasses and plates, leaving the oak table bare, save for an arrangement of greenery and the pewter candelabra.

Apart from the pop and crackle of the fire, it was blissfully silent. As she'd done many times, she almost had to pinch herself to believe that living and working in such a magnificent place was her job.

'Lara!'

Fiona Penhaligon strode across the floor towards her, a large vase of holly and ivy in her arms. A willowy platinum blonde in her late sixties, her formal title was Lady Penhaligon but she refused to let any of the staff address her by it. Her husband, Henry, was just as down to earth, considering he owned a massive castle.

Now was the moment to ask Fiona why Flynn had been appointed without her knowledge – as tactfully as she could.

'Are you all right, my dear?' her boss asked, placing the vase on the table with a concerned frown. 'I do hope your first tour wasn't too stressful. I passed some of the hordes on my way out. I must say they seemed very excited.'

'It went well,' Lara said, wondering how to introduce the subject of her new colleague. 'Um, I think everyone really enjoyed themselves.'

'Phew. That's a relief, although I can't say I'm surprised. You've worked terribly hard to organise all these events.'

'Thanks. It's always good to find that a plan works in practice. Christmas treats by the fire were very popular. Would you please thank Henry for lighting it?'

Fiona rolled her eyes good-humouredly. 'Oh, he loves lighting fires. Sometimes I worry he's a closet pyromaniac . . . Now, is there anything else I can help you with?'

Lara smiled again and took her opportunity. 'Well, I hear that you've found a replacement for Gerald.'

'You have?' Fiona screwed up her nose in discomfort.

'Yes, I – er – happen to have bumped into him earlier. He'd just arrived. It was quite a surprise.'

Fiona groaned. 'Oh, my dear, I am so sorry. It's all been so last minute. We only heard he'd accepted the job the day before yesterday and we were going to tell you, but with us only getting home from Hattie's in London yesterday evening, there hadn't been a moment.'

Hattie was one of the Penhaligons' two daughters and was a sculptor who had an art gallery in the capital.

'It's OK. I know how hectic things have been,' Lara said politely, seeing that Fiona seemed genuinely apologetic.

'Even so, we really should have warned you. Actually, we had planned to ask you and Flynn up to the flat this evening so we can all get to know each other better. Even better,' she added with a smile, 'why don't you come up to the flat at five and we'll have a glass of wine together? After all, we're all going to be working very closely together, so we want to get off on the right foot.'

Working very closely together. Lara's nerve endings jumped.

There was a crackle from the pocket of Fiona's ancient Barbour. 'Sorry, must get this.' She plucked a radio from her pocket. 'Hello. Jazz. Yes, yes, I'm on my way now. Give me two ticks!' She listened to Jazz for a few seconds before turning back to Lara. 'Sorry, Jazz needs me to finalise the menu for the reception. I must go. See you later in the flat. Well done, darling! You're a star.'

Lara could well imagine her friend and colleague, Jazz, tactfully trying to persuade Fiona to make a decision regarding the evening's menu. The reception was a PR and networking exercise for local suppliers, representatives from the tourist board, and hotel and accommodation providers. It had been Lara's idea as a way of showcasing Ravendale as an attraction at both Christmas and in the coming year ahead. It was important it went well and that they convinced the invitees to add Ravendale to their list of recommendations to guests.

Lara didn't see Flynn for the rest of the morning. Presumably he was settling into his cottage, and that afternoon she was busy dipping in and out of two more tours, conducted by other guides, to see how they were getting on.

As dusk fell, she took the chance to see how the light trail construction was going. The cables, bulbs and generators littered the grounds. The only illuminations at the moment were the harsh arc lights for the workforce as they hammered, banged and shouted to each other. Relief filled her. Although the trail had been her baby, she was more than happy to hand the technical duties over to Flynn.

It was past four, so after calling into her cottage to shower and change her fleece for a smart jumper, she headed back to the tower for her final and most important task of the day: checking that the Lucky Chalice had been taken back from the display case to the treasury safe after the last private tour. Lara trusted her guides, but her twelve years' experience managing historic properties and treasures had taught her never to leave anything to chance.

In the quiet of the treasury, she unlocked the safe and took out the blue leather box from among the other precious items of silver and gold. She put the box on the table and opened the lid. The chalice, about the size of a large gin glass, was nestled inside.

It looked pristine apart from an almost invisible fingerprint on its stem. Reverently, she removed it from its case, checking that the prints were the only marks on it.

She shuddered at the idea of what it was worth, yet it truly was priceless as a symbol of Ravendale and of its centuries of history. It had survived sieges, battles, family feuds and two fires.

'*Lara.*'

At the voice behind her, Lara started and lost her grip on the chalice. Time slowed down as it slipped through her fingers and tumbled through the air. With a soft thud, it landed on the oak boards between her feet.

'Oh God, no!'

Her cry of horror echoed around the room and her heart seemed to stop before she fell to her knees. The chalice was all that mattered now.

Chapter Three

Flynn knelt beside her. Over the past couple of weeks, Lara had often fantasised about having him in this position but she now wished he didn't exist.

'No! Please don't touch it!' She peered at the chalice, too scared to handle it herself.

'Bloody hell . . . it looks OK, though. It doesn't seem damaged,' Flynn said.

Lara met his eyes, which were full of remorse. 'We'd better hope not.'

'Maybe it's OK? These boards aren't like tiles or stone.'

'Maybe,' she murmured, finally lifting the chalice as gently as she could and standing up. She placed it on the table carefully, worried it might slip from her unsteady hands again.

'Can I do anything?' he asked, on his feet again but keeping his distance.

'Please don't touch it!' Lara said.

Wisely, he stayed silent as Lara peered closer at the glass, inspecting the rim, the bowl, the stem. It looked intact. She let out a breath.

Impossibly, there seemed to be no cracks. It *was* intact, which was a miracle after that fall. Somebody must be looking out for her.

She squinted at the chalice and her heart seemed to stop. *No. It couldn't be.*

'I think we got away with it,' Flynn said, with a sigh of relief. 'Phew.'

Lara stared at the glass, feeling sick. 'I don't think so.'

'What?'

'Look at the base. I think it's – I think it's chipped.'

He walked over to the table. 'Where? I can't see anything.'

'Look closer. It's only tiny but it's there.' She pointed to the edge of the base.

Flynn leaned over the chalice, his dark head of hair obscuring the chalice for a few moments before he turned back to her, his lips pressed together in a grimace.

'Yeah. I hate to say it, but I think you're right. It is only minuscule, and if you weren't looking for it, you probably wouldn't notice, but I'm afraid there is a tiny nick. I am so sorry.'

Lara sat down on a chair next to the table, her head in her hands. For six centuries, the Lucky Chalice of Ravendale had remained pristine and intact. Now, she'd done what sieges, battles, fire and flood could not achieve: ruined the most precious item that the Penhaligon family owned.

She glanced up. 'I could lose my job. I'll have to resign.'

'Whoa. Hold on. It can't be that bad, can it?' Flynn said gently.

Although on the verge of tears, Lara held them back. 'It is. I've destroyed a priceless object, the one thing that matters more to the family than everything else in the castle. I

15

must tell Fiona and Henry – but how can I?' A groan of frustration slipped out.

Flynn's hand was on her arm, his voice soothing. 'Hold on a minute. Take a breath. Let's think about this before we do anything rash.'

'It's too late for that. We, I – *have* done something rash. There's no way I can hide this from Henry and Fiona. I'll have to offer my resignation.' The enormity of the situation rolled over her like a truck. 'Just when I'd found a job I love and a place I want to stay.'

'Lara. Lara. I know this is upsetting—'

'Upsetting? It's a disaster.'

'Now wait,' Flynn said calmly, but with an edge of firmness. 'It's *not* a disaster. A fire burning the place down would be a disaster. Something awful happening to a guest or a member of staff or to you would be a disaster . . .'

She stared at him.

'What I'm trying to say,' he went on, 'is that this is unfortunate and not good, but it's not life or death, is it?'

'It might be,' Lara said, 'if you believe the myth around the chalice.'

He arched his eyebrows. 'And do you?'

'No, of course not!' She laughed bitterly, partly through embarrassment as she realised how dramatic she'd sounded. It wasn't like her to panic. She was cool, calm and competent. Normally. However, the combination of dropping the glass, the prospect of losing her job, and Flynn having a hand in it, had thrown all her normal rules of behaviour out the window. 'No, I don't believe the castle will fall and the family will have to leave Ravendale, but the fact remains. I've damaged a priceless piece of art and I have to do something about it.'

'If you're dead set on telling Henry and Fiona, then why not let me take the blame?'

She followed his gaze to the chipped chalice, which stood there, accusingly. Lara was acutely aware that he'd somehow taken charge of the situation and she needed to get a grip. 'Thanks for the offer, but you can't take the blame for the damage. For a start, I wouldn't let you. Besides, you haven't even started your job here. How can you go to the Penhaligons and tell them your first act has been to wreck the family's most precious heirloom?'

'Yet it's OK for you to do it?' Flynn asked. 'It was both our faults, but mainly mine, let's be honest.'

'I – I suppose they might not sack me,' Lara said. 'Even so, I'll feel my professional credibility has been shattered – not to mention their trust in me. I love working here. It's my dream job.'

'I already knew how much this place means to you,' he said.

That conversation had been almost three weeks ago, and since then she'd had to accept he'd been merely a guest passing through, like thousands of other visitors. She'd begun to think she might have imagined the briefest of kisses as he left and went off on his motorbike back to Cornwall.

Her shiver of desire ended when she caught sight of the chipped chalice again.

'I admire your honesty, Lara,' Flynn said gently, 'but

there is another solution, if you don't want me to take the blame or you to risk your job.'

'What?' she asked, torn between despair and hope.

'Don't jump down my throat before you've heard it, but can you get the chalice repaired – without anyone knowing, I mean?'

'I – well I suppose it could be – maybe.'

'You must know someone, with all your experience and contacts,' Flynn said. 'And won't it have to be restored anyway if you tell the Penhaligons? They'll need to claim on the insurance, surely?'

Either despite or because of her comment about the rarity of experts in the field, one name did immediately spring to mind. A name that caused a tiny spark of hope to flicker into life.

'Actually . . . I do know someone who might be able to help. A friend from uni. I've worked with her a few times before, but I'd still have to tell Henry and Fiona.'

Flynn raised his eyebrows. 'Would you really? I mean, do they look closely at the chalice that often?'

'No. Only me and occasionally the tour guides usually handle it. It was out for a special display today.'

'Do you think your restorer friend could be trusted?'

'To lie, you mean?' Lara asked, feeling nauseous at the prospect of such a charade.

'I mean to cover for you and keep a secret.'

'I suppose so . . . she probably would. I've put a lot of work her way and we've known each other a long time.'

'Then ask her.'

'I could, but it would be so wrong. I'd feel so bad about it. Lying and . . .'

'And what?' Flynn asked.

'And – nothing. I need to think about it.'

'I wouldn't take too long if I were you. Seize your chance,' he said.

He was right. Annoyingly right. Lara stared at the chalice. Even though the nick was tiny, it seemed to leap out at her like a giant crevasse – a gaping gorge of her stupidity and guilt. Why had she reacted so dramatically to Flynn's voice and appearance in the first place?

Flynn squeezed her shoulder briefly. 'Speak to your conservator friend and let me know how much the repair bill will be. We'll go halves.'

'Thanks. I do appreciate it,' Lara said, touched by his offer yet determined to take her destiny into her own hands. 'However, it was me that dropped it and I'll take the consequences.'

Chapter Four

Flynn opened the door to his staff cottage with a heavy sigh. He'd left Lara after she'd replaced the chalice in the safe and he still needed to decompress and change, ready for meeting the Penhaligons for welcome drinks in their private rooms in the castle.

After hanging his leather jacket in the vestibule, he decided a strong coffee was required.

His arrival at Ravendale couldn't have been more disastrous.

He'd hoped Lara would be pleased to see him. He'd *hoped* she'd been expecting him. He'd hoped his return to Ravendale wouldn't have turned into a horror show.

He'd brought his own coffee with him, but his hosts – now his employers – had thoughtfully provided a pint of milk, which was waiting in the fridge.

On closer inspection, he decided the one-bedroom Groom's Cottage must be a holiday let that had had been turned over for his use. It had that air of comfort yet minimalism and was too well maintained and smart for people to have lived in it full time. That suited him. He didn't like a lot of clutter and travelled light, both in life as well as on the bike.

It was pitch black outside at four-thirty. He thought of the modern apartment he'd left behind in Newquay overlooking Fistral Beach. It still wouldn't be dark there, due to the combination of the southern latitude, ocean and big skies all maximising the winter daylight.

Until a month ago, he'd been technical manager at a family-run Cornish theme park set in the grounds of an old estate. He'd enjoyed the job, even though he'd probably been in it too long. Sadly, times had changed, visitor numbers had dwindled, and the family had decided to retire and sell up. Flynn had taken it as an opportunity, as a signal that he should change his life and travel.

Yet here he was, plunging into the thick of a busy and unfamiliar role and already off on the wrong foot.

Flynn showered while the machine brewed his espresso, looking forward to a small comfort. He thought of messaging Lara, then decided not to put her under more pressure. The decision about the chalice had to be hers alone.

He'd managed to pull up his boxers when he received a message that drinks and nibbles were waiting in the sitting room and would he like to go along 'when he was ready'.

It was probably the first time a work induction with an employer had been framed in those terms, but he'd already met Henry and Fiona when he was their Halloween guest and liked them a lot. How could he refuse Henry's appeal for immediate help when the man, who was in his late seventies, had sounded so desperate and stressed out?

He felt terrible about startling Lara, and seeing her so conflicted about whether to tell the Penhaligons. He wished she'd let him take the blame, although he understood why she wouldn't. She was professional and honest; she played things straight.

The image of her in that crimson velvet dress at Halloween came back to him. That evening she'd worn her strawberry blonde hair long, so it had brushed the 'v' that had revealed her bare back. This afternoon, her hair had been restrained in a ponytail. Even in a Ravendale Castle fleece, eyes glittering with stress, he'd fancied her every bit as much as at Halloween.

No, he was lying. He fancied her *more*.

There hadn't been a day – or night – he hadn't thought about her since he'd left to ride home to Cornwall.

Deep down, he'd known from that moment that he'd take the castle job, despite his rational side telling him all the reasons why he shouldn't, like giving up his plans to take his first break from working in twenty years to follow his travel dreams.

He finished shaving hastily, nicking himself in the process and swearing again.

Ignoring the sting, he spritzed on the aftershave that he saved for special occasions. Finally, after hastily downing the now-lukewarm espresso, he decided what to wear. It wasn't a difficult decision when his wardrobe was 'capsule' at best, yet he hoped his shirt and jeans would be suitable for drinks with the Penhaligons.

Although he'd worked in and outside plenty of stately homes, he had to admit Ravendale topped them all for impact and grandeur. The castle – really a fortified house – had been built around a five-storey square tower with battlements on the top. Various wings had been added over the centuries and it was all surrounded by parkland that blended in perfectly with the rugged Lake-land landscape.

He'd been looking forward to taking the Harley out for some rides over the mountain passes, although now that he needed to take immediate control of the Winter Spectacular, that would have to wait until New Year. That is, if he lasted until New Year . . . his first day had hardly given him much optimism in that direction.

He'd swept and slicked his hair back as tidily as he could when his phone pinged with a message from Lara, whose number was still in his phone.

Still undecided. See you soon.

Still undecided . . . which meant he mustn't say anything about the chalice incident. Not that he would have dreamed of doing so without her permission.

He glanced in the mirror and sighed again. His first meeting with the Penhaligons as his employers – and with Lara as his colleague – was going to be challenging.

Chapter Five

'Ah, here he is! The man of the hour!'

Henry strode forward to meet Flynn, who wore a smile that looked as forced as hers.

In their brief exchange of messages, she and Flynn had agreed not to even mention their encounter in the treasury during the Penhaligons' welcome drinks. While the subterfuge kept Lara's options open, it also added another layer of deception. There would be many more, if she decided to go along with the plan of secretly having the chalice repaired.

Tonight should have been a chance to be introduced to Flynn as a new colleague. Instead, she felt as if her co-conspirator had walked in and the guilt was weighing on her like the granite the castle was made of.

Her butterflies weren't helped by the fact he looked like a Byronic hero, with his dark hair slicked back, black jeans, and a chunky jumper the colour of fir trees.

'Of course, there's no need to introduce you to each other.' Fiona's eyes twinkled.

Flynn put on a winning smile. 'No, we got to know each other pretty well at Halloween.' He looked directly into Lara's eyes, as if daring her to glance away, sending her temperature soaring.

Fiona invited them to sit down. Since Henry had chosen his wing-backed armchair and Fiona took a club chair, Lara and Flynn were forced to share the Chesterfield. She was close enough to inhale a subtle trace of his spicy aftershave, and tried not to fidget in her seat.

'Now, isn't this cosy?' Fiona asked, with a beam directed at Lara and Flynn as if they were her two favourite children.

Lara answered with a weak smile. 'Cosy' was not a word she would use to describe her sexy new colleague – and, she reminded herself, that was what he was. They would be working together in close proximity from now on and it would not be a good idea to get involved with him beyond a professional connection. She was still bruised and battered from her last workplace relationship, and she and Flynn needed no distractions from the important task in hand.

Henry huffed. 'It was blindingly obvious we should have taken on a temporary maintenance manager as soon as Gerald went off sick, but we kept bumbling on and letting other stuff get in the way of appointing a temp, until finally Gerald hinted he actually wanted to retire. All that time, poor Lara was shouldering the burden. Apologies, my dear.'

'Please don't worry, Henry. I was managing,' Lara replied. 'But some professional help will be very welcome . . .'

'Experienced maintenance staff are like gold dust in our remote little corner of the Lakes.' Fiona directed the comment at Flynn. 'And we didn't want to disappoint Lara – or the team – if you couldn't take the job.'

'And it was a long shot that he could hare all the way up here and start *tout de suite*. What time did you set out from Cornwall, my boy?' Henry asked.

'Actually, I set off yesterday and stayed overnight with a friend who lives up here,' Flynn said. 'But I'm fine. I like a good long ride.'

Lara felt a flush creep up the back of her neck. With her hair piled on top of her head, she was acutely aware her heightened colour would be visible against her fair skin.

'I'm sure. I did back in my day as well. I still haven't shown you my vintage Norton. Plenty of opportunity now, though, eh? I'll get us a sherry.'

Fiona rolled her eyes while her husband filled glasses from a decanter on the sideboard. 'I'm sure Flynn will be far too busy with his new role and the Winter Spectacular to tinker with motorbikes.'

'I'm sure he'll find the time. So, how are you settling in, old chap? How's the Groom's Cottage?' Henry Penhaligon was all rosy-cheeked affability as he handed a glass of sherry to Flynn.

Sitting in front of the crackling fire, Lara felt anything but affable. Her whole body was as taut as a wire.

'It's a great little place, thanks,' Flynn said, accepting the glass and sipping it. Lara would have bet her beloved old Land Rover that he'd never tasted sherry in his life.

'You're not far from Lara,' Henry continued. 'She's in Stable Cottage opposite if you need her.'

'How convenient,' Flynn said, exchanging an amused glance with Lara.

'Isn't it?' she ground out, wondering how he could joke at a time like this.

Fiona collected a platter of canapés from the sideboard. 'Our catering manager, Jazz, had these sent up. She's a gem.' She offered the platter to Flynn. 'You'll meet her soon enough. Won't he, Lara?'

'She's great,' Lara agreed. Having started working at Ravendale at a similar time, she and Jazz had hit it off very quickly and were now firm friends.

'These look delicious,' Flynn said, accepting a smoked salmon blini from a platter that also included Jazz's sticky mini Cumberland sausages and some mushroom tartlets. 'You needn't have gone to all this trouble for me, though.'

'Nonsense. I thought you'd need a bite to eat after that journey. If it makes you feel better, we have a candlelit drinks party in the banqueting hall tonight. Local businesses will be there. Jazz and the team were on duty anyway.'

'In that case, thank you,' Flynn said.

'These mini sausages are good,' Henry declared, helping himself to a second one. 'Grab one quick, my boy, before they're all gone.'

'You mean before you wolf the lot,' Fiona said, with an exasperated glance at her husband. She offered the platter to Lara. 'My dear? You must be famished after such a busy day and you know we won't get fed while we're mingling at the party.'

'Thanks,' said Lara, although her appetite was non-existent, even for the delicious sausages cooked in the chef's sticky, spicy marinade. They were speared on tiny sword-shaped cocktail sticks and she nibbled a small piece. Flynn, she noted, popped the whole sausage in his mouth. Clearly his conscience wasn't troubling him as much as hers was.

'I don't mind admitting I'm incredibly relieved that Flynn could start the job at such short notice.'

'You needed help and I was available. It was a no-brainer.'

'What will you do with your flat in Cornwall?' Lara asked, still not totally understanding the logistics.

'I'm going to rent it out. There are plenty of people who need a place to live in Cornwall, that's for sure.'

'Not left any broken hearts down there, have you?' Henry teased.

Fiona gasped. 'Henry!' She turned to Flynn, who sipped his sherry delicately. 'I'm so sorry. My husband has no filter these days.'

Henry looked perplexed. 'I've no idea what you mean,' he said, and Lara knew he absolutely didn't.

However, Henry's question made her wonder if Flynn was in a relationship or not.

'All my focus will be on Ravendale,' he said, answering Henry politely. 'And, on that note, can you tell me more about the Winter Spectacular?'

Lara was glad that he'd moved the conversation smoothly on to their jobs. They arranged a walkthrough of the site the following afternoon in order to do a trial run and spot any snags as dusk fell.

'We'll introduce you to the rest of the team properly in

the morning, and then I'm sure you'll want to get stuck in,' Fiona said.

Lara set her half-full glass of sherry aside. 'I'm afraid I have to pop back to the cottage to collect my radio. The drinks reception starts in half an hour.'

Fiona glanced at the elaborate clock on the mantlepiece. 'Gosh, yes! Time's flown by today! There aren't enough hours in the day at this time of year.'

Henry groaned and settled back deeper into his armchair. 'I could stay here with a whisky and a book. I'm too old for partying.'

'A, you're not old, and B, our guests will be expecting you, so I will surgically remove you if I have to,' said Fiona, with an arch of her eyebrows. 'It's only for a couple of hours, then you can slob around as much as you like.'

'I've never slobbed around in my life,' Henry protested.

'Then up you get,' said Fiona, with a wink for Lara.

The stratagem drew amused glances between her and Flynn too. He'd finished his sherry and stood up at the same time as she did, while Henry eased himself out of the armchair, muttering.

'I'll just touch up my warpaint in the bathroom,' Fiona said, 'while Henry gets his old bones moving.'

'See you at the reception,' Lara said.

Flynn insisted on her walking out of the drawing room, with a chivalry that would have amused her had she not been so troubled.

'I'd like to settle in and get an early night to be ready for tomorrow,' he said, as they walked down the stairs.

Once in the main hall, he made as if to head for the front entrance, but Lara stopped him. 'Not that way. There's a quicker route. Follow me.'

'You know all the secrets of this place by now, I guess,' he said, as they went through a small door behind the grand oak staircase.

'I know my way around,' she said. 'I'm sure you will too in no time.'

She had a feeling that he'd fit in anywhere he wanted to.

Her chest tightened momentarily as the cold night air hit her lungs. Flynn kept pace with her across the courtyard. A side archway marked 'Staff Only' led to another smaller courtyard, with offices and workshops and a gap cut into a yew hedge.

Her cottage came into view, a single lamp lit in the sitting-room window. Flynn's new quarters, almost opposite, were in darkness.

He stopped a few yards outside his front door. The winter moon shone down on his face and her heart did all kinds of things she didn't want it to do.

'Lara, I'm genuinely sorry to have landed on you so unexpectedly and caused such trouble.'

'The chalice was an accident,' she said. 'As for you coming to work here, Henry and Fiona are absolutely right. We – the castle needs someone to help. It's import-ant for everyone that these illuminations are a success. It's a major investment and we can't afford for it to make a loss.'

'It won't make a loss with you at the helm. Fiona told me

it was your idea to have the grounds illuminated. She said you've worked wonders since you first came here.'

'I wouldn't say wonders,' Lara said, keen not to hog all the credit and a little taken aback that her employers had spoken of her to Flynn. 'I've just tried to put a decent programme of events in place that we can build on.'

'And I'm here to support you. We can liaise on what you need at every step. You can call on me any time, night or day.' His serious expression told her he meant it.

'Thanks,' Lara muttered, wanting to look away from that handsome face. It was a face that could so easily melt a heart – yet he was a colleague and, now, a neighbour. She couldn't afford for him to become anything more. She'd learned the hard and very painful way what happened when you mixed business with pleasure. She shivered, surprised that the memory was still so raw over a year later.

'I need to get off to the drinks reception,' she said.

'OK. Have you decided about the chalice yet?'

Even the mention of the C word sent unpleasant shivers through her, yet the situation had to be faced. Henry had looked very tired at drinks, and Fiona seemed frazzled. She couldn't load any more worries onto them at this crucial time of year, especially when they thought some of their problems had been solved by the arrival of Flynn.

'I – still haven't decided 100 per cent. I'll sleep on it and then decide whether to contact my friend to ask if she could do the repair quickly and discreetly.'

He let out a breath of approval. 'I think that's a very good idea and, as I said, my offer to go halves still stands.'

'Well, I don't feel comfortable at all with deceiving the Penhaligons. I really need more time to consider all the ramifications. And if I do have it restored, my decision to pay for it myself stands too. But thank you. Now, I really have to go. I hope you get a good night's sleep in your new home.'

He smiled. 'Thanks, and I hope I do too. I've a feeling I'm going to need it.'

Chapter Six

Lara had to admit the banqueting hall looked incredibly festive. The fire blazed in the hearth and flickering candles were reflected in the coppery vases of holly and ivy. There were about sixty people in the room sipping wine, eating, and speaking loudly to make themselves heard. Catering staff, hired for the evening by Jazz, glided around, refilling glasses and offering canapés. The Christmas tree was lit with a thousand twinkling lights. No one could fail to be impressed by the venue.

Lara already had a dry throat from greeting people when she popped to the bathroom. On the way, she bumped into Jazz, who was talking to the head chef in a corner of the entrance hall under the staircase.

When the chef left, she took her chance to speak to Jazz. 'Hello! These canapés are so moreish. I've had about eight already. You've all surpassed yourselves tonight!'

'Phew. Good.' Jazz's smile was wide with relief and delight. 'I trialled a few before settling on those. Hopefully there's something to suit everyone. You have to think of so many different dietary requirements these days. I can't wait to go on holiday in the New Year.'

'I don't blame you. I'd like to be in Grenada now myself.'

'My grandparents can't wait to see me and the kids and we can't wait to see them,' Jazz said. 'But, wait, aren't you going to see your sister in Australia?'

'I'd like to . . . Mum and Dad are heading out just before Christmas and I said I'd join them.'

'So, you've booked the flights?'

'Not yet. I keep meaning to but I've been so busy.'

Jazz groaned. 'What are you like? Do it tonight. Otherwise, you'll have to pay through the nose.'

'I will . . .' Lara said, with a mix of guilt and regret.

'Look, let's try to find a time to go get a coffee in town. I need a break.'

'I'd love to.'

'Oh, and have you seen that new guy who's moved into the Groom's Cottage? I saw him earlier getting off a flipping Harley, for God's sake. Phew. He's hot, but don't tell my Luke I said that.'

'I – er – is that a new trouser suit? The colour really suits you,' Lara said, trying to change the subject and hoping Jazz hadn't noticed how red she'd gone.

'You like?' Jazz asked, smoothing the dark green matching trousers. 'I felt I ought to live up to the corporate image with so many events coming up. And it's festive.'

'It looks fabulous. And I like your hair like that.' Jazz was wearing her hair in a high bun with curly bangs.

'Good, because it took me ages! Now, I *have* to go. More vegan canapés are required and apparently two of the catering staff are having a domestic in the kitchen and the chef

34

wants me to read them the Riot Act because he's too busy. Speak tomorrow.'

When Lara returned to the banqueting hall, Fiona dinged on a glass and called for everyone's attention. 'Thank you, thank you, ladies and gentlemen. Don't worry, I'm not going to drone on, as Henry would describe it.' She gave him an indulgent glance before continuing. 'However, I must say a few words of welcome and thank you all for coming to Ravendale. I hope you enjoy a taste of the hospitality we can offer and hope you will see tonight as the first of many visits for you and your guests and clients.'

There were murmurs of appreciation from the guests.

'Now, many of you know that Ravendale is associated with many ancient tales and legends. We rather trade on them.'

Polite laughter followed Fiona's gentle joke.

'The most famous of these legends is our Lucky Chalice, which for those who don't know, was gifted to us by King Henry, who took shelter here one Christmas. He told the earl that Ravendale would never fall while it was intact.'

Lara broke out in goosebumps. It hurt to keep her smile in place.

'We are blessed with an incredible team of staff here at Ravendale, including our food and beverage manager, Jazz, who oversaw the delicious canapés and wine you're all enjoying. However, I'd just like to say a huge thank you to two more special people. One is our wonderful events manager, Lara Mayhew, who has transformed the events programme at the castle in the year since she joined us.' Fiona went on, oblivious to Lara squirming with embarrassment. 'Her energy, expertise and determination are having a significant impact on our revenue and, believe me, without an income stream, this castle really would fall. She is the ultimate professional.'

Everyone strained their eyes in an attempt to pick out Lara as Fiona mimed applause in her direction. Even though she forced a smile and tried to shrink modestly away, she was burning under the fire of praise she didn't feel she deserved. The moment the chalice had slipped through her fingers came back to her, making her feel light-headed.

Fortunately, Fiona had moved on to someone else.

'The second person I want to single out is my husband, Henry. He's been at my side for over forty years now and is my rock, although I did have to prise him out of his armchair like an oyster from his shell this evening.'

There was more gentle laughter as all eyes were now on Henry, including Fiona's own, giving him a loving look. Henry waved a dismissive hand in embarrassment, but Lara could see he was touched by his wife's praise.

How could she deceive these kind people? She'd have to admit her clumsiness in the morning. She'd tell Flynn that she couldn't go through with the subterfuge.

The speech ended with Fiona proposing a toast to Ravendale. Glasses were lifted high and, after that, everyone was chattering again. After half an hour, people began to drift away and Lara tried to recall all their names so she could make notes the next day. She had spoken to so many people: hoteliers, MDs of local companies, a tourist board PR guy . . . yet she couldn't remember much of what she'd said in return.

Soon, the hall was empty save for Fiona, Henry, and the catering staff clearing plates and glasses. Henry was complimenting Jazz and the head chef while Fiona made a beeline for Lara.

Her stomach turned over.

'Lara. I think that went very well. There were so many people who'd never actually been to the castle, despite it being on their doorstep, or they hadn't been for years. They were most impressed, I can tell you.'

'I'm not surprised. It's an incredible place . . .' Lara said, racked with angst.

'It's not merely the place. It's your ideas about showcasing it to the wider world. With a proper programme of events and nights such as this one, we look more professional all round and inspire confidence. A couple of people have said they'd love to hold corporate events here and one even asked if we can do conferences.'

'The MD of Fell Forest Products asked me about holding a summer conference too,' Lara said. 'He said his marketing team would be in touch next week.'

Fiona patted her arm. 'My dear, you have done amazing work. And I know managing the lighting contractors without Gerald was beyond your remit and added to your burden. Well, all that is over now. Flynn is here and, may I say, I now insist on you going straight to the cottage and to bed. You must be shattered.'

'I'm—' Lara was about to say fine, but decided to take the chance to escape and collect herself. Tomorrow would come round soon enough. 'I don't mind having an early night.'

'Then off you go and don't you worry about a thing.'

It came as no surprise to Lara that she didn't enjoy the restful night that Fiona had wished for her. When she eventually awoke at 7 a.m. the following morning, it was to the immediate recognition that she had to tell the Penhaligons that she'd damaged the chalice.

Fiona had been so generous the previous evening, praising her in front of the guests for being 'the ultimate professional' and lauding all she'd done for Ravendale.

Lara couldn't bear to keep harbouring this secret. And if – hopefully – they valued her as they said, she would admit her mistake, offer to pay for the glass to be restored, and they could move on.

That all sounded fine in theory, but she also couldn't forget that Fiona had mentioned the Lucky Chalice specifically. To Lara it was just an object: precious and beautiful, but she didn't for one second believe it had any magical powers. That was ludicrous.

A glance through her kitchen window showed a light in Flynn's own and she realised that she needed to warn him of her decision.

She wouldn't mention he'd even been in the tower when she had dropped the glass. It would only complicate things.

Things were complicated enough.

She drank a cup of tea and forced a slice of toast down

to give her energy for the ordeal ahead. Now all she had to decide was when. As Fiona had said, their days were so busy, but Lara was sure if she told Fiona that she had something important to say, her boss would find time.

She started typing a message to Flynn, but her decision and reasons were too complicated for a text. She could call him – or she could go across to his place and tell him in person. He deserved an explanation – just as long as he didn't try to dissuade her.

After throwing on a coat, she headed across to Flynn's, but hadn't even knocked on his door when Jazz hurtled from the archway that led to the castle courtyard.

'Lara!' she called. 'Have you heard?'

'Heard what?' Lara asked, meeting her a few yards from Flynn's door.

Jazz heaved in a breath. 'It's Henry. He's been taken to hospital! They think he's had a heart attack.'

Chapter Seven

'Lara? What's the matter?'

Flynn opened the door of the cottage to find Lara and another woman on his doorstep.

Lara looked up at him, pale with shock.

'It's H-Henry. He's been rushed into hospital,' she said slowly. 'Jazz just told me.'

Flynn pushed his hair out of his eyes. 'Shit, no. How is he?'

'We haven't had any further updates,' Jazz explained. 'I don't live on site, but I was here super early and saw the ambulance drive off. It had the blue lights on . . . Selwyn, the night porter, was around when Henry was taken ill in the early hours and said Henry had bad chest pains. The paramedics had him wired up. Selwyn said Henry looked in a bad way as they loaded him into the ambulance.'

Lara sat down heavily on the sofa. 'What if he dies? I'll never forgive myself if—' she bit back her words and Flynn guessed she'd been about to blurt out something about the chalice.

Flynn would have comforted her had Jazz not sat beside her and hugged her.

'It's not your fault, lovely,' she said.

'No, it isn't,' Flynn said hastily, realising why Lara might, in the shock of the moment, feel a degree of responsibility for Henry's illness. He was almost sure that Jazz, while clearly a good friend, wasn't privy to the chalice incident. 'Come inside, it's freezing out here. I'll make us all a cup of tea.'

In the end, Jazz didn't stay for a drink because she had to get back to supervising a business breakfast. It was now 8 a.m. and Flynn's own meeting with his new team was scheduled for half-past. Fiona had been going to introduce him, but that was now obviously out of the window. While Jazz said her farewells, he made a quick call to Carlos, the deputy maintenance manager, to postpone the meeting for an hour.

Seated at his breakfast bar, Lara sipped her tea. 'Did you put sugar in this?'

Flynn leaned against the worktop, mug in hand. 'Yeah. I thought it would be good for the shock. This isn't your fault, you know,' he added, before she could object to the sugar.

'I know – and of course I don't believe in the supernatural, but *what if*? What if there really is something in the legend? Henry collapsed less than twenty-four hours after I broke the chalice.'

'Henry's illness is just a terrible coincidence. Henry is – what? Seventy-five? He's responsible for a big estate and he likes to enjoy a few drinks and feasting from what I can see.'

'Seventy-seven. It's true he does live life to the full.' She sipped from the mug and didn't seem to mind his being rational.

'The castle is a huge responsibility and he said he didn't

feel that great last night. He attended a big event, he was on show the whole time, and I imagine up late. I'm very sorry to hear he's been taken ill, but that has nothing to do with a chipped glass,' Flynn said gently but as firmly as he dared.

'No. You're right . . .' Lara glanced up, seeming lost. 'When Jazz broke the news, I was on my way here to tell you I'd decided to confess about the chalice, but now . . . there's no way I'm going to add to Fiona and Henry's troubles. Sorting it out myself is the lesser of the evils. I'll call my restorer friend and see what I can do. Somehow, I must have it repaired without them knowing.'

'I think it's a good decision, but you don't have to sort everything out on your own. Please let me help in some way.'

'I – I'll see. Although I think the best thing you can do is carry on with your job. Ravendale needs us both more than ever now.'

Flynn nodded, relieved that Lara had decided not to confess in these circumstances. 'That's true for sure.' He was also glad to see a hint of pink begin to return to her cheeks, now that she'd decided on a course of action.

'I'll phone my friend and try to find out how Henry is, and then I'll come with you to the maintenance office and introduce you to the team myself. Let's just hope that Henry will be OK.' Her voice was steadier and, once again, Flynn glimpsed a steely core. You didn't become manager of a place like Ravendale without resilience and determination. However, he also wondered how much of Lara's cool professional demeanour was a defensive shell.

He still recalled her reaction when he'd kissed her cheek

and bid her farewell that frosty November morning. She'd seemed . . . bereft, as was he. He had also been unsure if he'd ever return, and uncertain that, if he did, it would be the right thing for either of them.

She put the mug down, a fresh resolve in her eyes. 'Belle likes to start work early. I'll call her now.' She picked up her phone from the breakfast bar.

'I'll give you some privacy,' Flynn said, leaving her in the kitchen while he went into his bedroom, where he'd set up a makeshift office on a dressing table.

He found the task list he'd written the previous evening, both for himself and his team. Later he had meetings with the lighting contractors and he'd have to be pretty full on with them so they knew that he wasn't going to be messed about. As Lara had said, it was now even more vital that the Christmas programme at the castle went smoothly, so that Henry could focus on recovering – if, Flynn hoped, he did.

He sent an email to his deputy and, once he'd stopped tapping at the laptop, he could hear Lara on the phone. While he couldn't make out all the words, he heard relief in Lara's voice and several 'thank you so much'es.

It was clear she was genuinely fond of the Penhaligons, just as he had been of the family who'd owned the theme park where he'd worked. He'd been sad when they'd had to sell up, and hell bent on seizing the moment to see more of the world.

However, wanderlust hadn't been his sole motivation for taking off in a new direction. It hadn't been that long since he'd been involved in a tangled romantic web back in Cornwall that had left him feeling betrayed and hurt.

What Lara didn't know was that it had been barely a year since Flynn had ended a relationship with a woman he'd met at a seaside pub. The break-up had stung, in so many ways, but mainly because he'd had no idea she was married until her husband had turned up in Cornwall out of the blue.

He'd had no inkling she was in any kind of relationship at all, and that, against every desire and instinct, he'd ended up the unwitting party in an affair. Having experienced the same kind of treatment in the past, and knowing how much it hurt, he would never have cheated on anyone. Ever.

Now he was truly free and single, though it was ironic that he'd absolutely not been looking for any entanglements. His road trip – seeing the world – had been his only focus until his Halloween visit, meeting Lara, and now this job coming up.

He still wasn't entirely sure why he'd gone and done the opposite of what he'd planned, though that was life, he supposed. It had a way of pulling the rug from under your feet when you least expected it.

'Oh! Thank goodness. That's such a relief. Though horrible for Henry.' Lara's voice had become raised and animated. It now sounded as if Lara was on the phone to Fiona. 'Please give him my best wishes. No, don't worry about a single thing.'

Some of the tension eased from his body as she continued and he listened harder.

'You just take care of Henry and yourself. We are absolutely fine.'

He walked into the sitting room, where Lara met him, shoulders slumped in relief. 'That was Fiona. Apparently Henry hasn't had a heart attack. It's gallstones. Apparently the symptoms can be similar.'

Flynn winced. 'I'm relieved it isn't his heart, though one of my managers at my old job was taken ill with gallstones and they're nasty. Poor old Henry. Is he staying in?'

'Fiona thinks he'll be kept for another couple of nights and then he's got to take things very easy and watch his diet. He might need an operation at some point in the future, but she said she feels confident enough to pop home for a change of clothes and a rest later this morning.'

'Well, I'm very glad to hear he's out of danger and being treated,' Flynn said.

Lara heaved a huge sigh, but her brief smile of relief melted away. 'I called my restorer friend, Belle. She said she might be able to look at the chalice the day after tomorrow.'

'That's good.'

'I'm lucky she said yes . . . I hate to do it, but it's probably a good idea if she comes to get it while Fiona and Henry are away. She said she could come over from Hawes tomorrow to collect it.' Lara swallowed. 'This still feels so wrong.'

'That's understandable but I think it's the right thing to do for everyone. Life doesn't need to be any more complicated for anyone at the castle at the moment,' Flynn said, hoping Lara wouldn't think his approval was only because he also felt partly responsible for the breakage. 'Like I said, I'm here to help in any way I can.'

'Thanks.' She seemed lost in thought for a moment before squaring her shoulders. 'Right. We have a lot to do. I told Fiona I'd introduce you to the team. Shall we meet in the estate office in ten minutes?'

'Absolutely,' said Flynn. 'I'm itching to get on with the job I came here to do.'

Flynn was grateful to Lara for introducing him to the staff he'd be working with. He could tell that they respected her. Her calm, quietly confident manner went some way to reassuring them that he might actually know what he was doing.

However, he still had a long way to go to win the trust of a team still shaken by the news of Gerald's early retirement and now Henry's illness. Gerald had obviously been well-liked – almost revered by Carlos – although his frequent absences in recent years had put pressure on the rest of the staff.

Flynn could tell they were wary of 'the new boss', with his funny accent and his direct style, and fully aware he had a hard act to follow.

After Lara had left, he spoke to them as a group, briefing them on what needed to be achieved. He also intended to speak to everyone individually over the course of the next day or two.

There were ten staff in total, covering all aspects of building services, including a painter and decorator, plumber, and two general handymen, all of them men older than Flynn, as well as two apprentices in plumbing and electrical work, both of whom were women.

Carlos was the most experienced, and had been acting as deputy to Gerald. A sharp-featured skinny guy around Flynn's own age, he sprawled over an old armchair in the corner, one leg crossed over the other, scrolling through his phone. Flynn thought he was letting Flynn – and everybody – know that this was his domain and he didn't like being usurped by some bloke with a country bumpkin accent.

'So, I know how well thought of Gerald was and is. I'm sorry he's had to leave but I'm ready to work with you and learn from you.'

Carlos snorted. 'I doubt you'll have anything to learn, boss.' There was an unmistakeable emphasis on the 'boss'.

'Flynn will do,' said Flynn coolly. 'This isn't CID.'

One of the apprentices, Holly, sniggered.

Carlos glared at her.

'Anyone else have any questions?' Flynn waited purely for effect, because he was damn sure no one would have any questions while Carlos was watching over everyone like a Rottweiler.

'OK? Great to hear you all know everything, then. But if you do want to ask me anything, you can come to me anytime.' He grinned. 'Send me an anonymous text if you need to.'

The junior electrician smirked and Holly gave Carlos a death glare. There was no love lost there.

Carlos huffed and went back to his phone.

After the meeting, Flynn was left alone in the office, mulling over the scale of his task. He'd already realised Ravendale came with a unique set of challenges: as a Grade I-listed historic building, sourcing materials and planning any kind of work would take far longer and be more involved.

Gerald had planned to move the fire alarm control room from a damp former dungeon to a purpose-built building. There were other urgent jobs on the list too: the replacement of the antiquated lift used to convey supplies and equipment to the upper floors, for example. The fire safety system itself also needed an upgrade. All of those would have to wait until New Year.

His immediate concern was the Spectacular, which was due to start in less than a week.

At lunchtime, Flynn walked out of his office while munching a bacon roll from a paper bag when he bumped into Lara.

'Lara. H-hello.'

'Hi there. Working lunch?' She had an amused glint in her eye, which heartened him, although it quickly faded.

'Literally. I'm taking it with me to the Ice House. The contractors have come to fix up the reindeer display on the roof. I might have been quite firm with them.'

'That's a relief!' Lara replied. 'I can't wait to see it up and running. We have *so* many bookings for the grotto already. It's my worst nightmare that it goes wrong and the children are disappointed – let alone the parents.'

'Don't worry, I've made it a priority.' He dropped the

remains of the roll back in the paper bag and grinned, then became more serious. 'How's Henry – any updates?'

'Fiona says he's not in pain now, but he is being kept in for more tests and monitoring.'

'He'll hate that, surely?'

'Oh, he will, but Fiona is just relieved he's being treated. She also insisted the "show has to go on" and asked me to pass on her thanks to you and everyone for managing everything while she and Henry are away.'

'No need. The last thing they need is to worry about the Winter Spectacular not going ahead or some maintenance issue. It's the job I've been hired to do and I am going to make sure everything runs as smoothly as possible.' Tendrils of her hair had escaped its ponytail and she was pink-cheeked, as if she'd been hurrying. 'But you must be even busier now that Fiona and Henry aren't around.'

'You could say that . . .' Lara said. 'The group tours are in full swing from now until Christmas, and there are a string of corporate events. For the next few days, it's just me in charge.'

'Not alone?'

'No. There are four permanent guides plus half a dozen seasonal ones, and we've taken on a team of temporary stewards for the Winter Spectacular. How did you get on with Carlos and your new team?'

He thought before answering, picturing the dubious-looking faces when Lara had left him alone. 'They were polite – perhaps too polite, and a bit quiet.'

'They were probably scared of you.'

49

He chuckled. 'Carlos wasn't.'

'I think it's possible,' Lara said cautiously, 'that he feels a bit put out.'

'Ah, so he's upset that I took Gerald's job? Or the job he'd hoped to have?'

'Both, probably. He can be a spiky customer, but he's actually quite insecure.'

'Insecure? That's one word for it. I'm going to have my work cut out winning him over.'

'You're more experienced than them. You're used to a bigger set-up and you're the one with the degree in live event tech.'

Flynn frowned in surprise. 'Has someone shared my CV?'

'I went on LinkedIn as soon as I heard you got the job. Impressive.'

He wasn't sure if she was being sarcastic or not. It was sometimes hard to tell with Lara.

'Most of what I learned came on the job. I had a screw-driver in my hand from the age of four.'

She smiled. 'I can actually picture that.'

'My parents ran a hotel in Newquay until they retired a couple of years ago. I grew up learning to be a jack of all trades, helping them fix the endless stream of maintenance problems that used to crop up on an almost daily basis.' He folded his arms. 'What else does my CV say? Or did you get bored and nod off?'

'Not at all. I know that you trained as an electrician after you left school and did the part-time degree. Then you worked at various places in the south-west and London and eventually you ended up as technical manager of Kernow Park.'

He mimed applause. 'Well done.'

'So, you were born and brought up in Cornwall – but you have connections up here?'

'Yeah. My mum's parents lived in Whitehaven. Sadly, they've both passed away. I have a mate who lives near Keswick too – he's the one I stayed over with the night before I arrived here to start the job.' He broke off when his phone buzzed with a message. 'It's Carlos. He needs me to OK a decision on something that I know he's been managing perfectly well up until now.'

'Like I said, he can be tricky to deal with at the best of times, let alone now that his mentor has quit and a strange southern bloke they're in awe of is in charge.'

'You're not in awe of me,' he said with a grin.

'Ah, but I know you better than them.'

There was a teasing gleam in her eyes that made Flynn's pulse flutter. Her eyes reminded him of the sea in a Cornish cove on a perfect summer's day.

'Do you?' he asked, revelling in the pleasure of being able to look directly into her gaze, which held a hint of mischief – maybe desire, if he were being fanciful. 'Even though, technically, we've barely got to know each other?'

'Perhaps. It just feels like much longer,' she said, then glanced away, speaking briskly as if she regretted their flirtatious moment. 'So Fiona's home and getting some sleep, but she's going back to the hospital when Henry has more tests, and Belle is coming over tomorrow morning while they're out.'

'That's good to hear. Let's hope she can help.'

She nodded – with very little enthusiasm, Flynn thought.

He switched to a topic he guessed she would be more comfortable with. 'By the way, Carlos was persuaded to walk the light trail with me earlier and we're doing the snagging now. I thought we'd have a dummy run at dusk after Belle has gone and wondered if you'd like to join me later to make sure you're happy with everything before we go live? We could meet here at the maintenance office. How does four-thirty sound?'

'That's good for me,' Lara said, and sighed. 'It'll be a relief to see something going well for the castle after the past few days.'

Chapter Eight

'Belle. Am I glad to see you.'

Lara inched open the door like a traitor letting an enemy into the castle. She'd asked her friend to park in the staff car park and use a rear door that led into a utility corridor that had once housed the butler's pantry and boot room.

Belle smiled and whispered. 'I take it no one knows I'm here.'

'Well, I haven't broadcast it, but if anyone asks why you were in the treasury, I can legitimately say you're here to take a look at that twelfth-century beaker. Thanks so much for coming at short notice.' Lara was so lucky that Belle had been available. It had only been a couple of days since she'd damaged the chalice, though it already felt like months.

Lara led her up the stairs and into the treasury. Her fingers weren't steady as she opened the safe. Part of her longed for a miracle: to see the chalice as pristine as the day it was presented to the castle by the king.

While Lara laid the case on the oak table, Belle unwound an impossibly long scarf and took off a tweed trench coat that made her look like a female version of Sherlock Holmes.

They'd studied History together at Birmingham University

and shared a student house together in their final year, keeping in touch ever since.

Lara stood by silently – although she could almost hear the beating of her own heart – as Belle examined the glass, occasionally frowning or huffing meaningfully.

None of these noises or gestures gave Lara any confidence and her sense of foreboding grew until she was almost ready to snap with the tension. She certainly felt as if she hadn't taken a proper breath the whole time Belle had been examining the chalice.

Eventually, Belle laid the chalice in its case and looked up at Lara.

'Is it bad?'

'Bad?' She frowned. 'In what way?'

'The damage?'

'Um. It's not irreparable, no.'

'*But*? I can tell from your face that there's something wrong.'

'Hmm.' Belle gave a small, sad smile and spoke softly. 'I'm sorry, Lara. You know that, in the words of the late great Meatloaf, I'd do anything for you, but I don't think I can do this . . .' she said. 'Or, more accurately, I don't think I *should*.'

Lara hesitated. Part of her felt like screaming in frustration but another part felt relief. 'I thought you'd say that. And, actually, I agree with you.'

Belle's eyes widened. 'You do?'

'Yes, because I've lain awake worrying about asking you to repair it. I half-wished I hadn't, but I'm glad I did because, deep down, I've always known it was a lost cause. You're a conservator, not a restorer, and this isn't *The Repair Shop*. No matter how much I want the chalice to go back to how it was, I know that the chip is now part of its history. Restoring it would be an act of vandalism, for which I would be responsible.'

Belle sighed. 'This must be so difficult for you, but you are 100 per cent right. Of course, I could repair the glass. There are some near-magical materials these days and perhaps no one would notice, even on a pretty close inspection. Even so, I could never make my repair invisible.'

'And nor should you. I'm so sorry I hauled you over here for nothing and sorry I put you in this position.'

Belle patted her arm. 'It's fine. It really is. I'll admit I had all kinds of misgivings about the idea, but I needed to see the job first and I was sure you'd agree with me. Now I've had my hands on the object, I am 100 per cent certain that I shouldn't do anything to it.' Belle peered at the chalice again and frowned, as if she was willing the object to magically restore itself, just as Lara had many times.

'It's unique, isn't it?' Lara said mournfully. 'And so beautiful.'

'It's certainly both of those things . . .' Belle returned her attention to Lara. 'So, if we agree to leave it as is, what will you do?'

'I'll break the news to Henry and Fiona . . . eventually. When the right moment comes. Maybe after Christmas . . .' The thought of keeping the secret all that time made her feel slightly nauseous.

'Will they need the chalice in the meantime?' Belle asked.

'Unlikely. It does sometimes go on display when the castle runs a particular exhibition. We don't show it all the time because it's so important, and so that we can make a splash when it *is* out. Over the past few days, we have been showing it off to some guests who'd paid extra for a private Christmas tour of the castle's treasures. It's now been put away until February half term, when we hold our History of Ravendale week.' Which, ironically, Lara thought, was one of her own ideas.

Belle gave her an encouraging smile. 'I know this is easy for me to say, but they seem like reasonable people. I'm sure they'll be understanding. And then I'll be more than happy to do any conservation work required if that's the way they decide to go.'

'Thanks, and thanks for coming, even though you must have thought it was a terrible idea. It was brave of you to tell me the truth.'

'I've always told you the truth. Remember when I told you to dump that physicist at uni, even though you were mad on him?'

'Yes, I remember. You saved me there. Turned out he was sleeping with another History student and the Egyptology lecturer.'

'Then you know I'll always look out for you.'

Thinking about how simple and carefree those uni days had been, Lara locked the safe and shivered. The treasury was cool at the best of times but it felt icy cold today. She ought to get Flynn to check the temperature control system.

Feeling the chill, she turned to Belle. 'You don't believe that there's anything at all in the old chalice curse?'

'I thought it was meant to be a blessing, not a curse,' Belle said, then rolled her eyes. 'Do you even have to ask me? Look, you've had a stressful time, it's three degrees outside and this place, genuinely, is freezing. In fact, why don't we get out of here?'

'Great idea. And why don't I buy you lunch?'

Belle's eyes lit up. 'I never say no to lunch in a castle.'

By the time Belle left, the sun had already begun its descent to the horizon. The castle was situated only three miles inland from the western coast of Cumbria and the sun, dipping low over the sea, had painted the fells in fiery hues. There was snow forecast for the higher tops overnight, and Lara knew it would look magical.

The beauty of the sunset reminded her why she'd wanted the job so much in the first place, and made her all the more determined to keep it.

Darkness was falling by the time she arrived at the maintenance office a few minutes early. Two of the apprentices were inside having a coffee break, but they said they didn't know where Flynn was. Lara checked her phone and hoped he'd turn up soon.

Outside, the contractors were still busy 'snagging' and making sure that everything would run like clockwork from the very first visitor to the last. Their vans occupied a large portion of the maintenance compound. Cables snaked to and from humming generators screened off from the public areas.

Although Lara had seen digital mock-ups of the trail at presentations, this was the first time she would be able to experience the complete trail in its full illuminated glory, even if it was far from ready for the public.

It seemed like an age since she'd first started working with the illumination contractors, Wizard, which had been almost as soon as she'd joined Ravendale. In January, they'd met to discuss the initial concept, which would showcase key moments in the castle's history with light and sound installations around the grounds.

She was determined that Ravendale's lights would inspire awe and delight. Ticket sales were healthy, thanks to ongoing advertising since late summer, but the Spectacular had been a substantial investment and needed to become an annual fixture.

The two apprentices left and Lara was checking her phone again when Flynn bounded into the office.

'Hi there. Sorry I'm late, I was held up on a call with the Wizard creative director.'

Lara's antennae twitched. 'And is everything OK?'

'Just going through final snagging.' Having seen her anxious expression, he smiled. 'We're almost there. Everything will be fine on the night, I promise. Are *you* OK?'

'Yeah. Well, not really, but – can we talk about it later? I really need to have something go well today.'

'It's not Henry, is it?'

'No, he's doing well. Staying in hospital tonight and Fiona said they might let him out tomorrow. Belle, my conservator friend, came to have a look at *it*.'

'Ah.' He grimaced. 'How did that go?'

Lara checked no one was in earshot. 'She can't do it. Or doesn't think she should, and I agree. But I'm not going to tell anyone about it . . .' She lowered her voice further. 'Can we talk about it another time?'

Flynn nodded. 'Definitely. Shall we see the light trail?'

From the moment Flynn had shown her the brightly lit archway at the entrance, Lara had felt her emotions bubbling up. This was the culmination of all her team's hard work.

The route had begun in the shrubbery, where the topiary yew hedges were lit with a changing palette of pink, blue, orange and white light that highlighted illuminated dragons, chess pieces and a griffon like the one on the Ravendale coat of arms.

'Here we are: Santa's Grotto!' Flynn declared.

The Ice House, normally a dank cave built into a small slope, had been transformed into a magical fairy cavern inside and out. All the trees and bushes leading to it were glowing with lanterns, while two full-sized illuminated reindeer grazed on the roof.

'It looks way better than I'd ever imagined. Like a fairyland.'

'I'm glad you like it. Is it OK that the reindeer are on the roof? I know the design showed them outside the entrance, but when the contractors set it up, I asked them to move the figures to the top. I think they have more impact and you can see them from further away.'

'I don't mind at all. I think they look brilliant up there. Almost real.' She laughed.

59

'The kids will absolutely love it.'

'Phew. I'm pleased it's worked out. Don't worry, I haven't tinkered with any of your other designs.'

All along the trail, the garden statues were aglow with coloured lights. At the formal gardens, the pond and central fountain were illuminated and accompanied by dramatic classical music.

'Pretty impressive, eh? The music really elevates the effect. I hear you chose it.'

Lara could only nod, dumbstruck by the spectacular beauty of the light display and the stirring music rising to a crescendo.

They moved on through the children's play area adorned with glowing figures of the woodland creatures that often visited the estate: red squirrels, badgers and foxes. There was also an interactive floor area where the children could set off a video of fish swimming through a pond.

'This might be my favourite,' Flynn said, leading the way to the Great Oak, one of the estate's oldest trees. Bright beams played over its trunk and lit up the canopy and the branches like skeletal fingers reaching for the night sky.

A shuttered cabin nearby would be aglow once they opened, selling hot chocolate and toasted marshmallows and mulled wine – as would the Castle Café. They hadn't even reached the courtyard, where projections of giant snowflakes would circle the castle walls, or had a chance to take in the dramatic green and purple lights highlighting the tower.

'Imagine everywhere full of excited kids, and with the choir singing carols in the courtyard,' Flynn said wistfully.

'It's . . . lovely . . .' Lara managed, too full of emotions to speak much. Embarrassingly, she felt a tear threatening to escape.

'Hey,' Flynn said, turning to her with a concerned frown. 'Are you OK? What's up? You're not . . . disappointed, are you?'

'No, no,' she insisted. 'The opposite. It's just such a relief to see everything in place and looking so much better than I even dreamed. Planning and organising it has been such a long slog and, at times, I wondered if it would actually happen, let alone be this good.'

'Well, it is, and that's down to you.'

She shrugged off the praise even though she secretly liked it. 'And the designers and techies at Wizard. They worked really hard, even if, up until a week ago, I was worried it would never come together.'

'Your vision and ideas started it and brought it to this point. I only took over at the very last moment.'

'Maybe, but Henry and Fiona have put their faith in me.'

'From what I hear from the staff, it seems as if everyone has been waiting to see the castle illuminated. This is a moment to take a breath and pat yourself on the back.'

'Hmm. I might do that when it's all over after New Year. You've done a lot in a couple of days, and I'm not sure we'd have been ready to open on time without you being here. Now Fiona and Henry can't be as involved, I don't think I could have juggled everything.'

'We haven't opened yet and I've only helped project-manage the final stages, but I'm glad I turned up too, even if you weren't too sure when I first appeared.'

'It was a shock. I'd expected to be . . .'

'Consulted? I promise you there was no plan to keep you in the dark. Look, we both need a break. Why don't we get off site and decompress and get to know each other properly? Is there somewhere we could go for coffee or a lunch later this week?'

'I ought to stay here . . .' Lara said. 'But I agree that a few hours away from the castle would do me good, especially after all that's happened.'

His eyes lit with pleasure in a way that made Lara tingle with excitement.

'Where do you suggest?' he asked.

'A new café opened in the village a couple of months ago but I haven't had the chance to try it yet. We could meet there?'

'Sounds like a plan,' Flynn said, digging his buzzing phone out of his pocket with an apologetic grimace. 'Sorry. Need to take this. I'll message you about coffee.'

Lara went back to her own office to make some calls and answer more emails – and agree on a time to meet Flynn at the Waterwheel Café later in the week. With the Christmas programme ramping up and her employers out of action for a while, she'd have precious few moments to herself and she sorely needed the café outing to look forward to. It wasn't a date, so it didn't break any of her rules. After all, what could possibly happen over a cup of coffee and a slice of cake?

*

The following morning, Lara was keen to see how Henry was when Fiona brought him home from the hospital. She found him sitting in his favourite armchair with a tartan rug over his legs and a cup of tea at his side.

'I'm hugely relieved to be home, even if I'm on a cocktail of painkillers and antibiotics,' he told Lara.

'And strict instructions about his diet!' Fiona declared. 'Low-fat healthy eating from now on. No port, cheese or rich sauces.'

'It's the privation that hurts the most.' Henry grasped his wife's hand. 'Seriously, I'm grateful it wasn't my ticker.'

'You need to look after that too,' Fiona said.

'I know, my dear. I'll be a veritable saint from now on.'

'Glad to see you still have your sense of humour,' Fiona said wryly.

Lara was glad he had too, but she was also dismayed to see that Henry had aged years overnight, which was no wonder when he'd been in pain and wasn't able to eat properly. Under his smile, he was a worried man, and Fiona's face was grey with exhaustion.

'We're both going upstairs for a nap,' Fiona said, before turning a sympathetic eye to Lara. 'And how are you coping, my dear? I am so sorry to leave you in the lurch. How is the planning for the Winter Spectacular going?'

'You mean, our own version of Blackpool Illuminations?' Henry declared with a chortle that turned into a cough and a wince.

Lara smiled. 'Not quite on such a grand scale, but I think you'll be pleased when you have the chance to see them.'

'And how's Flynn getting on?' Fiona asked. 'He's been thrown into the deep end.'

'Don't worry. I introduced him to the team and he seems to be getting on fine with them and the contractors. We did a walkthrough yesterday evening and they truly are spectacular. I don't think the visitors will be disappointed.'

Fiona's shoulders visibly relaxed. 'That's a huge weight lifted. I shall go and see them for myself tonight. I don't know what we'd do without you.'

Lara managed a smile. 'I only want the best for Ravendale.'

She had to hold off with any more shocks until after the New Year celebrations, and she only hoped Henry would feel up to those. He'd certainly be out of action for quite a time as far as work was concerned, and Fiona would be busy looking after him.

'I know and it's such a hectic time . . .'

'Especially with us oldies being *hors de combat*,' Henry chirped up.

'Quite, although I'm not sure I'd describe myself as an oldie yet, Henry.' Fiona shared a knowing look with Lara. 'Please make sure you have a break too. I know what an added burden you now have.'

'It's OK. Flynn being here and taking charge technically is a load off my mind.'

'Good. I'm still sorry we didn't warn you before he turned up, but I'm glad it's working out well.'

With a cheery nod for an answer, and hoping that her employers would be able to properly relax at last, Lara left them, thinking of her praise for Flynn.

On her way back to her office, she kept thinking that Flynn was working out almost *too* well. He had taken charge very quickly and seemed extremely competent. As for her reaction to him, it alarmed her how much she was looking forward to spending a few hours with him at the coffee shop.

It must not turn into anything even resembling a date. It was more important than ever to do a good job with the Winter Spectacular, because, she reasoned, the more indispensable she became, the more likely the Penhaligons would be to forgive her.

Chapter Nine

Flynn had considered offering Lara a lift to the Waterwheel Café on the Harley but was pretty sure she'd have said no. In the end she asked him to meet her there, as she had some shopping to do beforehand.

The village of Thorndale was about two miles from the gates of the castle. In summer, so he'd been told, there was a lovely walk to it across footpaths, but on a soggy late November day, Flynn didn't fancy getting soaked. There wasn't much to see anyway, with the fells hidden beneath low clouds as he rode to the café.

Newquay felt like a capital city compared to Thorndale, whose slate-roofed cottages were clustered around a tiny village green. At its heart lay the church, shop and pub, with the café situated on the road out of the village towards the dramatic lake and mountains of Wast Water.

As its name implied, the café had clearly once been a watermill, and its wheel was still in place over the beck, which tumbled down the valley. Flynn thought it was all very picturesque as he carried his helmet into the café. He hadn't spotted Lara's vintage Land Rover in the car park so didn't expect to see her yet.

He was greeted inside by a young server with red streaks in her hair.

'Just me and a friend,' he said, when she asked how many the table was for.

'OK. Table for two. Can I get you a drink while you wait?'

'Thanks. I'll have a cappuccino, please.'

'No problem.'

The place was half-full and Flynn took out his phone to check there were no urgent messages. He noticed a couple of the waiting staff steal a look at him when they thought he wasn't watching. Some people seemed to regard bikers as a threat and it amused him to think of their reaction if they knew he had a responsible position in the employ of the local aristocrats.

The waitress with the red streaks brought his coffee. 'Here you go.'

'Thanks.'

She didn't leave. 'I – er – saw your bike outside.'

'You did?'

'Yeah. Actually, I heard it before I saw it. My cousin has a Harley. Used to take me on the back of it sometimes.'

Now Flynn knew the reason for her interest in him. She wasn't wary of him, she was interested in his bike, which was much more palatable.

'Ever thought of learning to ride yourself?' he asked.

She snorted. 'Me? No way. I don't have the cash to buy a bike or pay for the lessons even if I wanted to.'

'Molly.' An older woman, who seemed to be in charge,

had appeared at the table. 'Do you mind helping out at the door? We have customers waiting for a table.'

'Sorry,' Molly said with a grimace. 'Coming.'

One of those customers proved to be Lara. She waved at Flynn and his heart gave a schoolboyish skip of pleasure. He heard her explain to Molly that her friend was already in the café before making her way over.

'It's warm in here,' Lara said, with a nod to the wood burner in the corner of the café.

'Very cosy,' Flynn replied, while she unwound a scarf from her neck and took off a puffa jacket. Her cheeks were tinged rose pink, either from the cold or from rushing about doing her errands. Her neck was lovely too – had he ever admired a neck before? And her eyes were beautiful. What was happening?

Oblivious to the desire surging through him, she sat down and nodded at his cup. 'How long have you been here?'

'Um. Only five minutes.' He snatched up a menu. 'Would you like a coffee? Or one of the hundred other fancy hot drinks they seem to offer?' he joked, to hide his discomfiture.

'Think I'll have a mocha, please. Best of both worlds: chocolate and caffeine.'

Flynn caught Molly's attention and she took their order but didn't linger this time, with her boss looking over her shoulder.

'Shopping go well?' he asked, still tongue-tied at having Lara sitting opposite him, not for any work-related reason but purely because she, presumably, wanted to be with him.

'As well as shopping can. I picked up some supplies from the farm shop.'

'I didn't know there was one nearby. I thought I'd have to go miles for my groceries. Sounds like I need to pick your brains about the local area.' He had a sense of being outside himself: going through the motions of polite chit-chat while fighting a powerful urge to take her in his arms and kiss her in front of everyone in the tea shop.

'If I'd known you were taking the job, I could have sent you a welcome info pack,' Lara said with a wry smile.

'Yeah ...' he said, returning her smile with his own sheepish grimace. 'I definitely haven't had much chance to explore yet, and I'll need to visit the bank and dentist. And I don't want to live on take-outs from the Castle Café, no matter how good the food is. Talking of which, shall we grab some lunch while we have the chance?'

'Good idea.' Lara picked up a menu. 'I hear their avo and poached egg on sourdough is good.'

'I might take the hint. My diet consists of Cumberland sausage and bacon at the moment.'

Away from the pressures of work, she was definitely more relaxed. Flynn certainly wasn't going to sour the moment by mentioning any recent unfortunate incidents or waste their time talking about work.

Over lunch, they chatted about the area, with Lara reeling off a list of places he could get stuff, from bike parts to a haircut.

'Not that you need a haircut,' she added hastily.

'Oh, I do. I don't want to end up with a man bun.'

She wrinkled her nose. 'Yeah, not sure I want to see that.' She seemed to regret such a personal remark and changed the subject. 'Anything else you want to know about the area? Best walks? Good pubs?'

'Both of those. You obviously know the place inside out. How long have you been working here?'

'Not that long, really. Not compared to some of the staff. I joined last autumn.'

'Wow. I thought you'd been here a few years at least.'

'It's a small community so there aren't many places to get to know – not in terms of shops and pubs. The fells are vast, of course. You could live here all your life and never try all the walks and hills.'

He smiled. 'I'd like to explore. It's very beautiful. Did you once tell me you used to work at a house in Warwickshire? Was it National Trust or private?'

'Private. Same as Ravendale but I worked for the Trust when I was younger.' Staring intently into her coffee, she said, 'The time was right for a change. I don't think it's good to stay in one place too long.'

'Maybe . . . but you seem very happy at Ravendale.'

'I was. I am. It's a dream place to work.' She looked at him very directly. 'How about you? Do you miss Cornwall? Have you left family behind?'

'I haven't had time to miss Cornwall yet and I do have some family there. My parents live in Falmouth and I have a brother who's a plumber – he moved to Walthamstow. I have mates back there too, but they understand that I need to travel for work. Two of them worked with me at Kernow Park, but in our line of work you get used to moving around and settling in different communities. As you know, I was going travelling solo anyway.'

'You do a lot of things solo?' she asked, resting her chin on her hand.

Such directness.

'If you mean do I like being independent, I guess so. Like I said, it goes with the territory.'

'Never been tempted to put down roots?'

He smiled. 'Tempted, yes. A couple of times. But it didn't work out.'

'But you wanted it to?' Lara asked.

'Yeah. I wanted it to. Once, I wanted it very badly.'

'Do you mind me asking what went wrong?' Lara asked tentatively.

After taking a sip of his coffee, Flynn said, 'She was married.'

She let out a gasp. 'Oh . . .'

'I didn't know she was married. You can believe that or not.'

'Why wouldn't I believe it?' she said, frowning.

Flynn immediately regretted his throwaway remark. 'I don't know . . .' Because he thought Lara might have formed an impression of him as a Jack the Lad? He wasn't going to say that out loud, so he shrugged. 'I don't know why I said it. Ignore me. I really didn't know Abigail was married, though. She'd kept it quiet from everyone. I met her at a local

71

pub and we hit it off straight away . . .' Flynn checked himself. The last thing he wanted was to talk about his feelings for another woman, which at the time had been powerful. 'We started a relationship, but at no point did she mention her husband to me or anyone else. Turns out he was working in Qatar and I didn't find out until I – until things came to a head between us.'

Flynn had noticed the cute smudge of chocolate on her top lip and wanted to wipe it away with his finger but didn't dare even mention it.

'How did you find out about the husband?' she asked.

'Well, I thought we might make a go of it. Settle down. I even suggested she might move in with me. I'd been seeing Abi about six months by then.'

Although Lara was listening, her lips were pressed together, almost as if she'd been physically trying to hold back her comments, but she broke her silence. 'That was the crunch moment . . . and things could never be the same . . .' Her comment was laden with experience.

Flynn was sure she knew exactly what he was talking about. 'You're right. I think me asking her to move in was the moment when she realised that our relationship couldn't go any further and she admitted she was married.'

Lara was aghast. 'How cruel to lie to like that!'

'I thought so for a long time, but I've come to accept she was lonely and unhappy in her marriage and looking for an escape – a fantasy. She said she was heartbroken about us splitting up, and admitted it was all her fault.'

'I'd have been the same,' Lara said, 'if I found out I'd been living a lie . . .'

'She said she'd never meant things to go so far between us and then fooled herself into believing we could have a future, but, in the end, she didn't want to leave her husband and I refused to continue being part of the affair. I didn't even want to be part of encouraging a split. Even if she *had* wanted to leave him, my trust was shattered. That's not how I want to live my life.' He paused. 'I understand people have problems, but to be honest, I felt used.'

'I can understand that . . .' Lara said, finally meeting his eyes fully. 'Surely she wasn't happy if she'd turned to you?'

'She definitely wasn't.' Flynn paused. He had left out the part where Abigail had also said he 'was the kind of man who was exciting and great to have a wild fling with but not to settle down with'. Perhaps she'd been trying to console him with the kind of thing she thought he'd like to hear, but her words had cut him deeply.

He'd also wondered if there any truth in her comments? When he was younger, he'd have been delighted to be considered exciting. Who wouldn't? He'd been very happy to travel, meet new people, and play the field. He'd been drawn to women who felt the same way. With Abi, it was perhaps the first time that he hadn't wanted a relationship to end. He'd been surprised how much he hurt and for how long.

Those words had nagged at him ever since. Had it been love? Had he had his heart broken? He'd felt crushed at the time: angry, foolish, and it had made him wary of getting serious – and hurt – again. And no one who might have threatened his heart had come along. He'd had a few short-lived relationships and 'friends with benefits', but mostly thrown himself into work, travelling on the bike and seeing friends.

Lara cut into his thoughts. 'I'm sure she did care about you, despite knowing what she did was wrong.'

'I think she did, but in the heat of the moment and for a while after, I couldn't believe it. We split up as soon as I found out. Once her husband was back in the UK for good, she decided to try again with him.'

'What a horrible situation to be in,' Lara said soothingly, making Flynn realise not only what a kind person she was but also that he'd been doing the one thing he'd vowed not to: going on about a previous relationship.

'Yeah.' He refocused on her lovely face and thought how lucky he was to be here with her. 'I'm not sure that dragging up the past is the best way to spend our precious free time,' he said with a warm smile. 'And anyway, I think the waitress is about to bring our lunch.'

Their conversation during and after steered clear of personal matters – both to Flynn's relief and, from what he could gather, to Lara's.

She left before him, driving off in her old Landy. Flynn stood by the bike, watching the beck tumble down the valley next to the old waterwheel.

'Friends' was how they had described each other to Molly and they were right to do so. There wasn't really any other appropriate word and 'friend' covered a multitude of possible permutations. Flynn knew he shouldn't really want to add complications to their relationship – they hardly knew each other, they were colleagues and Lara had more than enough on her plate. He needed to take things slowly. Perhaps he'd wait until New Year to try to take things to any kind of a new level.

Although considering the way he reacted when he saw Lara enter the café, he seriously doubted if he could stick to the plan.

Chapter Ten

Tonight was the night: the launch for the Winter Spectacular. Lara didn't mind admitting she'd had butterflies in her stomach from the moment she'd woken up – and she hadn't had the best night's sleep either.

The castle was shut for the day, with every effort over the past few days having been directed at making this evening run smoothly. A regional TV crew were arriving as dusk fell and before the public arrived, and Lara and Fiona had already given interviews to local newspapers, the county magazine, online blogs and influencers in the weeks before.

Despite every rational thought telling her that the chalice couldn't have any influence on the event's success, a splinter of superstition had lodged in her mind. What if there was a disaster, like a terrible accident or a lightning strike? It was unlikely, she decided, having checked the forecast. It said there would be stable high pressure hanging over the Lakes for a few days, which would bring cold, clear nights.

She was just stressed out and needed a break to centre herself. Even so, she'd allowed two cups of coffee to go cold in the staff room while answering calls from panicked staff and scrolling through messages she didn't need to be copied in on.

'Be calm. Take a breath.' Jazz came up behind her as she tipped the second coffee down the sink. They'd managed to squeeze in a quick working lunch at the Castle Café the day before, but any more ambitious plans for a night out would have to wait for Jazz's upcoming birthday.

'I am calm,' Lara said, then sighed. 'How do *you* look so calm?'

'I only have several thousand visitors to feed and not poison. I'm completely chilled.'

Lara laughed.

'Right. Here are my orders. Firstly, let me finish making you a coffee that you will drink. Secondly, eat this.' She presented her with a paper bag.

'What is it?'

'A cranberry-and-white-chocolate flapjack. Local bakery makes them by the thousands for us. They're great, and, believe me, I taste-tested a lot of them.'

Lara tucked in while Jazz poured hot water on the coffee granules and added milk. She really did need the boost to her blood sugar. Breakfast had been a very rushed affair a long time ago.

'Verdict?' Jazz asked, handing over the mug.

'Delicious. Thank you, I really needed this.' Lara sipped her coffee.

'Good.' Jazz leaned against the countertop. 'Now, as for worrying about tonight, it's natural, but I've done a lot of these events and I promise you, it'll work out OK. If you expect the unexpected, you'll get through it. The time to worry is if you haven't done your preparation and you have absolutely prepared this to the last detail.'

Lara bit off a large chunk of flapjack, feeling a little calmer. 'Thanks. I still think there's more I could have done and stuff to be sorted. One of the toilet blocks is out of action, and two marshals are off sick. A big branch came down and damaged one of the statues, and I just heard that badgers ate through a cable to the grotto.'

'All of those things can be handled by other people. That's why we have catering and cleaning teams and maintenance and security managers. Flynn's responsible for the technical side. Leave it to him.'

'I'm sure he'll do a good job. He just doesn't know Ravendale that well.'

'I think he's learning fast. Are you going to make me stand over you while you finish that flapjack?'

Jazz left and Lara went back to work, reminding herself that she was as prepared as she could possibly be. Even so, never had a day gone by so fast. Morning turned to afternoon and, in what seemed like a heartbeat, the sun was sinking over the distant sea.

She zipped up her puffa coat. It would be a very chilly night but at least it wasn't raining, which would have added an extra layer of challenges, like slippery paths, mud, and cafés packed with wet and cold punters.

Dusk was falling as she did one final walkthrough of the site, past kiosks where staff were stocking up with hot dogs and checking coffee machines and mulled-wine urns.

Carlos and the apprentices were mending the fence that had also been knocked down by badgers overnight while technicians fixed the cable. Flynn was deep in conversation with a contractor by the grotto. Lara left them to it and prayed they could fix it.

The golf buggies that whizzed about the estate seemed to be everywhere, along with people in hi-vis shouting. The constant beeping of trucks reversing came from the technical area along with the hum of the generators. There seemed to be an awful lot of scurrying and shouting and urgency with only two hours to go until the first visitors were allowed in at six.

Then, as the night deepened to velvet black, the pathways began to clear and the hubbub died down. The technical staff thinned out, retreating to the control hub, to be replaced by the stewards, who moved into their places along the route.

All around her, lights twinkled and shimmered in tree canopies, statues glowed, and the castle walls were painted in white light. Projections of stars washed over the walled garden and the orangery. Carols and Christmas favourites rang from the speakers. In the formal garden, the fountain danced with violet, red and green to classical music.

The aroma of cinnamon, hot chestnuts and frying onions filled Lara's nose as the kiosks prepared for the onslaught of hungry, thirsty people eager to warm up on the cold night, all ready to tell themselves: Christmas has started!

And then, the first visitors walked in. Families and couples, babies in buggies, toddlers on shoulders, people with big cameras, teenagers with mobiles, laughing, pointing, stopping, capturing it all or simply marvelling.

Lara felt a tear roll down her cheek, of relief and pride and hope.

It was here. It was happening. And that was thanks to everyone at the castle. They'd all pulled together to make her vision a reality – and Flynn had been instrumental in that. They worked well together and they had chemistry that she couldn't deny, even if she was trying not to act on it.

Chapter Eleven

Since his lunch with Lara, Flynn's feet had barely touched the ground as he prepared for this moment.

Even though he'd helped run sound and light events before – and bigger ones than this – he'd found himself stressing about this one more than usual. That was partly because he was so new to the venue, but also because he had such a personal stake in the game. He wanted it to go well, not to keep his job or to get a pat on the back, but for Lara.

The event was her baby: one she'd conceived and nurtured. It had to be a triumph. Flynn had beads of perspiration on his back from running around, making sure every aspect was working, answering the slightest query, and constantly checking in with the contractors that there were no glitches.

He'd been so busy that he'd only had one glimpse of Lara at a distance, talking to Fiona by the fountains. Thank goodness she hadn't known that the fountains weren't working five minutes before the gates opened or that the power to the Castle Café had briefly been cut off. Flynn had liaised with Jazz the catering manager and his own team to restore it before Lara had even realised or had a chance to worry.

It was now seven-thirty, and the place was heaving with

what felt like every human for miles around. How did such a remote location have so many people?

Flynn had to slow his pace as he made his way from the contractors' control room towards the grotto, drinking a can of Red Bull.

'Oh, hello.'

His way around the corner of the Ice House was blocked by a very young woman with red streaks in her hair pushing a buggy. She was familiar and he racked his maxed-out brain for a name. Melanie? Milly? No, *Molly*.

'Hello,' she said again.

Flynn didn't have time for chit-chat but he also wanted to be polite and friendly.

'Hi,' he said, with a smile for Molly but mostly for the baby in the buggy, who was wearing a pink-eared hat and staring wide-eyed at the lights. 'Enjoying the illuminations?' he asked, wondering if the baby was Molly's or not. She did seem pretty young to be a mum – probably still in her late teens or very early twenties at the most.

'Yeah. It's amazing. Esme loves it too.'

'Molly! Here I am!' An older woman with a cardboard carrier of coffees bustled up, her breath misting the air. 'Sorry, the queues at the kiosk are so long. Bet you thought I'd been kidnapped.'

'No, Nan,' Molly said wearily. 'Who would kidnap you?'

'Cheeky! You'd be surprised,' the woman said, bringing a smile to Flynn's face despite his haste to be gone.

His radio crackled with a message. 'Glad you're having a good time. Don't miss the Great Oak and the children's play area, though the baby's probably too young to appreciate it.'

'A bit,' said Molly, but smiled at Esme and held her hand. 'But she loves the lights, don't you, Esme? Your eyes have been like an owl's all evening.'

So, the child was Molly's, Flynn thought, giving her a wave before he hurried away. He didn't think he'd see his own bed before midnight.

Chapter Twelve

Lara was en route to the grotto when she spotted Flynn striding off as she delivered some water and a mince pie to Santa.

She'd recognised a number of people from the village
around the grounds and also recognised one of the women
queuing as Molly, the waitress from the Waterwheel Café.
She had a baby in a buggy and was chatting to an older
woman with cropped grey hair who, Lara presumed, was
probably a grandmother, auntie or older friend.

Santa's Chief Elf – normally one of the office admins –
asked the visitors near the front to wait a short while in the
small entrance tent, which was decorated with LED figures
of elves and woodland creatures.

After checking that Santa was surviving, she headed out
of the tent via a side flap and through a gap between the
walls and a line of Christmas trees that was out of bounds
to the public.

It was possibly the only place on site where she could
remain unseen while she sipped her own bottle of water and
had a few minutes' breather.

The evening was going better than she could have imagined and the reactions from visitors had brought happy tears
to her eyes more than a few times. The superstitious worries

that had nagged at her could be safely put down to lack of sleep and stress. While she sipped her water and thought about how much she'd like to hide in her nook for the rest of the evening, she heard Molly and her companion talking as they waited to be admitted to the grotto.

'Do you know that tall man you were talking to, Molly?' the older woman asked. 'He's one of the workers, isn't he?'

'Must be,' Molly said. 'He came in the café the other day.'

'He's handsome.'

'He's old.'

'Old?' Nan spluttered. 'What? He can't be forty yet. Probably nearer thirty-five.'

'Like I said, he's old,' Molly replied, then added mischievously. 'Still too young for you, Nan.'

From her hidden position, Lara stifled a chuckle.

'Of course he's too old for you, but I'm still allowed to say that he's a good-looking man!'

'Nan! You can't say things like that. Not now you're a great grandma.'

'I just did, Molly. I didn't lose my ability to give my opinions when you gave birth to Esme. And, you know, I think I've seen him somewhere before.'

Molly snorted and Lara pictured her pulling a face. 'Probably in one of those old-fashioned dramas you like watching. The ones where all the women are downtrodden and work in factories.'

'If you mean Catherine Cookson, then you could learn a lot from watching them. Thank your lucky stars you live now, not back then.'

Lara pictured Molly rolling her eyes.

'And he's handsome enough to be in one of them, but no, I haven't seen him on the telly. Those programmes were made forty years ago and I'm sure I've seen him somewhere more recently.'

'Have you?' Molly asked, but their attention was drawn by the Chief Elf, who was approaching them.

'Who do we have here?' the elf asked them.

'This is Esme. She's nine months old,' Molly said.

'Hello, Esme. Are you ready to meet Santa?'

Judging by the wail that emerged from Esme when she was lifted out of the comfort of her buggy, Lara guessed the answer was a resounding 'no'. Molly and her nan were still trying to persuade Esme that seeing Santa would be wonderful as they vanished inside the grotto.

Chuckling to herself, Lara slipped out from behind the trees and looped back to the main light trail. She'd found it hilarious that Flynn was considered good-looking and costume-drama hero material by a great-granny. She wondered if she should tell him, just to see his reaction, and decided that she definitely wouldn't. It might lead to him thinking *she* thought he was good-looking. Then again, he'd probably worked that out already.

Chapter Thirteen

'Hello, my dear! I'm afraid you've caught me red-handed.'

Henry was hanging decorations on a tree in the corner of the sitting room when Lara walked into the family apartments the next morning to give an update on the launch night.

He grinned sheepishly at her. 'I'm as bad as any child, but I always like decorating the tree for Christmas.'

Cardboard boxes surrounded him and the room smelled like a pine forest.

'It looks great,' she said, pleased to see him looking a little more like his old self. 'And the scent is wonderful.'

'The gardening team brought this spruce up here this morning. They cut it on the estate. Normally I go and help choose it myself but I haven't been able to this year.' He looked downcast. 'I love decorating it. My mother and father always insisted on waiting until the week before Christmas, but I wanted to do it as soon as I got home from boarding school for the holidays. I hated it when it all came down on Twelfth Night. It meant I'd be back at school soon.'

His eyes were suspiciously bright and Lara felt sorry for him. His recent health scare must have brought back some mixed emotions and memories.

'That must have been tough,' she said kindly.

'I hated being sent away, but that's what everyone did then. We refused to send Tara and Harriet. Ironically, they actually wanted to go, but we insisted on a day school. They seemed happy enough, though, and we didn't miss so much of their childhood.'

'Sounds like the right decision for everyone,' Lara said, gladder than ever that her parents hadn't been able to even contemplate sending her away to school. Her bog-standard local comp had suited her just fine. She couldn't imagine sending her kids off to board – if she ever had any.

Her eyes stung without warning. For a time, she'd foolishly allowed herself to imagine having a family with her ex, Rob. In fact, she'd done more than imagine. She remembered the day she found out she was pregnant – and the day she discovered she wasn't any more, memories still sharp enough to stop her in her tracks.

Henry was peering anxiously at her. 'Are you feeling all right, my dear?'

'Yes, only a tickle.' She pulled a tissue from her bag, dabbed at her nose for show and smiled. 'Thought I was going to sneeze but I'm not. You were telling me about Christmas when you were young.'

Henry picked up a glass reindeer that had seen better days. 'It's because I felt so bleak at the end of the Christmas festivities that I persuaded Fiona to revive the tradition of a Twelfth Night Ball after my father passed away and Mother moved into the Dower House until we lost her too.'

The Dower House was now a luxury holiday cottage. 'It's a beautiful property. Everyone who stays loves it.'

'Mother is probably turning in her grave at the prospect of people partying in her sitting room and children trampolining on the beds.'

Lara smiled. 'I like to think of guests enjoying themselves.'

'So do I, my dear! And that's why we wanted to give people something to look forward to in the dark days of January. Years ago, there was always a ball for the staff and estate workers on Twelfth Night, but it lapsed when the First World War broke out, so we revived it.'

'I'm so glad you did. Last year's was so lovely.' Lara reminded herself that she'd only accepted dances with men over sixty. She'd still been raw after the break-up with Rob and determined not to give anyone the slightest impression she was interested in romance. Perhaps, she thought, this year might be different, once the hard work was done and she could relax a little. Then she remembered the chalice sitting in the safe, flawed and imperfect.

'It's our way of saying thank you to all the folk who work here or volunteer or supply the castle,' Henry said. 'I just hope I'm fit enough to dance this year.'

'I'm sure you will be. And you're not the only one who leaves the decorations up until Twelfth Night. My parents are the same.'

'I like them already. Are you going home to see them for Christmas?' Henry asked.

'Not this time. My parents are off to Melbourne to visit my sister and her family.'

'Oh. Won't you miss them?'

'Yes, but they'll be back in the New Year and I hope to go and see them myself as soon as the Twelfth Night Ball is over.' Lara didn't add that she couldn't possibly travel at such a busy time of year, even though her parents and sister had offered to jointly fund her ticket. She hadn't wanted to accept it, though – and she definitely couldn't afford the time off.

'Harriet is coming back to the castle with her brood,' Henry said. 'Tara is going to her in-laws.'

Lara found it funny to hear Tara's in-laws, a marquess and marchioness, described this way. 'I'll be fine joining in here, although Jazz has invited me to spend Boxing Day with her and the children.'

'That sounds like fun,' said Henry.

It definitely would be, Lara thought, but not as nice as being with her own family.

Fiona walked in carrying a box of tinsel. 'Henry, haven't you finished the tree yet? He spends too long looking at the decorations rather than hanging them up.'

'I like looking at them,' Henry protested. 'I like to remember where each one came from. Remember when we bought this glass globe on our honeymoon in Venice? We spent ages deciding on the colour. Harriet knitted this angel, not that we could recognise it as an angel when she handed it over.'

Fiona put the box on the floor and took the 'angel' from her husband's hand. Its woollen hair and gown had almost unravelled.

'That angel's looking rather the worse for wear now.

Sometimes I wonder what the future holds now we're so much older. I dread to think what might happen if one of the children doesn't decide to take over. Who will take it on?' she asked. 'I'll help you in a minute, Henry. I just wanted to discuss with Lara face-to-face how well last night's launch went.'

'I've heard how super it was,' Henry said. 'Even though I wasn't able to visit myself, I did see the set-up and I knew it would be brilliant. I could hear the buzz from the visitors up here.'

'The reaction from everyone I spoke to was "wow",' Fiona said. 'The children's faces were a picture and it was a stroke of genius to use the Ice House as a grotto. You and the team have worked so hard on it all. I can't thank you enough. I'm so glad we managed to persuade Flynn to join us too.'

Lara agreed. There was no denying that the launch had gone very well. There had been only minor snags and Flynn, the in-house team and the on-site contractors had quickly fixed those. Her main takeaway from the evening was the expression on visitors' faces, particularly the children.

'I must admit I didn't hear a single person say they were disappointed and so many seemed to love it.'

'I wish I'd been able to see the lights in the flesh, so to speak. But Fiona says I have to stay inside for now.'

'Hopefully you'll be able to go see them before the Spectacular ends,' Fiona said.

He snorted. 'Good God, Fi! You can't keep me wrapped in cotton wool for ever. A bit of fresh air won't hurt me and I don't intend to go on any long walks. I'm not staying in here like a mole!'

Fiona patted his arm. 'I just don't want you to get cold or overdo it until you've had time to rest a bit more. That's why I arranged to have all the Christmas decorations brought up here – to cheer you up.'

'They look absolutely lovely,' Lara said.

'Mother let me make paper chains too . . .' Henry said wistfully, gazing up at the tree. 'Even though the rest of the castle was grand, even in those days our apartments were cosy, like every other home.'

Not quite, thought Lara, but she didn't say anything.

Fiona rubbed her hands together. 'Now let's not get maudlin. This is the trouble with Christmas. It brings back so many memories, happy and sad.'

Lara thought wistfully of her own home. Her mother wouldn't have taken their artificial tree out of the loft yet but she would very soon, even though she was heading off to Australia as soon as the primary school, where she was head teacher, broke up. Her father worked from home as an IT consultant.

She wished she could find time to go home before they went to Australia, but it was impossible. Ten thousand miles suddenly seemed a very long way indeed compared to two hundred.

Henry insisted on making them all tea in the apartment kitchen, even though Lara was worried he should be resting.

'Let him, my dear,' Fiona murmured, once her husband was out of earshot. 'It's good to see him getting back on his feet and wanting to do more. He may sound full of bravado, but he's had quite a scare. At least the doctors are keeping an eye on Henry now. He's not amused and he feels he's "in their clutches", but I'm very glad he is.'

Lara was amused, even though she felt for Henry. 'I can imagine.'

'When he collapsed and I was in that ambulance, holding his hand, I genuinely thought that our luck had run out. But now that last night has gone so well, I do feel our fortunes are turning again.'

Lara was keen to move away from the topic of luck and onto the Spectacular. 'I'm so pleased that you think that everything went well last night . . .'

For the next twenty minutes they all discussed the evening, what had worked well and also any minor glitches. Lara found herself using Flynn's name a lot. 'Flynn fixed it . . .' and 'Flynn suggested . . .'

She really must try to stop herself.

After lunch, which consisted of a cinnamon bun, coffee, and a catch-up with Jazz in the Castle Café, Lara had a meeting with the guides to discuss the following week's tour schedule. She then had to go up to the treasury to return a miniature painting of the nativity that had been out on display.

She went to turn the key in the oak door and found it already unlocked. Had it been left open or was someone inside? Her pulse rate rose as she walked inside.

'Fiona! What are you doing up here?'

Fiona glanced up with a frown of annoyance and immediately Lara realised how rude she'd been.

'I'm so sorry. I didn't mean it to come out like that. I was just taken aback to see someone in here when I thought the door was locked. How rude of me. What I meant to say was: how can I help you?'

Fiona smiled. 'It's all right, my dear. I didn't mean to startle you. I was only in here to collect one of our special treasures from the safe.'

Lara felt light-headed. 'You were?'

'Yes. Some woman from the telly is desperate to see St Anselm's finger. We all know the bone is from some long-dead and unfortunate animal, but she insisted on seeing it for herself.'

'Oh. I see, yes, of course.' Lara stifled a sigh of relief.

'I hope you're not cross. This woman – Lucy Wotsit – gosh, I keep forgetting her surname – called me this morning and said she's doing some research up here for a programme about fake relics and could she call in? I should have told her we're far too busy but I didn't dare.'

'No. She might give Ravendale some publicity.'

'She might, until she sees this old piece of bone. I had wondered whether to show her the chalice . . .'

Lara's throat seemed to seize up.

'However, it was St Anselm she was interested in. I'll mention the chalice to her. Though, frankly, the sooner I can get rid of her, the better. I'm taking Henry to a hospital appointment at four.'

'Do you want me to see her?' Lara offered, hoping to take control.

'Would you? You're so busy.' Fiona's phone went off. 'Bugger. The woman's here already.'

Lara dived in. 'I can bring St Anselm down to you if you want to go and greet her. It's no trouble!'

'That would be wonderful. We'll be in the drawing room having coffee.'

Lara waited until she heard the doors on the lift being slid back and a faint whirr as the lift descended. Once Fiona was safely gone, she heaved a sigh of relief, closed the strong room door, unlocked the safe and retrieved the carved wooden casket that contained the 'finger'. The box was about the size of a small jewellery box, with a carving of Saint Anselm on its lid.

She placed it carefully on the table while she relocked the safe and scrambled the combination.

'Hi there. Not thinking of doing a runner with the chalice, are you?'

Lara turned around, her pulse rate taking off like a bonfire-night rocket. At this rate, she'd be the one having a heart attack, not Henry.

Somehow Flynn had crept into the strong room without her realising.

'Would you mind not doing that, please!'

'Doing what?'

'Creeping into a room suddenly.'

'I'm sorry,' he said, with a downturn of the mouth, then

grinned. 'The door was ajar and I heard you muttering in here. Or praying, I wasn't sure which.'

'Both, and don't joke about it.'

'Are you OK?' he asked, serious now.

'Just about.' She lowered her voice. 'I had a very close shave with Fiona. She was here when I walked in and about to open the safe.'

'Jesus. Not to get the chalice?'

'No, but, for all I knew, she might have been about to. In the end, she only wanted St Anselm's finger.'

'His *what*?' Flynn pulled such a face that Lara almost laughed.

'His finger bone. It's actually been proven to be an animal bone passed off as a saint's relic, but the reliquary that holds it is thirteenth century and very beautiful. It's on the table over there, actually. No, please don't touch it.'

Flynn held up his hands and curled his lip in horror. 'I wouldn't dream of touching St Anselm's finger.'

'It's not funny,' Lara said in exasperation, although under other circumstances, she'd have had a fit of the giggles at his expression. 'I just managed to stop Fiona from opening the safe and offered to take the reliquary downstairs. Why are you up here anyway?'

'I had to come up to the attics to collect an old stereo set and speakers and stuff for the recycling centre. I also just dropped off some new Christmas lights for Henry's tree. I'm going down now with the electrical junk. I'll give you a lift. Ha ha.'

'Very funny,' Lara said, then sighed. 'Come on, then.

Knowing my luck, if I take the stairs, I'll probably fall down them and break St Anselm's finger.'

Flynn called the lift and wheeled a small truck loaded with the dusty sound system, a tea urn and a plate warmer inside.

It was an old-fashioned goods elevator, much larger than a passenger lift. It had a metal grille and a heavy door that you slid back before stepping out. Lara stepped gingerly inside and Flynn closed the door and metal grille. With the truck inside, there wasn't lots of room left.

Flynn sniffed at the control panel with its brass buttons. 'This is a real museum piece. Look. There are only two buttons. Up or down. That's it.'

He pushed one and there was a clanking and whirring noise before the lift started to descend slowly.

Lara cradled the reliquary in her hands, observing Flynn. Even with dusty hair and in dusty jeans, he still looked gorgeous. In a confined space, he seemed taller and rangier than ever.

'Colleting old stuff from the attics seems a trivial job for you,' she said, as the lift made its arthritic way down from the third floor.

'I wanted to sound out Henry and Fiona about the Spectacular. The Christmas lights and attic stuff gave me an excuse. They seem very pleased with how it went.'

'They are. We are definitely in their good books.'

'If only they knew the truth . . . Whoa!'

Lara steadied herself with a hand on the lift wall. The cabin had juddered and stopped.

Flynn rolled his eyes and pushed the button again. Nothing happened.

He peered at the panel. 'Hmm . . .'

'What does "hmm" mean?'

Flynn pushed both buttons but the lift stayed motionless. 'Hmm,' he said again. 'I suppose I could try to take the panel off, but I don't have my tool kit with me.'

Lara waited a few seconds, then said, 'So we're stuck?'

'Yes, but I'm sure we'll soon be out of here. You won't be trapped with me for long.'

Lara suppressed a sigh. Knowing her luck, she wouldn't bet on it. Now she had Fiona and the TV historian waiting in the drawing room for St Anselm's finger. What if Fiona decided to go back up to the treasury herself?

What's more, she was acutely aware that she was now stuck in very close proximity with a man she fancied like mad.

Chapter Fourteen

'I should have known not to get in here with you. This lift has always been a bit dodgy,' Lara said, trying not to dwell on Flynn's muscles as he leaned forward, examining the control panel.

Flynn turned to her. 'Yeah. Carlos told me, and the engineer's scheduled for next Tuesday. Not that it's any help to us now.' He tried a winning smile, which she assumed was meant to cheer her up.

'No, it isn't.'

He waved his radio. 'Shall I call someone or do you want to? Who normally rescues people from lifts around here?'

'Well, I'm one of the designated rescuers myself. I know how to use the emergency crank system in the basement.'

'Great!' Flynn gave an exaggerated sigh of relief then said, with mock surprise, 'Oh, wait. You're stuck in a lift.'

'Well spotted. Henry and Fiona also know how to use it, but we won't want to bother them. Gerald also knew, of course.'

'Ah.' He blew out a breath. 'So that would be my job now?'

'Yes, but luckily Carlos is also familiar with the crank system.'

Flynn closed his eyes and opened them again. 'He's going to love this. The boss being stuck in the lift.' He held up his radio. 'God, this is embarrassing.'

'Better that it's us and not Henry or Fiona,' Lara said, although she wouldn't have minded Fiona taking her place at that moment. She was trying not to dwell on the worst-case scenario of Fiona taking the historian into the treasury.

'I need to let Fiona know that her guests won't be seeing St Anselm's finger any time soon.'

Luckily, Fiona was more worried and embarrassed about her staff being stuck in an antiquated lift. She said she was giving her celebrity guest a tour of the ground-floor rooms and hoped they'd be out of there 'in a jiffy'.

Flynn, however, had less upbeat news to deliver from Carlos. 'He says it's going to take at least half an hour to crank us down to the ground floor.'

'I could have told you that. Good job I'm not claustrophobic,' Lara said, staring at the walls and the ancient two-button mechanism and the modern safety warnings: do not use this lift in a fire.

She suppressed a shudder. Even though she knew they'd be rescued sooner or later, it still gave her the creeps to be suspended halfway to the top of the tower, even with Flynn for company.

She sank down with her back to the wall of the lift.

'This bloody lift is now my top priority,' Flynn grumbled, peering at the control panel again. 'This whole system should be on display in a museum.'

'I doubt there's any money in the budget.'

'OK, then we need a new mechanism or a better failsafe than a hand crank system. We'll fix it ourselves in-house.'

'That's Ravendale, I'm afraid. Nothing moves too speedily and making do is the name of the game.'

'I'm going to change things.' He sighed, then the corners of his mouth curved upwards. 'Still, I suppose there are worse places to be stuck.'

In close proximity, and with no excuse to look away, Lara was forced to meet his gaze full on. If she was honest, it was no hardship, although that glint in his eye was sending her hormones haywire.

He slid down on the opposite wall, his feet reaching alongside hers to her calves. Luckily the lights had stayed on although the bulb was dim.

'I suppose I ought to expect situations like this in somewhere so ancient,' he said.

'The lift's from the 1950s. We're lucky it isn't listed.'

'Hmm.' Flynn put his radio on the floor, returning his attention to Lara. 'Ever thought what it would be like to actually own a place like this yourself?'

Lara snorted. 'No way. It's bad enough managing it. Owning it would be way too much responsibility. Look at Henry and Fiona. Their kids don't really want to take it on.'

'I wondered about them and where they are,' Flynn said.

'They have two daughters in their forties. I've only ever met one of them once, when she and the family came up for Fiona's birthday. Hattie's a sculptor and Tara is a paediatrician in London. They seemed nice enough but neither made any mention of giving up their career to run this place. But if they don't, Henry and Fiona might have to give the place to a trust or sell to a leisure corporation and they don't want to do that.'

'I'd no idea . . .' Flynn said.

'Don't worry, I don't think it will happen any time soon. Or I didn't until Henry was taken ill. Now we'll have to hope one of the daughters comes through and wants to run things the same.'

'And is that likely?'

'From what Fiona has hinted, Tara, the doctor, isn't interested at all. Hattie, who's the sculptor, has agreed to move her family here "if it becomes necessary".'

'*If*? I'd say *when* is more realistic,' Flynn murmured.

Lara nodded. The uncertainty of the situation around who might take over the castle had been the one drawback to accepting the job at Ravendale. However, every other consideration had outweighed that downside and, if she were honest, she had been desperate to get away from Rob. 'I wouldn't want to own a place like this. I know it seems like a dream come true for many people, and the owners are incredibly fortunate, but it also ties you down. It's not just the fact that you're tied to it for your whole life, but you have the responsibility to your family and future generations, and all the people who feel they have a stake in an historic property. How can your kids pursue their own lives?'

'I agree. It's not something I'd want to deal with,' Flynn said. 'There's no doubting that it's a very privileged position to be in, but I still wouldn't swap. However, I didn't own my own place until about five years ago, when my gran passed away and left me the deposit I used to buy the Newquay flat. It's a shame she never got to see the place.'

'It's rented out, isn't it?'

'Yes, but not formally. I let a couple of friends move in. They do pay some rent, but well below the market rate. I don't mind. There's a housing crisis in Cornwall and they could never afford the place at the going rate, and they have a baby on the way . . .'

'That was generous of you,' Lara said. Allowing his friends to move in must also mean he was committed to staying here too. Her heart warmed a little more to him.

'I was more than happy to help them out. You have to look after your friends, don't you?'

'You do and, to be fair, Henry and Fiona are lovely and do try to be kind and accessible and as normal as possible. Or as normal as they know how to be.'

Flynn returned her wry smile.

'But not everyone is like them. I think you could easily forget what life is like for most people. I'd hate to start thinking I was above anyone.'

His gaze became more serious. 'You sound like you're speaking from experience.'

'To a degree, I am.' She wasn't completely sure why she'd started this thread of the conversation. He looked wistful. She wondered how he felt being on his own at – thirty-nine?

Up close, she noticed the tiny scar on his chin, his thick

eyelashes, and the tiny threads of grey in his otherwise black hair. He had a kind heart, he was loyal, and he made her laugh, even if he could be annoying. Even when he was annoying, he did it with charm and wit.

They were interrupted by a call on Flynn's radio, which he stood up to take. 'Hi Carlos. Yeah. OK, thanks. How long? Wow . . . well, if that's what it takes. We're not going anywhere.'

Lara pushed herself to her feet, stretching to loosen her shoulders while listening to the radio exchange. Flynn stood up too.

The lift juddered and began to inch its way downwards.

'Oh!' Lara cried, 'I hope—' but then her optimism was dashed when the lift came to an abrupt halt.

With an apologetic grimace, Flynn said, 'I'm afraid you're going to be stuck with me a while longer.'

'How awful,' Lara murmured, then made a decision. She felt that if she didn't clear the air now, she never would.

'Flynn. There's something I want to say about why I've ended up at Ravendale.'

His forehead furrowed in surprise. 'You don't have to share anything about your personal life that you don't want to.'

'I know, but when you told me about your ex and the way she wasn't what you thought – that she'd been keeping secrets . . . Well, I didn't say anything at the time because it touched a nerve with me. We probably have more in common than you think.'

'We do?' Intrigue lit his eyes.

'I was seeing someone while I was at my previous job. He was the lord of the manor, to be honest. Literally.' She sighed. 'What could possibly go wrong?'

Flynn winced and said, 'Ouch.'

'Yes. Ouch.' She paused, recalling the pain, and the effects that had lingered far longer than she'd ever expected. Hopes crushed. Dreams shattered. A loss that she hadn't thought she deserved to mourn. She could never forget her mother's well-meaning words when she broke the news that she was leaving the manor and why.

'That's love,' her mother had said, kindly.

Yet Lara doubted it had been love – and definitely not on Rob's side – and if sacrificing her independence and having her heart shattered was the price of that kind of 'love', she wasn't sure she could ever risk it again.

'You don't have to tell me this if it's making you feel bad,' Flynn said, his words like a soothing balm on a raw wound.

'It isn't making me feel bad to tell you. The way I was treated at the time made me feel bad. Remembering it used to make me feel worse, but you were honest and open with me about Abi and I held back in the café. I want you to know what happened.' *Some of what happened* . . . Lara felt she should return his trust by sharing some of her own story, but she was still determined to keep back one part that still felt too raw to reveal. She wasn't sure Flynn would or even could understand.

'Rob's family had owned the place since the seventeenth century and he'd inherited the title. He was a baronet: Sir

Robert, to give him his full title, and I promise you he liked to use it. I was only allowed to call him Rob when we were on our own. Not in front of the staff or visitors.'

Flynn snorted in contempt. 'He sounds like a right tit.'

'He did turn out to be a bit of a tit. I wouldn't say we were going out officially, because he didn't want to go public, but we were very close.'

It had meant sleeping together and going out for dinner or lunch from time to time when they could both get away and Rob thought no one would see them. That had seemed romantic at the time. Clandestine, a thrill ... Lara was in love with him.

'After a while I began to get fed up with having to creep around as if our relationship was shameful. I couldn't see why Rob wouldn't go public about us. He said enough of the right things in private to make me believe he was serious about me.'

In fact, he'd as good as proposed. He'd told her he'd love to spend the rest of his life with her. He'd even joked about walking her up the aisle at the family chapel and whether his dog – a golden retriever, obviously – could be a bridesmaid.

Flynn cut gently into her thoughts. 'This doesn't end well, does it?'

'It depends on what you define by an ending,' she said. 'I certainly didn't get the kind of happy ending I'd expected. Perhaps that was my big mistake: expecting anything of Rob. I'd been there two years, and we'd been seeing each other for eighteen months, and he kept saying we'd be a great partnership – which I took to mean as a couple, as ...

life partners.' She stopped and took a breath. 'Then he went away for four weeks to manage some business interests in Dubai.'

'Business interests?' Flynn echoed. 'They sound dodgy.'

'They were – kind of. The day he came back, he called me into his study and said he had something important to say. I thought – well, let's not dwell on what I thought. What he wanted to tell me was that he was engaged to the daughter of a business acquaintance.'

It was the same day that Lara had also planned to share some news with him. It was news she never got to tell him, but perhaps, in the end, that had been a good thing. He might not have believed her anyway. Time had helped her realise that.

'Engaged? And he'd never mentioned this other woman before?'

'It turned out *I* was the other woman – not her,' Lara said. 'Rob told me they'd been university friends and they'd dated before I started working at the manor, but they'd split up when she'd moved to Dubai.' She halted because telling Flynn was like probing at a freshly healed wound: the shock and disbelief of that conversation, standing in front of his desk while he sat behind it, barely able to meet her eye. All the time bearing her own secret. 'He said that while they'd been together in Dubai, they'd realised they should never have broken up and they'd decided to get married.'

'Tit is too good a word for him! How did he have the balls? Actually, it sounds like he had no balls.'

Despite the painful memories, Lara managed a smile

at Flynn's attempt at sympathy. Rob may have had noble ancestors, and Flynn humble ones, but, ironically, it was Flynn who was the true gentleman. 'He said that one of the reasons he'd never got round to asking me to "formalise" things was that he was worried he was still on the rebound from his ex. He thought it was a good thing we'd never made things public, because it would have made things so much harder for me.'

'People make up any excuse to justify their actions when it suits them. What a tosser.'

'I've come to realise that now, but, for a long time, it hurt.' She'd shed so many tears lying in her bed in her cottage on the estate, knowing that Rob was with *her* – his fiancée. 'What really hurt, though, was when he told me it might be less painful for me if I were to look for a new opportunity elsewhere.'

'The bastard.' Flynn snorted in contempt.

'Yes. I felt I'd fallen for the oldest trick in the book or that I was living in some cheesy historical saga where the hired help falls for the lord of the manor and he lets her down. Except fortunately these days we have a thing called education.'

'He still forced you to move jobs, though,' Flynn said.

'He did. And, at the time, I was absolutely heartbroken, but now . . .' She paused. 'I should thank him, because without him being such a shit, I probably wouldn't be here.'

It was also a role that Lara might never have dared to apply for while she was blinded by the stars in her eyes, working for Rob. She'd hoped – expected – to be running the manor as his partner, a prospect that now filled her with horror. She was more angry with herself for being duped and for somehow allowing her hopes, career and her future to rest in the hands of one person.

Rob had never considered her as a priority in his life – she'd come way down the list after the estate, his title and being seen to make a suitable marriage. Was it selfish to want to be the most important – or at least one of the most important – priorities in a future partner's life?

'For what it's worth, Lara . . .' At the use of her name in his soft Cornish accent, a frisson of desire rippled through her. 'I'm glad you left Rancid Rob's poxy little manor. If you hadn't come to Ravendale, I'm not sure I'd be here either.'

Flynn abandoned his radio on the floor of the lift and moved closer. The warmth in the lift and his physical proximity made her flush with desire. She was a heartbeat away from flinging herself into his arms, yet she had to hold back.

'You didn't come here just for me . . .' It was a statement and question in one.

'You're wrong. I did. I only booked in to the Halloween night because I'd heard about the possible job on the grapevine and I wanted to see it. The castle is great, the job is interesting, but I don't think they would have been enough to change my mind without *you* being here . . . *you* tipped the balance.'

'No.' Trembling inside, she forced herself to laugh off the comment. 'You can't make a decision like that based on someone you knew for less than a day.'

'I'm just saying that sometimes life throws up these forks in the road. You have a plan and then *bam* – you decide to take a risk.'

'But I don't take risks any more,' Lara said. 'I can't afford to.'

'Rancid Rob has done that. Whoa . . .'

The lift juddered sharply and, with a cry of shock, Lara grabbed his arm to steady herself. She quickly removed her hand, but Flynn took it in his and pulled her closer to him.

She could have backed away, *should* have backed away, yet the adrenaline and desire surging through her made it impossible to act in any rational way. Instinct kicked in, and she tilted her chin up and met his mouth; his soft, warm, delicious mouth. It was her holding him around the waist and pressing even closer against his body. Her loving the sensation of his fingers brushing at the nape of her neck and tangling in her hair. Her loving what their proximity was doing to his body. It was Lara who kissed him harder and started to pull his shirt out of his work trousers.

'Wow . . .' he murmured, then started to kiss her back and unzip her fleece.

Rules and resolve didn't exist while they were cocooned inside that capsule, suspended in space where no one could see them or what they were doing. But Lara's thoughts were interrupted by the radio crackling from the corner. 'Flynn. Come in. Over. Flynn, are you OK? Over.'

'No. Not now . . .' Flynn murmured against her mouth in exasperation.

Lara opened her eyes before reluctantly pulling away from him. Flynn let out a groan. 'Sorry, I have to answer it in case they think something's happened in here.'

Something has happened in here.

He scooped up the radio while Lara leaned against the lift wall, trying to steady her breathing and tame the fire that still burned inside her.

Flynn was nodding, saying 'yes' and 'OK' and ending with 'Thanks, Carlos.'

Lara was coming down, slowly, reluctantly, when a familiar voice calling over the radio jolted her out of her post-kiss trance. It was Fiona.

'Are you OK? This is awful. Don't worry, we'll have you out of there in a jiffy!'

Lara snapped to attention. 'We're fine. Don't worry!'

'We're OK,' Flynn reiterated.

The moment he'd turned off the radio, Lara said, 'This can't happen again.'

He frowned. 'What? Ever? Or only until after Christmas?'

'I – I don't know, but I can't do this. Not so soon, so fast. Not when I'm on my way again. I can't lose everything again. I can't get involved with another man again, not another colleague. Not someone I'd have to work with when it all goes . . . Please, respect that.'

'I do respect it. I will respect it. But you can't ask me to stop having feelings for you. Ask me to stop hoping to bump into you, fantasising about ways to bunk off work to see you.'

'We hardly know each other,' Lara scoffed, in an effort to hide the fact she had very similar fantasies about him.

He raised his eyebrows and smirked. 'You could have fooled me after that kiss.'

'Shh. I wish you wouldn't look at me like that,' Lara said.

'Like what?'

'Like . . . a wolf scenting – a fluffy bunny!'

He laughed loud. 'No one would ever describe you as fluffy, Lara. Now, fierce like a mother bear is a different matter . . .'

'Flynn, stop it!'

'Hello! Are you two OK?'

A sliver of face appeared through the crack between the floor and the bottom of the lift. It was Carlos. She could hear Fiona behind him, asking him to be as quick as he possibly could.

'Fine. We're fine,' she called down, before glaring at Flynn. 'Just a bit bored.'

Carlos scoffed. 'I bet you are.'

'Bored?' Flynn mouthed with a mock-hurt expression.

'Hold on,' Carlos muttered.

There were more voices and the lift inched down until there was a space large enough for them to crawl out. Lara slid back the metal grating and refused to look at him.

Carlos crouched by the opening, grinning. He was clearly loving every moment of the drama. 'There you go. You should be able to get out now. We won't move the lift again so you can get out.'

'Thank you,' Lara said, as she got up again to find Flynn leaning against the lift wall, looking fed up.

'We'd better go,' she said.

'Pity,' he murmured, peeling himself off the wall and leaning close to her ear. 'Your hair has come down,' he whispered, before holding out his arm. 'After you.'

Still feeling his breath against her earlobe and the glow in her body, Lara dropped to her hands and knees again. Her dishevelled appearance was the least of her worries. She was desperate to escape from another few minutes in close proximity to a man who made fireworks explode in her stomach when he looked at her – and threatened to blow all her resolve and careful plans sky high.

She crawled out and Flynn followed, finding the space a tighter squeeze. He stood up, brushing dust off his jeans.

Carlos and Fiona were waiting, Carlos with a knowing smirk on his face. Did he suspect that anything unprofessional had gone on between her and Flynn?

Fiona was all aflutter. 'Have you been all right in that horrible thing? I'm so sorry it took so long to get you out. I told Henry that antiquated contraption was a liability!'

'We've been absolutely fine,' Flynn said before Lara could answer. 'Lara's made me aware that some things at the castle can't be rushed.'

Chapter Fifteen

'So, exactly what was it like being stuck in the lift with Flynn?' Jazz asked Lara a few days later while they queued for tickets at the cinema in Keswick.

Jazz's birthday was coming up and she was going spend it with her husband and two young children, but this was a 'grown-up' outing on one of the few evenings when she and Lara had a night off – and Jazz's police-officer husband, Luke, was on a day shift, so he could look after the kids.

'To be honest, it was pretty boring,' Lara said. 'We were in there for over half an hour.'

She'd said that same thing to at least a dozen of her colleagues since the incident. Every time she said it, she was sure that her nose grew an inch and the word 'Liar' flashed across her forehead in neon lights.

Being the butt of jokes had been the least of her worries, but, fortunately, Fiona hadn't decided to show the historian the chalice and she had left after examining the relic, hinting that she might return in the New Year to film a proper piece about Ravendale's treasures. Lara would have to have everything sorted by then – if she was still in her job.

Jazz shuddered. 'I'd have freaked out. I'm so claustrophobic. I'd rather climb those tower stairs ten times a day than get in that lift.'

'Then let's not talk about it. I've heard so many lift jokes, it's driving me mad. Everyone for miles around seems to know we were stuck.'

'Well, you know what the Ravendale rumour mill is like. At least Flynn's had the engineers in to fix the thing, so I suppose that's a positive. I'm still not ever getting in it, though.'

They reached the front of the queue.

'This is so nice,' Jazz said, with a dreamy sigh as they headed for the bar and kiosk. 'Obviously, I love the kids to bits, but it'll be nice to see a film that doesn't involve talking animals, talking cars or witches having an existential crisis.'

They collected their drinks and popcorn from the bar and took them into the cinema, an arthouse place with small screens and plush red seats. It was great to be away from the castle and from the drama around the Winter Spectacular, the chalice, and Flynn.

The latter, however, proved to be a distant hope, because they hadn't long taken their seats when Jazz mentioned the man himself again.

'How do you think our new techie is settling in? Seems like he knows what he's doing.'

'He does . . .' Lara said, and not only with his job, Lara thought, recalling being in his arms with an electric thrill. 'He certainly seems to have found his feet quickly.'

'He definitely has. The catering team are impressed, and not only at his expertise with a screwdriver.' Jazz smirked.

Lara didn't want to go there but was too intrigued to change the subject. 'Oh?'

'Yes. He's caused quite a stir. One of the café team dropped a whole tray of crockery when he walked into the café for his bacon butty.'

'Now you're joking!'

'Only half joking. He's a popular customer when he comes in. Is he single?'

Lara shrugged. 'I think so, but I couldn't say for sure. I don't know him any better than you or anyone else at the castle.'

'Oh, come on. After being trapped in a lift with him, I thought you'd have had plenty of time to chat . . .'

'We were only stuck for half an hour,' Lara protested.

The cinema screen sprang into life and the speakers boomed out with music for a car ad. Jazz spoke loudly into Lara's ear. 'But you must have been *close* in that confined space.'

'We were *fine*,' Lara said, refusing to rise to the bait and even hint at what actually happened – and what almost had.

'He is very handsome, if you like that Mr Rochester-slash-Heathcliff kind of vibe,' Jazz said, during an ad with soft classical music. 'I bet he's left a trail of broken hearts from Land's End to er . . . wherever the top of Cornwall is. Maybe that's why he took the job here – to get away from someone.'

Lara wouldn't have been keen on dating either of those fictional heroes. 'I – don't think him leaving was anything to do with a relationship. I just think he wanted the job. And it's Launceston,' Lara added. 'The top of Cornwall.'

Jazz ignored this and her eyebrows lifted in delight. 'So, you *have* talked to him – about his past, I mean?'

It was natural for her friend to want to know about their newest member of staff. He was probably the most intriguing and exciting character to have joined since they started working there. 'Yeah, we've talked.'

'And?'

'He was seeing a woman a while ago but it fizzled out. He hasn't mentioned being involved with anyone else recently. That's all I know,' Lara said, hoping she'd satisfied Jazz's curiosity without breaking Flynn's confidences. 'I'd appreciate it if you didn't share that with anyone. I'd hate for Flynn to think I'd been discussing his personal life with all and sundry.'

'I'm not "all and sundry", but of course I'll keep it to myself. But I asked because I'd also heard something about him.'

'What?' Lara blurted out, just as an ad ended abruptly.

The sharp-faced woman behind them, who'd been kicking the back of her seat, tapped Lara on the shoulder. 'I do wish people wouldn't talk through the film.'

'Actually. These. Are. Just. The. Ads,' Jazz enunciated, without turning round. She shared a grin with Lara, who, although a little embarrassed, was also highly amused.

'I'll tell you more later,' Jazz whispered, plunging her hand into her popcorn and crunching it noisily.

Lara settled back and the film, a new adaptation of *Jamaica Inn*, began. She was ready to banish all thoughts of a certain brooding colleague from her mind right until the anti-hero, Jem, appeared, and she couldn't help wondering how perfect Flynn would have been in the role.

After the warmth of the cinema, the biting cold outside made Lara catch her breath. It was dark now and the Christmas market was in full swing. It was the first time Lara had been and she was blown away by the atmosphere, the aroma of *glühwein*, and a choir singing carols. Even though she was surrounded by it at work, experiencing the season as a 'layperson' rather than a professional made Christmas suddenly feel very close and real.

'Wait,' Jazz said with a hiss. 'Isn't that him over there?'

Across the street, Flynn was standing by a Czech-inspired craft stall selling beautiful Christmas straw dollies with a woman carrying a baby. They were a distance away and Flynn's companion was bundled up in a thick scarf and bobble hat. She was laughing at something Flynn said and he was smiling back. They didn't seem uncomfortable together or as if they were strangers.

'He might just have bumped into her . . .' Jazz said. 'She seems pretty young.'

'Agreed,' Lara said. Even from a distance, she and Jazz could sense that the woman was at least ten years younger than them: her clothes were on trend and she had a kind of bubbly effervescence as she laughed with Flynn and with her baby.

It was then that Lara finally twigged that the girl was Molly, the waitress.

'Shall we go for Italian, Greek or Thai?' Jazz asked, taking no further interest in Flynn. 'It's early, so we can probably get a table without having to book.'

'Yes. Yes . . . of course. You choose. Call it a birthday treat from me.'

They walked in the opposite direction and chose the Greek taverna on the square, got a table and ordered mezze. With a gin cocktail in hand, Jazz told Lara about her family birthday plans and Lara listened patiently, determined to focus on her friend.

Even so, when Jazz went to the ladies, Lara's mind turned back to Flynn and Molly. They'd obviously bumped into each other and were having a quick chat. But they did seem very friendly – friendlier than you'd expect from two almost complete strangers who'd spoken only twice previously. Twice, as far as she knew at least. Lara didn't track Flynn's movements. He might have been to the café after the first night of the lights.

Jazz returned and they tucked into the mezze while the bouzouki music rose in volume.

The restaurant was filling up and a couple walked in and sat down at a table across the way. They were clearly loved up, constantly touching each other on the arm or linking fingers and leaning over the table to whisper things to each other.

Jazz lowered her voice and murmured, 'They're having an affair.'

'How do you know?' Lara mouthed back.

'He supplies our veg. She's not his wife,' Jazz whispered, plunging her pitta into the taramasalata.

'Ouch,' Lara whispered, selecting a stuffed vine leaf while worrying the couple might overhear.

'You never know what secrets people keep,' Jazz said, still *sotto voce*. 'Oh, that reminds me. I was going to tell you what I heard about Flynn.'

Chapter Sixteen

After checking out an issue with the extractor system, Flynn walked out of the castle kitchens and into flakes of falling snow that settled on his hair and face.

It was bitterly cold after the warmth of the kitchen, so he sheltered in a vaulted porch that led out into the courtyard. The sky was heavy with low clouds that obscured the fells completely, hiding all their beauty. A check of his weather app confirmed the news from earlier: the snow wouldn't stick around long. The forecast was for a warmer spell with rain.

Weather brought its own challenges for the light trail, although they wouldn't cancel unless high winds or heavy snow were forecast.

He was about to step into the courtyard when he saw Lara enter at the opposite corner through the gated archway marked 'Staff Only'. She was headed straight over the cobbles towards the porch where he was standing. With her mobile clamped to her ear, she didn't seem to have noticed him lurking in the doorway.

Flynn waited for her to glance up, slightly apprehensive of what her reaction would be.

He'd barely glimpsed her since their lift kiss a few days

earlier. Though disappointed, it didn't surprise him that their paths hadn't crossed. She was probably rushed off her feet dealing with the Christmas tours that were taking place at Ravendale during the day.

His own schedule had been non-stop too. Although the initial fevered activity of the launch was over, there was still enough to keep him occupied every minute of the working day and beyond. It was a miracle he'd managed to find time to go to Keswick the other evening, but he'd been in dire need of a break and some company from outside the castle.

After ending her call, Lara finally noticed him and slowed. Her expression – wary and inexplicably guilt-ridden – spoke volumes.

'Hello,' she said. Snowflakes had nestled in her hair and lay on the shoulders of her fleece, adding a fairy-tale Christmas-card effect to her pretty looks.

Lara clutched her phone to her chest defensively, clearly not having the same kind of romantic thoughts. 'Hi there,' she said.

'How are you after the other day?'

'What do you mean?' she asked.

'After being trapped in the lift. What else?' He tried a charming smile.

'Absolutely fine.'

'Don't let's stand in the snow and get cold. Let's go inside.'

'I don't have long,' Lara said, glancing around her as if she was looking for an excuse to leave.

'You're busy, I know. We both are, but we haven't had time to talk at all lately.'

She joined him in the entrance porch. Melting snow-flakes glistened in her lashes. He wanted to kiss them away.

'No. We've both been working . . .' She paused and then seemed to brighten up. 'Although I did go out with Jazz to Keswick on Friday. We saw a film and went to the Greek taverna afterwards.'

'Oh? Were they any good?' he asked, pleased that she was engaging with him. 'The film and the meal, I mean.'

'The film was good. It was an adaptation of *Jamaica Inn*, the Daphne du Maurier novel.'

'I don't think I've read the book.'

'You don't need to in order to enjoy the film. The Greek place is great too. I recommend it.'

'Thanks for the tip. I didn't know you could get Greek food round here. I must check it out. Where is it exactly? I was there myself the other night and I didn't see it, but I was only going to the barber's and then for a quick pint with a friend.'

'A *friend*?' Her voice lifted and she was obviously prompting him to give more detail.

'Harvey. He works at the National Trust house on Der-wentwater. In fact, Harvey is the one who first mentioned the Penhaligons were looking for a replacement for Gerald. I think I might have told you I stayed with him the night before I arrived at Ravendale,' Flynn said, keen to keep the conversation going.

'Oh.' She frowned and Flynn instantly regretted putting his size ten in it. He knew it was still a bit of a sore point that Lara hadn't been informed about Gerald. 'I hope you enjoyed yourselves.'

'We did, although we didn't have long together. Harv had to get back in time for his kids to write their letters to Father Christmas and I was keen on an early night.'

'Of course. It's a busy time.'

'Yes. Erm . . . So, you had a good evening? With Jazz,' he added, changing the subject but desperate to keep her talking.

'Yes. Yes, it was . . . We both had a night off, which was why we took the chance to go out.' She rolled her eyes. 'Not sure that'll happen again this side of Christmas.'

'No. Best to take the chance while you can . . .' Flynn was floundering a little. It was strange to be making small talk like this, or perhaps it was understandable that they were both skirting around the issue that was occupying his mind much of the time, and was probably occupying hers too.

The fact that they had jumped on each other in that lift, and if someone hadn't banged on the door and rescued them, who knows what might have happened? Then again, maybe Lara was horrified that they might have had sex in the middle of the working day at their place of employment.

Thinking of it in those terms, Flynn was also horrified – though probably not as much as he ought to be.

'Hmm. Oh, I also saw someone we both know in town. You didn't happen to bump into Molly, the waitress from the café, did you?'

'Molly?' Flynn was hamstrung for a moment. It seemed an odd but very specific question. 'As a matter of fact, I did.

She'd been to a kids' party at the soft play centre and was at the market waiting for her friend. Why do you ask?'

'I only wondered.' Once again, Flynn thought how beautiful her green eyes were. 'Well, I'm glad you found time for a break and to sample the delights of Keswick.' She hesitated before adding, 'I was on my way to see Fiona about the Twelfth Night Ball. We talked about it – the other day.'

'In the lift,' he said, partly because Lara obviously wasn't going to allude to the incident and partly because he felt wicked.

'Yes,' she said haughtily, then her tone softened. 'You will be there, won't you?'

'I wouldn't miss it,' he said, picturing Lara in a little black dress with her hair piled on her head and him slow dancing with her. It seemed like the kind of old-fashioned affair where people would do that and, if so, he was all for it.

'Good, because I'm not sure I mentioned that it was fancy dress.'

'What?' He swore softly and Lara bit back a giggle – or was it a snigger – and Flynn shook his head while giving her a wry grin. 'Ah, you're winding me up, aren't you?'

'Not at all. Everyone joins in. It's great fun. Even the people who hate fancy dress seem to enjoy it. They did last year, anyway.'

He sighed deeply. 'The last time I wore a costume was at primary school. I was a king in the nativity play.'

'You could do the same for the ball. The theme is historical costume.'

Flynn made a spluttering noise that caused Lara to dissolve into laughter. It gave him great pleasure to hear her laughing, despite his horror at the prospect of dressing up. If his discomfort was the price of seeing her relaxed, it was almost worth it.

'I don't think so,' he said. 'Can't I come as a grumpy biker?'

'No. Sorry.'

'Grumpy electrician, then?'

'Would anyone notice the difference?'

He feigned hurt. 'That's a bit harsh.'

Lara rolled her eyes good-humouredly. 'Well, give it some thought, because the staff and locals tend to reserve their costumes months in advance and there's only two fancy-dress hire shops within a thirty-mile radius. And the ball is less than five weeks away. It rolls up at an alarming rate.'

'Oh f—f—that's not very long.'

'No. Look, as you're new and I appreciate the ball has kind of landed on you, I could help, if you like. We keep a few costumes for the guides on re-enactment days. You could borrow one of those if there's something you like and it fits you?'

'There won't be anything I like,' Flynn said. 'I can't see myself in a harlequin outfit with jingly balls on my hat, can you?'

Lara put her hand over mouth, clearly trying to stifle her giggles. 'Oh, I don't know. I think you could pull it off.'

'Ha ha.'

'There's a limited choice, but still a choice. If you can spare the time in the next couple of days, I can show you and you could try a few on?'

'Great,' Flynn muttered. 'I mean, thanks. I think. I'm very grateful.'

'You sound it,' Lara said, narrowing her eyes. 'It's not compulsory.'

'No, I mean, I am genuinely grateful. And, yes, I *would* like to try some on, as long as I don't have to wear anything with one of those things.'

She frowned. 'What things?'

'Those things that Henry the bloody Eighth stuffed down his breeches.' He screwed up his nose. 'A codpiece.'

Lara squeaked with mirth and Flynn heaved a sigh. 'You're loving this, aren't you?'

With a saintly expression, she held up her hands. 'No, not at all. And for your information, I think we have gentlemen's costumes that don't require a codpiece.'

'Thank God for that. I'd never live it down if the apprentices saw me in a codpiece.'

'I don't think I'd ever recover either,' said Lara, adding, 'Byeeee! See you soon!' before flitting off through the door to the great hall, spluttering with laughter.

Flynn had the feeling she would be giggling about him for the rest of the day.

Even as he lingered, trying to work out their puzzling conversation, he found himself smiling too. Their flirting – if you could call it that – had brought a flush to her face that accentuated the emerald of her eyes.

Yet she had been so wary when she'd first bumped into him, quizzing him about his evening in Keswick as if she was trying to catch him out – though God knows why. Still, the encounter had ended far more promisingly than it had begun and he'd gladly make a prat of himself in a stupid costume if it made her happy.

Chapter Seventeen

Lara chose the stairs to reach the family apartment in the castle. She certainly wasn't going to take the lift and risk having to be rescued by Carlos or Flynn.

Her conversation with him the previous day had helped set her mind at rest. The 'rumours' about his personal life were nothing more than the gossip that inevitably circulated in an enclosed community like Ravendale. They were vague and largely involved Flynn having been seen with a woman in a pub and having left behind a trail of broken hearts in Cornwall. Both stories were based on speculation, from what Lara could work out.

To be fair, Jazz had stressed at the restaurant that she didn't give any credit to such tittle-tattle either. Now Lara was annoyed with herself for even wondering why Flynn was talking to Molly at the Christmas market. Of course he would be polite and pleasant to her. She knew him from the café and the Spectacular and she – and her grandmother – clearly loved a chat. Flynn was very good with people, despite claiming to be grumpy.

Lara was pleased he had his friend, Harvey, living nearby, so he wasn't completely isolated from his old life. She wasn't even that miffed that he'd mentioned knowing about the job again. She was just relieved that there was no 'secret woman' or whatever had been implied by the Ravendale rumour mill.

She'd already agreed with Jazz that he'd have had to be a fast worker to start seeing someone in Cumbria so soon after starting work at the castle.

Well, someone other than *her*.

But Lara was annoyed with herself for caring what Flynn did in his private life. She was well aware that she'd been acting inconsistently: pushing Flynn away yet being jealous about who else he might be seeing.

She needed to behave more professionally from now on.

She knocked on the door of the Penhaligons' apartment and Henry opened it. He was wearing his Barbour and a tweed hat and had an excited gleam in his eyes.

'Sorry, I can't stay, my dear. I'm off for a drive around the estate with the estate manager. Fiona's finally agreed to let me out for good behaviour.'

Fiona gasped. 'You make me sound like a prison warden!'

'You'd make a good one,' Henry replied, kissing her on the cheek. 'See you later, and enjoy making the arrangements for the ball. I know you will.' With a wink, he exited into the corridor and Lara heard him talking to the estate manager, a man with a distinctive Highland accent.

'I do hope he's careful,' Fiona said, a worried crease between her brows.

'I'm sure he will be. He looks very excited to be going out. How is he?'

'Still waiting for further tests but, in himself, a lot better.

Thanks for coming up here. Why don't you make us both a coffee while I fetch something I promise you'll find interesting?'

Wondering what Fiona could mean, Lara went into the kitchen. She was unsure whether to make real coffee or instant, but she could hardly delve into the cupboards for the real stuff, so she decided instant would do.

She went back into the sitting room with the mugs but Fiona was still nowhere to be seen. Lara thought she could hear a dull thud of a door opening and closing towards the corridor that led to the family bedrooms.

Sipping her coffee, she marvelled again at what a strange life it must be to own and live at Ravendale. Although it was mid-morning, a fire burned in the hearth and the lamps were on, making the tinsel and baubles shimmer in their light. Lara still hadn't managed to decorate her own cottage, and now she'd have to give up some of her spare time to help Flynn find a costume. Actually, why had she done that? He hadn't asked and now she'd have to spend half an hour with him getting undressed and dressed in various outfits.

Not that she'd be there when he got undressed, a prospect that sent a thrill right through her.

Argh, why hadn't she said Flynn could take the costumes back to his cottage to try them on? She didn't need to supervise, and Flynn's outfit should have been the least of her worries. She hadn't even decided what she was going to wear herself.

'Penny for them?' Fiona broke into her thoughts. She was

holding two photo albums and Lara hadn't even heard her re-enter the room.

'Oh. Sorry, Fiona. I was well away.'

Fiona's eyes crinkled with amusement. 'Yes, you were staring into that fire as if it held the answers to life and the universe.'

'Er, I was just thinking about what I might wear for the ball.'

Fiona's eyebrows lifted. 'Haven't you decided yet?' She laid the albums on the Chesterfield sofa and beckoned Lara to sit down in the armchair nearby. 'I thought you'd have got everything sorted out by now.'

'Not yet. I've been so busy.'

'Gosh, yes. I should have realised. I didn't mean to sound critical.'

'I know you didn't,' Lara said. 'And I can easily borrow one of the re-enactment costumes. I just can't decide which one.'

'The guides' costumes?' Fiona wrinkled her nose. 'They're getting a bit long in the tooth now. I was thinking we ought to invest in some new ones. You don't really want to wear one of those, do you?'

'Well, they're probably more authentic than anything I could find in the hire shops. With everyone booking for the ball and other New Year events, they'll probably only have giant bananas or Elvis left by now anyway. I don't think Bananaman counts as a historical figure.'

'Oh, we can't have that,' Fiona declared. 'But the re-enactment costumes are huge.'

Lara accepted this was true. They all had drawstring waists that could be pulled in, but they were still very much 'one size fits no one'.

'And I think I can help.' Fiona tapped the top photo album. 'These two albums contain photographs from the balls that took place between the wars.' She handed over a large leather-bound album to Lara. 'This is the one from 1920 to 1928.' She kept the other on her lap. 'And this album covers the years up to the Second World War.'

'Wow, these must have so much history. I'd love to look through them.'

'I thought you might, and what's more, I have an ulterior motive for showing you. Have a flick through both and then I'll share my plan with you.'

Twenty minutes later, Lara had browsed through scores of black-and-white photographs of guests, all protected by leaves of embossed tissue paper. There were groups and individuals in a huge variety of costumes, from Roman emperors to pharaohs, alongside fictional heroes such as Robin Hood and King Arthur.

'The family always employed a professional photographer, right from the 1920s,' Fiona said, turning the pages and smiling. 'Family and guests could pose in the hall by the tree when they arrived. It was a novelty to have a photograph then.'

'What a brilliant memento of the ball,' Lara said. 'And of your family.'

'I'm ashamed to say that some of the outfits would now be considered, quite rightly, entirely inappropriate,' Fiona said, grimacing at one of the photos of a group of men in First Nations dress.

Lara winced. 'Hmm. You could look on it as a historical record of the changing times,' Lara said, and turned the page to a group dressed as Peter Pan, Tinkerbell and Nana the dog. 'Some seem to have interpreted historical figures very loosely.'

'We're pretty relaxed on the theme now, and no one who works here would ever wish to cause offence. The thing is, Henry and I – well, me, really – have decided to take inspiration from these albums and choose a costume referencing something one of our ancestors wore. One of the acceptable ones,' she added hastily.

'Oh? That sounds interesting.'

'Hopefully. I also thought that, as you haven't decided what to wear yet, you might like to choose something too.'

'Oh. I—' Lara had to think before replying. 'That's incredibly generous of you, but won't it be a lot of trouble? And take a lot of time?'

'We've already chosen our outfits and Tessa has measured us. It's really cheered Henry up.'

'If you've already given Tessa the measurements, will she have time to fit me in?' Lara asked, thinking of the very clever seamstress who lived locally and was an expert in historical costumes.

'Of course. She won't mind. She's a treasure.'

With only four weeks to the ball, Lara was afraid that Tessa would mind quite a bit. 'It's very kind of you, but I really don't want to put anyone to that much trouble.'

'Nonsense. You've worked so hard and the ball is designed specially to thank the staff, so it's the least we can do. Please do take the albums and have a look overnight. Why don't you decide if there's something you like in there, unless you have any other ideas. We only used the albums for inspiration. Then let me know what you fancy and Tessa can measure you up.'

'I – well, that's very kind of you. I'll enjoy looking at these,' Lara said, realising that refusal might cause offence. Besides, she really did need a costume and a made-to-measure outfit would solve all her problems. Her mind was already buzzing with medieval princesses and Regency ladies. Then again, Flynn was definitely no Mr Darcy. A pang of guilt struck her: she'd be forcing him to wear a tatty second-hand affair while she'd be making an entrance in a made-to-measure costume.

Setting the albums and her fantasies aside, she refocused on the organisation of the ball, discussing the latest responses from the guest list and the period musicians and entertainers she'd booked. This included a troupe of jesters, fire eaters, a Regency quartet, and a swing band for later to get the real party going.

Lara had already shown Fiona a YouTube video of the fire eaters.

'Good grief,' Fiona said in awe. 'That's pretty impressive, but I hope the whole place doesn't go up in smoke on my watch.'

For a moment, Lara thought Fiona was going to mention the Lucky Chalice and its curse, but instead she asked if there were enough car-park stewards.

'Plenty. The same company who are marshalling the illuminations are sending a smaller crew for the ball. They've coped with thousands of visitors, so they can handle a few hundred. And there's enough room in the staff and disabled parking area without using the grassed areas.'

'Good. We can't have anyone tramping through the mud in their finery.' Fiona applauded Lara. 'Looks like you have everything in hand. I hope you can fully relax on the night. That's the general idea – that all the staff can let their hair down after a hectic season.'

'I'm sure they will,' Lara said, although she knew she wouldn't be able to fully relax when she'd been in charge of the organisation. At least Jazz had finalised the menu and was overseeing the caterers, so she didn't have to worry about that.

Once again, Fiona had been so kind to her and yet Lara was keeping the secret of the chalice. She almost confessed there and then, but realised it would be terrible timing when Fiona was so happy and Henry was recovering. It might even set him back.

'What have you decided on for your costumes?' she asked, sounding even to herself like she was strangled with guilt. 'You haven't said yet.'

Fiona tapped the side of her nose and said mysteriously, 'Oh, we're keeping ours a surprise until the big night. But let's say it will be linked to a key moment in Ravendale's history.'

'Oh? That sounds intriguing,' Lara said.

'Yes, but I've hinted too much already. Our lips are

sealed. Please don't even breathe word of our conversation to anyone. Henry and I want to make a real entrance at the ball. I think it will be great fun for everyone.'

'I'm sure it's going to be amazing,' Lara said, picking up the albums. They weighed a ton, rather like her conscience. 'I promise I'll make a decision tonight and bring these back tomorrow.'

Lara spent ages leafing through the albums before she took them back. Although Fiona had said she could choose any costume she wanted, she was mindful of poor Tessa and didn't want to pick anything too elaborate. That was pretty difficult, however, because the more she looked, the more she realised that the wealthy guests of the past had really been out to impress.

There were a few pictures of servants and locals, but they were in much plainer outfits that they'd clearly made themselves.

Most of the photos that had made the album were the poshos. There were peacock feathers, velvet cloaks, hilarious wigs, buckled shoes that had obviously been made purely for the occasion – and, yes, a sprinkling of codpieces worn by portly men with their hands on their hips, trying to channel their inner Henry VIII.

Yuck. Who would ever want to channel a psychopath, thought Lara, rapidly turning the page. What could she wear that would be simple, appropriate and, because she wasn't immune to vanity, flattering? She wanted to look nice, not so much to make an entrance, but to feel confident and not look ridiculous. Every time she wondered what Flynn would think of her being a shepherdess or in a crinoline, she dismissed the thought.

She should choose solely on what she'd feel comfortable in.

Even so … she half-wished he was here to give his opinion.

'No. No!' she said out loud, then started laughing.

In the end, she realised she'd returned time and again to a page with a group of people dressed in medieval costumes and an idea dropped into her mind with such a clang that she burst out with a 'Yes!'

Flynn would be bound to ask what she was wearing. She was filled with childish glee. She wouldn't tell him. Like Fiona, she'd be keeping it a secret until the night.

Chapter Eighteen

On Sunday, Flynn grabbed the opportunity to have a few hours' break from the Spectacular. Flynn had decided to go for a bike ride and then meet Harvey for Sunday lunch at a Lakeland pub.

After breakfast, he donned his leathers and set off. On this still, crisp winter day, there was no thrill like it and his spirits lifted as he leaned into the bends on the twisting roads and whizzed past snow-topped mountains on one side and mirrored lakes on the other.

The roar of the engine sounded like a symphony or poetry to him, not that he'd admit it to anyone but another biker.

They hadn't had long to talk the other evening in town, so Harvey had suggested the lunch. By the time he reached the pub, nestled between Loweswater and Crummock Water, he felt more exhilarated than he had for a long time. His decision to move to Ravendale felt like fate.

He wondered if he would ever be able to persuade Lara to ride pillion with him. He'd thought there was no thrill like riding the Lakeland roads, but he was wrong, because if she was behind him, her arms around his waist, he'd think he'd gone to heaven.

It was difficult to miss Harvey, because he was six foot

five – four inches taller than Flynn himself – and of Antiguan heritage. He played rugby in the winter and cricket for a village team in the summer. Harvey had a table by the window and already had a cappuccino in front of him. Vintage Christmas rock 'n' roll played over the speakers: Flynn supposed it made a change from the classical music at the gardens, which he had now heard approximately one hundred times.

Harv was occupying a settle at a table near the fire and got up when Flynn arrived. 'Hello again,' he said. 'We must stop meeting like this. People will talk.'

Flynn laughed and pulled back the chair opposite. 'Twice in three days. This must be a record.'

A waiter took their orders for a Guinness Zero and a Coke. Turkey was on offer, but Flynn was so maxed out with anything festive that he ordered roast beef. Harvey, a traditionalist, went for the turkey with all the trimmings.

'I never asked you what you're doing for Christmas Day,' Harvey said.

'Not much, I expect.' Flynn had been wondering what Lara would be doing but wasn't ready to mention her name to Harvey yet. 'The Spectacular only closes for Christmas Eve, Christmas Day and Boxing Day. It's not really worth me making the journey south until the New Year.'

'What will your mum and dad say about that?' Harvey had met Flynn's parents a few times when he'd visited Flynn in Cornwall.

'They said they'll miss me but they'll have their hands full hosting my dad's parents.'

'Well, you're welcome to come over to our place.'

'Thanks,' Flynn said. 'Will Carmel mind an extra one for dinner?'

Harvey smiled. 'It was Carmel who asked me to invite you.'

'That was kind of her,' Flynn said, feeling genuinely touched by his friends' thoughtfulness. He wasn't sure how to reply, however, mainly because he didn't want to intrude on a special family occasion.

'You don't have to answer now, you can leave it as late as you want. I warn you that the house will be awash with wrapping paper and the kids will be hyper, but it might be more fun than sitting in your armchair in your cottage on your own.'

'I'm sure it will be.' Flynn laughed.

'Then again,' Harvey said with a sigh, 'I might be desperate to swap places with you by the middle of the afternoon. You also might have other plans, of course.'

Flynn hesitated that bit too long before responding. Lara was staying at the castle over Christmas and he couldn't imagine her being on her own.

'I would love to spend the day with you and it's very kind of you both. Can I hang on? I just need to check I'm not expected to stay at the castle. Obviously there isn't a light show on Christmas Day, but I had heard vague rumours of a staff dinner for all those who were working away from home and on their own on the twenty-fifth.'

Harvey's eyebrows shot up. 'Wow. That sounds like something from *Downton* bloody *Abbey*. All the staff gathering in the servant's hall whether they like it or not . . .'

141

'It does a bit. I don't know any details or even if it's definitely on. I suppose I don't *have* to go to it, either, but I ought to find out what normally happens as I'm the new boy. There are several people who are working over Christmas and won't be able to go home.'

He also assumed that Lara would be one of the people who was bound to go to the communal dinner if it was happening this year.

'I promise I'll find out and let you know.'

'If you do have to go to this thing, then you're welcome at ours on Boxing Day. We usually have a walk, go to the pub, and then come home and eat all the leftovers.'

'That sounds great. You can definitely put me down for that.'

The dinners arrived and the talk turned to all sorts, from the kids' Christmas presents to Flynn's motorbike and sport. Flynn wasn't a big football fan but he'd played cricket and rugby at school and once had a try-out for one of the junior teams at Cornish Pirates. Nothing had come of it and he was now rather glad that he hadn't ended up with a broken nose and cauliflower ears. He thought of Lara's reaction to him if that had been the case and suppressed his laughter.

They'd finished the roasts and were tucking into portions of Cumberland Rum Nicky, a date and rum pie topped with rum butter, when Lara messaged Flynn.

He read her WhatsApp and felt his mouth stretch into a grin.

When he put the phone down, Harvey was watching him carefully. 'Work or pleasure?'

'Erm. Neither . . . and possibly both.' The message had been reminding him not to forget the costume fitting at five.

Harvey scratched his beard. 'Now I'm really intrigued. Go on.'

'If I do, will you promise not to laugh too loudly?'

'I'll try very hard.'

Flynn dived in. 'I'm going for a historical costume fitting.'

Harvey spluttered. 'You what?'

'Mate, you promised not to laugh,' Flynn said, feigning a serious face.

'I – er—' Harvey covered his mouth with his hand. 'I never expected to hear that phrase come out of your mouth.'

Flynn sighed. 'It's for the Twelfth Night Ball. They hold it every year apparently, and it's fancy dress – well, historical costume – and I've been persuaded to join in. For the sake of the team, of course.'

'Well, if it's for the team and it's part of the job, I guess you've no choice, but . . .' Harvey sniggered again. 'You're not going to wear tights or breeches, are you?'

'Not if I can help it,' Flynn replied, struck with horror at the prospect of either. 'The castle manager is overseeing the fitting.' He hoped Harvey wouldn't ask who she – or he – was. 'I can't really wriggle out of it.' Not that he'd want to wriggle out of anything where Lara was involved. Plus, if any 'wriggling out' were to be done, he hoped it would involve Lara shimmying out of the red dress she'd worn when he'd first met her at Halloween.

Chapter Nineteen

'One hundred per cent no.'

'OK. How about this?' Lara asked, holding up a monk's habit.

Flynn snorted. 'I can't see myself as a monk.'

'Neither can I,' Lara muttered. 'OK. What about . . .' She plucked another hanger from the rail in the costume store-room. 'This one?'

'You're joking, aren't you?' Flynn muttered from behind her. 'I did say no jingly bells.'

Lara turned round to find him standing squarely, with his hands on his hips. Since he'd arrived at the room used to store the fancy dress, she'd avoided looking at him too closely, because the slim-fit tracksuit bottoms and T-shirt he was wearing showed off a lean yet muscular physique, honed from doing physical work his whole life.

'Actually, I wasn't joking, but I can see you're not keen.' Lara hung the jester's costume back on the rail with a secret smile. She'd guessed it was a long shot but it had been worth a try, and she'd wanted to see his face.

'I know but . . .' Half the costumes she'd selected had already been pushed to the end of the rail. So far, not one of them had even made it out of her hands. Flynn had scoffed, sworn, and laughed at all six.

'Why don't you come and have a look?'

'I have. There doesn't seem to be much choice.'

'These are the only ones I thought were remotely suitable. Half are female costumes, and while you're very welcome to wear one of those, they're almost certainly too small. There's also a bear, which I did think was very appropriate, but that you wouldn't even consider.'

His eyebrows knitted together. 'Are you trying to say I'm grumpy and scary?'

'Well, you're definitely not cuddly.'

He let out a growl and made a clawing motion. 'Grrrr.'

'And three of the others that might have done have cod-pieces,' she said, stifling her giggles.

Flynn curled his lip in contempt like a pirate – Blackbeard, say.

Lara felt a lightbulb go off in her head and broke into a grin.

'What?' Flynn asked, unearthing a pair of curly-toed slippers from a box on the floor and pulling a face.

'Just an idea. I'm not sure it would work, though . . .'

He dropped the slippers back in the box.

'There is something else I found in the costume cupboard but I didn't bring it out.'

'Why not?'

'Well, I thought it was a bit of a cliché, but the main thing is, it's almost certainly too small. I suppose we could do something about that if we're desperate.'

'If it's not a wild animal and doesn't come with breeches or jingly bells, I'm willing to try it.'

'Well, it does have breeches, technically.'

Flynn opened his mouth to object, but Lara held up her hand.

'Please can you keep an open mind? I'll fetch it. Otherwise, I'm out of ideas and I'm afraid you're going to have to resort to the fancy-dress shop. And at this late stage, good luck with that.'

'So, what do you think?' Lara asked the question as nonchalantly as she could, because Flynn had actually taken the costume out of her hands and was examining it. So far he'd refused to even touch anything, so this was progress.

After a few seconds, he uttered the momentous words. 'It's – er – I suppose it's not quite as bad as the others.'

With an inner punch of the air, Lara carried on casually. 'It's more a bit of fun than historical. I don't really know why it's here, because I've never seen any of the guides wearing it.'

'Wasn't Dick Turpin a historical figure?' Flynn asked, slipping the eighteenth-century-style frock coat off the hanger. 'Or was he made up?'

The black coat, made of wool felt, had a short cape attached. Lara had kept back a fabric bag containing the accessories. He needed time to come to terms with the coat first.

'Oh, Turpin was real enough. He was a horse thief and a burglar and, unfortunately, he killed at least one man, although his exploits have been wildly romanticised since.'

146

Flynn didn't seem put off and inserted his arm through the sleeve. This was progress.

'You see, I wondered if you really wanted to be associated with a highwayman. And Turpin has nothing to do with Ravendale. You could just be a general highwayman, the kind that probably did lurk up on the fells waiting to ambush travellers in the eighteenth century.'

Flynn grunted a reply, busy trying to put his other arm through the other sleeve. He managed to get the coat on but it was obviously too tight across the shoulders.

'Hmm,' he said. 'Bit snug.'

'I knew it would be too small, but maybe . . . I can get someone to add a panel in the back.'

'That sounds like a lot of trouble,' he said.

'Well, a local seamstress is making a costume for me, so I could ask her to do it at the same time as she makes my costume.' She didn't mention that Henry and Fiona had commissioned Tessa or else Flynn would definitely have felt too guilty to agree.

He was still wearing the coat, and not looking too embarrassed, which Lara considered a huge leap forward.

She held up the bag.

'You don't have to wear the breeches that come with the costume. You could just wear some black trousers or jeans, I guess, and there are some boots that would do from one of the other costumes. So you won't have to wear white stockings and add the buckles to a pair of smart black shoes.'

He laughed. 'I don't own those types of shoes and there's no way I'm wearing breeches and stockings, so I would

147

rather wear the boots.' He'd moved to the full-length mirror, turning this way and that and twisting his lips as he scrutinised himself. Lara was slightly worried the back of the coat would rip under the strain of his broad shoulders.

'It comes with a shirt that's quite roomy, but it does have a jabot – that's the lacy neck part. And, of course, there's a tricorne and a mask.'

'What?' He snapped round.

She pulled the shirt from the bag and handed it to Flynn. 'It needs a wash and iron.'

'I can do that,' he said, shaking out the crumpled cotton shirt with its lacy neck.

Lara took the offer as another positive sign.

'Can I try it with the coat?'

She shrugged as if watching Flynn strip off in front of her was all in a day's work. 'Be my guest.'

Seconds later, he'd slipped off the coat and was pulling his T-shirt over his head. Lara wasn't sure where to look, even though she wanted very badly to look at him.

He didn't seem bothered by her being there in the slightest and casually slipped the shirt over his head. Even so, she'd had more than enough time to drink in the sight of his broad shoulders and toned stomach. She clutched the bag with the hat and mask to her, digging her fingers into the cloth bag while attempting to look cool and professional. Not that she supposed it was at all professional to ask a colleague to try on a highwayman's outfit in front of you.

'I suppose it's OK,' he said, tugging at the jabot while the shirt brushed midway down his backside. He still had the tracksuit bottoms on, so it looked slightly strange until he donned the coat as well. With the shirt underneath, it really was a very tight fit.

She pulled the hat and mask from the bag and offered them to him.

'Thanks,' he said, but didn't attempt to put them on. 'Do I really need to wear these?'

'Yes, or you won't look like a highwayman, just a bloke in a funny shirt and coat.'

He smiled briefly then grimaced as he tried to put the mask over his head. Instantly he was transformed into a rakish rogue and Lara's stomach flipped. Was it wrong to feel lust at the sight of Flynn dressed as such a disreputable figure?

He lifted the hat, muttering, 'I'm not sure how this goes . . .'

'The usual way is with one point facing forwards but you can wear it different ways,' Lara explained. 'Sailors often wore the point at the back for a better view of the sea, but soldiers liked to have the tricorne pointed to the left so they could rest a musket on their right shoulder.'

'I'm not a soldier or a sailor . . .' he said, adjusting the tricorne hat so the point was forward.

When he was satisfied, he stood back while he looked at himself in the mirror.

'I look ridiculous, don't I?' he growled.

'I wouldn't say that,' Lara murmured, stifling her laughter. 'Though with a scowl like that on your face, you do look pretty mean. I wouldn't like to bump into you on a dark night, that's for sure.'

Flynn turned back to her with a roguish grin. 'I wouldn't mind bumping into you.'

Heat flooded her cheeks. 'I can see you're getting into character.'

He swished the coat and declared, 'Stand and deliver!'

Lara's pulse spiked but she managed to roll her eyes and say coolly, 'I'm sure highwaymen only ever said that in old black-and-white movies.'

'How disappointing . . .' Flynn replied silkily. 'What about, "Your money or your life"?'

'I doubt it. They were probably thugs, not the romantic gentlemen thieves they're made out to be.'

Flynn stepped closer, his eyes gleaming behind the mask and a tantalising half-smile on his lips. 'Yes, but I could be the exception that proves the rule.'

Lara didn't flinch and met his gaze full on, even though she was finding it hard to stop herself from jumping on him.

'Why don't you come to the highwayman's lair for a drink?' he said, looking down into her eyes.

'I don't think that would be a good idea,' she murmured.

'Why not? Don't you dare?' he said, challenging her.

Lara forced herself to laugh. 'Of course I dare.'

'Then come over to the cottage for a glass of wine. What else are you going to do on a Sunday night?'

Lara couldn't think of a single thing to say. Watching a box set with a glass of wine on her own could hardly match up to spending the evening with a handsome colleague, even if it was a hundred times safer.

'Maybe just a quick drink then. But I won't stay long.'

Flynn whipped off the hat and bowed with a flourish. 'I'll look forward to it, and I promise to behave like the perfect gentleman.'

Chapter Twenty

'Thanks,' Lara said, accepting the glass of red Flynn offered her. 'For the wine and the supper.'

Flynn put the platter of cheese, biscuits and olives on the coffee table so that they could both help themselves. He was thrilled – and surprised – that she'd agreed to come over and it felt natural to offer food along with the wine.

The highwayman outfit hung on the back of the bedroom door. Back in his normal clothes, he and Lara had returned to something akin to colleagues sharing a drink.

'It's not much, but I had lunch at the pub earlier,' he said.

He sat down beside her and Lara took a plate, cut herself a piece of Lancashire, and topped a cracker with it.

'It's perfect. I had a good lunch earlier too. I met Jazz and her family for a walk and we ate at a café afterwards.'

'I went to the Kirkstile Inn with Harvey – the friend I met in Keswick when you were at the cinema. The ride over was great.'

'I can imagine,' Lara said. 'It must be exhilarating.'

Flynn took his chance. 'Maybe you should experience it some time.'

Her mouth was full but she shook her head firmly until she'd finished. 'I don't think so. I'd be petrified.'

'It's not that scary and I wouldn't go fast. I'd choose a straight bit of road for your first time.'

She laughed nervously. 'There are no straight stretches of road round here, as you well know.'

'I'd go slowly, then.'

'Sure you would . . .' Lara said, meeting his eyes, her own filled with doubt yet also sparkling with amusement. Her face was only a foot from his, her leg just inches away. He wanted to lean in and kiss her but he was worried that it was too soon.

She glanced away and sipped her wine, the only bottle he'd had in the cottage. Fortunately, it was a decent Malbec he'd picked up on his way back from the pub along with the cheese and olives.

Lara nodded to the costume hanging off the door frame. 'You'll have to let me have your measurements for the coat so I can ask Tessa about the alterations.'

'Thanks. I am very grateful for your help, even if I didn't sound it earlier. If the coat's an issue, I'll just wear the rest of the outfit as it is.'

They were chatting about the work involved in organising the ball and the traditions behind it when Flynn had a message from his mum.

He glanced at it briefly, smiled, and put his phone down again.

'Something nice?' Lara asked.

'It was Mum. She messages me regularly, usually with some spurious question or reason. I know why. She's always worried that I've come off the bike.'

153

Lara smiled. 'Were your mum and dad disappointed that you decided to move up here?'

'A bit. I used to see them every couple of weeks. They moved to Falmouth after they sold their hotel a couple of years ago. Mum was pretty cut up, to be honest, although my dad had pointed out that Cumbria was probably safer than Mongolia. I pointed out that it wouldn't have been on my South Asian itinerary without quite a detour.'

'Will you get to Cornwall for Christmas?'

'No, it's too far. I promised to go back in the New Year and I've asked them to come north in the spring. I was going to ask you about Christmas. I heard a rumour that there's some communal Christmas dinner here for the staff.'

Lara nodded. 'There is. I went last year and, with the Spectacular and all the events this time, I also don't think I can go home, even if my parents weren't going away.'

'So will you go to it? Is it compulsory?'

She laughed. 'No, it's not compulsory and, yes, I will go. I should, as castle manager.'

Damn, thought Flynn. Bang went his fantasy of a cosy Christmas Day curled up by the fire with Lara.

'What about you?' she asked.

'I do have an invitation from Harvey's family, but I don't want to let that side down either.'

'Don't feel obliged,' she said, adding earnestly, 'I mean it. You're new. You don't have to spend your Christmas Day with a bunch of relative strangers.'

'I don't consider you a stranger,' Flynn said, realising that Lara's presence was the only thing that made this communal dinner attractive in any way. 'Is it in the servant's hall?' he asked, topping up Lara's glass and his own.

She burst out laughing. 'Why do you think that?'

'I dunno. Just something I'd imagined.' Or assumed, he thought, without any evidence. He still had a lot to learn about Ravendale. About Lara. About himself.

'The castle doesn't have a servants' hall these days. The lunch is held in the Castle Café. Everyone mucks in and Henry and Fiona keep well away, apart from paying for it. It's actually quite fun, and if last year is anything to go by, everyone gets pretty merry.'

Flynn nodded. 'I think I ought to go to this Christmas lunch.'

'I'll add you to the list then,' she said. 'Who knows, you might even enjoy it.'

Chapter Twenty-one

Two hours later, the bottle of wine was empty and Lara was curled up on Flynn's sofa, stifling her giggles while listening to anecdotes about his theme-park days.

'You're not serious,' she said. 'They didn't really try to have sex on a Waltzer?'

'They did. It was after we'd closed and they'd sneaked into the vintage fair. Apparently it had always been a fantasy for the woman and her boyfriend was keen to oblige.'

'And you actually caught them?' Lara asked, tears of laughter in her eyes. 'In the actual Waltzer?'

'Well, we knew they were there, so I suggested turning the ride on to . . . alert them, shall we say . . . and so all the lights started flashing and the organ stated playing.'

Lara let out a squeal of mirth. 'The organ?'

'Yes, it was a vintage ride with a huge organ.'

'You can say that again! What happened to the couple?'

'They were a bit shocked and very embarrassed, but, in the end, they were relieved not to get into any trouble.' He smiled. 'You must have caught visitors up to no good during the course of your job?'

She giggled. 'Not actually having sex, though we did

throw two people out for lying on a four-poster bed. They were only kissing, though.'

'Only kissing?' He waggled his eyebrows. 'Are you sure? Were you watching?'

'No, I wasn't watching, but I did have to walk in on them. I could hear the noises so I started to . . . hum outside the door . . . to give them time to stop anything that they might be thinking of doing.'

'What were you humming?'

'The first thing I could think of – 'The Birdie Song'. My dad is always whistling it when he's doing DIY and it just popped into my head.'

'That'd put anybody off!' Flynn said.

She was laughing out loud, her sides almost hurting. 'I – s-so w-wish you'd stop doing this.'

'What?'

'Making me laugh or get mad or do something I shouldn't and that I'll regret.'

'I don't mean to.'

'R-really?' She dabbed at her eyes with a tissue, knowing her mascara must be smeared. She expected Flynn to make a teasing remark but instead he gave her that intense and serious look that made her melt inside.

'I don't want to be something you'll regret. I'm not the bastard lord of the manor. I'm not someone who makes promises he can't keep. I'm someone who cares about you and is ready for a new relationship against all his expectations and fears and plans. I'm someone who just happened to come across you. And you happened to come across me.'

He'd switched the mood in an instant, from sexy banter to serious grown-up stuff. She could feel blood pulsing through her, making her body tingle from her scalp to the tips of her toes.

'Have I overstepped the mark?' he asked solemnly.

'No. No, and let's get this straight. You're about as far from the lord of the manor as it's possible to get.'

His mouth lifted at the corners and his eyes lit up.

'But it doesn't matter. It's the being ready for a new relationship that's holding me back from taking this – *us* – any further. You know I lost my job, my home, when I split with Rob. I don't want that to happen again.'

'If it did – and I hope it won't – I'd be out of the door before you even had to think about asking me. I'd *never* put you in that position.'

Somehow, Flynn had picked up her hand and held it, as if to emphasise his point.

'I – believe you. I truly do, but I also don't want to be hurt again. After Rob, I couldn't handle getting involved with someone who's tied to anyone or anything else. I know I can't predict or control the future but I'm only trying to protect myself.'

'I do understand what it's like to find out someone's not what you thought they were, but I don't have any skeletons in my cupboard.' He stroked the back of her hand and gazed into her eyes, making every nerve ending come alive. 'And I also know there's no true happiness in life without taking risks. We both have no ties . . . us getting together may, possibly, be a disaster waiting to happen . . .'

Lara found herself smiling and shaking her head, disagreeing with him – perversely – for some insane reason. The insane reason being that she was wavering and she was tired of denying herself a chance of happiness and the chance to kiss him and be in his arms and know what it would be like to be close to that gorgeous body. To wake up next to him.

'What if a disaster doesn't happen?' he asked, moving closer and resting his hand on her cheek. 'What if this is a good thing and stays a good thing for . . . a very long time?'

Her skin turned molten under his touch. 'Why do you always make me doubt myself?' she murmured, uncurling her feet and turning to face him.

He shook his head. 'I don't want you to doubt yourself.' He withdrew his hand and she felt as if she'd turned her face away from the sun into shadow. 'I want you to be sure. That you're not just doing this because you've had half a bottle of wine.'

'Half a bottle?' She laughed. 'That's not enough to make me do something I don't want to.' She ran her hand along his arm, resting it on his bicep and squeezing gently.

'And tomorrow?' There was a raw edge to his voice. 'What happens when we have to face each other in front of everyone? How will you feel about me then?'

'I don't want to think about tomorrow. This is now and I want to do something before I can change my mind.'

It was Lara who closed the space between them and knelt astride him. It was her choice to kiss him and push him back against the sofa. If his lingering doubts were gone, she'd thrown hers to the winds. His mouth was like warm velvet and he tasted of wine. Sparks exploded inside her, and she gripped his shoulders, pushing against his mouth greedily.

She found herself lifted off the sofa, and wrapped her legs around his waist so he could carry her into the bedroom. Reckless joy filled her as Flynn lowered her onto the bed, kissing her again, over and over.

There was a moment when he stopped kissing her to strip off his shirt, but then he was next to her again, taking off her jumper and dropping soft kisses on her collarbone and chest.

Any thought of anything beyond giving herself up to Flynn and his body had vanished.

What a night; the best night. Lara thanked the Lakes' long winter and the need to spend the dark hours huddled up together under his duvet, keeping each other warm. And the warm glow that suffused her body when she woke to find he was beside her, his dark lashes against his cheek, one arm flung over the pillow, still fast asleep.

It hadn't been a disaster. It had been a night of joyful, hot sex and, now, even the gloomy Lakeland morning seemed like a bright new dawn. She was so glad she'd set her fears aside and taken that leap, but now she had to face reality. She certainly wasn't ready for her colleagues to know she was – what? – seeing Flynn? Sleeping with him? Dating him?

Telling herself to live in the moment, she lifted the duvet off her, swung her legs out of bed, and fumbled for the clothes that were still scattered on the rug next to the bed.

The room was pitch black and she'd no idea how she was going to get dressed.

'Morning.'

The gravelly voice from behind her was accompanied by a warm hand trailing down her back. Lara turned to find Flynn sitting up, his hair rumpled, and blinking in the lamp he'd just switched on. Lara was dazzled too, and not only by the light. Her desire kindled again at the sight of that honed torso with the sun tat on his right pec. She'd kissed it last night and asked him where he got it.

She knew almost every inch of him now and she was way past blushing.

'Do you have to go?' he asked.

'It's half-six already. I ought to go back to mine before every man and his dog are up.'

'Pity,' he said, smiling up at her. 'But I understand.' Flynn lay back on the bed with a sigh, hands behind his head. 'I'll see you later?'

'Bit difficult not to.' She zipped up her jeans.

He watched as she found her bra and fastened it with his hot gaze raking over her. 'How will I cope, knowing what I do now?'

OK. Maybe she *could* still blush, she thought, feeling her cheeks warm. 'You'll have to pretend nothing happened. We still have to work together.' She felt that she'd be wandering around Ravendale with a big sign on her back: *Yes, I slept with Flynn and I can't wait to do it again.* The thought made her want to laugh but was closely followed by a flutter of unease.

'You won't tell anyone?' she asked, sitting down on the bed, holding her top.

Flynn pushed himself up. 'Of course not. I'm not that guy, Lara. I'd happily shout about us from the rooftops if you want to, but we're going at your pace.' He took her hand and she kissed him, a heartbeat away from getting back into bed.

However, he ended the kiss and said, 'I'll get dressed and act as lookout for you.'

He threw off the covers and got out of bed completely naked. Lara reluctantly tore her eyes from his body and put her top on while he dressed.

She nodded. 'I left the light on all night in my hallway. That's unusual.'

He turned to her. 'It's hardly suspicious.'

'No, but this is such a tiny community. The gossip is terrible.' She now felt guilty at taking Jazz's rumour even slightly seriously.

'I can imagine. It was the same wherever I've worked.'

'Has that been your fault?' she asked jokingly.

'Sometimes, maybe. Not as often as I'd have liked . . . I'm joking, by the way.'

Even the sneaking around – checking that no one was watching – had held a sexy frisson. She'd behaved like a nun for so long, obsessed with being the perfect employee. Rob had made her into a romantic recluse even after she'd begun to get over the broken heart. It was time she took a risk.

From his sitting room, Flynn peered round his curtains. 'Coast is clear, though it's so dark out there I'm half guessing. It's icy too, so be careful or there really will be a drama to explain.'

'I'll be careful.' She joined him by the front door for one final lingering kiss before he opened the door just enough for her slip out, hiding behind it himself.

'See you later,' he whispered, with a glint in his eye that almost trashed her resolve.

She answered with a nod, flitting out of the door, then gasping at the cold air and almost tripping over the boot scraper in her haste to get across the courtyard to her cottage.

A few seconds later she was safely inside, high on adrenaline, still not quite able to believe her daring. The spectres of the past: lost loves, superstitious fears, and future music to be faced had receded into the shadows. This bright new hope in her life – Flynn, moving forward, and leaving the past behind – was far more dazzling and joyful than any Christmas lights.

Chapter Twenty-two

Flynn practically skipped down the steps from the castle after his late afternoon meeting and emerged into the courtyard.

He was almost tempted to whistle before realising how cheesy that was and also that it was so out of character that it would definitely arouse suspicion among his team. All that hearts and flowers stuff, red roses, etc. – he'd never been into it. He'd rarely had to do the running or wanted to do the running. Yet, with Lara, he was acting the opposite of cool, pursuing her and thinking about her all the time. Last night had been incredible and he was eager to repeat it as soon as possible.

The Spectacular was on the brink of opening for the evening. Generators hummed and the lights glittered through the trees and on the castle walls. As he walked along the light trail to check all was well before heading to the lighting contractors' control room, he was caught up in the excitement of the evening as never before. Perhaps it was because he felt he had things under control, that he was finally able to relax a little and experience the trail from the visitors' point of view.

Or maybe it was because he felt his life – his inner, fullest life – had been reignited again.

Families began to appear, kids shrieking and laughing, their parents pointing out the glowing figures and shimmering trees. Over the hum of chatter and generators, he could hear the classical music from the terraced gardens.

He bought a coffee, checking with the kiosk staff that all was well, then took a short cut to the Ice House grotto to make sure everything was in order, as its damp location had made it the most prone to glitches.

The Christmas tree entrance was ablaze with lights, the reindeer grazed peacefully on the Ice House roof, and a queue to meet Santa had already formed.

Flynn stopped, sipped his coffee, and watched as the helper elves crouched down by pushchairs and soothed the small children clutching their parents' and grandparents' hands.

'Hi there . . .'

Flynn hadn't noticed Molly appear at his side with Esme in her buggy.

'Oh, hello. You're back again?' he said, surprised.

'There was a half price discount for a second visit.'

'Are you going to see Santa?' he asked, smiling at the face peeping out of a furry hood, a rattle in her hand. 'I mean, is the baby going?'

'Esme?' Molly laughed a little nervously. 'Not this time. But my friend's little boy is. That's Kaden, there in the queue, second from the front?'

She pointed at a boy of around three-ish – Flynn was hopeless with kids' ages – wearing a Gruffalo onesie and tiny wellies.

'Lovely,' Flynn said, having nothing else he could think of to say. 'Um, have a lovely evening. I was on my way to the control centre. Just grabbing a quick coffee.' He threw the cup in an adjacent bin to signal he was leaving.

'Flynn . . .' she said.

He turned back from the bin, surprised to hear her use his name. She must have overheard Lara using it in the café.

'Yes?'

Her knuckles whitened on the handle of the buggy. 'I – er – wanted to talk to you.'

'To me?' he asked, knowing he should be getting back to work but sensing that she needed him to stay. When she didn't say anything, he asked, 'Is everything OK?'

She shook her head. 'Not really. I mean, it's nothing awful but – oh God – I've wanted to say this for so long but now it feels so scary, I don't know how to do it.'

Flynn's skin prickled yet he had no idea why. He didn't know this girl. He'd never seen her in his life until very recently. 'I think you'd just better say it,' he said, as gently as he could.

She put her hands over her face as if she'd lost courage, then blurted out, 'You're my dad. And Esme's grandad.'

Chapter Twenty-three

'I kept waiting and waiting to see if you had any clue. Mum's always said you didn't know about me.'

'Your mum?' Flynn said, thinking he must have misheard what Molly had said, because what she'd said was impossible.

'Imogen,' Molly said slowly. 'Imogen Harrison? Don't you remember? Buttermere 2006?'

'I er – don't—' Oh, God. 'I – *do*.'

Flashes of waves lapping a moonlit shore came back to him. Of a dark-haired, very pretty girl he'd met on a visit to see his grandparents in Whitehaven. He and some friends had gone camping for the night at a tiny Lakeland site and ended up drinking round the fire with some other young campers. He'd also ended up with one of the girls.

Her name was Imogen – or Immy, as she'd introduced herself. She'd worn an ankle bracelet and she had a Northern accent and a laugh as warm as the sun. After they'd virtually ripped off each other's clothes and had sex down by the lake, they'd sat together drinking cider, Immy wearing his sweatshirt to ward off the evening chill – until her friends came for her. She walked away, laughing and refusing his pleas for her number.

'Don't spoil it, Flynn . . . Let it be perfect like this for ever. You know it can't go anywhere. We live too far apart and I have plans.'

She had plans. And he'd have bet his right arm they didn't include having his child.

'It's coming back to you, isn't it?' Molly asked, staring at him with the same disapproval that his own mother had always shown when he'd come home late after being out on his bike. 'You and my mum hooked up on the last night of the holiday. She said you'd drunk loads of cider and had sex by the lake. That's when I was conceived.'

'Oh God.'

She'd pushed the buggy to the side of the Ice House where it was a little quieter, but Flynn was still conscious of the world rushing by while he was trapped in a surreal bubble.

'Mum was on the pill but she'd had a stomach upset and you were both too drunk to use a condom. You told her that, even though you were Cornish, you hated surfing, had just passed your motorbike test and one day you'd have a Harley Davidson.' Molly paused before adding in a quiet voice. 'And that she had beautiful eyes . . .'

Flynn was too stunned by the details to reply, both the intimate ones and the specifics of what he and Immy had spoken about on that evening. It all sounded so reckless now, though, at the time, it had felt spontaneous and special. His throat felt very dry, his voice strangled when he finally recovered himself.

'I am – s-sorry.'

Molly looked hurt. 'Sorry I'm here?'

'No!' he burst out in horror. 'No, I didn't mean *that*. I'm sorry I never knew. Sorry that you had to find me and your mother never tried to find me. Are you – are you 100 per cent sure, though? That I'm your father?'

'I'm sure,' Molly said fiercely, 'but I guess it's a shock. We can do a DNA test if you like, but I know what it'll say.' She sounded so confident and she knew so much detail about that night that only her mother could have told her. 'Mum said she didn't even have your number so she couldn't find you. She knew your first name and what you looked like but, back then, you weren't online. It was only ten years later that she finally found out you'd joined Facebook.'

'I don't do social media . . .' Flynn said, having always had a horror of sharing his boring existence and innermost secrets with the ether. 'I didn't want to join then, but every-one had and was using it to arrange meeting up. I felt I ought to.'

'You regret it now, I bet.' Molly laughed. 'Because Mum did find you.'

'B-but why didn't she get in touch with me?'

'I was ten by then and she didn't want you getting involved. She'd managed on her own and met someone else. Her life had moved on. We all moved on without you.'

'How did you find me now?' he managed, hearing him-self dismissed as an irrelevance – someone who might as well not have existed – in his own child's life.

'I've known your name for a while. When I was four-teen, Mum decided to tell me all about you. It was only when I had Esme that I knew how much I wanted to find you myself. Esme changed the way I saw myself – and my place in the world, I suppose. I realised what being a parent means when she came along. Her dad isn't much of a part of her life and so I appreciated what my mum went through to bring me up – on her own until I was four and she met my stepdad. I wanted to know who my birth father was.'

From the buggy, Esme let out a wail. Or it could have been a gurgle of excitement or hunger or cold – Flynn had no clue what his granddaughter – *his granddaughter* – wanted or needed. All this time . . . He'd had no clue his daughter existed.

It made him feel almost dizzy. He thrust his fingers through his hair. 'I swear I had no idea . . .'

'I can tell that,' Molly said. 'It's a shock and I wish I'd told you another time, not at your work, but I've been holding on for so long now that it just burst out.'

'What made decide to you tell me – now?'

'Maybe I still wouldn't have searched for you, but I overheard two of the castle workers in the café talking about the new man that had started. They said your name: Flynn Cafferty, and that you used to live in Cornwall – in Newquay.'

'How the—' Flynn bit back the expletive, some inner filter reminding him that his child and granddaughter were present.

'I almost dropped a tray. I knew straight away it was you. I didn't know what to do after that.'

'Does your Nan know who I am?' Flynn asked.

'She knows your name but she didn't connect it with

you. When she was going on about you being handsome, I thought she might guess, but she's only seen one photo of you from years back. You had short hair and were wearing a baseball cap and you looked younger.'

'I've aged a lot recently,' Flynn muttered – and most of it in the past five minutes.

'You don't go online much,' Molly said. 'Not for a bloke your age. Most are forever sharing photos of themselves on holidays or in the gym trying to look cool.'

'I'm sorry to disappoint you. Still, you did well to track me down.'

'I also saw that you updated your LinkedIn,' she said proudly.

'My LinkedIn?'

'You sound very impressive.'

'I promise you I don't mean to.'

Esme shrieked in delight – or derision. Was she old enough to be sarcastic? Of course not, but Flynn didn't actually know how old she was. Seven months? A year? It was a complete guess.

Molly smiled and placed Esme's toy penguin within her reach again. 'So that's why Nan had no idea that she was talking to my father, and . . .' Molly grimaced. 'Saying you were handsome. Sorry about that. I love her to bits but she can be very embarrassing.'

Flynn made an unintelligible noise. He couldn't form a coherent response in the face of this one huge revelation. It was like a giant sun, irradiating every other thought. He had a daughter, and a granddaughter. He was a father and his child and her child were here in front of him and apparently living down the road.

'I – I am – sorry . . . I – um – do you want to get a coffee?' he asked, wondering what excuse he could make to leave the Winter Spectacular and where could they go to speak privately.

'I don't think that's a great idea. Esme needs her bedtime milk and, anyway, do you really want to talk about this in public?' she added, reminding him that they were standing in the middle of hundreds of people, his work colleagues a moment away. It was a miracle no one had called him on the radio yet to ask where he'd been.

'No. Yes. I mean you're right,' Flynn said, realising Molly was more mature than he had given her credit for.

'I could meet you tomorrow, though?'

'Yeah. That would be good.' *Good? Was it?* 'I can get some time off,' he said, vowing that he'd make time.

'Should I come here? I don't want Nan to know I've found you yet. She might have a heart attack.'

She's not the only one, thought Flynn, his body stiff with tension. 'Yes, if you don't mind. You could come to the cottage. I can meet you in the visitor car park. We can talk at my place.'

'OK.' She beamed.

Esme let out another wail and, this time, even Flynn could tell it was a cry of demand.

'OK, sweetheart. I know. It's almost bedtime.' She looked at Flynn with an eye roll. 'She probably needs a clean nappy too. I'd better get home fast. I don't want to change her in the public toilets here. Too busy.'

'You could use my cottage . . .' he offered, before he'd really known what he was saying. But Esme was his flesh and blood.

'Thanks. But I'll get her home. I can see your place tomorrow—' she hesitated and, for a second, he thought she might call him Dad, but instead she grasped the buggy handles and said, 'See you tomorrow. What time?'

'Six-thirty?' He dragged up a smile from somewhere because he thought it was how he ought to react. 'I'll look forward to it.'

The words came out of his mouth but they hadn't seemed to come from his brain. They had just emerged as a pleasantry he might say to an old friend, to Harvey, or to Lara. Oh God, Lara . . .

'Me too, and we can definitely arrange a DNA test if you want to. It might give us all some certainty, even if I am sure,' said Molly.

'Yes. Probably a good idea.'

She lifted Esme's hand in a wave.

'Bye,' said Flynn, and lifted his own hand and somehow managed a smile for the baby and his daughter.

Molly wheeled the buggy away between the flanking yew trees and he watched until she turned a corner and vanished.

He was alone again, and his first thought was that he had woken from a very vivid dream. It wasn't a nightmare, and it wasn't a joyful dream that he wanted to step back into. It was a strange out-of-body experience. Had he been hallucinating? Was he drunk? Was there another layer of consciousness that he needed to pierce through?

He looked up at the spiky branches, sparkling with a myriad of lights. He could hear shouts and laughter again, and a child screaming 'I want to see Santa!', and the cannon boom of Tchaikovsky's *1812 Overture* from the fountains.

He was definitely fully awake. Molly and Esme really had been there. And what she'd said had to be true. She knew so much – the details. The lake, the dates, the cider . . .

Why would she make it up? And when he'd looked, really looked at Molly, he could surely see himself in her. Take away the red streaks in her hair and that was his own thick, almost black hair. And her eyes – a deep brown flecked with amber. Then there was her height, the confidence, the challenging gaze, and the direct manner . . . she had to be his daughter.

His daughter.

A rush of emotion surged through him: fear and shock, and joy that brought tears to his eyes. He hadn't cried for a decade or more and yet here he was, in the middle of a working day, tears on his face.

'Flynn! There you are. I need you.'

It was Lara's voice behind him, yet he dared not turn round, so he pulled a tissue from his pocket and covered his face, blowing his nose noisily.

'Sorry,' he mumbled, blinking and wrinkling his nose in an almost comic way. 'The cold got to me. Hope it's not flu. I can't afford the time off.'

'Me neither,' she replied. 'Seriously, I hope it isn't flu. Not at this particular moment especially. Everyone's looking for you. The lights have gone out in the Ice House – sorry, grotto, and we have a queue of kids and parents. Santa's resorted to his phone torch but we can't allow anyone else in because of health and safety.'

Flynn cursed softly, sighed, then heard his voice speaking calmly, as if disassociated from his body. 'OK. On my way. I'll soon have everything sorted, don't worry.'

Chapter Twenty-four

Lara plumped the sofa cushions again and checked she had enough good coffee – not that Flynn would notice a cushion if it fell on his head or care about coffee. She was annoyed with herself for even touching a cushion; it was a signal that she was starting to be too excited.

Yet she knew better than most that once you'd started to fall for someone, it was almost impossible to avoid that rollercoaster.

So, she decided to be kind to herself and accept the fact that she'd been on a high ever since she'd fallen into Flynn's arms and into his bed the evening before.

Not even the day's small trials could dampen her spirits: a Portaloo issue or the cancellation of a corporate Christmas event. On the upside, Tessa had kindly agreed to make her costume for the ball and to alter Flynn's highwayman outfit to fit his physique.

Flynn was on duty that evening and they'd arranged to meet up after the Spectacular had ended and he'd finished closing everything down. She hoped he wasn't too knackered after sorting out the grotto problem. He'd need his energy . . . a thought that made her want to laugh. At this rate, they'd both give the game away by looking permanently knackered at work. She'd already had to stifle a yawn during a health and safety meeting.

She checked her phone. The site closed at nine officially, but Flynn might be up to an hour after that. It was only eight-thirty, so she had a while to wait. She might as well relax and watch some TV or read a book, not that she could concentrate on either.

She'd restarted a historical documentary three times when Flynn messaged:

Grotto issue still not totally sorted. Probably damp :(Don't worry but it might be a late one. Don't wait up. F x

And that was it. Lara felt as if she'd been dunked into an icy lake. How disappointing. Poor Flynn. He must really be up against it to bail out. Still, it couldn't be helped. She might as well get an early night and catch up on her lost sleep even if he couldn't. There was always tomorrow evening when they were both off-duty.

She suggested he come over after her Zumba class and, with that pleasant thought to console herself, she settled down to watch TV with a hot chocolate and tried not to dwell too much on what she was missing out on.

'You're looking well, Lara,' Henry whispered at the end of the Christmas tour the following afternoon. One of the guides felt unwell and had to leave at the last minute, so Lara had stepped in.

'Thanks. You're looking better yourself, if you don't mind me saying.'

Henry beamed. His cheeks were ruddier again and he was more relaxed. 'Mustn't grumble. This diet is a nuisance, though I do feel like I have more energy and it's better than being carted off to hospital. I wonder if I dare have a mince pie. No, perhaps not. Fiona might catch me.'

Lara was not up for such self-denial. While the tour group admired the trees and decorations, she tucked into the mince pies that Jazz's team had served in the banqueting hall. With just over two weeks to Christmas, there was an air of excitement and anticipation that was infectious.

Her mood was also helped by a serious dose of anticipation and excitement that had nothing to do with presents or Santa coming down the chimney.

She didn't even have to wait until dinnertime, because she bumped into Flynn on her way out of the castle.

'Flynn. Hi.'

His mouth opened in surprise, as if he'd been startled by her. He looked very harassed.

'Problems?' she asked.

'What?' he said, frowning, almost angrily, before his expression changed to the wry grimace she was used to. 'The usual. Actually, I'm glad I caught you. You know you suggested I come over after your dance class tonight?'

'I *did*,' Lara said, with a wrinkle of her brow.

'I'd forgotten I was meant to meet Harvey for a drink. I've got some presents for his kids and I promised to hand them over and I'll be pretty late back. I've got a very early start in the morning, so I thought – um – maybe it's a good idea for us both if we sleep in our own beds tonight?'

'Oh,' Lara said, taken aback. 'I see – erm, well you can't let down a friend. It's fine.' It wasn't really fine but she wasn't going to make a thing of it. 'We can rearrange . . . I'll just have to contain myself a while longer,' she murmured, with a look that spoke volumes. She had thought of kissing him and not caring who saw them but didn't dare.

He flashed her a smile in return. 'Yeah. We can.'

'Speak tomorrow? It's not as if we won't see each other around,' she said, with a knowing eyebrow raise.

Flynn smiled back. 'No. Yes. We certainly will,' he said. 'See you. Have to go. Carlos is after me and I don't want him to think I'm skiving.'

'No, you don't want that . . .'

'Speak soon,' he said, and with a wave of the hand, hurried away without looking back.

Lara shivered as if a sudden cold wind had rushed down from the fells, heralding a storm to come. Then she sighed and walked back to the cottage. Flynn was busy and their relationship was barely a day old. He had a prior engagement – an unfortunate choice of words, she thought, but it described the situation well. Her life didn't revolve around him and she was looking forward to seeing Jazz at Zumba. How she would manage not to blurt out her secret about Flynn, though, she wasn't sure.

Chapter Twenty-five

Flynn baulked in surprise at finding Molly outside his door with the buggy. 'Esme too?'

'I had to bring her. My nan – Brenda – is out with her friends and I don't want her to know I'm here. I don't have a babysitter. Is that OK?'

'Of course it is. It's great,' he said, trying to sound warm and welcoming. 'Um, let me help you in.'

Together, they lifted the pushchair over the low step into the cottage and Flynn returned to the doorway. While Molly unloaded Esme, he glanced to left and right, making sure no one was watching. The last place he looked was Lara's window before he finally closed the door. The cottage was in darkness, as he'd expected. She should be at her dance class now.

After unstrapping Esme from her pushchair, Molly carried her into the sitting room ahead of Flynn. Esme stared back at Flynn like a baby owl. He wasn't sure whether to stare back, smile, or try to make conversation with her.

'This is cosy,' Molly said, looking around the room with unabashed curiosity.

'You think?' Flynn's palms were sweaty with nerves.

'It's smart. Minimal. I suppose I kind of expected it to be grander.'

He smiled. 'Not for the staff.'

'It still looks like a holiday let on changeover day. Too tidy to be a real home. If you know what I mean . . .'

'I do,' he said. 'I left a lot of my stuff in mum and dad's garage. You have to travel light on the bike and this place came fully furnished.'

Molly wrinkled her nose. 'Not very Christmassy, though, is it?'

'I haven't had time and, to be honest, I'm all Christmased out after a day surrounded by illuminated reindeer and Christmas tunes on a loop.'

Molly nodded. 'Yeah, I can understand that.'

'Would you like to sit down?' He grabbed a blanket. 'Esme can use this so she can play on the floor. Does she crawl yet? I can move anything that might be dangerous, but, like you say, I don't have much stuff.'

'Thanks, and she can crawl a bit.' Molly deposited Esme on the fleece blanket and sat cross-legged beside her. 'I'll stay down here to keep an eye on her. Would you mind fetching her bag from underneath the buggy?'

Flynn was very happy to do so, as it gave him a few extra seconds to compose himself. He marvelled at how well-organised Molly was. She unearthed a variety of toys from the bag, along with bottles, blankets and spare clothes, before repacking it. She was even more organised than Flynn was when he packed the bike.

'How's that, then, baba?' she asked, handing a plastic giraffe to Esme. 'Here's Sophie. It's her favourite.'

He smiled. 'That bag's like Mary Poppins' one. Bottomless.'

'I need to make sure I've got at least three of everything.'

'I must be hard work, managing on your own . . .' he said, watching his daughter playing with his granddaughter, and trying to get used to even thinking those two words, let alone using them out loud. Sooner or later, however, he would have to get used to it. The realisation hit him like a sucker punch: everything in his life had changed for ever.

'I've got Nan to help,' Molly said, as Esme crawled towards a wooden car. 'And Mum when she has leave from work or is between contracts.'

'What about Esme's dad? Does he ever look after her?' Flynn asked, trying to recover himself.

'We're not together any more, but that's fine with me,' Molly said, sounding as if she'd said the line many times before. She must have had a lot to deal with in her young life. 'He works at the nuclear power station up the coast. He does visit Esme sometimes, and he helps out a bit, financially, but he wasn't the one and I'm not wasting my time with someone who isn't the one.'

Flynn nodded and sat down, briefly at a loss as to how to reply. 'By the way . . . I do remember your mum. Even though we were only together . . . for a very short time, I thought she was a lovely person. She had a great sense of humour too.'

Molly smiled. 'We both do. Did you actually know where she lived?'

'Somewhere up north.' He grimaced.

Molly sniggered. 'Up north? That's a big area!'

'I thought she said Yorkshire. Sorry, I was nineteen and clearly geography wasn't a strong point.'

Molly rolled her eyes. 'I'm only nineteen and I know the difference between Cumbria and Yorkshire. And where Cornwall is,' she said, again making him feel like the child being told off by a parent. Then again, she'd had to grow up fast with Esme to look after. 'And she did live in Yorkshire. We both did until I was two, when we moved to Cumbria. That's where she met my stepdad. Ex-stepdad.'

Stepdad. So, another man had been part of Molly's life, rather than him? Flynn's stomach turned over with jealousy and guilt that he hadn't been there. It was an emotion he'd rarely experienced and it felt toxic.

'He didn't stick around long,' Molly said, as if she could read Flynn's thoughts. 'Mum kicked him out after a couple of years.'

Sitting up on her mat, Esme gurgled and batted the green frog on her baby gym.

'It's no use trying to change the past,' Flynn said, not sure if he meant that or not. What else could he say? 'You said your mum isn't often around? Do you live with her?'

'Mum's usually abroad. She's a holiday rep supervisor, so she moves around a lot. We both live with my nan. Mum shares the house with her. It saves rent and keeps Nan company since my grandad died.' Molly laughed, a warm laugh that triggered a powerful memory of her mother more than anything had before – because no memories had been triggered before.

183

'Esme and me are lucky to have a home with Nan, and Mum when she's here.'

'That must be tough for your mum, being away from you all.'

'She loves her job and obviously she needs the money, but it means she'll miss Christmas with Esme.'

'I understand,' he said, though he wondered if he would ever understand anything again.

Esme made grunting sounds, which Molly seemed to understand. 'She's overtired.'

'She looks lively enough to me,' Flynn said, as Esme bashed the living daylights out of her toy penguin. 'Can I get you a drink?'

'Water will be fine, thanks.'

When he returned with a glass for her and for himself, Esme was sorting through her wooden blocks, examining and trying to chew them.

Flynn was fascinated by every tiny movement and expression. Was she really his flesh and blood? He cleared his throat and sipped the water.

'What about you?' Molly asked from the floor. 'You haven't said if you have any other kids. Though from the shock on your face when I turned up, I assumed not. You're on your own, so I guess they could live with their mum, but I kind of assumed you didn't.'

He had to smile. She was a shrewd character, perhaps world-weary by nature – like himself. 'No, I don't have any kids. Any other kids,' he corrected himself, feeling like he would never get used to this new reality.

'Have you ever been married? Or is that woman from the café your girlfriend? She's the manager here, isn't she? I googled her too after you left,' Molly said.

'Did you know who I was before I came into the café?'

'I knew you'd started work at the castle. I'd overheard the gossip and, when you walked in, one of the staff mentioned it to my boss. She's the one who didn't want me hanging around your table.'

'Bloody hell,' Flynn murmured. 'Were you sure it was me – I mean that I was your dad?'

'I was pretty sure. I mean, I was sure, I suppose, but I couldn't quite believe it. It was so weird, seeing you sitting there with your friend – Lara, isn't it? – and telling myself it was you.' Molly fiddled nervously with a toy brick. 'Have you told her about me?'

'No. Not yet.' Flynn's heart sank. It was only two days ago that he'd told Lara he had no skeletons in his cupboard, no commitments. How was he going to tell her about this?

'Is she your girlfriend? Won't she want to know?'

'We're just friends,' Flynn said, not wanting to go into detail and still unsure of his exact relationship with Lara. Whatever it was – or was going to be – it would surely have to change. God, he didn't know how to tell her or how to deal with it.

'You seemed more than friends to me,' Molly said sagely. 'I can tell from the body language. I like watching people. I was doing Psychology A level at college before I had to take a break to have Esme. I'd like to be a child psychologist one day.' Molly ruffled Esme's hair but there was a wistful tone to her comment. She'd had to put her dream on hold at a very young age to devote herself to her daughter. He admired her for it. So many plans had been shattered in a moment.

'If it's not Lara, is there anyone else?' Molly went on, with the boldness of youth.

'No, no one else. Not now.'

'Now? You're thirty-nine, and you're still single?'

'Erm . . . I suppose I am,' Flynn said, not knowing how else to answer.

'It's not easy finding the right person to make a commitment to,' Molly said, handing a wooden block to Esme that was just out of her reach. 'You see, I thought Esme's dad might have been the one, but I soon realised he wasn't. He's harmless enough, according to Nan, but he's not for ever material or dad material.'

Not dad material. The words were like yet another sucker punch. They were a bit too similar to the words Abi had used about him.

'I've only just started my new job here . . .' Flynn added.

Esme bashed her penguin with a wooden hammer and babbled, 'Ba ba ba.'

'Hmm. OK. It's only I thought you might have taken the job because of Lara – or someone.'

'I didn't know her before I came to Ravendale,' he said, skating over the detail that he had met Lara before, although briefly. 'I was asked to start early. They needed someone urgently for the role and I thought the castle would be a great place to work. Who wouldn't want to live up here?'

'Oh, you see, when I first heard you'd moved, I did wonder if you'd found out about me.' For the first time, Molly's confidence seemed to wobble. 'But if you had, you would have said something when you saw me in the café.'

Flynn felt terrible, but he owed his daughter honesty – along with a whole lot more that he could hardly bear to think about yet. 'I wish I had known. I would have wanted to find you a long time ago.'

She nodded, seeming soothed by his response. 'Are you angry with my mum for not telling you?'

Flynn hesitated. His main emotion at that point was a shocked numbness, but how could he express that to Molly? 'I'm not angry. I'm still coming to terms with the fact I have a daughter and a granddaughter.'

Esme was chewing her penguin's beak. 'She loves Penguin,' Molly said, stroking her daughter's dark hair.

'Are you going to tell your nan about me?' Flynn asked.

'No!' she cried, the first time he'd really seen her in a panic. So far she'd been far more at ease with the situation than him, but he reminded himself she'd had a long time to think about how she'd handle it.

'She'll surely have to find out eventually.'

She sighed. 'I suppose so. I need time before I tell her too. I don't want her having a heart attack.'

Flynn smiled. From what he remembered, Brenda was barely older than his own parents, who were fit and healthy and enjoying an active retirement. 'I doubt that will happen.'

Molly pursed her lips. 'Well, I don't want her to know.

Not yet. Nor Mum. I want to get to know you myself first before I hear their opinions.'

'Do they have opinions of me?'

'No, because they don't know anything about you other than you ride a motorbike and worked at an old house and at the theme park. Why would they?'

Flynn felt slightly sick. He was a complete stranger to his own daughter and granddaughter. She didn't know if he was a criminal, a total bastard or a pillar of the community.

'I do know you're not a serial killer,' she said with a wry smile.

Flynn laughed. 'Well, I'm pleased you've established that much.'

'I've got a friend in the police. I asked her to run a check on you before I came here.'

'Christ. Isn't that illegal?'

'Yeah, but my friend owes me.'

'Won't they find out she looked me up?'

'No. Don't ask how,' Molly said with a grin. 'You don't think I'd just turn up here with Esme without making sure you aren't a psycho, do you? And I watched you for a while. With the people who work for you. With your friend. The woman. I could tell you were decent.'

That's a pretty short time to make such an assumption, thought Flynn, but didn't say anything.

Esme battered the penguin with the hammer again, gurgling with laughter. Flynn knew how Penguin felt.

Flynn sipped his water. He had that disturbing out-of-body sensation again. He'd wake up in a moment . . .

Esme had dropped her toys and even Penguin lay abandoned. She let out a cry that cut through Flynn. She had real tears on her cheeks and, for some reason, he felt devastated. He hadn't held Molly at that age and now he'd never have the chance. The pain of loss was sharp; it was physical. How could he react so strongly to losing something that, a day ago, he'd never even known he was missing?

Molly dabbed at her daughter's cheek with a tissue. 'Poor baby. She's tired out. I have to go home soon and feed her and get her to bed.'

'Of course,' he said. 'She's – she's beautiful.'

'She is,' Molly said with pride, lifting her daughter up from the blanket. Esme immediately stopped crying and was all smiles again. 'Do you want to hold her?'

'Um—'

'It's not compulsory.'

'I do want to hold her. Of course I do. She seems happy at the moment, though. What if I start her crying again?'

Molly smiled. 'You won't.'

Flynn wouldn't have bet on it.

'Esme,' she said, bringing the baby closer to Flynn. 'This is your grandad. Grandad Flynn.'

Flynn's throat was choked with emotion. He felt a tidal wave of emotion bearing down on him.

Esme reached out her hand to touch him and her fingers rested on his cheek.

'Hello,' he said. 'Hello, Esme.'

She tugged his hair with surprising strength and he yelped, 'Ouch!'

'Now, now. Don't pull Grandad's hair.'

'It's fine. It's OK.'

She gave the baby to him, and Flynn was amazed by how heavy she felt. Molly was stronger than she looked. Esme looked into his eyes in the frank, almost unblinking way that very small children had but that he'd always smiled at or ignored. Now, he found he could not tear his eyes away from this child.

Molly laughed. 'That's her owl stare.'

Esme let out a sudden and heartfelt wail.

'Sorry,' Flynn said, as his eardrums throbbed.

'You keep saying that. What are you sorry for? That I found you? That you made a mistake that night in Buttermere?'

Esme settled down to pulling his hair, which gave Flynn the chance to utter a few comic 'ouch'es and scrunch up his face before he answered. 'I actually meant sorry for making Esme cry, but I don't feel I made a mistake. I'm sorry I didn't know about you. Sorry that your mum didn't feel able to tell me. Sorry for all the things I've missed.' He tried not to sound bitter, because he honestly didn't know how he felt about missing his own daughter's entire childhood. He'd lain awake wondering how his life would have been, trying to decide if he felt angry or cheated – it was all so new that he didn't know what to feel.

'I'm sorry too. That Mum didn't want you to be part of my life. At first, when I was born, she said it was because she couldn't track you down, but I think she could have. We both could have.'

Flynn was too choked with emotion to reply.

Esme wriggled and Molly said, 'I really must take her home now or she will be a nightmare all the way back in the car. She's already over-excited by all the Christmas disruption.'

'Christmas?'

Molly took Esme from him and laughed. 'Yeah, it's happening in two weeks' time. Less. I'd have thought you'd have noticed, running a Christmas Spectacular?'

'I – of course. I get so caught up in the work aspect, I forget that it's a real event, if you know what I mean. It must be exciting – Esme's first Christmas.'

'It is, though more for me and Nan. Mum's really sad she can't be there but can't wait to call her. But she has been out a lot more. Playgroup Christmas party, shopping with Nan, and now you, of course. Her routine's all over the place but I don't mind.'

Tell me about it, thought Flynn. His routine had been blown to smithereens, along with his life.

Molly put Esme back in the buggy and said she'd send off for a DNA test kit that evening. She knew the process. It was obvious she'd given it careful thought. Flynn agreed, even though he knew what the outcome would be.

He offered to walk her to her car in the visitors' car park but she said no, so he watched her walk across the courtyard pushing the buggy. The castle walls were washed with white and violet, and the buzz of excited families filled the night air. It would soon be Christmas and he had a family. He wasn't just responsible for himself. He wasn't free and single and surely no one who was a grandparent could describe themselves as young, even at thirty-nine.

He watched Molly strap Esme into her buggy and tuck a blanket around her.

After Molly left, Flynn closed the door and stood in the sitting room, unable to move. Then, he sat on the sofa, put his head in hands, and wept.

Chapter Twenty-six

'Phew. That was intense. I wasn't sure how'd I cope with those new moves at the end. After two kids, it's all turning a bit dodgy down below.' Jazz collapsed into giggles, setting Lara off. 'Sorry, too much information.'

Lara swigged from her water flask in the local village hall after their Zumba class. 'I must admit that I thought I was going to have to ask for oxygen at one point. It was all so fast.'

'I thought I was going to pass out by the end.'

The upbeat music of her Zumba classes always cheered her up. Lara had enrolled through the autumn months to give her something to brighten the dark nights and as a total contrast to her work at the castle. Jazz, meanwhile, had carved out a precious night away from childcare duties that didn't involve 'stuffing my face with a sharing bag of crisps and a giant glass of wine'.

Who cared that the music for this final week of the 'term' was Christmas classics? At least Lara didn't hear Mariah Carey blasting out at Ravendale.

She even felt a little more optimistic about the chalice, although she wasn't going to tell the Penhaligons about it just yet. And the ticket sales were beyond everyone's expectations, driven by word of mouth on social media as well as some cold but dry spells of weather.

En route to the ladies' cloakroom to pick up their sports bags, Jazz asked, 'Shall we go to the pub on the way back?'

'Do you have time?'

'I can spare half an hour and it *is* my night off. Luke is in charge. Anyway, I want to leave it long enough to give him an outside chance of getting the kids to bed. They were totally hyper after the school Christmas mini disco. In fact, they've been in a permanent state of over-excitement since the middle of November.'

'No wonder. How many times have they been to the Spectacular?'

'Three so far, and Oscar says he wants to go every night once school finishes. I've tried to tell him that Mummy spends all day there anyway but he's adamant.'

Lara could imagine Jazz's two lively little ones, aged five and seven, badgering her day and night. They were lovely kids, hyper and exhausting but also sweet-natured and funny. Not for the first time, she imagined how her own child or children might be if she'd had some. Would they be lively and sporty? Geeky and quiet? Redheads like herself? Blond as Rob was . . . her heart squeezed with the echo of loss and her jaw ached with the effort of maintaining a smiling face to hide her pain.

'Wouldn't be without 'em, though, and I know these days will fly by soon enough. Oscar is already asking some awkward questions about Santa and why he was living in the Ice House at the castle but we've fended them off so far.'

'Oh, I hope you get a couple more years of magic yet.'

Jazz held up her crossed fingers. She wasn't aware that Lara had been pregnant when she and Rob had split up. That was too personal a secret to share yet – if ever – and Lara certainly didn't want to be a cloud of gloom, especially on an evening that was meant to be devoted to relaxation and fun.

The village hall had no showers, so the only option was to spritz themselves with body spray and put on jeans, clean T-shirts and hoodies. It wasn't ideal but they hadn't exactly been running a marathon. Most of the class members had headed straight home, but there were still a couple of regulars in the cloakroom, also changing.

Lara peered in the mirror to put on some lip gloss.

Jazz frowned at her from behind.

'What's up?' Lara asked, lip gloss wand in hand.

'Nothing. The opposite, in fact. You look glowing.'

'Do I?' Lara laughed and turned round. 'It's my sweaty post-Zumba look.'

'No. It's not only the Zumba. You have an inner glow. You have for the past few days now. Your eyes are shining and you look happy.'

'Compared to my usual harassed frown, you mean?'

'You rarely look harassed. Though I think you hide the stress well. You're the Miss Cool, Calm and Collected of the Castle.'

More like Miss Panic, Lara thought, remembering the state she'd been in over the chalice. 'But thanks. I do feel life's on the up.'

'Is there a specific reason?'

'I—' she was about to say no, but realised that Jazz deserved her honesty. Besides, Lara was bursting to share. 'Come on, let's freshen up and I'll tell you at the pub.'

The Fellside Inn was nothing special but it was cosy and welcoming, and they passed it on Jazz's way to Ravendale, where she would drop off Lara before heading to her own house in a village a few miles further on.

Because of the route, Jazz usually drove, which gave Lara a chance to relax over a drink. She decided to try the pub's 'homemade' mulled wine and took her glass and Jazz's elderflower cordial back to the table. The pub was quiet midweek but there was a fire crackling in the hearth and the beams were adorned with fairy lights.

Lara sipped her wine and felt her limbs relaxing very pleasantly.

'So, what's the secret behind the inner glow?'

'I think you might have guessed, but before I tell you more, please promise me that you won't let on to anyone. Flynn and I – we're such an early days thing that I've no idea if it will last or what. I feel I'm tempting fate by even telling you that we're – well, I don't know what we are.'

'Wow! You're having hot sex with the hot biker guy?'

'Jazz!' Lara squeaked. 'Please, please don't say that in public. Or at all.'

'Why not if it's true?' Jazz asked with a cheeky grin. She did lower her voice however. 'I'm very happy for you. Both of you. He seems a nice, decent guy and he's hot. And I have to apologise, as I feel like a total cow now for passing on that stupid gossip. I should have known better.'

'It's OK. I'd have done the same, if our roles had been reversed. I know you didn't mean it maliciously and you'd no idea we were – interested in each other.'

'That's very generous of you. Oh, this is so exciting for you, Lara.'

Lara nodded, wanting to grin from ear to ear but still cautious. 'I didn't think it was fair to keep you in the dark. We're having to skirt around each other and pretend there's nothing going on. I don't want to be the centre of attention and Flynn definitely doesn't. Also, I can't shake off the worry that I've gone and done something I swore I'd never do.'

'Oh . . . what's that, then?'

'Date a work colleague. After Rob, I swore never to do it again, because the fallout is just so huge.'

'Only if it goes wrong.'

Lara sighed. 'Yes.' She also could have added that she'd also been determined not to fall for any man who wasn't willing to make her a priority in his life.

The fire glowed in Jazz's brown eyes. 'And he'd be the one who'd be out on his ear, not you. He isn't the lord of the manor here. You're top dog: he'd have to go.'

'He said that too, but . . . I don't want anyone to have to leave. Even by getting together, the risk is that both of us could get hurt and he'd probably end up quitting.'

'Lara, stop projecting so far forward. I get that His Shitty Lordship made your life impossible, but this isn't the same situation and my gut tells me that Flynn is one of the good guys. Who knows, he could even be the one?'

'Hmm,' Lara said, trying to shake off the sense of unease that niggled at her despite her friend's wise words. 'I'll admit that would be very nice.' Very nice indeed, she thought, as a memory of Flynn lounging in his bed wearing zero clothing came into her mind.

'Let's drink to it, shall we?' Jazz said, smiling as she lifted her glass. 'To "the one" and to a much happier Christmas than the last one. You deserve to let your hair down and celebrate more than anyone I know.'

The Spectacular was winding down when she arrived, so she was grateful for being able to cut in to the private staff car park and avoid the crowds queuing to leave. She slipped across the courtyard to the gate that led through to the staff cottages area but stopped under the archway. Flynn was helping a woman with a buggy down the step from his place. In the light spilling from the doorway, it was unmistakably Molly the waitress and her baby.

Lara dipped back into the shadow of the gateway. Flynn was saying something to Molly but she couldn't hear what. She wasn't sure she *wanted* to hear, but one conversation was ringing in her head.

'I'd forgotten I was meant to meet Harvey at a pub. I am sorry.'

So why wasn't Flynn meeting Harvey at the pub? Lara had expected him to be out until much later. Why was he here with Molly?

She could accept that his plans to meet Harvey had

changed, but what was Molly doing in his cottage? With her baby too?

It could hardly be anything suspicious with the baby in tow, but it was very odd. She was probably half his age and, as far as Lara knew, they were strangers.

He'd tell her as soon as he could, she thought. She could even knock on his door now and ask him, yet something held her back.

Why should she hassle him? It would seem needy, and she would never ever be needy again. Not after Rob. Not ever.

No, she would wait for Flynn to explain, as he surely would.

Telling herself there would be a perfectly reasonable explanation, she walked to her cottage and went inside, turning on the lights.

Who knew, Flynn might pop over at any minute with a 'You won't believe what happened tonight' tale they could both laugh at.

Chapter Twenty-seven

By late afternoon the next day, Flynn still hadn't popped over to her cottage. Despite having spotted him three times around the estate, he hadn't come up to her to offer any explanation at all.

Lara refused to be the one to ask him why he'd lied to her and why Molly had been at his cottage. She'd wasted plenty of time coming up with answers to both scenarios but not a single one of them made her feel any better. Speculating was useless; she had to hear the truth willingly from his own lips.

They bumped into each other as darkness was falling and Lara was on her way back to her office after leading a tour. He was striding along a path that skirted the rear of the kitchens in a way that suggested he didn't want to be held up. When he spotted her, he pulled up suddenly and looked startled.

She wasn't sure she even wanted to speak to him, but there was no escape now. 'Hi there,' she said, cheerfully enough.

'Hi.' He grinned – nervously? Or was she being paranoid? 'How was your class?'

She felt it was a strange choice for the opening of their

conversation. 'It was – it was good. How was your evening with Harvey?'

'Harvey?' His brow creased in confusion. 'It was – OK.'

Despite her sinking heart at his lie, Lara kept a smile on her face. It was just about possible Flynn had decided to meet his friend locally and then Molly had turned up the moment he'd got home.

'Where did you meet?' she asked.

'Oh, the White Hart at Ravenglass.'

She nodded in approval. 'Nice old place. Christmas menu, was it?'

'Um. The usual stuff. Turkey, Christmas pud.'

Lara looked into his handsome face and felt queasy.

He looked around as if hoping someone would come to his rescue. 'I'm sorry, I can't stop. I have to go. I was on my way to sort out an issue with the grotto.'

She raised her eyebrows and said lightly, 'Again?'

'Unfortunately.' He grimaced, but in a charming way. Even so, Lara felt a chill spread from the roots of her hair to her toes. 'Catch you later.'

Flynn never did catch her later, although he didn't have much chance. Lara had gone back to the cottage, then gone for a costume fitting at the Penhaligons' apartment. The linen toile Tessa had made for her to try fitted like a glove, and the fabric she'd chosen was so beautiful she wanted to cry. Even so, it was very hard to keep smiling and joking while Tessa pinned her and made tiny adjustments with Fiona hovering around like a mother hen.

She went home and called her parents. Then she got involved in a long exchange of messages in a WhatsApp group of uni friends from Birmingham days. She watched a Christmas special of a favourite comedy and then went to bed, at which point she finally had the opportunity to think about the reasons why Flynn would openly lie about his relationship with Molly.

It was the following evening, after she'd finished work, that he finally knocked on her door.

'Hello,' he said. There was no trace of the charming smile and his serious expression set alarm bells jangling immediately. 'Are you busy?'

'Erm. Not really.'

'I – think we need to have a chat.'

Goosebumps popped out all over her body. Even though she'd known that something sudden and not at all good had happened between them, the realisation still made her legs feel weak. 'You'd better come in,' she said.

'Thanks.'

She closed the door behind him and joined him in the sitting room.

'You've put your Christmas tree up,' he said, almost in wonder.

'Yes. I thought it would be too late if I didn't do it soon.'

'I haven't got round to mine. I don't think I will now.' He brushed his hand over his chin. 'For all kinds of reasons.'

Of all the statements he could have made and all the ways of leading into a conversation that she knew would not end well, this was the one she'd never have guessed.

'What do you mean? Why would you not have a tree up? Are you – are you leaving Ravendale?'

'No! Nothing like that. No.'

She felt her shoulders slump in relief but then said, 'But something's wrong. I know it is, and I know that you didn't meet Harvey at the White Hart the other night.'

'You do?' He raked his fingers through his hair. 'Oh, shit. Damn. I am so sorry, Lara.'

'For lying?'

'Yes. I – I couldn't think of anything else to say in the moment.'

'I guessed that. But all you had to do was be honest. If you were meeting Molly from the café, all you had to do was say. If there's something . . . between you, then you only had to tell me.'

'Something between me and Molly?' He had an expression of horror on his face. 'No. No. It's not that. It could *never* be. Lara, I can't believe you thought that.'

'What else was I to think when you lied about seeing her and I saw her at your place with the baby. Is Esme yours?'

'Oh my God. What a bloody mess . . .' He sat down heavily on the sofa. 'Esme isn't my daughter. She's my granddaughter and Molly is her mum.'

Lara steadied herself with a hand on the mantelpiece. Nothing he said made sense. At no point had she even dreamed of such a scenario. 'You mean that Molly is your *daughter*?' she managed, after a few seconds. 'But . . . you don't have any children. You're too young. It can't be . . .'

'I thought I didn't until last week. Molly presented

Esme to me and told me the truth and, believe me, I am old enough. Molly's only nineteen and I'm thirty-nine.'

Lara sat down on the chair. 'But you had *no* idea about them at all?'

'No. I had a one-night stand with Molly's mother, Imogen, which resulted in Molly. She didn't have my contact details to tell me she was pregnant and then, once the baby was born, she decided not to try and find me.'

'You mean she kept the fact you had a daughter from you for all this time?' Lara could barely believe anyone would deprive a parent of knowing their child.

'Yes.'

'That's – that's awful. And – you're 100 per cent sure?'

'We've sent off our DNA – me, Molly, and the baby. The results will be back soon, but I know it's true. The details all add up and now I'm face to face with her, she does look like me.'

'I hadn't noticed, but, then, I wasn't looking for any resemblance. I can't believe her mother didn't tell you before, though. To keep you from seeing your child is awful . . .' Lara added, then regretted her blunt statement and realised she probably wasn't helping. 'Sorry. I'm a bit stunned.'

'Trust me, I'm struggling to understand why Imogen did it too, but I have to think of Molly and Esme first, and not how – how robbed – I feel. I might see things differently in a few days or months, but, right now, I'm still in shock and living from one day to the next.'

'Why did Molly choose to tell you *now*?'

'She'd known who I was for a while from social media and

then found out I'd taken the job at the castle. I think it became impossible for her not to tell me the truth, especially as having Esme had made her realise what being a parent means.'

Everything Flynn said made sense and yet Lara was too stunned by the news to think straight. And if she was stunned, how must he feel?

He leaned forward in his seat and reached out his hand, then pulled back. 'I am so sorry for not being honest with you about where I'd been the other night, but it was a hell of a shock. I wasn't thinking straight and I needed time to process a bombshell like that myself before sharing it with anyone. You're the only person I've told.'

Lara felt the gravity of him choosing her to confide in. 'Has she told her mother or her grandmother that she's tracked you down?'

'Not yet, although I've asked her to. She's not keen for now, but I don't feel comfortable with them not knowing.'

'You must want to speak to Imogen, though. You must want to know from her why she didn't tell you about Molly for so long?'

'Of course I do, but Imogen is working abroad and I'm respecting Molly's wishes for now. If I'm to build a relation-ship with her, she needs to learn to trust me.'

Lara nodded. 'I don't suppose you can do any different if that's what she's asked of you.' Even so, thought Lara, Molly was making some big demands of Flynn.

'Thank you,' he said, sitting back and sighing with relief. 'Thank you for listening, and I know you won't tell anyone else.'

'Of course I won't. I wouldn't.'

He took her hand. 'I know I can trust you and, for that, I can't tell you how grateful I am.' He hesitated. 'Lara, my head is so messed up right now, I think I need some time to process everything.'

'I'm glad you've been honest with me,' she said, hiding her misery with a bravery she didn't feel one bit. 'And you know what I think? You need time to come to terms with everything and so, until then . . .' she said, not knowing if there would ever be a 'then' when he suddenly had a whole new family and lifelong commitment to embrace. 'I mean, I think we should probably take a step back from this – from us.'

Although she was saying what she thought were the right things – for both of them – part of Lara hoped he might disagree and insist they should carry on as they were, despite all the turmoil in his life. On the other hand, she didn't want to force Flynn to tear himself into pieces trying to give everything to a new relationship as well as a new family.

'I never wanted things to end up like this. So soon after we . . .' he began in a voice full of anguish. 'But, even though it's killing me to say it, you're probably right that we should take a breather.' He stepped forward and brushed her cheek with his fingers. 'Oh God, it feels as if I don't even know *who* I am right now.'

'Life will never be the same . . .' Lara said, forcing herself to sound upbeat. 'For the best, though.'

He enfolded her in his arms even though she was itching to get away and lick her wounds. 'And how can I expect you to deal with all of this stuff?' he murmured 'And now that Molly has reached out to me, I owe it to her and Esme – and to myself – to try to make sense of it all and give them what they need.'

Lara was trying to hold it together and say the words a sensible, loving friend would say, even if those words weren't the ones she wanted to say. 'I get it. Of course you need to focus on your family. They need you and you need them. But I am here. I am always here if you need me. As a – a friend, if you want.'

'Thank you, thank you,' he said, looking down into her face. 'I know you've been through a messy relationship already and I'm so sorry this happened now. It's terrible timing.' He seemed almost on the edge of tears himself.

Gently, Lara extricated herself from his arms. 'It's OK.'

'It's not,' Flynn said gently.

'No . . . but it is – what it is,' Lara said, even though it was a phrase she hated and had never believed in. You could always take your fate into your hands, or at least how you reacted to it. She wouldn't stand by and be passive again after waiting around for Rob. More than that, how could she ever come between Flynn and his family? She'd wanted her own so much and she would never jeopardise his newfound joy. 'I'm so happy for you, Flynn. This is a wonderful discovery even if it's not the perfect way to find out. You need to seize every moment and make up for lost time.'

'Lara . . .' he said, with a look of tender agony in his eyes that almost made her burst into tears.

'You know where I am if you do need me or want to talk.'

'I do. I will.' He let out a groan. 'My phone is going off again. I wish I could ignore it, but it's Molly – it might be about the test. I – I'll catch you later. And Lara, thank you for being so understanding. You're a wonderful person. I'm so sorry.'

With that, he walked away, phone clamped to his ear.

Lara forced herself not to watch him go and turned away, compelling herself to walk back into the sitting room, all the words she'd left unsaid silently screaming to be let out.

She wanted to scream that the timing of this revelation was absolutely shitty. That life was unfair. That she would have been devastated to be deprived of her daughter for nineteen years. That she would have been shocked and overwhelmed too, but that she would have welcomed the chance to share the burden – the new dimension – with someone who would listen and try to help with navigating this scary, wonderful thing that had exploded into his life.

Chapter Twenty-eight

'Now, isn't this all terribly exciting?'

'Very.' Lara answered Fiona through gritted teeth while Tessa bustled around her like a seamstress from a bygone age. She'd never had a made-to-measure outfit of any kind and it felt weird trying one on.

The three of them were in the Penhaligons' apartment, with Lara in her leggings and T-shirt. Henry had been banished to the estate office with the head gardener and the doors were locked.

'Can't have anyone walking in,' Fiona had declared, turning the key in the lock. 'Not while you're trying the costume for size.'

'Would you mind keeping still just for a few moments longer?' Tessa said, holding out the almost-finished costume. It was stunning and only needed some final adjustments.

'Sorry, it's me. I'm distracting her,' Fiona said. 'Honestly, I ought to be too old for dressing up, but I feel quite giddy with excitement. The children keep asking me to send photos, but I've told them they have to wait until the ball.'

So the dynasty would turn up for the ball, then, Lara thought.

She didn't think Fiona could ever be giddy with excitement but she did start to laugh before Tessa gave her a glare that wiped the temporary mirth off her face. It was a brief moment of levity since Flynn had told her about Molly the night before.

'Fiona, it would help if you didn't keep distracting Lara,' Tessa said.

'Why don't I go and make us all some refreshments?' Fiona still sounded more gleeful than guilty.

'And I'll stop fidgeting,' Lara added, slipping the costume over her head.

The final fitting should have been exciting. Lara had been looking forward to dressing up and to the ball. She'd imagined the look on Flynn's face when he saw her Lady of Shalott outfit, an updated take on the medieval costume she'd spotted in a photo of one of the previous guests at the ball.

She had no choice but to continue to focus on the Twelfth Night Ball, seeing as she was one of the chief organisers, but now the thought of attending it herself, dressed in her finery and making merry, was about as appealing as being thrown in the dungeon.

Now she was rueing the day she'd ever chosen such a doomed character as a lovelorn woman pining for one of the Knights of the Round Table.

With some umming and inaudible mutterings, Tessa finished her pinning, then marked a few things in a notebook and rose to her feet.

'OK. You can breathe again now,' she said, and called in the direction of the kitchen, 'You can come back in now, Fiona!'

Fiona walked in carrying a tray with a china tea set and a plate of mince pies.

Lara drank the tea but declined the mince pie. Mince pies were way too festive to suit her mood right now. Talk turned to Christmas plans, but Lara was itching to get away.

'How are the plans for the staff Christmas lunch going?' Fiona asked.

'Um. Good. It's all in hand.'

'How many people do you think will be going?'

'Eight or nine. Not quite sure yet.'

There was a knock at the door and Henry called, 'Am I allowed in yet?'

'What's the password?' Fiona joked, before unlocking the door.

'It's F.L.Y.N.N. He's with me now,' Henry said.

'In that case, you can come in.'

Lara almost dropped her cup. If it had been her decision, the door would have remained locked.

'Flynn gave me a lift back in his truck,' Henry said, entering the room with a beaming smile.

Flynn lingered in the doorway, unwilling to cross the threshold.

'Thank you, Flynn,' Fiona said.

'No problem.'

He caught sight of Lara and Tessa and nodded a polite greeting. Tessa seemed frozen to the sofa, teacup in hand, her eyes out on stalks. Even in his work combats and Ravendale hoodie, Flynn could have that effect on people.

211

'Tessa's been fitting Lara for her Twelfth Night costume,' Fiona said.

'I already told him we might not gain admittance to the boudoir,' Henry said with a chortle.

'It is not a "boudoir", Henry,' Fiona said icily, 'it's a salon. Two quite different things.'

'I stand corrected,' Henry said, with a twinkle in his eye. 'I bet you looked lovely,' he directed to Lara. 'Don't you think, Flynn?'

Lara wanted to sink through the cushions of the sofa.

'I'm sure she did,' Flynn managed without catching Lara's eye. He was as tense as a coiled spring in his obvious urgency to escape.

'We were just talking about the staff Christmas dinner,' Fiona said. 'Are you going to be joining the rest of the team?'

'Er. I – um – I'm not sure yet.'

'I thought that as you were so far from your family, you might enjoy it,' Fiona said.

'Flynn might have other options, my dear,' Henry said, perhaps sensing Flynn's discomfort. 'Now, am I allowed to have a cup of that tea before it's stewed? It's parky out there.'

'Of course. Flynn, would you like a coffee? I can make one.'

'No, thanks. I really must get back to work. I'm meeting the builders about a quote for relocating the fire systems from the dungeon in the New Year.'

'I won't keep you from that,' Fiona said. 'It's long overdue.'

Flynn beat a hasty retreat. Lara wanted to make her own exit but also leave enough time for Flynn to be out of the way first.

'Isn't he wonderful?' Fiona said dreamily after he'd gone. 'One of our better decisions.'

'I'd say so,' Tessa chirped up. 'I was quite discombobulated. I'd love to see him in his full highwayman costume.'

Henry sniggered. 'When he first turned up at the castle, we thought the ghost of Sir Roger – a long-gone ancestor who'd vanished on the moors – had materialised. He made a dramatic entrance in the middle of our Halloween dinner, dripping wet in his motorcycle leathers.'

Lara would never forget Flynn's arrival at Halloween either, not long after the other guests had been hearing about Sir Roger's disappearance.

Tessa fanned herself with her hand. 'Oh my, I'd like to have seen that.'

'I have to be going too!' Lara clattered her cup rather too hard in the saucer. She found it impossible to deal with the Flynn Appreciation Society any longer. Any moment now, Tessa would set up a Facebook fan page and be making TikTok videos about him.

'Oh, of course. We're keeping you from your work.'

'Not at all. I'm very grateful for the costume. I'm sure it will be amazing and thank you for the tea. But I have to meet a party of Japanese tour operators for lunch and persuade them to include Ravendale on their Lakeland tour itineraries.'

'Gosh. I'd almost forgotten about that. I'll be down in time for lunch too,' Fiona said, 'once I've smartened myself up.'

Lara left, once again avoiding the lift in case Flynn was called to rescue her from it. She didn't need rescuing – never had and never would, but it was hard not to feel the weight of disappointed hopes as she trudged down the staircase to the ground floor.

It was embarrassing to mope over a man she'd only known for such a short amount of time, even though she understood his reasons for cooling things with her.

'Lara.'

She jumped. Flynn peeled himself off the wall outside the exit to the courtyard and shoved his phone in his pocket.

'I wish you wouldn't keep doing that,' she said.

'Sorry, I was waiting for you.'

She also wished he wouldn't do that. 'I thought you were busy.'

'I guess we both are but I had to talk to you. I feel so bad that it's my complicated life – my relationships – that have made things so difficult for us .'

Lara was about to tell him that she didn't want to cool thing but then reminded herself that 'complicated' was the exact opposite of what she'd been looking for. In fact, she hadn't been looking for anything: Flynn had roared into her life.

'You – you have too much to deal with at the moment,' she said mechanically, before adding, in an attempt to lighten the mood, 'It's not as if we'd started anything serious, is it?'

'Anything serious . . .' he echoed her words, a deep frown etched between his brows.

'We've only known each other a few weeks. We hadn't even gone public, which is a good thing.' Apart from with Jazz, she thought, and how she regretted that now.

'No. I suppose that's something to be grateful for,' he murmured.

She was trying to convince him she was fine – and herself – and probably doing a terrible job of both. 'Flynn, it's not ideal but it's not the end of the world.'

'No, I was only wondering . . .'

She let him founder and finish his phrase.

'I – you're right, it's not the end of the world. I don't want to drag you into my mess.'

'It's not a mess. It's – a shock, but, actually, I think it's pretty amazing. And you should . . .' Only now did she feel emotion clog her voice. 'I think you should make the most of every moment. Like I said, I'm here, as a friend, to help if you ever need it or just to talk. If you want to.'

The stables clock struck twelve.

'I have to go. The Japanese delegation will be here any moment and I want to greet them at the front door.'

Abandoning Flynn, she hurried off to the banqueting hall without a glance behind.

It was impossible to prevent bitter memories from resurfacing. Was it being with the Penhaligons and hearing their comments about their children, who would turn up for special occasions and, eventually, take up their inheritance?

Lovely as Fiona and Henry were, they existed in a different universe. Like Rob.

'The estate needs an heir. It's a bore, but it's down to me to continue the family line.' Rob had actually said that to her.

You could never be sure whether Rob was in earnest. He liked to throw out one-liners, often just for effect or to be witty or shocking. Even if you knew him very well, as Lara had thought she did, it was occasionally hard to tell when he meant what he said.

However, no matter how often he might joke about providing an heir for the estate, and how 'bored' he affected to be on this topic, Lara had always known he was deadly serious.

And the fact that he said it several times while they were actually in bed together, having had amazing sex, did make her wonder if he meant she was the one he wanted to continue the family line with. She'd been crushed with humiliation when she'd learned the truth: that Rob had probably never even considered 'carrying on the family line' with her.

'You said you loved me. Did you ever really mean that?' She had asked him when he ended it.

'Of course I did. I still do, and you'll always be special to me, but with Tabby and I, it's on a different level. We've been around each other for so long. We're like an old pair of slippers.'

He had laughed. Lara hadn't.

'An old pair of slippers.' She would never have described Rob's fiancée as that. Tabitha struck her as the type of woman who wouldn't be seen dead in slippers. She was more a spike-heeled pair of patent Louboutins that had only touched a pavement to move from a chauffeur-driven car to a five-star restaurant.

Lara was the pair of slippers: well-used, well-worn, but never meant to be seen in public and now consigned to the bin. And she felt foolish now, for making such a leap, but still angry with him for leading her to believe they had a future.

'I mean, you must have realised that you and I were never going to be a long-term thing. You're a realist and you must have known the score.'

She'd always been a plaything to be discarded once he found a suitable person to carry on the dynasty – and an ordinary peasant like herself was never going to be it.

She never told him her 'news' because, a few days after their conversation, she realised she wasn't pregnant after all. She'd lost the baby. It didn't matter that the miscarriage had been very early – only a few weeks: she was still devastated. She'd gone home and in the depths of despair and told her mother what had happened. Her mother, naturally horrified, and angry with Rob, had blamed him for causing Lara so much worry and stress that she'd miscarried.

Lara would never know, but the shock couldn't have helped, and when she returned to work, she resigned.

She was thirty-four. She did want a family one day. It was just that 'one day' now seemed further in the distance than it ever had – and she had begun to fear that the one day would never come, not with a partner she loved.

She'd only known Flynn for six weeks but she'd started to believe that they might have a future too. Was it just her? Was she someone who jumped to conclusions or misjudged situations? She'd never wanted to be the cliché and yet now she felt she had been – twice.

Flynn had done the running. Flynn had wanted them to get together despite her misgivings, but he hadn't forced her. She'd made the decision, and she genuinely believed that he had had no idea about Molly. She understood that it was a huge shock to him and firmly believed that he needed to put his new family first and take time to come to terms with this huge change in his life.

So, why did all these rational explanations fail to lessen her feelings of disappointment that clung to her like freezing fog?

Then again, she thought, conscious of the now-imperfect chalice nestled in its blue satin case, maybe she was just plain unlucky.

Chapter Twenty-nine

The following morning, Flynn had a few hours off and so handled the total implosion of his life in the only way he knew how: he took off on his bike.

Twisty roads took a lot more skill and concentration but, most of all, you forgot everything else except your ride. He felt like he was going a lot faster and it was more exhilarating than a long straight road.

He wasn't a fair-weather biker, although only a fool deliberately sought out ice and snow. Black ice was the worst nightmare. If you were already banked over and hit a patch, you were off. But even if today wasn't a clear, relatively mild day, he might still have risked it just to get away from the castle and the maelstrom of thoughts inside his head.

He rode up the west coast towards Keswick, the mountains and lakes whizzing by. He stuck to the speed limit and didn't take any risks, but he knew damn well he was riding at the limit of his abilities.

Eventually, he pulled up at a roadside café at the top of Bassenthwaite Lake for a coffee and comfort stop.

The keen wind whipped up whitecaps on the lake and chilled his face. Flynn allowed himself the time to dwell on the damage he'd inflicted on the person he'd begun to care deeply about: Lara.

What was she going through? Was she really as OK and as understanding as she'd led him to believe? Or was that all part of an act to make him feel better?

Suspecting the truth, Flynn didn't dare to delve any deeper. He had started to come to terms with his new family, getting to know them – and persuading Molly to let her mother and grandmother know that he was now part of their lives.

He couldn't see them being any happier about the new reality than Lara. Probably less so. He also wasn't sure how he was going to react when he met them: if he'd only known about Molly sooner, he could have built a relationship with his child, watched her grow up, and played the role that fathers were meant to play. It wasn't as if he'd abandoned Imogen or Molly.

Flynn put his helmet back on and closed the visor, keen to shut out the world for another hour or so while he headed back to Ravendale.

His route back was slower but every bit as challenging: over the Whinlatter Pass and across to the western coast road.

The sun was low over the coast, tingeing the mountains pink.

Signs along the road had read:

Ravendale Winter Spectacular
Celebrate the Season of Magic and Joy
At this Unmissable Family Festival of Light and Sound

Once that word – family – had been almost invisible to him. Despite working at so many family attractions, he'd never really thought about what it meant. Now he did: fear, panic, duty – along with a sense of purpose and responsibility that eclipsed all of these things.

He slowed the bike on the bend and thought for a moment about continuing past Ravendale's gates and heading south to Cornwall, or east on the trip he'd always planned: the trip that would have meant he'd never have met Lara or known about Molly or Esme.

It was impossible. Now he knew about them, he could never run away.

Chapter Thirty

Lara's answer to stress was, as ever, to immerse herself in work, which wasn't difficult now it was the week before Christmas.

There were tours and festive afternoon teas at the Castle Café until Christmas Eve, plus a host of events to finalise and organise for February half term, Easter, and then Mother's Day. Magazines needed features several months in advance and Lara had to help supply details to the castle's part-time PR officer, even though blossom festivals and egg trails were the last things on her mind, what with Christmas tunes and fairy lights surrounding her.

She was meant to have a day off, but she had so much catching up to do that she spent it hidden away in her cottage where no one would disturb her.

She only emerged to meet Jazz for coffee at the Waterwheel Café. With Molly working there, it felt strange, but it was convenient for Jazz, who was on her way to see her youngest in the school nativity play.

Jazz had just got out of her car when Lara parked next to her in the Landy. Her heart skipped a beat and sunk simultaneously when she spotted Flynn talking to Molly near the entrance. He was holding Esme and making faces at her.

He didn't look totally comfortable, but he was obviously making a good attempt at entertaining her.

Lara climbed out of the Landy and the expression of amazement on Jazz's face didn't surprise her. 'Flynn seems to know Molly very well,' she said to Lara from the shelter of the open car doors.

'You have no idea . . .' Lara said. She heaved a sigh. 'I need to tell you something and I don't want it to go any further. And I think I should tell you before we go inside the café.'

Acknowledging Flynn was unavoidable, so Lara raised her hand to him and threw a smile at Molly. At first, she thought that they would say their goodbyes and part, but her heart beat faster again as he walked over to her with Esme in his arms and Molly alongside.

'Oh, God, they're coming over. Jazz – help.'

'Why help?' Jazz asked with a puzzled frown.

'Because . . . because . . . he's Molly's dad and the baby's grandad.'

'What the—' Jazz cut off the expletive. 'No. You're joking! He can't be. He's too young.'

'He isn't and it's true, and I only found out a couple of days ago, and it's all been very awkward and stressful – please, just act dumb for now. I mean, just nod and smile. I'll tell you everything after they've gone. Promise.'

Leaving a stunned Jazz standing next to her, Lara steeled herself and pasted on a smile. She wasn't even sure if Molly knew that she knew about her.

'Hello!' Lara trilled when Flynn, Molly and Esme

reached them. Her voice was far too shrill. She tried to take a breath.

Flynn gave a very awkward smile, holding Esme in his arms. The child stared at Lara most disconcertingly, as if she could see right into her mind.

'Hello,' Molly said, nervously Lara thought. It made Lara suspect that Flynn had told her that Lara was aware of the situation.

Flynn finally found his voice. 'We – er – met up here for coffee.'

'That's nice,' Lara said. 'It's a lovely café, but you know that because you work here. Obviously.'

Molly laughed nervously and Flynn just looked pained.

'I don't like meeting friends here normally because it's work, but it was convenient for Flynn. He has to go back to the castle. He says you're all very busy.'

'It's a busy time of year,' Lara said. 'Isn't it, Jazz?'

'Er – yes. Very.' Lara dared not even glimpse her friend's face. Was no one going to mention the elephant in the room?

A few wet flakes of snow had started to fall, and one landed on Lara's nose. Esme let out a little moan.

'It's cold and it looks like sleet,' Molly said. 'I should take Esme home.'

'Good idea,' Flynn said. 'I should get back to work.'

'OK,' Molly said, taking Esme from him. 'Grandad's so busy at the moment but we'll have more time to see him after Christmas.'

Jazz had a coughing fit.

Flynn was grinning in a slightly hysterical way.

'See you soon. Wave to Grandad,' Molly said, but Esme buried her face in her mum's shoulder.

'I'll message you,' Molly said.

'Great,' said Flynn. 'Take care on the roads.'

'I will,' Molly said, although she seemed amused at his concern.

She walked back to her car, but Flynn was momentarily frozen to the spot.

'Have a nice lunch,' he said, his eyes telegraphing agony and regret to Lara. 'See you later, I'm sure.'

'I'm sure.'

'Bye Jazz,' he said, then walked away, got on his bike, and rode off before Jazz could manage to speak.

'Well,' she said, with a huff of breath. 'That wasn't awkward at all, was it?'

Lara heaved a huge sigh. 'It was awful! Shall we get back in the car so we can talk before we go in the café?'

Inside the vehicle, Jazz swore softly. 'Sorry, but this is the last thing I'd ever have expected. Flynn – well, he doesn't look like a dad. I mean, he's such a cool guy, I can't imagine him as a grandad.'

'He's thirty-nine and Molly's only nineteen. Flynn and Imogen – Molly's mum – had a one-night stand when Flynn was on holiday up here at his grandparents. He was only a teenager himself then.'

Jazz's contorted expression seemed to reflect the whole tangled situation. 'But – but is that why he came up to Ravendale? To find her?' she asked.

'No. He had no idea Molly existed until she confronted

him at work. Apparently she'd known who he was for years but only decided to get in touch when she became a mum herself – and then she found out Flynn was coming to work here.'

Jazz exhaled sharply. 'Wow. That's a turn up. One hell of a shock for Flynn, and you.'

'Yes, you could say that.'

'How do you feel about it? Seeing a grandad?'

'Well, I'm *not* seeing him at the moment. Flynn's finding the situation all a bit overwhelming and I can't blame him, so I decided that we should cool things for now.' And Flynn had – reluctantly – agreed, which was what she wanted . . . wasn't it?

Jazz's eyes widened. 'You did?'

'I felt I had no choice. Flynn's life has been turned upside down, and starting a new relationship is too much on top of finding out he has family he never knew about. And after Rob, I don't want to be part of any kind of tangled relationship.'

'I understand, but this is different. How does Flynn feel about you backing off?'

'I—' Lara felt a stab of regret. 'He said he was gutted but I think he also feels torn between his new family and me. I don't want him to feel like that and so I thought it better for both of us, all of us, to take a step back.' *A huge step back*, Lara thought. She already felt there was a gaping hole in her life.

'I'm so sorry. Have you two talked much about it?'

'Not that much. He's still processing the bombshell of Molly and I suspect his way of dealing with it is to shut himself off. I think he feels it's his problem to handle, all alone.'

Jazz snorted. 'Typical man.'

Lara was inclined to agree but she'd also been out – briefly – with a guy who'd spent their dates unloading all his angst about his previous relationships, his job, even his problems with his unruly dog, who had 'severe separation anxiety'. Lara had never been able to get a word in. Flynn had taken the opposite approach.

'I think Flynn's also used to dealing with stuff himself. He's been on his own, or at least without any ties, for a long time. Now, a huge load of responsibility has been dropped on him in one go.'

'Hmm. No wonder he's feeling like a rabbit in the headlights.'

'Or a wounded one who's run away to lick his wounds,' Lara said, remembering the misery of telling him they should back away from each other. 'Shall we go inside and have a coffee? Now you know why I didn't want to tell you this inside the café.'

'If I'd known, I'd have chosen somewhere else.'

Lara steeled herself. 'Well, we're here now, and Molly is clearly happy to share the news, so I'd better get used to the new normal.'

Chapter Thirty-one

The following morning, Lara opened her curtains and knew straight away, even though it was still dark, that that evening's illuminations would have to be cancelled. Several inches of snow had fallen overnight and thick flakes were swirling around outside with no prospect of a thaw until much later that afternoon.

Her phone had already pinged with messages from Flynn and Fiona. As soon as she was dressed, they met in the office to make the final decision.

'It can't be helped. If we only lose a couple of nights, we'll have done well,' Fiona said.

'It looks bad. I don't think I've ever seen that much snow in Newquay,' Flynn said, grimacing through the window, where some of his team were already spreading grit on the snowy cobbles.

Fiona laughed and even Lara smiled. 'This is nothing! A mere sprinkling. Gosh, I remember when there were drifts six feet deep on the main road outside and we were all stuck for almost a week.'

'We don't have much snow by the coast,' Flynn said. 'Though we had to close the theme park because of high winds at least once a year.'

Lara had been checking the Met Office app. 'The forecast is for a low-pressure front coming in. Temps are going up by ten degrees by the early hours, but that won't help us now, even if it means we should be able to open tomorrow. I'm afraid we'll have to let everyone know and refund their tickets.'

'That's it, then. I think we can all agree it's not safe to open. Lara, can you activate the emergency cancellation plan, please?'

Flynn left to liaise with the contractors and the maintenance team while Lara helped the comms team get the word out on social media.

She wandered out of the office, bundled up in a padded parka and feeling as if she were off to an abandoned castle in an Alpine fairyland. Under the thick blanket of cloud, the light was eerie. Snow had added dunce's caps to the covered statues and iced the roofs of the food cabins, turning them into gingerbread houses. The topiary bushes in the gardens reminded her of frosted cupcakes and a sheen of ice had stilled the water in the fountain.

Ravendale was eerily quiet, as the guided Christmas tours, like the illuminations, had all been cancelled and the café was closed for the day. The only activity involved snow clearing and that had to be done with great care to avoid damaging the foliage, garden features and stonework.

By late afternoon, the thaw had begun. Water dripped off trees and bushes and flowed down the gutters. Every so often a load of snow would slide from a roof or a branch with a rattle, making Lara jump. With the winter equinox approaching, the eerie half-light soon turned into full darkness.

Without the illuminations, Ravendale seemed a melancholy place, with an added undercurrent of tension as exhausted staff continued to clear paths and fix snow-related problems to ensure the castle was safe and ready to reopen the following day. Lara and the other admin staff had also had a day of non-stop firefighting, fielding calls from groups who hadn't got the message about the cancellation and rescheduling tours.

Finally, at six-thirty, Lara made it back to the cottage and shoved a ready meal in her microwave. She ate it in front of the TV and took a sip of the large glass of white wine she'd poured. An early night was called for: the past few days had been fraught, to say the least. She was exhausted but, thankfully, Christmas was on the horizon so they could have a couple of days' break.

The glass was at her lips when there was a loud rap on her window.

Flynn called through the glass. 'Lara! Are you in there?'

Who else would be inside? She abandoned the wine glass on the coffee table, fearing some work-related crisis was going to derail her evening of exhausted wallowing.

She opened the door to Flynn, who stood there with a panicked expression and dripping wet hair. 'Oh no! What's the matter?'

'It's Molly and Esme. I need to go over to their house right away.'

Chapter Thirty-two

'Are Molly and the baby OK?' Lara asked.

'They're both fine. They've had a burst pipe in the house and there's water running down the walls and all over the electrics. The ceiling came down over the cot while Molly was changing Esme and they're wet through. Brenda's away in Manchester and Molly's panicking, understandably.'

'I'm not surprised. It must have been terrifying.'

'It could have been catastrophic . . .' He shook his head. 'Molly's turned off the stopcock but she has no idea what to do next. She's asked if I can go round now.'

'How scary for them. What I can do to help?'

'I can't take the bike in these conditions and it'd be useless if I need to give Molly and the baby a lift anywhere. I don't like to borrow the castle van on a – um – personal matter. I hoped you might be able loan me the Land Rover.'

'I could and it *is* insured for other drivers, but I know the roads and the Landy has its quirks.' Lara thought on her feet. 'Why don't I take you?'

He let out a sigh of relief. 'Thanks so much. I was hoping you'd say that, but it's a real imposition to make you come out after a busy day.'

'Don't worry. We all need help sometimes.'

'Thanks. They're in the dark and cold right now and they're not safe.'

'Then let's go.' Without a moment's hesitation, Lara pulled her coat from the rack and scooped up her keys.

It took half an hour to reach the coastal village where Molly, Esme and Brenda lived. Flynn was largely silent, sending messages to Molly while Lara drove along the unlit road, concentrating hard in case there were any lingering patches of slush.

Brightly lit homes heralded their entrance to the village, with trees twinkling in people's windows and glowing reindeer grazing on front lawns. Some people had really gone to town, and while none of it could measure up the Ravendale light show, Lara found it touching. It gave her a pang of homesickness for her own family home. She didn't think she'd see them now until well into the New Year, when they returned from Australia.

And the consolation of sharing a communal Christmas lunch with Flynn was now gone; he'd be sure to spend it with Molly and Esme, which was only to be expected. She hoped that Flynn and his new family would be able to get to know each other better by then – meaning that Molly would have to tell Imogen and Brenda.

'We're only a couple of minutes away,' Lara said, turning off the main street into a residential area.

'It's number twenty-eight,' Flynn said, scanning the houses for Molly's.

'On the left. Might be that one with the Santa in the garden?'

Lara slowed and stopped the Land Rover outside a stone semi-detached cottage where the street lights showed a blow-up Santa tethered to the front lawn amid patches of melting snow.

'There are no lights on, so I think it is.'

She turned off the engine and headlights, but Flynn seemed frozen to the passenger seat.

'To think they were here all this time,' he said, looking out of the window. 'And I had no idea.'

'I know . . .' Lara thought of the switchback of emotions that the past couple of months had brought. Flynn walking into her life so dramatically at Halloween, breaking down her defences and giving her the hope of a fresh start – and now the future had been turned on its head again.

She took the keys from the ignition. 'Come on, we don't want to keep them waiting any longer. It's past 10 p.m. already.'

Flynn snapped into life and carried his toolkit and torch into the house, where a pale-faced Molly let them in. Flynn had already told her Lara was coming too, so her presence wasn't a shock.

Flynn set up a powerful torch that doubled as a lamp.

Molly had her coat on but was still shivering. It was almost as chilly inside as out.

'I brought the travel cot down here,' she said. 'Luckily Esme's now gone off to sleep.'

'That's one good thing, then,' Lara said, smiling at the sleeping babe while Flynn opened up his toolbox.

233

Molly was still agitated. 'I'm sorry to call you, but I didn't know who else to ask,' she said. 'Nan's gone to a *Strictly* Christmas show in Manchester. She took the car or I would have driven myself. She'll go spare when she sees the damage but I'm not telling her until she gets home. I don't want to ruin her special trip.'

'It's not your fault,' Lara said.

'Burst pipes and leaks can happen to anyone,' Flynn said kindly. 'Can you show me where the worst of the damage is?'

'I can sit here and keep an eye on Esme,' Lara offered, aware that she was even more of a stranger to the baby than Flynn.

Molly nodded and took Flynn into what seemed to be a kitchen area.

Ten minutes later, they both returned to the sitting room, much to Lara's relief. Esme had woken up and she hadn't dared let her crawl around in the dark, so she'd been entertaining her with YouTube kids' videos on her phone.

Flynn set up his torch so they could see each other while he delivered his verdict on the damage.

'It's not great,' he said, with a grimace, although Lara could tell he was trying not to over-dramatise the situation for Molly's sake. 'The water has leaked through the floor of Esme's room, through to the utility room below and damaged the circuit breakers there, which is why there's no power or light.'

'It's bad, isn't it?'

'I've seen far worse, but the most important thing is that you're both OK. The ceiling can be fixed, but that's a bigger job and I can't even call anyone to see when they can repair it until morning. We'll also need to call out an emergency plumber and clear up the mess. I can check the electrics properly myself tomorrow and fix any issues.'

Lara thought it was very fortunate for Molly that Flynn was an experienced maintenance manager.

Esme let out a snicker of protest and Molly took her from Lara. 'I can't let her sleep in the dark and cold.'

'No way can you stay here. I can't be sure how safe the electrics are until at least tomorrow. Is there anywhere you can go?'

'Friends?' Lara prompted.

'All the friends my age live with their parents or in house shares. There's my Auntie Jane in Keswick, but that's over an hour away and her flat is tiny. And before you ask, I am not staying with my ex! He lives with his brother and the place is pigsty. No way am I taking Esme there.'

'It is very late,' Lara said, then found herself blurting out, 'You could always stay with me for the night, if you wanted to.'

Flynn stared at her in amazement.

'Could I? You mean at the castle? Won't they mind?'

Lara smiled. 'I don't live *in* the actual castle. I have a cottage in the grounds – opposite Flynn's place, in fact. If you want, you and Esme are welcome to stay with me tonight. It's not very big but it's warm and dry.'

'That's very kind. Are you sure?' Flynn said, wondering if Lara had offered because Molly might feel more comfortable staying with a woman than him.

'I'd be very happy if Molly is.'

'I think it's a great idea.'

Esme wasn't happy about being disturbed, and Lara was worried that her car seat wouldn't tether to the old Land Rover's rear seats, but Flynn and Molly managed to fix it and they set off, surrounded by cots, a highchair, a pack of nappies, and several bags of clothes and toys.

It was half-past eleven when Molly lifted a sleeping Esme from the car seat and followed Lara to her cottage while Flynn unloaded their stuff from the Land Rover.

Lara showed Molly her room and left her trying to settle Esme in her travel cot while she found fresh sheets.

Flynn had been on shuttle runs to the Land Rover with the rest of Esme's paraphernalia and Lara opened the front door for him as he brought the last of it into the cottage. He put the bags down on the step and glanced over her shoulder, checking that Molly wasn't listening.

'Lara,' he said in a low voice, 'thank you for offering to have them. I was going to myself, but— I wasn't sure if she would feel comfortable if I suggested it. I'm her dad but she hardly knows me.'

'She hardly knows me either, but I thought it might feel more natural – an all-girls-together kind of thing, like a sleepover . . .' Lara grimaced. 'I make it sound like we're all ten! You know what I mean.'

Flynn smiled. 'It's a great solution. I can't thank you enough.' He looked as if he were about to hug her.

'You don't need to. I'm more than happy to help.'

'I won't disturb Molly if she's settling Esme. Tell her I

said goodnight to them both. See you tomorrow. It'll have to be early: seven-thirty according to Molly?'

Lara smiled. 'I think I'll be lucky if I make it to six without waking up.'

'Yeah. Look, I really am so grateful.'

'Flynn. Stop being grateful.' I don't want you to feel guilty, she could have said. I don't want you to try to compensate for a decision that must have felt impossible. That must still feel impossible. 'Get some rest. I think you're going to need it more than I do.'

Lara closed the door with an inner sigh before putting on a smile and carrying the things into the sitting room. Molly was in the kitchen pouring water into two mugs. 'I managed to get Esme off to sleep and I found some teabags.'

'Thanks,' Lara said, getting milk from the fridge while trying to process that Flynn's daughter – and granddaughter – were in her cottage, making *her* a drink.

Molly dropped the used teabags in the bin and added a splash of milk to her tea before leaning against the worktop. 'It must be incredible living by a castle. I've always wanted to stay here. Not under these circumstances, of course.' She laughed nervously.

'It's nowhere near as exciting as you might think,' said Lara, thinking that the past couple of months had been even more eventful than the previous eighteen. 'Shall we take these in the sitting room? You must need to decompress a bit before you go to bed. It must have been a stressful day.'

Molly sat down on the sofa, which was to be Lara's bed for the night.

'My friend said you were nice,' she said.

'Your friend?'

'Rachel. She's a cleaner here. She needs the cash while she's studying. We were at college together until I had to take a break to have Esme.'

'Will you be going back?'

'Yeah. I have to. I want to. I need to get a good job to support Esme. She'll have a nursery place three days a week and Nan will help out.'

'What about your mother? I heard she works abroad.' Lara could not help herself. She was so curious about the woman who'd given birth to Flynn's daughter.

'She does help when she can, but her job means she's usually away. She needs to work and this is how she helps us. She saves loads.'

Lara nodded, imagining the sacrifices Imogen had made to bring up Molly. Even so, it must be heartbreaking for Flynn to have been denied the chance to help. 'Does your mum stay with your nan when she's back in the UK?'

'Yes. She does have a flat in Bootle, but she rents that out long-term. She can't usually use it, so she may as well have the revenue.' Lara noted there was no mention of a partner but didn't dare push it.

'Have you told your mum and nan about Flynn yet? People might start talking, seeing you spend so much time at the castle. And I'm not sure if you realise that you let it slip about Flynn being Esme's grandad in front of my friend Jazz.'

'Oh, shit!' Molly clapped her hand over her mouth. 'Did I?'

'I'm afraid so, but don't worry, Jazz won't tell anyone, and I certainly won't. I told her the situation is delicate, if that's OK? But you can see how hard it's going to be to keep such exciting news a secret,' Lara went on, hoping she hadn't caused trouble.

'It's hard. I *do* want to tell people, and I will have to. It isn't fair on Flynn to expect him to keep it all to himself, but that means coming clean to Nan.'

'Won't your nan ask what happened in the house and who fixed it?'

Molly pulled a face. 'I've thought of that. I don't think I can lie. I don't want to.' She heaved a deep sigh. 'I do think I'm going to have to tell her the truth.'

'But you'll talk to Flynn first?' Lara asked, slightly horrified that Molly might not.

'Of course I will. There's no way I'd go behind his back with something that big. He seems like a nice guy. I don't want to cause him any more trouble than I already have.'

She put her mug down and frowned at Lara. 'Are you and him . . .? Do you two have a *thing* together?'

'No. No . . . we're friends, but we work together and that complicates things.'

'Oh. OK. I get that. Cos I wouldn't want to ruin anything between you both by turning up.'

'Don't worry, you haven't,' Lara insisted, wanting to scream out loud but realising she was meant to be the adult here.

'OK. That makes me feel better. I've probably caused enough trouble as it is. I bet Flynn wishes he'd never moved up here.'

'I'm sure he doesn't feel like that,' Lara said. It wasn't her place to speak for Flynn, but Molly was seeking reassurance – validation – for her decision.

Molly nodded. 'Goodnight. See you in the morning. And thank you, Lara.'

Even though Molly wasn't her long-lost daughter and this wasn't her newfound family, somehow Lara felt she'd taken on a tiny share of the burden of responsibility.

The following morning, Molly was in the kitchen when Lara walked in, mashing up a banana and adding it to a Weetabix in one of Lara's nibbles bowls.

She grinned over her shoulder. 'Hope you don't mind me getting on with things. Esme's starving.'

Esme was sitting on a blanket on the floor, bashing a pan with a wooden spoon. There were toys and kitchen implements strewn on the carpet and a bumper pack of nappies by the bin. Baby bottles and formula powder littered the worktops.

'Not at all. Can I help?' Lara asked, still not fully awake and definitely not at ease with the weird situation.

'You could put some water in a cup. I found a plastic one in your cupboard. Was that OK?'

'It's fine.' Lara had completely forgotten where she'd acquired the pink picnic tumbler and half filled it with tap water.

'Would you mind setting up the highchair by the worktop?'

'Um. I'll do my best,' Lara said, feeling ham-fisted at taking more than a few seconds to manhandle it into place.

'Thanks.' Molly slotted Esme in the chair and sat on a breakfast stool next to her, feeding her with a plastic spoon.

'Would you like a coffee?' Lara asked.

'Yeah. Thanks.'

Esme reminded Lara of a baby gannet with the way she opened her mouth to guzzle whatever was on the spoon. It was as if another greedy gannet chick might swoop in and get to it first. Weetabix was plastered around her mouth and she was banging the high-chair tray with her own spoon.

She was so gorgeous, though, with her fluffy dark hair. Even so, Lara wasn't going to offer to feed her. She was sure that the baby would scream the place down or she'd shovel too much food in her mouth.

She made the coffee, trying to work out how she felt about having Flynn's daughter and granddaughter in her home. She'd told Flynn she'd help in any way she could, but having the family to stay had never featured on her list of possibilities.

Lara made some toast for all three of them and they ate it, Esme happily chewing her toast 'soldiers' with the few teeth she had. There were pieces of toast and Weetabix all over the kitchen floor and Weetabix in Esme's hair and on Molly's top. Lara tried not to look.

'Was that nice?' she asked Esme.

Esme couldn't reply because her mouth was full.

'I'll go and try to clean her up and get her dressed. She goes to nursery today so I can go to work,' Molly said, seemingly oblivious to the chaos wrought on Lara's neat cottage

241

by one tiny person in the space of a few hours. 'Thanks for the breakfast.'

While Molly was changing and dressing Esme in Lara's bedroom and en suite, Flynn knocked the door.

'Morning,' he said, taking in the chaos in the sitting room and kitchen. 'Jesus . . .' He winced and lowered his voice. 'I was going to say I hoped they haven't been too much trouble.'

'No trouble at all,' Lara said, managing a half-smile at his horrified expression. His own rumpled hair and unshaven chin added to the general air of chaos surrounding them.

'I'll help you clear this up,' he said.

'Thanks, but I can manage, and Molly will need a lift to nursery and work.'

Flynn looked around him again and grimaced. 'If you're sure.'

'It'll be easier when they're gone. I mean that in the nicest way. Once the decks are clear, it won't take me long.'

'I can't thank you enough for this.'

'It's OK. It's been an experience, and Esme is gorgeous. You're very lucky.'

'Am I? I know I am, but I don't *feel* like I am. Not yet.' He sighed. 'But we've been a burden to you long enough.'

At that moment, the burdens walked into the sitting room, Molly in a clean top and jeans, and Esme wearing a pink jumper with an otter on it. She smiled and babbled 'Ga-ga-ga' in Flynn's direction.

Lara saw his face. The sheer incredulity and astonishment – and love. Her own heart felt as if it was squeezing and she wanted to cry, but she didn't know whether it was for herself or him.

'You're chatty this morning, baby,' Molly said, smiling and obviously unheeding of the cauldron of emotions seething around her.

'When you're ready, I'll give you a lift to the nursery and the café,' Flynn said. 'I've – er – borrowed one of the maintenance vans. I need to collect some kit from the electrical wholesaler and it's on the way to the nursery, so I don't feel so guilty.'

'I don't think anyone would mind anyway. It is an emergency,' Lara reassured him. 'Although I suppose no one knows about Molly yet, do they?'

'Not yet,' Flynn murmured.

Lara was reminded how difficult this situation must be for him and suddenly wondered how she was going to explain Molly's presence in the cottage, which probably hadn't gone unnoticed.

'I'll be back in five minutes, OK?' he said, recovering his composure.

'Yeah. Thanks.'

Lara held Esme as Molly repacked their bags and was surprised by how heavy she was. She wouldn't have liked to hold her for long. Esme wriggled a bit but then decided to pull Lara's hair and make a grab for her earrings.

'I've been thinking about what you said – about me telling Nan and Mum that I've found Flynn. You're right. If I want him to be part of my life, and Esme's, I'll have to.'

'There's no other way, is there?' Lara said.

'No, and the thing is, I really would like Mum to meet Flynn again, because she's on her own and he is too, and, you know, they must have connected with each other once. The chemistry must have been there even if it was twenty years ago. It could happen again, couldn't it? It's not impossible.'

Lara didn't know what to say. She'd denied any connection with Flynn beyond friendship, so she simply said, 'It's not impossible, no.'

Molly sighed. 'Thanks for driving Flynn to mine and letting us stay here. I had no idea what I was going to do. I feel so much better now.'

'You're welcome,' said Lara, as cheerily as she could manage.

Flynn bustled back in, sounding harassed. 'Right. I've parked the van as close as I could. Shall I carry the bags and buggy while you bring Esme?'

'Yeah.' Molly brought Esme closer to Lara and helped her wave her chubby arm. 'Bye then, Lara. Thanks so much for everything.'

'No problem.'

Lara let them out and closed the door, unwilling to draw attention. It was just starting to get light and staff were already up and about, starting work in the kitchens and café and castle.

Molly couldn't help her hopes for her parents to reunite. They were understandable and reasonable, in the circumstances. Yet, Lara thought, understanding a situation was one thing, while accepting and liking it was far far harder.

Her role was passive: to leave Flynn to work things

out and, in this case, temporarily support Molly through a minor crisis.

Fixing the burst pipe and tidying up the cottage was the easy part. Standing by cheerfully while Molly tried to rebuild a relationship between her mother and father would be almost impossible.

Chapter Thirty-three

After Flynn had dropped Esme at nursery and Molly at the Waterwheel Café, he'd hardly been able to function at work, but he had managed to get the evening off from the illuminations to go round to their house that evening.

He'd borrowed some dehumidifiers to help dry the affected rooms out. Molly had cleaned out the cot and moved it to her own room. The plumber had been earlier to fix the leak and Flynn had booked someone to repair the damaged ceiling the following day.

Flynn had just finished replacing the circuit boards and was sweeping up dust and bits of wire when Molly rushed into the utility room, waving her phone.

'Oh. My. God.'

'What now?' Flynn's stomach lurched. She looked pale as a ghost. 'Is everything OK?'

'Yes. I mean. No.' She let out a squeak. 'I hope so. It's here. The email's here.'

Flynn broke out in a sweat. 'You mean the DNA test results.'

'Yes.'

He longed for and dreaded the result. If it was negative, Molly would be devastated and Flynn had no idea how he'd cope. He'd been on such a rollercoaster over the past week that, if Molly wasn't his, he would feel he'd lost her, even if having found her had lobbed a bombshell into his life and caused a rift with Lara.

He leaned the brush on the worktop, trying to sound calm. 'You haven't opened it, then?'

'No. I thought we should do it together. I want it to be a yes. I really do.'

'So do I,' said Flynn, feeling a bit sick.

'Let's do it, then.' Molly showed him her email inbox with the DNA test company's message.

'OK,' Flynn said, clenching his trembling fingers by his side.

Molly opened it and, within seconds, she'd burst into tears.

Flynn put his arms around her and held her as she sobbed. It was probably a good thing she couldn't see the tears in his own eyes as he realised, without a shadow of a doubt, that he was holding his daughter. He was filled with warmth and wonder and joy, and, at the same time, sadness at realising that he'd missed out on that for so many years.

'It's true,' Molly said, leaning back and looking at him. 'You are my dad.'

His throat was clogged, so he nodded before saying, 'I knew from the moment you told me.'

'But it's good to be sure, or you might always have wondered.'

'You're very wise,' he said, smiling, as Molly wiped her face with a tissue.

247

'We should open champagne or something, but I don't have any and you're driving.'

'We definitely need to celebrate,' he said.

'I've got ginger beer. Nan likes it.'

Flynn laughed. 'Go on, then.'

Molly collected Esme from her playpen and Flynn had found the bottle and two glasses from the cupboard when lights swept up the driveway.

'Oh my God. Nan's back.'

Hearing these words, you would have thought Brenda was a Gorgon waiting to turn Flynn to stone. His pulse rose, his palms were sweaty, and he had the urgent desire to leap out of a window, jump on his bike, and head straight for the Far East as he'd once planned.

'Oh. Right. OK . . .'

'You look terrified,' said Molly.

'Should I be?'

Instead of laughing as he'd expected, Molly suddenly burst into tears again. 'I thought I wouldn't be, but now I am. Oh . . . shaving cream and fluffing hell! Argh. That's what I have to say now Esme's around. Fluffing, fluffing, fluffing hell!'

Under other circumstances, Flynn might have laughed: the sheer surrealness of the situation had struck him so many times since he'd first found out about Molly.

'I don't think I can't do this! What will Nan say when she sees you here? Hold Esme while I find a tissue.'

Esme was bundled into his arms like a parcel while Molly dashed into the loo.

Flynn was left holding the baby in every way possible,

and Molly's comments about her nan hadn't helped his own nerves either.

Molly dashed back into the sitting room with a bundle of loo roll just as Brenda's key scraped the lock and the front door opened.

'Hello! I'm home. What's that damp smell? Bloody hell! What happened to the ceiling? Molly!'

Brenda entered the sitting room and stopped dead. Her mouth dropped open and she looked from Molly to Flynn and Esme as if they were ghosts.

'Hello, Nan,' Molly said. 'This is Flynn. He's my dad.'

Brenda sat on the sofa with Esme on her lap while Molly made her a mug of tea.

'I don't understand,' she kept saying. 'How come you're working at the castle? Did you come to find us?'

'No, Molly came to find me. She found out that I'd moved up here and decided she wanted to meet me. I appreciate it's been a shock.'

'A shock?' She fanned herself. 'I thought I was going to have a heart attack.'

'You say that all the time, Nan, and you never do,' Molly said, walking into the room with a tray.

'It's a wonder!' Brenda declared.

'Drink this. I put sugar in it. Yours too, and a drop of whisky in Nan's,' she said to Flynn, who'd perched on the chair. 'Let me take Esme.'

Molly lifted the baby from her grandmother's arms and put her on the playmat next to her baby gym.

'It was a shock for me too,' Flynn said, as calmly as he could. 'As I'd no idea she even existed.'

'No . . . I—' Brenda stared at him then closed her eyes briefly. 'I bet you hate us all, don't you?'

'I don't hate anyone, Brenda. I must admit I'd rather have known about Molly, but it's too late to go back now.'

'I've said we're sorry, Nan. I explained that Mum didn't have any way of contacting Flynn and then, when she did, it was too late.'

Flynn begged to differ. It had never been too late. He felt a sharp tug in his gut and realised that it was loss. Increasingly, he'd begun to feel hurt and anger – but now wasn't the time to give vent to feelings like that.

'Now you're here,' Brenda muttered after sipping her tea, 'I'd like to know what's going to happen next.'

'Well, I've made the electrics safe but you're going to need the ceiling restoring and plastering.'

'I didn't mean the bloody ceiling! I meant, what's going to happen with you?' Brenda asked, leaning forward on the sofa and glaring at him.

'Flynn's not going to take us away from you, Nan, if that's what you're worried about. We only met each other less than two weeks ago.'

'This has been going on for weeks? So you knew – that night at the illuminations?' Brenda said, incredulously. 'And you let me say those things about—' She nodded in Flynn's direction. 'About him?'

Great, thought Flynn. Brenda couldn't bring herself to utter his name.

'I hadn't told Flynn – Dad – then. I only went to see him for myself.'

Flynn swallowed a lump in his throat, hearing Molly call him Dad. Would he ever get used to it?

'Oh, dear Lord,' Brenda said, fanning herself again.

'Mrs Carver,' Flynn said, as calmly but firmly as he could muster, 'Molly's absolutely right. We all need time to adjust to this – situation.'

'It's Brenda. You can call me Brenda.'

'OK, Brenda,' he said firmly. 'You can call me Flynn. It's certainly preferable to "him".'

Molly stifled a gasp that might have been due to him – or anyone – standing up to her nan.

'Your mother will have to know about this.' Brenda directed this at Molly. 'I'll have to tell her.'

'No!' Molly burst out, causing Esme to look up sharply. 'I want to tell Mum. I've found Flynn and I ought to be the one to break it to her.'

Flynn felt that he also ought to have some say. And being referred to as being 'found' made him feel like a grime-covered artefact that had been discarded and unearthed centuries later. Christ, he didn't know whether to laugh or cry.

'God knows what she'll say. I mean she hasn't seen him since the day – the thing happened.'

Thanks, thought Flynn.

'When's Imogen actually coming home?' Flynn cut in, trying not to be cross at hearing Brenda referring to the moment that had resulted in her granddaughter and great-granddaughter as 'the thing'.

'Not until after Christmas. That's much too long away. I can't lie to her about this. She's my daughter . . .' Brenda clutched Molly's hand. 'Love, you must understand that I can't keep something this big from her. How would you like it if you were in my situation?'

Molly pulled a face and tears glistened in her eyes. 'If it hadn't been for the burst pipe, she wouldn't need to know. You wouldn't know.'

'I think,' Flynn dared, 'that your nan would have had to find out sooner or later.'

'And I'm glad I have! How long were you two planning on keeping this a secret from me?'

'Don't blame my dad,' Molly said. 'He didn't ask to be found.'

'But your mum will have to know about him. She has a right to.'

She pulled her hand out of Brenda's. 'Yeah, but she – and you – didn't think he had a right to know about me!'

Flynn had now decided that he was spectator at a gladiatorial battle. Actually, no, he'd been thrown into the arena with the lions.

'Hold on!' he said, standing up. 'I think this is a decision we all need to make together and it should be in Molly's best interests. What's best for her and Esme?'

Molly sniffed loudly and Brenda stayed silent for a few seconds before nodding. 'He – Flynn – is right. It's all about you two now.'

'Why don't you take a little while?' Flynn offered, taking Brenda's agreement to his proposal as a huge step forward.

'At least sleep on it. Things might seem clearer in the morning.' He didn't really believe they would for a second but he needed to defuse the tension somehow and carve out some time to take it in himself.

Molly nodded. 'Yeah. Maybe. I know we have to tell Mum, but I'd rather do it face to face.'

'That's not going to happen. You'll have to do it over the phone.'

Please don't ask me to join this particular call, Flynn pleaded silently.

'I know.' Molly looked at Esme, who was playing with Penguin, and her lip quivered. Flynn knew why. Everything they did now must be in the little one's best interests and arguing wasn't going to help. His own heart lurched with an emotion that he'd never felt before. Still, he knew instantly it was the most terrifying emotion of all: unconditional love. With it came the fear of the unthinkable: losing his daughter and granddaughter.

He hadn't asked to be in this situation and every day brought a fresh challenge that he had no idea how to deal with. He had a family he never knew existed and had the joy of holding his granddaughter and being called 'Dad' – yet, in some ways, he'd never felt more alone in his entire life.

Chapter Thirty-four

The medieval Christmas evening at Ravendale – another of Lara's ideas – was fully booked. Eighty guests were packed into the banqueting hall to enjoy a concert of traditional seasonal music against a backdrop of flickering candlelight.

The sound was so pure and lilting and just so *Christmassy* that Lara had to fight back tears as the choir's voices seemed to lift the ceiling. Combined with the tang of evergreen from the tree and the lingering scent of woodsmoke, she didn't think she'd ever experienced such a perfect seasonal combination. People were dabbing their eyes with tissues as the singers and musicians performed versions of the 'Coventry Carol', '*In dulci jubilo*' and '*Gaudete*'.

The ancient hymns reminded her that the season was about the birth of a baby and Esme came into her mind – followed by the one she'd lost at such an early stage. Her eyes stung, though she tried to tell herself it was probably the smoke from the flickering candles.

The previous Christmas had been emotional enough – for all the wrong reasons – and she'd been looking forward to this one being at least calmer and less draining. Then Flynn had roared into her life and she'd begun to think her Christmas would be joyful . . .

Now, their paths had diverged again.

The choir finished with a rendition of 'Deck the Halls', which the presenter explained was based on an old Welsh song. The guests joined in and the applause raised the roof. The moment the concert ended, waiting staff moved in with mulled wine and festive canapés. Lara forced herself to smile and chat with the guests and, soon, Fiona found her way over to Lara. Her eyes sparkled with happiness. 'My dear, this is a triumph. What a superb idea.'

'Thank you,' Lara said, genuinely delighted with her boss's warm approval. 'I hoped it would be a hit. The singers are amazing.'

'They're brilliant.' Fiona looked around her. 'It really reminds you that Christmas is around the corner.'

'It's easy to become jaded and cynical and forget to celebrate when you're so caught up in the day-to-day business of the season,' Lara said.

'Hmm. Everyone's starting to get a bit weary and look frazzled by this stage. We're like the proverbial swans paddling away for all we're worth tonight, making it seem that an event like this goes on serenely and seemingly with no effort. However, I know how much work has gone into it by you and Jazz and the whole team.'

Lara agreed. Amid her own problems, there was still a job to be done. Tempers had been fraying. Jazz had had a set-to with her head chef over some curdled brandy butter, of all things. The housekeeping manager, Rebecca, had what Henry had called a 'ding dong' with Fiona and threatened to walk out. Lara had tried to pour oil on troubled waters and found herself patiently listening to Jazz moaning about the chef 'making a drama over trivia'.

'Thank you for speaking to Rebecca on my behalf,' Fiona said to Lara. 'It was all a misunderstanding. I really do appreciate all she does and I know she'll always go the extra mile for us.'

'I'm just glad that things are back on track,' said Lara.

'Talking of irreplaceable people, how is Flynn? I've barely had a chance to speak with him. He always seems to be flying here and there.'

'I think the poor man looks completely frazzled,' Henry remarked. 'I hope we're not working him too hard. Lara, you must remind him to take some time for himself.'

'I don't think he'd listen to me,' Lara said.

'Oh, I think he would,' Henry said, with a knowing smile.

Fiona piped up. 'Oh, I almost forgot! Tessa's bringing your ball costume round tomorrow. And she's altered Flynn's outfit too. I'm sure he'll look terribly dashing in it.'

'I'm sure he will,' said Lara, gritting her teeth yet again. She'd grind them right down at this rate. 'I'll pop in to collect them, shall I?'

On Saturday afternoon, after she'd collected their costumes, Lara saw Flynn in the topiary garden sitting on a bench, gazing out over the view as if seeking solace or answers in the snow-topped hills. She thought of avoiding him and then took pity. He looked so alone and at a loss.

She walked up to him and said, 'Hi. I just picked up your costume from Fiona.' She handed over the suit carrier, glad to have it off her hands. The two together were surprisingly heavy.

'Oh, shit,' Flynn said, before looking skywards. 'Sorry, ignore me. Dressing as Dick Turpin at a ball is the last thing on my mind right now.'

'I'm sure,' Lara murmured, thinking that she wasn't in the party mood either.

'I appreciate it. Really.' Finally, he smiled, and her pulse sped up.

'You're welcome. How's it going? If I dare ask.' She sat beside him and rested her own costume on her lap.

'Work or the other stuff?'

'Both, although you seem to have the work stuff under control.'

'It might look like it, but I lost it a bit with Carlos the other day.'

'He can be a difficult character to deal with.'

'Yeah, but it was unprofessional of me.' He scuffed the gravel with his boot. 'How about you?'

'OK. It's the final day of the guided tours, thank goodness. We have a guide down with flu and we're trying to spread ourselves way too thin. Tempers are fraying all round. People are tired and trying to juggle work and getting ready for Christmas.'

'And I'm worried that I'm turning into the kind of grumpy sod I always resolved never to be,' Flynn said, with a wry smile that made her stomach do an annoying flip. 'Actually, I'm glad I bumped into you. I have a favour to ask and it's probably bloody cheeky considering, but . . .'

'Unless you ask, you won't know,' Lara replied.

'OK. I, um, wondered if you'd help me choose a Christmas present for Molly and for Esme? I agonised over whether to get them anything, but it seems weird not to and I want to . . . but I've no idea what to get them. Now I've said that out loud, I realise that it's probably an incredibly cheeky thing to do and I shouldn't have asked.' He banged his forehead with his palm. 'Argh. I expect you're far too busy, and shopping for Molly and Esme is hardly top of your agenda.'

'Hold on.' Lara thought it was quite satisfying to see him in a state of flustered confusion. Was this the man who'd strolled into her life with such cool self-confidence? She wasn't sure she was qualified to help him shop for his new family, or quite how she felt about it, but he looked so desperate and he *was* reaching out to her by asking for her help.

'I am busy, we all are, but . . . I could spare some time on Sunday, if you really think I could help? In fact, I had fancied going to Keswick Christmas market on Sunday. The Landy is in for a service from Friday until Monday, though, and I daren't cancel it now in case it fails its MOT.'

'Oh.' He seemed stunned she hadn't said no. 'If you really were thinking of going anyway, I could give you a lift.'

'In one of the castle vans?'

'Um. I was thinking of on my bike.'

Lara snorted unattractively. 'You're joking.'

'No, actually I was deadly serious.'

'But – but what about the presents? How will they all fit on the bike?'

'As long as we're not thinking of buying a table and chairs, you'd be surprised how much the lockers and panniers hold.'

'I – don't think I can.'

'I promise I won't go too fast. And the roads to Keswick are pretty good.'

'What about—' she started. *About my safety? My sanity? My life?* 'I – I don't have any leathers for a start.'

'I could nip round to Harv's tonight. His wife rides a bike. I'm sure he'll lend me a spare set.'

'I think it would be much easier to borrow a van.'

He grinned and, for the first time in ages, she glimpsed the old Flynn. 'But not as much fun. Go on, I dare you.'

Chapter Thirty-five

'What are you staring at?' Lara felt like a kinky Tellytubby in the leathers, which were actually Kevlar textiles. The helmet was surprisingly heavy too and she hadn't even put it on.

'Nothing. You just look . . .' he said, obviously too wary to finish the sentence.

'Like the Michelin man?'

He was obviously struggling not to laugh. 'No. You look like a biker.'

She curled her lip. 'Funny that, when I'm dressed like a biker . . . you *have* taken a passenger before?'

His confidence seemed to waver. 'I'll let you in on a secret. You're the first one.'

Lara squeaked in horror. 'You are joking!'

'Yeah, of course I am. I'm not crazy. I've taken hundreds of passengers. I promise, I know what I'm doing.'

'Hmm.' Lara had no doubt he was as experienced as he said, yet it was difficult to overcome her nervousness. Then again, if she was going to get on the back of a powerful machine for the first time, she couldn't think of anyone she'd rather do it with than Flynn.

That image, with all its erotic associations, made her burst out laughing,

'What's so funny?' he asked.

'Nothing. Nervous laughter.'

'No need to be nervous,' he insisted. 'All you need to do is trust the rider. It's 100 per cent *my* job to ride the bike. You don't need to do anything. You don't have to lean or move. You just brace against the top case, hold the sissy bars . . .'

Lara was sure she'd misheard him. Nobody used a word like that these days. 'The *what* bars?'

'The sissy bars,' he said sternly. 'The grab bars if we're being technical. I'm sorry but that's what everyone calls them – they originated in the sixties in America, but we won't go into that now.'

'I don't think you should,' she said tartly.

Flynn went on. 'All you need to know is that you hold on to them, and don't make any erratic movements. But I know you're cool in a crisis, so that will be fine. Got that?'

'Oh yeah. Easy. There won't be a crisis, will there?' she added, feeling the need to clear her dry throat.

'No. I'll show you how to get on and off, and what to do when I need to slow down or speed up at traffic lights or park up.' He smirked. 'If you do what I say, I promise everything will be OK.'

'This is all very autocratic,' Lara muttered, using sarcasm to hide her nerves.

'Yeah, I guess it is, but I'm responsible for everything that happens to us both. Don't look so worried. I promise that, when you get used to it, you're going to wonder why you've never done it before.'

Don't move, don't bounce, don't – as if! – take her feet off

261

the pegs and above all, hold on – like she was planning to start waving her arms around and screaming as if she was at a nightclub, Lara thought, as he issued a stream of further instructions.

Even getting on the bike had a special technique. Lara leaned back against the top box and found the sissy bars.

'When we slow down, I'm afraid you will have to hold on to me or brace on the fuel tank. I'll show you your options.'

'I have options?' she asked, with an eyebrow raise. 'I thought this was a not-so-benign dictatorship.'

He rolled his eyes.

'You're enjoying this, aren't you?'

He grinned then turned serious again. 'I only want you to be safe. Now, shall I show you how to get on and off and we can take some drills round the car park so you know what to expect? If you really hate it, we don't have to go.'

She probably would really hate it, thought Lara, but, no matter how much, there was no way she'd embarrass herself by chickening out now.

'Let's put our helmets on.'

A minute of fiddling later and Lara felt she'd entered a new realm. No one from the castle or among her friends would have ever imagined serious, geeky Lara as a biker chick. Lara herself would never have dreamed of it either.

'So, are you ready to live dangerously?'

Lara's stomach turned over. 'I wish you hadn't said that!'

'I was joking. We're as safe as houses.' He flipped her visor down and held the bike steady while she climbed on the back of it.

It was only as the Harley's engine roared into life and the vibrations swept her body that she remembered the chalice and its chip. If by some twist of fate their luck was going to run out, she just prayed it wasn't during the next few hours.

By the time Flynn pulled into a layby next to the shore of Bassenthwaite Lake, she had no idea how much of her life had flashed by.

Lara also wasn't sure she'd ever hear anything again. The power of the Harley was astounding and riding behind Flynn was nothing whatsoever like anything she'd ever done. It was like getting on the back of a wild horse compared to her old faithful Land Rover.

'You can let go now,' he called, kicking the stand down.

'Oh.' She realised that her arms were wound tightly around his waist. They had been since the first set of traffic lights when she'd transferred them to him and forgotten to let go.

'And it's safe to get off.' Flynn twisted round, his visor now open and his eyes gleaming.

There was so much tension in her body, she wasn't sure she could lift her leg. It felt like a wrench to take her hands from his waist, and how had the scent of leather and petrol never turned her on before?

Her legs felt wobbly but she made it safely onto the tarmac. She flipped up the visor.

Flynn had taken off his helmet and pushed his hair back off his face. 'You're alive,' he said, rather gleefully, Lara thought.

'B-barely,' Lara said, taking off her own helmet.

'How was it?'

'You s-said you w-wouldn't go very fast.'

'I didn't. I stuck to the speed limit or lower all the way.'

'It felt like we were doing a hundred miles an hour.'

'Not today.' His dark eyes glinted wickedly. 'Great, isn't it?'

She tried not to think of all the biker clichés about throbbing power and being exposed to the elements, but the rush on the corners and the straights had been mind-blowing. The mountains and lakes had flashed by her in a blur of brown and white and indigo.

'Are you OK to go on?'

Lara wasn't sure she could speak again so she nodded. 'Of course. Bring it on.'

The latter part of the route was more sedate as they rode into Keswick, found a parking spot for the bike, and headed into the little town, where the square was buzzing with stalls set up for the Christmas market. With the big day imminent, the stalls were doing a roaring trade as everyone scrambled for gifts and festive food.

Lara took off the helmet and was glad she'd tied her hair back to keep it from turning into a bird's nest. Even so, she could barely believe that the biker girl reflected in the shop windows was her. She wished her parents could see her. She rather hoped they'd be horrified.

'What's funny?' Flynn asked, outside the Peter Rabbit shop.

'Nothing. Nothing at all. Shall we go inside? I think we'll

find something for Esme in here. I don't think you can go wrong with Peter Rabbit, and it is *very* Lake District. Beatrix Potter lived and wrote her books here.'

Flynn wrinkled his nose and heaved a sigh.

'What's up? You look nervous.'

'I need to tell you now that I have never in my life been inside a Peter Rabbit shop.'

Lara laughed. 'No need to be scared, although you might be when you see the prices. Come on. Let's do it.'

The reaction to two bikers entering the store was interesting. It wasn't large and had lots of nooks and crannies, so Flynn filled the space quite quickly. There were glances from some of the more traditional customers and some admiring looks from others.

Half an hour later they emerged, Flynn carrying a large Peter Rabbit bag containing a Jellycat toy that had cost an eyewatering sum, two board books, and a Peter Rabbit-themed sleepsuit, dress and leggings chosen by Lara. Lara had also indulged, buying gifts for Jazz's children and an old friend's new baby.

With Esme catered for, Flynn was now fretting about what to get for Molly. Lara suggested they go into the bakery café for a spicy sausage roll and some stollen.

'What do young women want for Christmas these days? I don't want to get anything weird or fogeyish.'

'Make-up, clothes, hair stuff, tech, books? I bet she's so busy looking after Esme that she doesn't have time for herself – and not much money.'

'Money, I – that's another thing. I need to think about helping to support them both.'

'That's not my area,' Lara said. 'I'll leave that to you.'

'I know what you're thinking. I've thought it too. How do I know that Molly is really mine?'

'I – I wasn't thinking that,' Lara said, taken aback that Flynn had admitted such a personal concern.

'She offered to do a DNA test and I agreed. The results came back last week. She is mine.' His smile broadened into one of pure happiness. 'I always knew it. The timings are exactly right for her birthday and she looks like me – God help her – you have to admit that.'

'Yeah. She does.' Lara had thought it several times.

'Or is that wishful thinking?' he asked.

'No, it's understandable, and—' She paused. 'I'm so happy for you, Flynn.'

'Thanks. Thanks for being so understanding. I'm sorry that things have turned out to be so complicated for us.'

Lara agreed but she would never ever wish away his joy, even if that joy reminded her again and again of what she might have had.

'You know, two months ago, if you'd asked me if I wanted to discover a child I didn't know about, I'd have laughed and been horrified. Why would anyone want that kind of bombshell in their life? Not me. I was free and single – still youngish – free to do what I wanted and—'

'And now?'

'Now I don't know what I'd do without them. Though I still wake up in the morning, remember they exist, and think it can't be true. But now they *are* here, I would never wish it any different. I just wish I hadn't missed the earlier part of their lives. Oh no, I've made today all about them when I wanted it to be a day we could . . . enjoy as friends, with no pressure.'

Lara found it hard to reply. It was all about Flynn and his new family, and she got that, she totally did, and she felt for him – but this was his life, and while she might be helping him choose gifts for them, that was as far as her help could possibly go.

Having had lunch, they dived back into crowds even thicker than before. There was an air of urgency, panic even, but it all added to the festive buzz she loved at this time of year. A school choir was singing carols in the market-place, the children bundled up in coats and bobble hats. The aromas of spiced hot apple and turkey rolls mingled with the tang of holly and mistletoe for sale on the greengrocers' stalls.

Lara bought a small print of the Lakeland fells from an artist's stall to give to a friend at home when she visited in the New Year, along with some orange and cinnamon soaps for Jazz and sloe gin for Luke. She'd sent her parents' gifts with them to Australia and had had to be very creative, choosing small light items, such as jewellery. Come to think of it, she mustn't go mad today because everything had to fit in the Harley's top box.

Flynn had stopped and was looking at the butcher's stall, where pheasants and rabbits hung from hooks.

'What about Brenda?' he asked, turning back to Lara. 'I want to get her something small. I can't go to her house empty-handed.'

'Hmm . . . in my opinion, you probably can't go wrong with some really nice chocolates, as long as she's not allergic.'

'She's not allergic to whisky,' Flynn said bluntly. 'But I don't think a bottle of single malt would be tactful. She might think I'm implying she's an alcoholic.'

'What about some nice whisky-flavoured chocs – some with liqueurs in?' Lara pointed up the street at a large store whose windows were at least three shops wide. 'I know the perfect place.'

It took Flynn almost as long to choose the chocolates from the Friars store as it had to decide on the baby gifts. They both walked out with bags full of delicious treats for not only Brenda but their friends and families.

'Well, I'm going to need a second mortgage, but at least I've solved my Christmas present dilemma,' Flynn said, eyeing the carrier bag of chocs ruefully. They'd decided to stroll down the lakeside path back to the bike. Lights had been strung between the street lamps and were twinkling as afternoon drew on.

'When will you tell your parents about Molly and Esme?'

'I'd said I'd visit early in the New Year . . . but now I can't decide whether to tell them they have a granddaughter and great grandchild before then.' He stopped by the lake shore, gazing out over the fells, which were topped with snow and turning a soft pink in the late afternoon sun.

'Will they be shocked?'

'Initially, yeah, but they'll probably be thrilled once they get used to it. They've been on at me to settle down with someone for years. They never found out about Abigail, fortunately, and that she was married – I'm not sure they'd have believed me when I said I didn't know. Did your family know about your relationship with Rob?'

'I tried to keep it fairly low key. I was living on site in the "gardener's cottage" at the manor, and he'd never really interacted with my friends or family. I think I didn't see as much of them as I should have either, in hindsight. It can be a very isolating life, living and working somewhere like Ravendale or my last place. You have to work extra hard not to make it the centre of your life.' Which was even more reason not to make someone you work with the centre of your life, she reflected.

Flynn smiled. 'I know . . . Lara, I am really grateful for your help today. I wouldn't have had a clue what to buy. These are my closest relatives and I don't know them at all, but this isn't really your problem, and I didn't want to lay it on you.'

'I think I can handle a bit of Christmas shopping.'

'Thanks. This whole situation has totally pulled the rug from under my feet. There I was, so sure of where I was heading. So sure of what I wanted—'

She'd been sure he knew too – so sure that she'd set aside all her misgivings and launched herself feet first back into the deep waters she'd avoided for so long.

He gazed out over the lake again as if searching for answers in the mountains and December sky before turning to her. 'One moment you have a plan, and then, *boom*, life throws you a hand grenade.'

'A very cute hand grenade. Two, in fact.'

'Yes. Two.' He managed a smile. 'Don't get me wrong, I know how lucky I am to have a family, even one that was kept a secret for so long. But it's tough, and I feel I'm failing all the time. I'm feeling my way every day and every day seems to throw up a bigger challenge. Getting to know Molly and Esme, worrying about other people's reactions . . .'

'You're not failing. You could have run away by now. Some people would have. You stayed, you're trying to learn, and trying to make things work.'

'Yeah. Maybe.' He kicked at the gravel on the shore and rested his gaze on the lake where the Christmas lights shimmered on the surface.

'Does Imogen know yet? She could help share the responsibility and,' Lara added gently, 'answer some of your questions.'

'Hmm. I don't know if I dare ask her some of the questions that keep me awake at night. And no, she doesn't know Molly found me yet. Molly keeps putting off telling her. My worry is that, if she doesn't tell her mum, Brenda will do it for her, and I'm not sure that's the best idea.'

From nowhere, fireworks burst into the darkening sky.

The sound jolted Flynn and he turned to her with a melancholy smile. 'I think we should be getting back. I've dragged you into my dramas long enough. Are you ready for the return ride?'

'Not really . . . but you know I'm always here as your friend,' she said, as they walked back to the car park.

'You're more than a friend,' he said with a look of tenderness. 'You're special to me.'

The comment stabbed at her. It was what Rob had said and, even though Lara knew that Flynn was a good, decent man – the opposite of Rob – she'd ended up in the same situation. Alone. This time she had no intention of walking away from her job or her home so the only option was to protect her heart as best she could.

They'd reached the bike. 'I'll always listen. As a *friend*,' she emphasised again, and bustled ahead, trying to forget his comment and cover it with practicalities. 'There is one thing I need to ask. Jazz is badgering me to give the final numbers for the Christmas lunch at the castle. I hate to hassle you about it but are you definitely not coming?'

His brow furrowed. 'Why would you think I wasn't coming?'

'I'd assumed you'd be going to Molly's.'

'I am – but I already told her and Brenda that I'll be at Ravendale for the lunch. They invited me for tea afterwards. Not that I'll have room for tea, but it seemed the best solution.'

'Are you sure?'

'I said I'm going to be at the castle for the dinner. Wild horses wouldn't keep me away.'

Chapter Thirty-six

Somehow Lara survived the journey home, although she found the last half of it pretty hairy, because darkness had fallen and a lot of the route was unlit. Once again, it was easier and more reassuring to hang on to Flynn.

Even so, her arms and legs ached from the tension of holding on, and she needed a large G&T to help her unwind after a day of physical and emotional ups and downs.

She fell asleep, dreaming about riding behind him without a helmet, her cheek pressed against the leather of his jacket, the wind tugging at her hair and the roar of the bike obliterating every sound. She dreamed that she'd somehow flown off the bike, high above the lake and fells – yet she hadn't been scared.

Over the next few days, Lara was running around getting ready for the last hordes before the Christmas break, solving the lack of loos problem, and finalising arrangements for the staff Christmas lunch. When the final visitors left on the 23rd, everyone heaved a sigh of relief.

On Christmas Eve morning the staff worked hard to make everything secure and address any minor glitches to be ready for re-opening. That way, they could finish early and get back to their families – or the pub.

Lara wasn't sure if that would be Flynn's plan – she only knew that he'd messaged the group chat to say he was looking forward to the Christmas dinner.

At 4 p.m., Lara changed into a Christmas jumper with a glittery Rudolph, put on her reindeer antlers, and headed to the formal drawing room for another of the Ravendale Christmas traditions: Christmas Eve drinks.

The stars were twinkling in the velvet Lakeland sky and the tower clock was striking the half hour when she walked up the steps into the castle.

Most of the staff who were staying on site over the holiday had gathered, along with a few of those who lived off-site but wanted to wind down and socialise before driving or getting a taxi home.

There were around twenty people laughing and chattering in the drawing room, including Jazz, Carlos, Rebecca the housekeeper, a few of the gardeners, and the head porter. Henry and Fiona were standing in front of the Christmas tree talking to Flynn.

'Ah! Lara!' Henry said. 'Help yourself to a glass of fizz. Well done on surviving.'

Lara plucked a glass from the table and joined them.

'Hi.' Flynn had a slightly strained smile.

Henry was overflowing with festive bonhomie and looking a lot healthier. 'Hello there! I bet you two are so glad that it's almost over and we can all take a breather. Time for you both to relax and have a chill out.'

Lara looked at Flynn, expecting an amused glance in exchange, but his hand was on his pocket where he kept his phone.

Henry chatted to them a while more, talking about how much he was looking forward to their two daughters and their respective families visiting, before leaving them together by the Christmas tree.

'He's a sweetheart but I suspect he's never had a "chill out" in his life.'

'No,' Flynn said, with the wry and crooked smile that still had the power to throw her off kilter and make her want to sweep him off to bed.

She cleared her throat and sipped her fizz. 'This must be an exciting time for Molly,' she said, in a low voice, making sure they couldn't be overheard. 'Tonight will be fun for her and Brenda.'

'It will,' Flynn murmured, distracted by a phone message. 'Excuse me,' he said, and glanced at the screen before breaking into a smile that lit up his face. 'Sorry. That was Molly. She sent a picture of Esme dressed in a reindeer outfit at the nursery party yesterday.' He showed the screen to Lara. Her heart ached at the photo of the smiling baby in her outfit.

'She looks very cute,' she said, realising that Flynn must be itching to reply.

'She is,' he said proudly.

'I'll leave you to it,' she said, as cheerfully as she could muster. 'I ought to be going. I promised to check in with my parents and get an early night. See you tomorrow for lunch.'

Chapter Thirty-seven

'G'day from Down Under! Happy Christmas!'

'Happy Christmas!' Lara answered, taking in the small and beaming crowd gathered round a table on the covered terrace of her sister's spacious bungalow. It was early evening in Melbourne and the sun was still dazzling through the screen. They were all wearing Santa hats, along with their T-shirts and summer dresses.

Lara pulled the duvet up higher, longing to feel the warmth of that Aussie sun on her face and blot out the dark wintry morning. She'd emerged into the chilly cottage long enough to grab a mug of coffee and a croissant and pop a pair of glittery antlers on her head before returning to bed with her laptop.

'I'd have thought you'd still be having a barbie on the beach,' she joked.

'It rained earlier,' her sister, Mel, declared. 'It does do that sometimes, even in December, and anyway, you can't park by the beach because of the hordes of people wanting to do the same. Sun's out now, though. We're quite happy to chill out here.'

'It looks wonderful,' she said with a sigh.

She'd had an early night in front of the TV, so that she'd

275

be fresh for the busy day ahead. She drank her coffee and ate her croissant while her family tucked into grilled prawns and salad. The laptop screen was crowded with smiling, excited faces while her parents, brother-in-law and nephews – and Lara herself – opened their gifts in front of each other.

Then everyone, apart from Mel, waved goodbye and went outside to the pool to watch the kids play with their new inflatables.

Mel stayed online, having taken her laptop inside for some shade. 'Is it really cold there?'

'What do you think? I'm still in bed under the duvet and it isn't even properly light yet.'

'Is there snow? I do miss the snow . . . I bet it looks wonderful there too. A snow-topped castle must be amazing. Turkey and all the trimmings isn't quite the same when it's thirty-five degrees. That's why we've had prawns and salad. To tell you the truth, if Mum and Dad hadn't decided to visit, I'd have rather liked to come home . . .'

Lara was taken aback. It was the first time in the three years since Mel had gone to Australia that she'd expressed any regrets. 'Well, the fells are covered in snow but it's only frosty down here . . . do you mean that about coming home?'

'We might. Vince is coming round to the idea. His contract is ending this summer and so it will be decision time. I don't want to move the kids once they start their next school.' She smiled. 'So you must come out here next year – I mean after Christmas. You promised, and you ought to visit us while you still can.'

The heavy hint wasn't lost on Lara as her throat was full

of emotion. 'I'm going to book a ticket as soon as the madness here is over. I promise.'

'Come in the autumn – that's March – when it cools down and the crowds have gone. And if there's someone you want to bring with you, you'd both be welcome.'

'Why would I? You've just seen me wake up in bed on my own.'

'I can see you in bed on your own *now*,' Mel replied, with a shrewd look. 'I know you too well, Lara. If there was anyone you'd like to wake up with, you'd have made sure he wasn't around.'

'Well, there isn't anyone I was planning to wake up with,' she said.

'Then there should be. I hope there will be. You deserve to find someone gorgeous and who isn't a bastard after that prick Rob.'

'Don't hold back with the opinions,' Lara said.

'It's the Aussie influence.' She grinned.

Lara snorted. 'You've always been outspoken. Don't blame your friends and neighbours!'

They both laughed and Lara said, 'I promise I'll make my travel plans as soon as the Christmas programme here is over. I promise.' She crossed her heart and ended the call.

It had been fun and lovely to see her family but, as she leaned back against the pillows, she felt a bit hollow. Tears formed in her eyes. She'd rarely felt more desolate and alone in her life: perhaps not since the days after she'd spilt with Rob and realised her pregnancy was over too soon.

She was no tragic case, in that she worked in her dream

job in an amazing location. How many people could say that? She had a rich and fulfilling life and yet all that had happened in the past eighteen months had reminded her how much she valued family, and that, one day, she'd like to start one of her own. Was it selfish to want that for herself or even to hope for it with someone she respected and loved deeply – and who felt the same about her?

The clock on the castle tower chimed eight and the first hints of daylight found their way through the curtains. Lara opened them to find a crisp coating of frost on the shrubs outside and rooftops above. The lights were on in Flynn's cottage, which meant he was already awake, perhaps messaging his Cornish family – or his new one.

She set her regrets aside for the time being. Mel was right about one thing: spending Christmas Day at a fairy-tale castle was a magical experience and, no matter what happened from now on, she was going to make the most of it.

Chapter Thirty-eight

Flynn had been awake since 5 a.m. but his sleeplessness had nothing to do with wondering if Santa had been. He got up, made a strong coffee with the new machine that his parents had sent, and flicked through the various TV channels full of carol services and Christmas versions of kids' cartoons until he wondered why he was wasting his time.

Then he dressed, had a shave, and hoped he didn't look as knackered over WhatsApp as he had in the bathroom mirror.

Finally, he summoned up all his nerve and called his parents on the phone.

Their smiling faces greeted him, his mother in her dressing gown. 'Wow, Flynn. This is early even for you.'

'Ha ha. You know I'm used to waking up early.'

'Not when you were a teenager.' His mum chuckled. 'It looks very dark up there.'

'It is, but it'll brighten up later and there's snow on the hills. Where's Dad?'

'Steve!' His mother called, over her shoulder. 'It's your son!'

At the mention of that one innocuous word – son – Flynn's stomach lurched with so many emotions, he could hardly speak.

'I'm coming.' His father appeared wearing reindeer antlers with jingly bells on the tips.

'Morning, Dad,' said Flynn.

'Hello. Sorry. I was putting the turkey in. It almost didn't fit in the oven and we'll still be eating the damn thing at Easter.'

Flynn smiled as they started to chatter and ask him questions that were easy to answer, yet which only delayed the inevitable.

'Yeah, I'm fine. Yes, the fells are covered in snow. It does look very Christmassy . . .' Flynn took a deep breath. 'Thanks for the vouchers. I opened them this morning. And for the coffee machine. You've spoiled me. I'll bring yours when I see you . . . yes, I—'

The conversation went on. He smiled and joked, while feeling he was about to burst with the tension of keeping his secret.

Suddenly, there was a loud screeching from somewhere in his parents' house and his mother said, 'That's the smoke alarm. Steve, please don't tell me you left the grill on. Is that burning bacon I can smell?'

'Jesus. Yes! I have to go!' His father jumped up.

'No!' Flynn heard himself shout above the shrieking of the alarm. 'Don't go. I have something to tell you!'

Chapter Thirty-nine

Lara was tucking serviettes into wine glasses when Flynn walked into the Castle Café. He wore black jeans and a red jumper with 'Ho Ho Ho' on it and made a beeline for her.

'Hello. Happy Christmas. Can I help?'

She handed him the packet of serviettes, thinking that he looked good enough to eat. 'Happy Christmas. Make those look pretty?'

He grimaced. 'Can I do something easier?'

She smiled despite the tension in her body. 'Not unless you want to peel potatoes with Mrs Danvers. She's very particular about how they're prepared.'

'Mrs Danvers?' Flynn's brow furrowed in confusion.

Lara smirked. 'Jazz and I call Rebecca Mrs Danvers. Because she rules the castle with a rod of iron and can be a bit scary.'

'Er . . . sorry . . .' Flynn was nonplussed.

'Don't worry about it,' Lara said, handing him another wad of serviettes. All the light banter was their way of dancing around each other, trying to defuse the tension.

'I think I'll pass on Mrs Danvers. I'll do my best to be artistic instead.'

'Good decision. To be honest, everything seems under

control in the kitchen and I'm not going to interfere with Mrs D – Rebecca – in charge.'

'Hmm.' Flynn folded a serviette, frowned and re-folded it. 'Fluffing hell.'

'Sorry?'

'Nothing,' he said and stood back. 'You look lovely.'

Lara was in her crimson velvet dress and a tinsel head-band. 'Thanks,' she said, and nodded at his chest, where the 'Ho Ho Ho' was stretched across his pecs. 'Nice jumper.'

He gave a wry smile. 'I thought I ought to enter the fes-tive spirit. And I don't want to get a reputation as a party pooper.'

'Why ever would anyone think that?'

'Because I've been cracking the whip since I got here. This is my one chance to show I'm a nice, harmless, normal human being.'

'I don't think you'll ever achieve that.' She took the crum-pled serviette from his hand, folded it and popped it into a glass. 'Can I get you a drink?'

'Yes, please. No alcohol obviously, because I'm riding later. Though I'd like a large whisky, to be honest. I just told my parents about Molly and Esme.'

'Wow,' Lara said. 'How did they take it?'

'They were stunned. Shocked. Mum cried and Dad kept saying "bloody hell".' They both think they're far too young to be great-grandparents and are desperate to know more and meet Molly and Esme.' He blew out a breath. 'I was on the phone for an hour, trying to tell them that Imogen didn't even know yet, so they'd have to keep everything to themselves for now.'

'I bet. But Molly will tell Imogen when she comes home after Christmas?'

'Yes, she's promised she will. Now I need to try and unwind for a few hours. Have you got anything remotely festive with no booze in it so I can pretend I'm getting pissed when I'm not?'

Lara laughed. 'I think we have some zero beer and gallons of elderflower fizz. The bar's over here.'

Flynn found a beer and Lara decided that, at half-past eleven on Christmas morning, it was allowable to have a small glass of Prosecco, though she intended to pace herself. She'd learned from bitter experience that, with free booze on tap and a long day ahead without family looking over their shoulders, some of her work colleagues did have a tendency to get plastered.

Though it *was* tempting to drink the free bar dry, Lara knew there was always the possibility she might have to turn peacemaker or help someone back to their accommodation – not to mention that last year one of the gardening team had set fire to the kitchen bin. They'd narrowly avoided a callout from the fire service.

Most of all, she wanted to be in full control of anything she might say to Flynn. He must be in turmoil after breaking the news to his parents, and even Lara had found her video call with her own family to be way more emotional than she'd expected.

For now, she threw herself into the celebrations and one glass of fizz led to several others. After everyone had mucked in with preparing and serving lunch, Flynn proved a dab hand at carving and they ate enough to be fit to burst. Once she'd got over the oddity of sharing Christmas dinner with people she worked with every day, Lara found herself relaxing. She had to hand it to Flynn – he was clearly keen to join in.

People were talking about missing family and Rebecca piped up from the head of the table.

'I always volunteer to work over Christmas,' she stated. 'I can't stand the forced jollity and my mum insists on having my aunt and cousins round. They're total snobs and the kids are feral.' She grinned. 'Can someone pass the roast potatoes? And I wouldn't mind some extra gravy.'

They'd just finished forcing pudding down themselves when someone suggested playing games.

Lara, two of the gardeners, the deputy housekeeper, and a finance officer called Troy, who she'd only ever spoken to once, actually had a lot of fun. They had a 'reveal one silly fact' about yourself, which had resulted in Troy revealing he used to work in a circus. He then fetched a unicycle from his cottage and rode it round the courtyard to prove it. Rebecca had had a go and fallen off, but fortunately it was into a hay bale.

One of the apprentices revealed he'd once played for the Man United youth team, and the deputy head gardener, a burly guy with a shaven head and bushy beard, confessed that he'd once reached the final stage auditions of *Britain's Got Talent*. He was then persuaded to sing 'Have Yourself a Very Merry Christmas'.

People's eyes were still suspiciously moist after his performance when Mrs Danvers was thrust into the spotlight.

She leaned back in her chair. 'Well, when I was working at a – let's say a very famous and historic palace in the southeast – I once caught a cabinet minister doing something very naughty with his permanent private secretary in the linen storeroom.'

'Oh!'

'What?'

'Who?'

The others bombarded her with questions.

'I can't possibly say, but it involved, according to what I overheard through the door, hiding the – hic – sausage.'

Laughter erupted and Flynn joined in.

'What about you, Flynn? What's the thing we don't know about you?'

'Could be anything!' Mrs D declared. 'He's only been here two months.'

'OK. OK. I once did something really stupid. I had to be rescued by the RNLI after I jumped into the sea off a cliff for a dare. I hit the water at a funny angle, except it wasn't funny. It was like hitting concrete and I passed out.'

Lara stared at him in horror.

'Silly boy,' Rebecca muttered. 'Hic.'

'Yeah, it was stupid. Lucky for me, some guy in a kayak got to me and the RNLI fished me out. I was OK after a night in hospital, but Mum and Dad went mad and grounded me for the rest of the school holidays. I learned my lesson.'

'So you went out and got a motorbike instead?' Lara commented.

'I was eighteen by then. They couldn't stop me.' He grinned. 'I was a bit of a rebel but I'm very sensible now.'

'Of course,' Lara said. 'You'd never do anything risky now.'

'It all sounds extremely reckless,' Mrs Danvers said, before sloshing more fizz into her glass. 'And rather wonderful. Your turn, Lara.'

'Oh no. You know everything about me.'

'No, we don't, you play your cards very close to your chest,' said Mrs Danvers. 'You must have seen a lot in your career. I bet you're keeping loads of secrets.'

She thought of the chalice and tried not to catch Flynn's eye. So many secrets, none of which she would ever reveal to her colleagues.

'My secret is that my boss once tried to persuade me to break up with an old flame for him because he was too cowardly to do it.'

'Urgh!'

'What a pig.'

'How were you to do this evil deed?' Mrs Danvers asked. 'In person or on the phone?'

'Neither. He wanted me to compose an email to her, as if the message had come from him. He said I'd be a lot more sensitive and tactful about it than he would.'

She should have known then that Rob was a bastard,

Lara thought, but she hadn't known him long and he'd sold her some story about the woman turning into a stalker.

'I didn't do it,' Lara insisted. 'I refused, so he had to write her a letter instead.'

'What a creep,' Flynn murmured.

'Well, it's clear there are some total shits about.' Mrs Danvers waggled her glass. 'Is there any more Prosecco about? If their lordships are paying, I feel it's our duty as their vassals to drink it.'

It was half past two when Flynn took Lara aside in a quiet corner near the rear door of the café. 'Lara . . . I hate to do this, but I have to bail out or I'll never make it to Molly's. I've really enjoyed myself.'

'Against your expectations?' she said archly.

'Maybe,' he said, grinning. 'I'm sorry to leave you.'

'Don't be sorry. I'll be fine.' There was an edge to Lara's voice that she couldn't suppress. 'And you'll enjoy being with Molly and Esme on Christmas Day.'

'Will I? Molly's excited and Esme is a delight, but Brenda's none too sure about me. I think she's finding having a man around quite a struggle. They have their own family traditions and I don't want to upset them.'

'It can't be easy for anyone. But you'll make new traditions. Together,' she added cheerfully, hiding her disappointment at him leaving.

'Are you staying over at Molly's tonight?'

'No. I think that would be a bit much for all of us. We're all still taking baby steps. Literally.'

'And Imogen?' Lara asked.

'Molly's promised to tell her tomorrow on FaceTime.' He grimaced. 'If she doesn't, Brenda will. And what about you? How will you spend the rest of the day?'

'Join the *Wallace and Gromit* watch party. Eat my own weight in chocolate truffles. Make sure no one falls in the fountains.'

He laughed. 'I hope not.' His smile melted away. 'I wish . . .' he said, with an expression of longing that made Lara's resolve wobble.

'Don't wish. Never wish.'

'You're probably right.' He gazed upwards in frustration. 'But this is tearing me in two, Lara.'

'I don't want to be the reason for ripping anything apart. This is a special time for you and for Molly. I wouldn't expect you to do anything other than give your whole self to it. You'll regret it if you don't, I promise.'

'I know, but . . .' There was such tenderness in his voice and eyes – such longing and gratitude that Lara almost threw her arms around him.

He glanced upwards. 'How ironic,' he murmured, 'that we're standing under the mistletoe.'

'*Some* mistletoe,' she qualified, as her heart pitter-pattered. 'There's mistletoe all over the castle.'

With him so temptingly close on a day when people were meant to come together, she was struggling. It would be so easy to imagine his hands cradling her face and those warm lips pressed against hers.

She instinctively stepped back. 'And it wouldn't be a good idea to use it.'

He closed his eyes and subsided into a silent sigh. 'I'm sure you're right. It would be a very bad idea. And I really must go.' He glanced up at the mistletoe again, then back at Lara before leaning in to press his lips against her cheek. 'Happy Christmas, Lara.'

'Happy Christmas, Flynn,' she said, as her heart hollowed out. 'Wish the family a good one, from me.'

'I will.'

He walked away and, the moment he was out of sight, Lara lifted her hand to her cheek, feeling – imagining – that the skin was still warm from his kiss.

It had been the innocent kiss of a friend, yet Flynn could never be her friend. In that moment she realised she could not stay and work and live with him here as her friend.

She closed the door, readjusted her tinsel headband, and went back inside to join the party.

Chapter Forty

Flynn unloaded the presents from the bike's top box and stood on the pathway outside Molly and Brenda's house. He'd found it so hard to ride away from Lara; he'd felt he'd abandoned her on a special day and now he was so nervous that he'd almost ridden straight back.

Darkness had all but fallen by the time he reached the house. The cul-de-sac was crowded with cars and vans, and there were lights in almost every window. Everyone was home for Christmas and probably passed out in a post-turkey haze.

The curtains were drawn at Molly's but he could imagine the scene inside. Brenda flopped on the sofa with her feet up, a glass of port in her hand. Molly on the floor, surrounded by a sea of wrapping paper, boxes, furry toys and upturned crates of Duplo. Esme bashing Penguin with a hammer or trying to crawl off. He still couldn't imagine himself in that scene and yet he had to insert himself into it.

He took a deep breath, walked up the path, and rang the bell. There was the usual kerfuffle when guests arrived at doors: voices, the TV, squeals from Esme, and the door opened.

Yet it was neither Molly nor Brenda who answered the

door but a tall, tanned woman his own age. Flynn froze on the threshold.

The woman's jaw fell open in shock. *'Flynn?'*

'Imogen.'

Even now, after twenty years, even without the benefit of having seen her profile picture on Facebook, he'd have recognised her instantly. The pretty girl by the lake; the mother of his child.

'What the hell?' Imogen murmured.

Flynn was spared from speaking by Molly appearing behind her mother. 'Oh my God! I meant to answer the door. Don't be angry. I didn't know she was coming. I tried to warn you both. Oh, shit.'

Flynn was still paralysed with shock, his arms full of presents. 'Imogen, I'd n-no idea you'd be here.'

'Same here,' Imogen said, staring at him. 'No bloody idea at all.'

'For the love of God, will someone let the man in?' Brenda materialised behind Molly with Esme in her arms. 'I knew this would happen! I'm taking Esme upstairs to put her pyjamas on. She doesn't need to hear this. Molly, love, don't get upset. It can't be helped now.'

Imogen opened the door as Molly shrunk back into the hallway. 'I suppose you'd better come in.'

'Are you sure? This doesn't seem the best time . . .'

'You were obviously expected.'

While Flynn hadn't quite known what kind of welcome to expect, he had hoped that the afternoon could be a chance to build more bonds with Molly and some bridges with

Brenda. That had gone out of the window, because never in a million years had he expected Imogen to be there. She looked as shocked – and dismayed – as he was.

'Come in,' Molly said, not adding 'Dad', which Flynn thought was wise considering the thunderous expression on her mother's face.

Imogen walked into the sitting room and sat down heavily on a chair with Molly standing in front of her.

'Mum, if we'd known you were going to rock up out of the blue, we'd have told Flynn not to come.'

Flynn glanced back at the doorway, wondering if he still had time to bolt. He felt ridiculous with his bags of gifts. 'Maybe I should come back another time.'

'No,' Imogen finally spoke again. 'This was obviously all planned. And no one knew I was coming until I turned up after lunch.'

'We thought she was in Tenerife,' Molly said, hugging herself.

'Well, I wasn't going to miss my granddaughter's first Christmas and I wanted to see you and Mum,' Imogen snapped. 'I managed to get the time off and wanted to surprise you.'

'That was—' Flynn was going to say 'nice of you', but he decided it was better if settled for 'I'm glad you could get here.'

'Yeah – but – why are *you* here? It looks like you've been hanging around a while.'

'I wouldn't describe it as hanging around,' Flynn said, feeling annoyed. He was aware that Imogen had zero insight into the events of the past few weeks and he didn't want to inflame the situation, for Molly's sake, but he had a bunch of questions of his own for Imogen. In this highly charged atmosphere, though, now was not the moment.

Molly finally found her voice. 'I am so sorry, Mum. I swear I was going to tell you tomorrow – over FaceTime.'

'FaceTime?' Imogen echoed. 'I suppose it would have been better than nothing.'

'And Flynn. I tried to message you as soon as I could after Mum arrived.'

'I didn't look at my phone. I was at the castle at the staff Christmas lunch. I didn't even think to check my phone because I was late and rushing over here.'

'I'm sorry. It wasn't meant to turn out like this.'

'It's OK,' he soothed his daughter. 'But I can see it's a shock for your mum.'

Imogen stared at him. She was still very like the girl he'd lain with by that lakeside fire, albeit her hair was even darker than it had been then, almost black. She was very tanned, as you'd expect from someone who worked in the sun a lot, and there was something harder-edged about her features than he remembered. Maybe twenty years of working to support a child on her own would have done that, he thought bitterly.

He wanted to ask her why she'd felt the need but he stopped himself. All in good time. God knows what he looked like to her.

He dragged his eyes away and smiled at Molly. 'This is pretty awkward, isn't it?'

'You can say that again,' Imogen said. 'Molly, any chance of a large glass of that pink gin I brought?'

Molly scurried off to the kitchen and seemed to take a long time making a G&T and finding a zero beer for Flynn. In an ideal world, he would have had several shots of Harvey's decent whisky to cope with the drama. However, he was stuck here now and there was no escape. He wouldn't have left anyway, though, because Molly and Esme needed him.

'It's unfortunate Molly didn't alert either of us, but it means I have no idea why and how you're here.'

'I work at Ravendale Castle. Molly heard my name mentioned around and kind of tracked me down. I think that's something you need to talk to her about, though,' Flynn replied.

Brenda came back into the lounge with Esme in her arms. 'My, she is getting so heavy. Do I need to referee?'

Flynn almost managed a smile. 'Not yet, Brenda.'

Imogen's eyes flicked from her mother to Flynn, perhaps sensing the glimmer of an in-joke between the two of them. 'How long has this been going on?'

Molly re-entered the room, a tissue in her hand.

'Only a few weeks. Well, Flynn's only known about us for a few weeks. I was kind of stalking him online for a while before that. So were you, Mum, so don't deny it.' Molly handed her a gin and tonic.

'Stalking? If you mean I was interested in what the father of my child was doing, then, yes, but I had no intention of contacting him. Jeez, Mum, why didn't you both tell me before?'

'We didn't have time. And I wanted to, Immy, I wanted to, but Molly was – Molly was worried and scared.'

Molly took Esme from Brenda. 'I was going to tell you tomorrow, Mum. I swear.'

'Hold on. I am here,' Flynn said. 'May I suggest we have this conversation when Esme is in bed?'

'I think that's a very good idea,' Brenda said, placing Esme on the carpet, where she started to crawl towards the cat, who shot out of the door before its tail was grabbed.

'I can see some presents,' Molly said, with a forced cheerfulness.

'Yes. Why don't you open them now?' Flynn said, wondering what Imogen would make of it all.

'So many presents . . . You really have got your feet under the table while I've been away,' Imogen said, chilling the mood like a squall of winter sleet. But even though the temperature had nosedived, Flynn was determined to stay as civil as he could.

At least, he thought, he could leave at the end of the evening. He would not have wanted to be a fly on the wall after he'd gone.

'I'm making up for lost time,' Flynn shot back.

'It's a lovely thought,' Brenda said, with a glare for Imogen.

'I'm going into the kitchen,' Imogen declared, and didn't even bother giving a reason. Flynn guessed that she was surprised that her mother had come to his rescue.

'Come on, let's open them,' Molly said, 'before Esme is too tired and decides to get aggy.'

Flynn decided that the only person in the room who had seemed 'aggy' was Imogen and he was relieved she had decided to let them open the gifts in peace, obviously not wanting to be part of the proceedings

Molly's eyes widened in surprise when she opened her gift.

'This is beautiful,' she said, lifting the lid on the luxurious hamper before giving him a shrewd look. 'Did someone help you choose this?'

He silently thanked Lara for suggesting he pay the extra to have it gift-wrapped in the shop. Even though he didn't want to drag her into his dramas, he half-wished she were here now with her calming presence. She seemed to understand him so well, even after such a short time.

'Erm . . .'

Flynn was saved from completing the sentence by Esme, who had stuffed the wrapping paper from her new wooden blocks in her mouth. The next ten minutes were taken up by Molly helping Esme open her presents and admiring the Peter Rabbit outfits.

Brenda opened the chocolates and shared them round, thanking Flynn and telling him that Friars was her favourite shop. 'They're lovely. Thank you.'

'You're welcome.'

'I got you something,' Molly said. 'Actually, Esme made it at nursery.'

Flynn was taken aback. He had completely overlooked the fact that he might receive a present too.

Molly handed over a card with a foot-shaped paint

splodge that had been turned into a creature Flynn recognised as a reindeer.

'That's Esme's footprint,' she said.

Flynn opened the card and sucked in a breath. It read:

to Grandad Flynn, love from Esme xxx

To see his name written like that: Grandad Flynn. It sounded ancient, and a few weeks ago, he'd have been frankly horrified at the very thought, and yet . . . he was the opposite of horrified. He felt privileged.

'It's – it's brilliant,' he said, recovering himself and smiling at Esme. 'I love it. Thank you, Esme.'

Esme responded with a smile and bashed her blocks on Penguin.

'And there's this. I think you can guess what it is.'

Molly handed over a rectangular present, which Flynn unwrapped, even though he could have bet the Harley on what was inside. It was a photograph of Molly and Esme at the Winter Spectacular, Molly pointing at the reindeer on the grotto. It was a photo so full of joy and life that he felt the prickle of tears behind his eyes and struggled to reply.

'It's at Ravendale. Obviously,' Molly said, smiling. 'I thought it was one of the best of us together and, being at the castle, I thought you'd like it, and that you wouldn't have a photo yet.'

'I do – I – love it. It's perfect. Thank you.'

Brenda fetched a tray of mugs and slices of Christmas cake, which Flynn didn't dare refuse. It was lovely cake and

Brenda had made it herself, but he was too full of emotion to eat much.

After, he helped Molly clear up wrapping paper and packaging from the carpet. Esme was already rubbing her eyes and ready for her bottle and bed.

Brenda went back into the kitchen, leaving Molly alone with Flynn again while she gave Esme her milk.

'I am sorry about what happened. I honestly was going to tell Mum and I did try to warn you.'

'I know.'

'Would you have come over if you'd found out she was here?' Molly asked, allowing Esme to hold her own bottle. Her eyes were fixed on Flynn while she was drinking and his heart did that squeeze of love that always took him by surprise by its suddenness and intensity. He already knew he'd die for them both if he had to and that was terrifying.

'I – probably would have waited for a more convenient time,' he said tactfully.

'I thought so. It's been a shock for you and Mum, and I'm not looking forward to what she'll have to say later. I bet you want to talk to her . . .'

'You could say that. But today isn't the moment.'

'Nan says she'll come round.'

'Yeah.'

'And that it hasn't been fair to keep you in the dark about me. I wish I'd asked Mum to get in contact sooner. I never wanted to upset her . . . but when this one came along, I realised how much being a parent means. I wasn't even sure if you'd want to get to know us after all this time, but I'm glad you did.'

'So am I,' Flynn said.

Molly took Esme to bed, allowing Flynn to kiss her cheek. In the brief moment before Brenda and Imogen returned to the lounge, Flynn looked around, experiencing one of the many 'pinch-me' moments he'd had lately. The artificial tree in the window, bedecked with tinsel and baubles, and the cards from people he'd never met but who meant a lot to his new family.

The card and photo on the sofa next to him: this was his family now.

Imogen and Brenda returned, but Flynn refused the offer of cheese and sausage rolls, saying he was still stuffed after the Ravendale Christmas dinner. His appetite wasn't great and he had the feeling he'd outstayed his welcome – with Imogen at least. Brenda wanted him to take a 'doggy bag' of buffet snacks, and he didn't want to offend her, so he accepted it.

Molly hugged him. Brenda gave him a smile and thanked him for coming warmly enough for him to know she meant it.

Imogen stood by in the hall, arms folded, like a shaken bottle of pop about to go off.

Esme had started to cry, so Molly trotted upstairs. Brenda seemed to have conveniently vanished and only Imogen remained.

'I'll let myself out,' Flynn said, picking up his helmet from the coat rack.

'I need to talk to you.'

'We both need to talk,' he said calmly. 'That's the under-statement of the year, but I thought we'd agreed now wasn't the best time.'

'Yes, but I want you to know something *now*.' Imogen folded her arms. 'I know what you're thinking. Why didn't I tell you about Molly? I bet you hate me.'

Flynn hesitated. 'I don't hate anyone and Molly's given me some idea why you kept her existence a secret, but, yeah, I'd like to hear it from you. You could have got in touch as soon as you found me on social media. Maybe before then.'

'I could have but I didn't. I managed to bring up Molly on my own. We were a one-night stand – there was never going to be an 'us'. We had no future. We were young and our hormones were in overdrive. You were handsome and I fancied you rotten, but let's face it, you could have been anyone.'

Flynn snorted. 'Jesus, Imogen. Don't hold back!' Remembering where he was, he lowered his voice. 'Yeah, I *could* have been any man but I wasn't. I'm *not*. You could have given me the benefit of the doubt and asked me if I wanted to be part of my child's future.'

'I could have but I decided not to. I had to carry Molly and give birth to her and, once I'd got used to bringing her up on my own – and with Mum's help – I realised I didn't need a man in my life.'

'Did you not think Molly might have needed a father in hers?'

Imogen pressed her lips together. 'Of course I thought about that, but even after we knew where you were and how to contact you, I couldn't tell you.'

'Why not?'

'Because I was scared you'd try to take Molly and Esme away from us. I still am. You can hate me for that if you like, but I love them too much to see them hurt.'

'I'll never hurt them.' Flynn could not help his sense of injustice and loss, but his overriding emotion was sadness for the time he'd lost – and despair that Imogen had decided he was the kind of man she could never trust to be a parent to his daughter. 'I'm part of their lives now and I intend to stick around. And it's going to take a long time for us all to get used to this – but it's what Molly wants and I have no intention of missing a moment more of her life or Esme's.'

He stomped down the path and got on his bike, revving the engine a bit too hard, knowing it would probably disturb the neighbours. It was childish but he didn't care: tonight had been way more turbulent than he'd ever imagined. He'd held his emotions together for so long, trying to be the grown-up in the situation, and now the dam had burst. And the one person he wanted to be with right now, the person he knew would soothe and calm him, was Lara.

Chapter Forty-one

Lara woke with a dry mouth and fuzzy head despite her restraint the previous day. She got up and dressed, wrapping up warm for the Boxing Day outing with Jazz and her crew. For the umpteenth time since he'd ridden off from the staff lunch, she wondered how Flynn had got on at Molly's.

That peck on the cheek under the mistletoe had been so bittersweet, leaving her longing for so much more. She hoped he'd had a great time and had pictured them all laughing and opening their gifts round the tree. Family time was so important and she always looked forward to catching up with hers. Online only made her long to be with her loved ones in person all the more, but, she reminded herself, today would be fun. Jazz's crew were always up for a laugh and she was always warmly welcomed there.

Her mobile rang and she scooped it up, expecting to hear Jazz's voice making arrangements, but it was an unknown caller. She was in two minds whether to answer but, in the end, she risked it.

'Er. Hello. Is that Lara?' It was a man's voice.

'Er. Yes . . .' she said warily.

'It's Harvey Sinclair here. You don't know me but I'm a

mate of Flynn's. You borrowed my wife's leathers not long back?'

'Yes, I did.' Lara was confused and then the tiny hairs on her arms stood on end. Flynn's best friend calling her: his voice weary and unsure.

'I'm afraid I'm calling you with some not very good news. It's Flynn. He's been in an accident.'

Lara collapsed back onto the bed, her heart pounding.

Bad news. Accident. The words sliced through her.

'Oh my God. Is he OK? Oh, please don't say he's—'

'He's alive,' Harvey said. 'I'm sorry to have upset you and I don't have many details, but he was in a pretty bad way from what I could gather.'

Tears of shock rolled down her face but she forced herself to ask. 'How bad?'

'I'm not sure, but I think it was nasty. Flynn's dad phoned me about an hour ago. Understandably, he was upset and not that coherent. The police found Flynn's parents' details as the emergency contact on his phone. Apparently he came off the road on a bend, ended up in a ditch, and was airlifted to hospital in the early hours. He's in Whitehaven General. That's all I can tell you, but I thought you'd want to know.'

Chapter Forty-two

Flynn had been watching *The Snowman* on TV and then he realised he was actually in *The Snowman*. He was flying like the boy, holding the Snowman's hand and wearing striped pyjamas and an old-fashioned dressing gown.

As he soared over the snowy landscape, lights twinkled in the villages below. It was magical and peaceful. Then he found himself alone and falling.

The descent to earth was rapid and headlong. He twisted over and over until, once again, he was on the road in the dark, speeding along on the bike around twists and turns.

Something loomed ahead; something that had come off the fells and through the woods. It was a creature . . . not human. A memory stirred somewhere in the depths of his fractured consciousness . . . of a horseman riding across the fells and the devil springing up. Where had he heard that story before? He grasped at the memory but it eluded him, and then all he knew was darkness.

When he woke up, he had no idea where he was. It wasn't heaven – perhaps some kind of purgatory, because he couldn't move and the pain in his legs and head was so bad it made him feel sick.

People were talking but their voices sounded distorted,

like a recording in slow motion. He couldn't understand a word they were saying. Someone in a mask loomed over him. He tried to talk and no sound came out.

The next thing he knew, he was lying still in a dark room. Eventually the voices started again and he had the sensation of movement. There were lights so bright they hurt his eyes and ahead of him was a dark tunnel. He was paralysed, powerless to escape. The faces of people flashed in front of him; strangers and people he knew and loved. Work colleagues, his mum and dad, Molly, Esme, Harvey – and Lara. The tunnel crept closer and closer, becoming a giant mouth that opened wider, ready to swallow him up.

Chapter Forty-three

Lara didn't remember much of the journey to the hospital other than gripping the wheel of the car to stop her hands from shaking. Every dark thought imaginable – and then some – had raced through her mind. She'd managed to text Jazz the news before she left and then rushed out to the car, almost slipping on the ice in her haste.

Somehow, after what seemed like the longest and worst journey she'd ever made, she arrived in the midst of blue lights, ambulances queuing outside, and people being pushed to and from the entrance in wheelchairs.

It might be Boxing Day but the festivities were definitely on hold for some people. Her own life felt as if it was on pause too. The walk from the car park to the reception desk consisted of some of the worst minutes of her life.

For all she knew, Flynn might be dead. That possibility made her feel faint with terror. She wanted to race into the A&E reception, push everyone queuing aside, and scream: is he alive? Please let me see him!

Instead, she had to force herself to wait in line, digging her nails into her palm with frustration, and wondering what kind of person had devised the exquisite torture known as a casualty reception desk.

Then came the agony of trying to find out where he was and having to tell a lie that she was Flynn's fiancée, just in case they wouldn't give her any information otherwise. And the wait while the receptionist tapped away at her keyboard with all the urgency of a clothes-shop sales assistant checking if a particular pair of jeans were in stock. God, the woman even broke off to accept a colleague's offer of a cappuccino from the Costa at one point.

Lara was on the point of leaping over the counter and getting herself arrested when the receptionist finally located Flynn.

'He's been moved out of ICU into the HDU: the High Dependency Unit.'

Her first reaction – after she'd thanked the receptionist and managed to find an empty stretch of corridor en route to the HDU – was to hide between the drinks machine and the wall, take some deep breaths, and try not to cry with relief. He was alive and out of the intensive care unit. She had to be thankful for that.

Several wrong turns and corridors later, she finally reached the HDU.

She spoke to the nurse on duty, saying she was his girlfriend this time, and they told her Flynn was stable and had been knocked unconscious but was now reasonably alert and able to speak. He'd broken his knee and had cuts and bruises. The nurse also informed her that he already had two family visitors, but she could wait for a while if she wanted to. Then he left the station to deal with another patient.

His absence enabled Lara to venture a few paces beyond

their desk, where she could see the nearby bay where he was lying. The curtains were partially open and Lara caught her breath, stunned by the sight. Machines surrounded his bed. He was hooked up to a drip and monitors. His leg was under a dome and he looked grey and exhausted, but at least he was alive. Even so, to see this big, strong man reduced to a helpless figure made her feel shaky.

The urge to go to him was powerful, but Lara held back.

Flynn's current visitors perched on plastic chairs at his bedside. Lara recognised Molly instantly, but the woman next to her was a stranger. She was in her late thirties with jet-black hair tied back in a band. Her neck and arms were deeply tanned.

Flynn's hand lay on the bedclothes; perhaps he'd moved his fingers. Lara wasn't sure, because the tanned stranger leaned forward and placed her hand over his. A few seconds later, she moved her hand and put her arm around Molly's back. In that moment, Lara caught a better glimpse of the woman's face and realised that she had to be Molly's mother, Imogen.

She went back through the doors into the adjacent small corridor and sat down heavily in a chair. How was Imogen here? Flynn had said she wasn't meant to be home until New Year. Obviously, Imogen now knew about Flynn ... how long had he been in contact with her? She saw the gesture again: Imogen tenderly placing her hand over Flynn's. Anyone watching would think she was his wife or partner. And she *was* the mother of his child.

Lara wondered where Esme was – probably with Brenda.

She put her head in her hands, overwhelmed by the multiple shocks of the past few hours. Was it possible that Imogen had known Flynn longer than he had let on? Lara dismissed it; Flynn would have told her. And at least he was alive and stable, even though she didn't know anything certain about the accident.

'Hello. Are you OK, love?'

Lara lifted her head to find a stocky middle-aged man with greying hair speaking to her.

She sat up and managed a smile, feeling embarrassed at being caught feeling sorry for herself. 'Yes, I'm OK. I just feel a bit tired.'

'Oh. OK. I was worried you'd had bad news,' the man said.

'No. Not bad news. It's – just so stressful and strange seeing people you love in hospital, isn't it?'

'Tell me about it,' the man said. 'Bloody nightmare when you live so far away too. My son's in there. Been in a motorbike crash. I bloody hate that thing. Told him a hundred times to get rid of it.' The Cornish accent became stronger as he spoke. Lara pictured Flynn's reaction when, at the age of thirty-nine, he was told by his father that he couldn't have a motorbike. However, judging by the state of him at present, he was probably in no position to protest.

'Steve?' A woman arrived, carrying two takeout coffees. She frowned in concern. 'Everything OK?'

Lara smiled, partly to put on a brave face but also at the sight of Flynn's mother, who was tall, brunette, and had the same beautiful eyes as her son.

'Fine, Paula. I was talking to this young lady about Flynn and asking if she was OK herself. One of her friends is in this bloody place too.'

'Is she OK?' Paula asked, frowning in concern.

'He,' Lara said. 'I think so.'

'It's awful, though,' Steve said. 'Getting a call in the middle of the night, having to drive hundreds of miles up here, not knowing what you're going to find. We were in bits when we heard, weren't we, Paula?'

'He's OK, though,' Paula said. 'Here, get this down you. You can't take it into the ward. If I'd known you were here, I'd have asked if you wanted one too,' she said to Lara.

'That's very kind of you but I'm fine. Actually, I was about to leave so you're welcome to the chairs.'

'Don't go because of us. We've done enough sitting down over the past few hours.'

'No, really. It's time I went home.'

'Are you sure? Are you OK to drive?'

'I'll be fine now I know my – friend – is going to be OK. That's all I need to know and they have other visitors with them. They won't be on their own.'

Paula smiled wearily. 'I'm very pleased to hear it. You go home and get some rest. You must take care of yourself too. Your friend will need you when they're home.'

'Thanks,' she said, picking up her bag and vacating the seat for them. 'I hope your son is much better very soon.'

Lara trudged down the corridor, hearing Steve and Paula discussing 'that bloody bike', but also sounding hugely relieved.

She hurried past the crowded A&E, where two men dressed in Santa costumes were having to be pulled apart by security, past the Christmas tree in the hospital foyer, and out into the blinding sunlight of the winter morning.

Flynn was OK. Well, not exactly OK, but he would be. He was strong and still young, and he had so many people who cared about him and loved him – he'd be fine. And she had no doubt at all that he would buy another bike, no matter what his father said. Unless, as a father himself, he decided he no longer wanted to take the risk.

Flynn's parents knew about Molly and Esme and all of them – his next of kin – his family . . . were by his bedside.

Lara told herself to count her lucky stars and be thankful that Flynn was alive and would mend. Then she got into her car, leaned over the steering wheel, and sobbed her heart out.

Chapter Forty-four

Flynn wasn't sure whether it was better to be awake and in pain or drugged up with no control over what happened to him.

Either state wasn't a lot of fun.

He'd been amazed to find out from his parents that he'd missed the whole of Boxing Day and that it was now 27 December. The upside was he'd been moved to a regular ward and was feeling slightly less out of it.

His parents filled him in on what he'd missed and told him they'd been by his bed since they'd arrived. He was astonished to discover that they'd met Molly, Brenda and Imogen, and had struck up an admittedly awkward friendship born of necessity.

'They're letting us see Esme later,' his mother said. 'I can't believe I'm a great nanny. How is that possible? I'm not old enough . . .' She shook her head, tears filling her eyes. 'I just can't believe it and I'm thrilled, of course, but . . . fancy never telling us about Molly. I'm finding it hard to forgive Brenda and Imogen for that. Very hard.'

Flynn couldn't say he blamed them.

'Not now,' his father murmured. 'Not here. Flynn doesn't need it.'

'It's OK to feel angry and upset, Mum,' Flynn said. 'I – I haven't even got used to it myself. Imogen had her reasons for staying quiet. I—' He had to stop speaking partly because he still felt too weak to talk much, and also because his brain didn't always connect properly with his mouth. The thoughts had floated around at times, probably because of the drugs, but as they'd been gradually reduced, he was becoming more aware yet was also in more pain.

So many bridges needed building but he didn't feel he had the strength to even begin the construction process.

'OK. Another time,' his mother said.

'And at least we do know about them now,' his father murmured, patting his hand.

Flynn closed his eyes but then opened them again. 'Did you – have you spoken to Lara?'

'Lara?' They exchanged a glance. 'Who's Lara?'

'My – friend. We work together at the castle. Does she know about the accident?'

'Erm. I assume so,' his mother said. 'I think Harvey might have called the castle. We asked him to tell all your work mates because we were in no state to. We were only concerned with getting up here as fast as possible.'

Flynn nodded. 'OK. I'll ask him.'

His mum smiled at him. 'He did text us a couple of times and ask how you were. He said he'd come and see you tomorrow. He was very worried about you.'

'Tomorrow? I hope to be out of here by then . . . or soon afterwards,' Flynn said, with a vehemence that left him coughing.

His mum offered him a glass of water. 'I think they'll want to keep you a while longer. You've had a serious accident and they need to make sure you're OK.'

'I don't want to be in here a second longer than I need to,' Flynn insisted. He pushed himself up on the pillows even though it hurt like hell. 'Do you know where my phone is? Please?'

'Sorry, son. It was smashed up in the accident,' his father said.

'Shit.' Flynn sank back against the pillow.

'If you really want to message anyone, you can borrow mine.'

'No, it's OK.' Flynn desperately wanted to speak to Lara in private, and that thought forced him to work through the brain fog. 'I could really do with a new one. Any chance you can get me a new one?'

'You should be resting,' his mum said sternly.

'Yeah, but it would ease my mind.' Flynn tried his best puppy-dog look but his mother folded her arms. 'Please?' It felt ridiculous to be like a child again, at the mercy of his parents being willing to help him.

'I suppose we could,' she relented.

'Thanks. There's a retail park near the hospital. I'm sure you can get hold of one now the shops are open again. I'll settle up as soon as I can.'

His dad sighed then nodded. 'Look, if it would make your life easier, we'll buy you a new phone.'

'Thank you.' Flynn smiled, despite the pain. If he could get in touch with Lara, he'd feel a whole lot better. He was beyond grateful to the paramedics and medical staff who'd scraped him off the side of the road and saved him, but it was driving him mad to rely on other people. Once he'd spoken with Lara, he could focus on getting out of this place and take charge of his own life again.

Chapter Forty-five

'Lara! Have you heard? Flynn's home,' Jazz called to Lara from halfway across the snow-sprinkled castle courtyard.

Many people might be wandering around in a cheese-induced coma wondering what day of the week it was, but, at Ravendale, Twixmas was a time to make the most of bored families looking for places to get some fresh air and entertainment.

The crisp, clear weather over Christmas had helped boost visitor numbers to a record high, and all the Spectacular dates were now fully booked. With Flynn out of action, Lara was having to pick up some of the slack with his team, as well as for Fiona and Henry. However, she'd been glad of the work as a distraction from her almost constant thoughts about Flynn. She was certain that his families, new and old, must have wanted to be with him all the time. That was natural, even though Lara had been desperate to see him herself.

Jazz caught up with her, slithering in the slush on the flagstones. 'Mrs Danvers saw him being helped into the cottage by his mum and dad. She said he looked absolutely terrible and he's on crutches.'

'Well, he did have concussion and a broken knee,' Lara

said, doubting Flynn could ever look terrible even after a near-death experience. That thought made her shudder again. The accident had made her realise how fragile life was and how easily it could shatter.

She shoved the thought to the back of her mind. 'Mrs D exaggerates. You know that. I thought you might have spoken to him.'

'Not yet.' In fact, she hadn't heard from him since Christmas Day. 'His friend Harvey called me. He'd spoken to Flynn's mum. Apparently, his phone was damaged in the accident and I knew he was hoping to be discharged soon. I hadn't realised he'd be back this morning.'

'It's a huge relief, though. I know how worried you've been, hun.'

Lara nodded. 'I – I thought he might have . . .'

Jazz hugged her. 'But he hasn't. Will you go and see him now?'

'Yes, but I should let him settle in first. His parents will be with him.'

'Don't leave it too long. I'm sure he wants to see you. I know how much you like him as a friend, and friends matter, don't they, particularly when you are so far from home.'

Jazz spoke to her about work for a few more minutes, until Lara broke off to check a message that made her pulse race.

'Was that him?' Jazz asked, when Lara looked up again.

'Yes, how did you know?'

'The great big grin on your face? You look like you've won the lottery.'

Lara laughed – probably for the first time since Harvey had made that terrible phone call. 'I'm just so relieved. Jazz, we're not together. He needs the space.'

'No, but . . . you need to take this as a wake-up call to sort yourselves out. Go on, go and see him now and send him lots of love from me. In a friendly sense, of course.'

'I will.' Lara could not deny that she felt huge relief at receiving the message. He'd asked her if she would 'pop round if she could as he'd really love to see her', adding that his parents were out.

Hearing that was enough to make her almost run across the castle courtyard, but she managed to restrain herself to a brisk walk. She was aching to see him but trembling inside at what she might find.

'Come in! The door's unlocked.'

Well, his voice was recovered at least, Lara decided. She went into the sitting room, trying to tame her mix of emotions.

Immediately, Lara disagreed with Mrs Danvers' assessment of Flynn. He was pale, unshaven, and had some impressive bruises on his legs, but he didn't look a fraction as awful as when he was hooked up to the machines in the HDU. The sight of him, sitting on the sofa in shorts, with one leg in a black brace, was enough to make her stomach do a double somersault. A pair of crutches lay on the carpet by the sofa alongside a fleecy blanket.

'Hello, how are you feeling?' she asked, approaching the sofa but not daring to get too close, in case she was tempted to fling her arms around him and weep with relief.

'I've been better. You'll forgive me if I don't get up.' His half-grin, half-grimace made her want to dive on him and kiss him. 'The docs said I can start to put weight on my knee in a few days, but it's going to take six to eight weeks before it's back to anything like normal.'

'Phew. I'm glad it wasn't much worse,' she said, distracted by the muscular thighs. Was it wrong to focus on his body when he was an injured man? 'Very glad. When Harvey called me, I thought – well, let's not dwell on what I thought.'

'I thought some pretty scary things too, when I was drugged, but I've survived.' He swallowed hard. 'And I'm in one piece, though the hospital said I could only come out if I had someone with me here. Mum and Dad raced up here to help. I hate relying on other people but I'd have done anything to get out of there.'

'I bet . . .' Lara spotted the overnight bags by the coffee table. 'Um. Can I help? Do your mum and dad need anything? Bed linen, towels? I can ask housekeeping.'

Flynn hesitated then said, 'Thank you. That would be a big help if you could. Actually, they popped out to buy some spare clothes and toiletries and stuff. I had to beg them to leave me on my own, but I think they could see I needed a while to settle in. And I wanted to talk to you. To be honest, I wish they weren't staying with me. I'd manage on my own but they're fussing over me like crazy.' He gestured to the chair with a wry smile. 'Sit down, please. Put that stuff on the floor. I'm sorry I can't tidy up myself.'

Clearing a bag of medication off the chair, Lara smiled

with pure relief that he was well enough to joke and to want to look after himself. His condition was so much more encouraging than she'd dared to hope in those dark moments when she'd first heard about his crash. He was strong and fit, and a fighter; that must have all helped him. 'I'm sure your mum and dad only want to keep a close eye on you, but it *is* very small in here. The sofa beds are usually only intended for kids to use. You know, I could try and ask around if there's some other accommodation available on the estate?'

His eyes lit with up in relief. 'Would you? Honestly, it will only be for a day or two. Mum and Dad were supposed to be going to Madeira for a New Year holiday, and I really don't want them to miss it, even though they keep threatening to cancel. I love them but I don't want them hanging around nannying me. I left home when I was nineteen and I can't go back to sharing a house with them.' He grinned and Lara glimpsed the young Flynn.

'I can understand that. I'm pretty sure I can help with the overcrowding issue. It's a quiet time of year and I'm sure Fiona and Henry won't mind. In fact, I bet they'll be only too happy to help.'

He screwed up his face. 'Mmm. I shouldn't think they're impressed with me turning up and then putting myself out of action after just over a month. They're coming to see me later, but I wanted to speak to you first . . . I haven't heard from you and I haven't been able to contact you. Mum and Dad only brought me a new phone this morning, then the doc did his rounds and told me I'd been let out for bad behaviour.'

Lara rolled her eyes at his silly joke, determined to hide the agony of worry she'd been through and the disappointment at finding Imogen by his bedside. When was he going to tell her about *that* situation?

'Lara,' he said, suddenly serious. 'Joking apart, I've been so desperate to see you. I wanted you to be the first person from the castle I saw and to explain what had happened before I see the Penhaligons or anyone.' Close up, she was shocked by how anxious and drawn he looked. He must feel as if his world had imploded.

'So how are you?' she asked gently. 'Really?'

'Honestly? I feel like I've been run over by a bus. Which isn't far from the truth. How much have you heard about the accident?'

'Only what Harvey told me. He told me you'd had to be airlifted to hospital, which sounds scary, but I don't know any more details. Can you remember what happened?'

Flynn picked at a thread on the sofa cushion and sighed. 'Unfortunately, some of it's coming back to me. I was riding home and I'd reached Ravenscar Woods and something big jumped out of the trees into the road – I think it was a deer, though it had gone when the cops got to me. I braked and skidded on some black ice. The next thing I knew I was sliding over the road and ended up in a ditch. They say the bike landed on top of me but I blacked out after that and I can't remember much of the whole of the next day or so.' He shook his head. 'I'm more pissed off that they had to cut off my leathers. They cost a bomb.'

'You don't mean that,' Lara said.

'No. Not really. They did their job and stopped the road rash.'

She shuddered. 'I don't even want to think about it!'

'No – well, the next thing I remember I was being sucked into a dark tunnel, helpless to do anything about it.'

Lara's stomach turned over. 'Was it that touch and go?' she asked, her voice cracking in horror.

'No! Sorry.' He leaned forward towards her then winced in pain. 'Forgive the dark humour. I really did think I was being dragged into a tunnel, but it turns out it was the porters loading me into the MRI scanner. I was so drugged up on morphine I'd have believed the fairies had abducted me. In fact, I'd have let them.'

'It's not funny!' Lara burst out.

'No, I suppose not, but I'd go mad if I thought about what *could* have happened. If I'd hit a tree, not a muddy ditch. If a driver behind hadn't found me and called 999, if the air ambulance hadn't come along . . .'

'I don't want to think about any of those scenarios either.'

'Then don't. Lara . . .' He glanced at his hands then back at her, his face pale and drawn. 'I need to tell you something else. When I got to Brenda's house on Christmas Day, Imogen was there.'

Now was her chance to say she'd waited outside the HDU, how she'd rushed there in terror, but she wanted him to tell the story.

'Imogen?' she said, with mild surprise. Flynn's parents would surely recognise her as soon as they saw her, but it was up to Lara to admit that she'd actually crept into the ward and seen Molly and her mother with him. 'I – thought she wasn't coming home until the New Year.'

'She managed to swap with a colleague and get a last-minute flight home as a Christmas Day surprise.'

So Flynn had had no idea about Imogen turning up. 'That's some surprise . . .'

'Shock is a more accurate word. Molly had been trying to message me but I hadn't checked my phone. First I knew about it was Imogen answering the door.'

'And how did it go?''

'Awkward as you can imagine. None of us knew what to say or do. Imogen was stunned and not impressed that Molly and Brenda had been in touch with me behind her back. No one had warned her . . . and they were both hoping to stop me from turning up at the house. My parents are now angry with her for depriving them of their granddaughter for twenty years. I can't blame them but they'll all have to deal with it.'

'What a shock. How do you . . . feel . . . about Imogen turning up?' Lara asked, unsure of whether she wanted to hear the answer.

'Still stunned. Very confused. Jesus, I don't know how I feel.' He leaned forward on the sofa again, agitated now. 'I kept trying – still am – to understand why Imogen kept Molly a secret from me but I didn't want a confrontation on Christmas Day, and especially not with Esme there.'

'No. I can imagine.' Lara pictured the little one amid a bunch of warring adults and felt sorry for her.

'The two of us have a lot of talking to do,' Flynn went

on. 'I'm not sure she'll ever accept me being part of Molly's life but she'll have to. I don't know how I'm ever going to fix this.' He sat up sharply, wincing and rubbing his thigh above the brace. 'Feck. This bloody knee.'

'You need to rest,' Lara said, starting to rise from the chair.

'No, don't go! I don't look that bad, do I?' he added with mock hurt.

'No. I mean, you *have* been in a crash, Flynn,' she said, refusing to tell him how gorgeous he looked in spite of his injuries. 'Seriously, you need time to recover.'

He sighed. 'I've no choice for a while at least. I'm off sick officially. I can't ride a bike for weeks – even if I *had* a bike, because the Harley is a write-off. I can't drive before I'm signed off as fit by the doc. I can't do any physical work for a while either, but there's no way I'm lying around here being bored out of my mind when there's so much to be done. There are still eight more days of the illuminations and I'm not totally helpless.'

'And you're *alive*. That's all that matters . . .'

'Yes, I'm alive, but I feel torn in two.'

'I know it's a crap situation but try to get some rest. As for the business with Molly and Imogen, let it be for now and accept that even Flynn Cafferty may not be able to fix everything immediately. Some situations take time.'

'Maybe . . . On Christmas Day, I didn't leave the house on the best of terms with Imogen or in the best of moods. In fact, we were one step away from a blazing row, which is probably why I lost my focus on the way home. If I'd been paying attention, I might have spotted the deer or been able to control the bike better.'

'Might – if – they're pointless words. It was just bad luck . . .' Lara murmured, a shiver running through her. 'All you can do is look to the future now and, more importantly, be in the present.'

He held her gaze for a few moments during which she was sure he must be able to hear the beating of her heart. She wanted to throw her arms around him.

'You're right. You always are. Always the sensible one.'

'I'm not sure that's a good thing. I'm not sure I want to be sensible all the time.'

He winced and rubbed the top of his leg.

'Are you in pain?'

'It nags a bit. They gave me some painkillers but I can't think straight if I take them. I feel fuzzy.'

'If they help you sleep, though . . .'

'Yeah.'

She got up. 'I have to get back to work and you should rest up.'

He glanced up at her. 'Lara, before you go, there's something else I forgot to say.'

'Yes?' Her heart beat a little faster.

'I forgot to give you your present. It's not much but it's in my bedroom, in the wardrobe. Don't get too excited.'

What else had she expected him to say? She laughed at herself. 'I never get too excited.'

She went into his bedroom, recalling the last time she'd been in there, naked between the sheets with Flynn. It seemed like a lifetime ago – a moment when she'd cast off the shackles of her past and everything seemed possible. She was trying to understand, to accommodate, to suppress her real feelings, but it was almost impossible.

It was then she spotted a photo on his bedside table that definitely hadn't been there before. It showed Molly and Esme at the illuminations, both smiling, and Esme pointing at the reindeer on the grotto, her eyes lit up. It was such a happy picture. Lara wanted to cry for what might have been as well as for happiness on Flynn's behalf. She wanted a family of her own. There was no way she could express that to Flynn or tell him that she'd dared to dream she could finally put her previous heartbreak behind her.

She hardly knew him, even if she was in love with him.

Her gasp was audible with the realisation that she did indeed love Flynn. It hit her physically with a squeeze of the heart. Nothing she could do could change her feelings even if, now that he had so much to deal with, it was the very worst time to tell him.

She had to give him space, hoping that, when he was back on his feet – in every way – things might change, though she couldn't imagine how.

She dragged her eyes from the photo and opened the wardrobe. It wasn't hard to find the present. His wardrobe wasn't rammed like her own small one with stuff she hated to give away. The box lay at the bottom next to a pair of boots.

'Lara! Is everything OK? Can you find it?' Flynn was leaning against the door frame, his face grey with pain.

'Yes, I've just found it.'

'Good. I want you to open it with me.'

Before she could bend down to pick it up, she heard a squeal from outside and excited chattering.

He glanced at the bedroom window, where Molly, Esme and Imogen were on the path.

'You have visitors,' Lara said.

Flynn glanced back at her. 'I – Lara—'

There was a rap at the door and they heard Molly chattering excitedly outside.

'I didn't know they were coming,' he said.

'I expect they wanted to surprise you. Shall I let them in?'

'What about your present?'

She smiled. 'I can have it another time.'

'I know, but Lara – I want to say something,' he said in a desperate tone, hobbling forward. 'Shit! Ow!'

He almost tripped and fell, but Lara caught him just in time and steadied him, holding him up with her hands on his elbows. Their gaze met.

'Flynn . . .' Lara said. 'You have to be more careful.'

'I need to say something . . .'

'Hello! The door's unlocked so we're coming in!'

'I should go,' Lara said, leaving Flynn leaning against the door and hurrying into the sitting room where Molly, Esme and Imogen had just walked in.

Imogen's poker-straight jet-black hair hung down under a cream bobble hat, and Lara couldn't help thinking it made her look quite severe. Or maybe that was because she'd found Lara walking out of Flynn's bedroom. She stared at Lara in puzzlement.

'This is my mum, Imogen,' Molly said, turning to her mother. 'Lara works here at the castle.'

'Hi,' said Lara, turning on her best visitor smile.

'Hello,' Imogen said, with polite indifference. Understandably she had other concerns than socialising with a strange woman. She turned her attention immediately to Flynn, who'd hobbled into the doorway, and smiled at him. 'You look knackered.'

'I wasn't expecting you,' Flynn muttered.

Molly beamed and carried Esme forwards to meet him. 'Hello, Dad! Hope it's OK but we thought we'd surprise you.'

Dad. Lara would never get used to hearing Molly say that to Flynn, who looked torn between happiness and awkwardness. He struck her as a stranger blundering through a strange landscape, unsure if he loved it or was petrified. She was an observer, wanting to jump in and help him but unsure if she should or let him work out his path by himself.

'That's a lovely thought,' Flynn said.

'I'll put the kettle on,' Imogen said, and marched through to the kitchen.

'I'll leave you to it,' Lara said, feeling completely superfluous.

'Thank you,' Flynn said, 'for everything.'

Lara smiled, wondering what he'd been about to say when they'd been interrupted – and if she'd get another chance to find out.

Chapter Forty-six

Flynn sank back against the sofa, feeling as if someone had pulled a plug out of his body and drained his last reserves of energy. He wasn't used to feeling exhausted and not wanting to get up off the sofa, and he hated it.

He was grateful for the concern of his family – old and new – but the past couple of hours had literally floored him.

The cottage wasn't big enough for three people, let alone six, and when his parents had arrived while Molly, Imogen and Esme were still there, the conflicting emotions and agendas had totally overwhelmed the space and Flynn himself.

Esme had been wailing because she was teething and tired – Flynn knew how she felt. Molly had chattered away nervously, wanting everyone to get along, while Imogen had been sullen, and his own mother had barely been able to be polite. His father had tried to be jolly and ended up making awkward jokes that only served to make a tense situation worse.

As for Lara, she'd rushed off, clearly feeling out of place and eager to escape the whole desperate situation. Flynn didn't blame her but he was eaten up with frustration.

There was so much he wanted to say to her. To tell her the person he'd longed to see at his bedside was her. He'd been on the verge of saying how much he felt for her when Molly and the others had descended.

How could he tell her that, while he'd lain there, he'd wanted her to hold him? Maybe that was for the best. It wouldn't be fair to Lara when he couldn't give her the commitment she truly deserved and that he wanted to give.

Now that he'd experienced the whole of his family, old and new, descending on him, he was even more aware of how much he'd taken on and how he could not expect her to deal with that. He was also pretty helpless at the moment, which made him feel even more vulnerable.

He closed his eyes and tried not to think of how much his knee – and his head – ached. He picked up the bottle of painkillers by his side, tossed some down with a sip from a bottle of water, and lay back against the cushion.

The following morning brought a solution to one of his problems at least. Lara had arranged for his parents to move to a vacant holiday cottage the previous evening, which gave everyone some space. His pills had worked, the pain was easing, and while he wouldn't be carrying his toolkit up the tower stairs anytime soon, he was able to hobble around the cottage on his own.

The previous day, Fiona and Henry had thoughtfully messaged him, suggesting he might like to rest and settle in before they visited him. Flynn had gratefully accepted the offer. He managed a shave and a wash on his own and his parents took a stroll around the estate while he saw the Penhaligons.

They arrived bearing a basket of treats, which Fiona described as 'Just a few home comforts – cake, biscuits, tea and coffee you can all share.'

'You've used up one of your lives there,' Henry said, sitting down opposite him.

'I must admit I've had a few close shaves, but that was probably the closest,' Flynn admitted.

'I once came off, you know. I was riding an old Triumph over the fells from Coniston and hit a patch of gravel on the moor road. Didn't have the high-tech lids you lot wear today. Was knocked unconscious. Wonder I wasn't a goner.'

Fiona let out a squeak of horror. 'Henry, that's enough. That's the last thing Flynn needs to hear. Ignore him.'

Henry looked chastened, but said, 'I'll tell you all about it some time. You still haven't seen my bike collection, have you? You can borrow one of them until you get your new wheels.'

Fiona gazed heavenwards. 'I despair. But someone was definitely looking out for you that night, Flynn.'

'I was extremely lucky,' he admitted, the moment flashing back to him again as it had several times. Not that he'd admit it to anyone. He also remembered the dream in which the important people in his life had flashed before his eyes. Lara had been one of them – the last one he remembered, in fact.

He also, out of the blue, thought of the chalice. For a moment or two, when he was half in and out of awareness in the hospital, he'd wondered if the breakage had anything to do with his bad luck in meeting the deer.

331

Now he thought that the fact he'd survived the accident and that a vehicle had been close behind him on the lonely road was proof that his good luck had outweighed any curse that evening.

'We all need a bit of good fortune at crucial moments,' Henry said, cutting into his thoughts.

'We sure do.'

Fiona glanced out of the window. 'Oh, look. Your parents are back. We'll leave you in peace.'

'I'm sure they'd love to meet you,' Flynn said, 'and I can't thank you enough for offering them somewhere to stay.'

'When Lara mentioned it, we didn't hesitate,' Fiona said. 'And if there hadn't been a cottage vacant, they could have stayed in the castle.'

Flynn thought ruefully of how much his folks would have loved that. 'Thank you.'

They talked a little while longer, with the Penhaligons telling him not to rush back to work, that the Spectacular was nearly over, and that everyone else would pick up the slack until he had recovered.

Henry eased himself up and patted his shoulder. 'I expect this means we won't see you dancing at the ball, eh?'

In all the chaos and confusion since the accident, Flynn had forgotten about the event. 'Maybe not this year. I was looking forward to it too.'

As was Lara, he thought. He'd never dance with her now. Shit. He hadn't wanted to dress up, but he had wanted to dance with her, although in the current complex circumstances, she might well want to avoid him.

'At least you won't have to worry about a costume,' Henry said.

'No, there's that.'

'Here are your parents. Get well soon. If you need anything at all, you only have to ask.'

Fiona opened the door to his parents and they had a brief chat together until the Penhaligons left.

'They weren't what we expected at all. Well, they *are* posh – old-school posh,' his father said. 'But so normal and kind and not snooty at all and so generous. You're lucky to have them as your employers.'

Then Flynn had to submit to being fussed over and served soup and toast until he was forced to confess he needed a 'lie-down', which consisted of him lying on his bed and messaging family, friends and people he hadn't heard from for years, who somehow seemed to have found out about the accident. The whispers had grown, with one cousin under the impression he'd almost been decapitated and a former colleague from the theme park sure he'd been brought back to life at the roadside by a passing motorist who happened to be a heart surgeon.

Flynn banished these dark thoughts by scrolling through his phone, which these days lifted his mood instantly. He had pictures of Esme eating prune purée, Esme playing with wooden bricks, and Esme wearing the Peter Rabbit sleepsuit that Lara had encouraged him to buy. There were pictures of him with Lara at the launch of the lights, and one of them both at the Christmas dinner table with Mrs Danvers.

No wonder he felt exhausted and confused.

One minute he was Flynn the motorcycle tearaway, another a valued colleague, and another a grandfather.

The one person Flynn really wanted to be was the thing he didn't think he dared to be: a lover and a partner with a future. Henry's comment had made him think and think again. He *did* want to dance with Lara at the ball. More importantly, he wanted *her* to want him to dance with her. Which meant he had to show her how the accident had made him rethink his life. But he'd messed her around so much, how could he regain her trust?

He now had another unexpected visitor.

Carlos appeared, looking sheepish and carrying a bag. Flynn hopped over to the door and opened it.

'Sorry to make you get up. I won't stay long,' Carlos muttered, seeming reluctant to cross the threshold. 'But we – the maintenance and tech teams and the apprentices – had a whip-round and we got you this.' He handed the supermarket carrier to Flynn. 'It's some chocolates and some whisky, which you probably can't have if you're on medication.' He nodded at the pill packet by the sofa. 'Maybe you can drink it when the docs allow it.'

'I'll enjoy that, thanks,' Flynn said, taking the rather nice bottle of malt from the bag and admiring it. 'Tell everyone I'm really grateful for the presents and plan on being back on my feet – or at least back at work, as soon as I can.'

'Yeah, well, you should look after yourself. That knee looks nasty and we heard you were lucky . . .'

'Yes, I was . . . and I'm sorry to leave you in the lurch in the middle of the Spectacular. I really will be back in a few days, but I know you'll take it all in your stride anyway. You can manage without me.'

Carlos grunted. 'We can all get on without you being under our feet for a while. We'll do our best, but we'll be glad when you're back driving us nuts. Get well soon, *boss*.'

'Mum, you *must* still go. I'm *fine*. Everyone is waiting on me hand and foot – I'm getting far too used to it. Have your holiday and come back and see me afterwards.'

Standing by his chair in her coat, his mother seemed to be, even now, in two minds about leaving him behind to go on holiday. 'OK . . . if you're 100 per cent sure?'

'I am. You need a rest too.' Flynn meant it. His folks looked worn-out and no wonder after the worry, the sleep-less nights, the stress and the shock of finding out about Molly and Esme. Flynn didn't only think they needed a physical break, he thought it might do everyone good to have some space and time to reflect.

Flynn eased himself upright to prove that he could stand on his own two feet – well, one, but he needed to make his point.

'When you're back, I'll speak to Molly about making sure that, from now on, you can visit her and Esme.'

'We'd love to see them in Cornwall. Esme would love the sea.'

He patted his mother's shoulder. 'She's going to love it.'

His mum started to cry and Flynn knew exactly how she felt. All those years they'd lost, but it was time to move on.

335

'Don't cry, Mum. They're in our life now and we have so much catching up to do.'

'I just want to see you happy. You deserve it.' His mum wiped her eyes and said, 'Lara seems nice. She's done so much to help us.'

'Yeah, she's nice.' He didn't trust himself to say more.

'Oh, and we've been meaning to tell you. She was at the hospital in the morning when you were taken in.'

'What?' He thought he'd misheard. 'I didn't see her. You didn't say that before.'

'It was outside the ward in the corridor. We'd gone to get a drink while Molly and Imogen were with you and she was waiting there. We didn't know who she was until we met her the other day,' his father said. 'And she didn't tell you either?'

'No. No . . .' He was glad of the support of his crutch. Lara had rushed to see him, spotted Imogen and Molly by the bed, and decided to leave rather than intruding. He felt awful at the thought of her holding back her own fears and needs for his family's sake – and his.

'I think she felt awkward, not being one of the family,' his mum said. 'And we didn't say that we were visiting you by name at the time, and neither did she. It was only when we were moving cottages that we mentioned it to her. She said she just wanted to make sure you were OK but she'd clearly rushed there as soon as she'd heard. She must care about you a lot.'

His mother leaned in and kissed his cheek and his dad grinned awkwardly. 'We'll get on our way. It's a long way home. Take care, for God's sake, love. My heart won't stand this kind of drama again.'

'I promise I'll be careful. I'm a dad now and a grandad. Ready for my pipe and slippers.'

'You will never ever wear slippers or smoke a pipe!' his mum said.

'Now, off you go,' Flynn said. 'Have a great holiday and WhatsApp me when you arrive.'

'We will. Promise me another thing. You won't get another bike,' his mother said.

Flynn smiled enigmatically.

His dad shook his head. 'I wouldn't hold your breath, Paula. Come on.'

After they'd gone, he sank down in his seat again.

Lara had rushed to the hospital yet hadn't dared to come to see him: even though she was the one person he longed to see most. It was clear that Lara didn't feel part of his life – and the thing that tormented him most was he'd made her feel like that. He'd excluded her because he wanted to protect her, yet in doing so he'd caused her even more pain. It wasn't his decision to dictate what she could handle – it was hers.

He had to respect her ability to make that decision and yet he needed to show her that she was as important to him as anyone else in his life. But how?

Chapter Forty-seven

'It'll have to do,' Flynn muttered to himself, looking around his sitting room the following evening, hardly able to believe it was New Year's Eve.

The table was laid, ready for the Uber Eats delivery from the Greek restaurant that Lara had liked. He'd managed to order a bottle of fizz online, along with a pre-lit artificial tree plus baubles and tinsel. There was a vase on the table – thank God it had been a holiday let, as he'd never owned such an item – with some greenery that he'd foraged while hopping around the grounds nearest the cottage, along with some slightly wilting flowers that Mrs Danvers had left while he'd been in hospital.

The only thing missing was Lara. In half an hour, he hoped she'd arrive and he could spend the evening showing her that he wanted her to be part of his life: his present *and* his future.

She'd been out the previous evening; he'd no idea where and he'd had an anxious wait for a reply to his message asking her if she would come over to spend New Year's Eve with him. *If* she was free, that was, because there was a staff party happening at Carlos's place, and he was pretty sure she'd been planning to go to that.

It was 11 a.m. that morning before she'd messaged back:

OK. Sounds like it could be fun. See you later.

Good job Flynn had hedged his bets and ordered everything he might need the previous day: if she hadn't agreed, he was going to be a very sad and lonely figure with a takeaway for two next to his new Christmas tree.

Still, her message was hardly wild with enthusiasm, but he could hardly blame her for being wary. He'd messed her around so much, so caught up in his own problems, that he hadn't thought of her – yet expected her to help and support him when it suited him.

He checked his watch again and decided to get the plates out of the kitchen cupboards ready for the Uber delivery scheduled for 8 p.m. Hopefully it arrived after he and Lara had had time to talk and loosen up.

Twenty minutes until she was due to arrive. He was as nervous as a schoolboy on a first date, but he could hardly pace the room: his knee was already aching like the devil. He eased himself down onto the chair and waited for the knock on the door.

It came a few moments later, when he'd barely made himself comfortable. She was early: surely a good sign?

'Hold on a sec!' he called, limped to the fridge, and collected the bottle of champagne. Somehow, he managed to make it to the door with the bottle tucked under his arm and the aid of one crutch, gingerly taking some weight on his knee. It hurt but he didn't care.

'It's unlocked,' he said, standing back from the door.

The door opened and Flynn readied himself with his warmest smile.

'Happy New—' He stopped. '*Imogen?*'

'Wow. That's pushing the boat out.' Imogen had a supermarket carrier. 'I brought fizzy apple juice. I can't drink.'

Flynn hesitated. 'But what are . . .' Flynn's question died in his mouth even though it pulsed in his brain. What was she doing there?

'Molly said you wanted us all to spend New Year's Eve together. Mum's babysitting.' She looked at the table laid for two and frowned. 'Is she not here yet?'

'No . . . no . . . er. Come inside.'

'Molly had to twist my arm. I had my doubts but she was adamant. We do need to talk properly, though I'm not sure tonight is the best idea. She said it would mark a fresh start . . .' Imogen looked at the table laid for two. 'Oh my God. She's set us up, hasn't she? What's she said? That this is some kind of cosy date – just the two of us?'

Flynn was in mental agony. He didn't know what to say, or, rather, he knew what he had to say but not how to break it to Imogen that he'd been expecting another woman.

She narrowed her eyes. 'Hold on. Did you even know I was coming?'

'Not exactly, no.'

She covered her face with her hands and let out a cry of frustration. 'Oh, Molly, Molly, Molly, I love you but this is one of your worst ideas ever.'

'She probably had good intentions,' Flynn said, realising that he and Imogen had been set up.

'Yeah. She did.'

Imogen's gaze was drawn to the table with its flowers and candle. 'If you didn't know I was coming, then who's that for?'

Flynn took a breath. 'I invited a friend over.'

'That friend being – Lara, by any chance?'

There was no point in lying. 'Yes.'

She groaned. 'Shit.'

'I'm sorry, Imogen, but don't blame Molly. She has no idea about Lara. She just wants something that's never going to happen.'

'I know.' Imogen sat down. 'I've made a giant cock-up of everything.'

Flynn lowered himself into the chair too, his knee throbbing worse than ever.

'No, you haven't, and we really do need to talk but tonight isn't the best time.' Lara was due in ten minutes, and the last thing he wanted was her walking in on him and Imogen having a cosy chat.

'Do you want a drink?' he asked, desperate for Imogen to leave but not wanting to seem rude.

'Not champagne,' she said drily. 'I'm driving, but I could do with something cold before I go home.'

'I have Coke.'

'Thanks. I'll get it, shall I?'

'No, I can grab a can from the fridge.' He eased himself

up and went into the kitchen. While he was getting it, Imogen's voice came from the doorway. 'I don't want to cause any trouble and ruin your evening.'

He turned round, can in hand. 'I was only expecting an Uber from the Greek taverna up the road.'

'A Greek taverna?" She nodded at the laid table. 'That sounds fancy. We may hardly know each other, but I guess you're not into flower arranging as a rule?'

'No . . . it was all I could manage to find from the grounds near the cottage.'

She smiled. 'I suppose this is almost funny.'

Flynn tipped the Coke into a glass and handed it over. His leg was already aching again.

Imogen perched on his sofa. 'I suppose I could call Molly and say I'm not staying, but I think it would be better to talk to her face to face. I presume she's at home. She'd fed me some story about meeting me here after work at the café.'

'She clearly had it all worked out,' Flynn said, easing himself back into a chair and trying not to glance at his mobile.

Imogen sipped the Coke and briefly seemed at a loss for words, then sighed and picked up the carrier bag.

'Actually, the main reason I agreed to come, as well as keeping Molly company, was to bring you this.' She handed over the bag. 'It's a photo album. Old school. It's mostly Molly growing up, but I've added something.'

Almost too scared to look, Flynn opened the first page. There was a very young Imogen with Molly in her arms, blue eyes peeping out of a pink blanket; Molly in a paddling pool and on a beach with a bucket and spade; Molly in her school uniform, clutching her mum's hand tightly.

'Her first day at school,' Imogen said.

'She looks so – serious.'

'She was scared but excited too. She's always liked school.'

'I didn't,' Flynn said. 'Unless I was in the workshop, then I loved it.'

The photos went on, with Molly at a nativity play dressed as an angel; singing in a school choir; Molly in a workshop with safety goggles.

'She's good with her hands and at science. She was studying Biology and Psychology A levels until Esme came along.'

'She told me . . .' Flynn said.

The last page showed Molly in hospital, tired but beaming, with a very similar picture of her holding Esme in her arms. Imogen and Brenda were at her side, bursting with an unalloyed pride that had once been a mystery to Flynn – but wasn't now.

'The midwife took that,' Imogen said. 'Molly's useless ex declined to be present at the birth.'

Flynn murmured something unintelligible because he was seeing his child's life unfurl before him. A life he had missed, so many moments when he hadn't been there, hadn't even been aware were happening.

'I – I almost didn't bring these photos. Have I made a huge mistake? Are you angry?' Imogen said. 'I guess I would be, but it's too late now, so I thought that this ought to be the start of you catching up. I can't turn back the clock but I can involve you from now on. Not that it's my decision any more. Molly is an adult – and I should behave like one too. If you'll let me, you can see all the videos, all the photos, and ask anything you want to.'

Flynn nodded. He couldn't articulate an honest answer: that every new experience such as this would bring a fresh wave of emotions to deal with. Yet one thing he did know was that there was no point in raging and wallowing in bitterness, even if those feelings would have been natural. Perhaps he needed to allow some time – in private – to feel them, but not in this moment. Not now. When he was with Molly and Esme, he had to make the most of every second.

Finally, he came to a photo stuck to the rear inside cover of the album; it showed a skinny young man with his dark hair touching his shoulders, his arm around a girl in shorts and a vest. They were sitting by the lake, bottles of cider raised high.

He rested his fingers on the photo, somehow finding his voice. 'I don't remember anyone taking that.'

'My friend took it earlier in the evening. I added it to the album because that's the moment Molly came into being. Now I want you and everyone to know that you're part of the story. I will never be able to make it up to you for writing you out and all the years you've lost, but I promise you that I came here determined to say that tonight . . . will be a fresh start. A turning point in all our lives.'

'I—' He was choked with emotion. 'Thank you.'

'No, don't thank me. I don't deserve it, but if you can forgive me, then that will be enough. And don't worry, I'll speak to Molly about tonight and I won't be angry with her. There's been enough disruption to her life.'

'I'll speak to her too and explain that she'll always be part of my life now.'

'Good idea.' She glanced at her wristwatch. 'Thanks for the drink. I should be getting back now. No need to get up. Goodbye, Flynn. We were never meant to be together, but we're going to have a hell of a time being Nanny and Grandad.'

Chapter Forty-eight

Was it still snowing? Lara opened the curtains to see if the flakes that had been falling were going to stick when she spotted a visitor at Flynn's front door.

She had been wondering if she could make it over there in the new heeled boots she'd had as a present for Christmas when she saw Imogen on his step, wearing a cream furry coat. Flynn had answered with a beaming smile and a bottle of something fizzy.

Lara dropped the curtain and sat down heavily on her sofa.

Every rational thought told her that Flynn would never have invited Imogen over on the same evening that he'd asked Lara. It had to be a mix-up or a coincidence. There was the outside chance that he'd intended to have a party or some kind of family gathering, but she doubted it very much. The more likely scenario, her sensible side told her, was that Imogen had turned up unannounced – but why was Flynn so happy to see her, in that case?

Lara checked his message from the previous day again:

If you don't have other plans, do you fancy coming over for New Year's Eve dinner?

A minute later, he'd added:

No Pressure. We can just talk.

Lara hadn't had plans, exactly, but she had been included in an informal get-together at Carlos's flat. If last year's was anything to go by, it was bound to be raucous and boozy with terrible eighties music and probably end up with someone being carried back to their rooms. Pretty much exactly what a New Year's Eve party should be. She'd hinted she might go, but when Flynn's invitation had come through, she'd known she probably wouldn't.

We can just talk.

Did he really mean that?

Did *she* want things to go further?

If they did, wouldn't that just put them back in the position they'd been in before? They wouldn't be going forward or back. He was bound by the ties in the present and she didn't want to get hurt or be on the sidelines, on hand with consolation when he needed it.

Whatever the reason for Imogen turning up, it only reinforced that Flynn was in no position to sustain a new relationship.

Ten minutes later, Lara peered through the curtains again. It was seven-fifteen and she'd no way of knowing if Imogen was still inside. She certainly wasn't going to knock on the door and ask.

What the hell was she doing? Waiting for a man to make up his mind again?

It was New Year's Eve. A party awaited. She zipped up her boots, grabbed her coat and a bottle of wine, and decided that it was time she stopped hanging around and let her hair down for a change.

'Lara! Wait!'

Lara slithered to a halt halfway across the cobbles. She'd almost slipped in the slush once already.

'Lara!'

She turned round to see Flynn, in shorts and a T-shirt, hobbling towards her across the cobbles.

'Wait!' he yelled. A moment later, the crutch fell to the ground, followed by Flynn. 'Oh, f-fuck!'

Lara abandoned her bottle and dashed forward, almost falling over herself. 'Oh God. Are you OK? What did you think you were doing?'

'Trying to run after you,' he said, then groaned and swore repeatedly.

'Are you completely mad?' she asked, high on relief that he was OK. 'You could have done your knee in again.'

'Yes to the first and I bloody hope not to the second. Can you help me up? My arse is getting soaked.'

'I'll try, but you're not some elf, you know.'

'Ha ha. Ouch.'

Somehow, breathing heavily, Lara helped him to his feet and handed over the crutches.

'Thanks,' he said, breathing heavily. 'Where were you going?'

'To the party at Carlos's.'

'I thought you were coming to mine?'

'I saw you had a visitor and – well, I didn't know what was happening.'

He sighed. 'Neither did I – please come back to the cottage and give me a chance to explain. Then, if you don't like what you hear, by all means go to the party. Though—' he added with such hope in his voice that it made her melt. 'I very much don't want you to leave.'

'Molly set me and Imogen up,' Flynn explained, after he'd changed into dry shorts and a jumper in his bedroom. 'She told her mum that I wanted to have a family party and asked Imogen to meet us here. You didn't think I'd invite her when I'd already asked you?'

'No, not really, but what could I do? I wasn't going to intrude. There could have been an emergency or something. I don't know. I waited a while then decided to go to Carlos's party.'

'You still can,' he said, with a grin. 'Though if you do, I'll cancel the Uber Eats order and my flower arranging course will have been in vain.'

Lara noticed the table set for two and the greenery stuck in a vase with a couple of fading roses. She realised what a huge effort he'd gone to and was near tears.

'Oh, Flynn.'

PHILLIPA ASHLEY

He took her hand and looked serious. 'Please, sit down. Stay. At least until you hear what I have to say anyway.'

She sat next to him and he kept hold of her hand. 'That day at the hospital . . . why didn't you come into the HDU to see me?'

'How did you know I was there?'

'Mum and Dad mentioned they'd seen you. You must have known they would eventually.'

'I . . . suppose so. I thought they might have been too worried to have recognised me or too busy to say anything to you.'

'You should have told them who you were.' He squeezed her hand.

Told them who she was? She daren't let on she'd lied about being his fiancée when, in reality, she wasn't technically anything to Flynn. Yet now she knew he was the man she'd fallen in love with, despite her vain attempts not to. The man who'd coaxed her out of her self-imposed exile.

'Why didn't you come and see me?' he asked.

'I saw Molly and Brenda by your bed – and a woman I guessed was Imogen. And afterwards your parents saw me waiting outside and they had enough to worry about and you had enough visitors. Nurses wouldn't have let another one in. It wasn't a party.'

Flynn shook his head. 'God, I wish you'd come in to see me.'

'You looked out of it and I'd seen that you were OK – alive at least – and so I went home.'

'Do you know that, even though I was half-delirious,

I did know one thing: I wanted to see *you*. I wanted you to be there by my bed to hold my hand and tell me everything would be OK.' He lifted his fingers to her face and rested them there, making every nerve cell spring into life. 'You've seen me at my lowest, heard me struggle, and stood by while I tried to sort my life out. It's time that everything was all about you, Lara. It's time I made it all about you.'

'All about *me*?' she murmured.

'Yes. I want you to tell me what you're really feeling. The stuff you've been too afraid to say.'

'It's too soon for that deep, intense stuff. We've known each other less than two months.'

He laughed. '*Only* two months. I feel more has happened to me in those two months than in my whole life.' He stroked her hand tenderly. 'And it's plenty long enough for two people to decide to be honest with each other.'

He studied her hand for a moment, then held it tightly between his two warm ones. 'I'm a lost cause! I've let you down and messed you around because I felt overwhelmed by the stuff that was happening to me, but the accident . . . call it a cliché, but it has focused my mind on what I really want. Imogen calling tonight – Molly setting us up. That's crystallised what I want from life. Now I want to know what's holding you back from committing to me. I want to know everything about you, Lara Mayhew.'

'Everything?' She was glad he was holding her hand, because she wasn't sure she could stop herself from shaking otherwise.

'All of it.'

Telling Flynn everything would mean confessing her deepest fears and desires and risk scaring him away. Yet without doing that, there could be no future for them. She'd already thought there was no hope for them, so what had she got to lose?

'OK. You asked for it.' She paused for a breath and laid her heart on the line. 'I wanted a family with Rob. I thought he did too. He talked about it from time to time, about watching the kids run around the hall, climb the trees in the orchard, and how they'd take over the reins, as he put it. He talked about it when we were in bed, when we were alone together – more than a few times. I was naïve. I assumed he meant *our* children, when all along he'd only meant *his* children.'

'Go on . . .' He squeezed her hand when she faltered.

'And then – and I swear it was a complete accident – I realised I was pregnant.' She ploughed on, determined not to shed another tear for a man who had never deserved a single one. 'And I never got a chance to tell him before he broke it off and then – then—' Her throat was thick with a sob. 'I had a miscarriage, so he never knew.'

Flynn recoiled in shock before pulling her into his arms. 'Oh, Lara, Lara. I am so sorry for what you've gone through. None of what happened to you is your fault.' He looked into her eyes, his own full of empathy and passion. 'This isn't on you. It's all on *him*. A coward, a total bastard who will never face up to his responsibilities. God help his wife.'

'Yeah, though that doesn't make me happy. I feel sorry for her.' Through her tears, she managed a smile at his intense expression, so full of pain and anger on her behalf.

'You should have told me this before . . .' he said, gently lifting a strand of hair away from her tear-stained face

'No, I couldn't,' she said. 'I couldn't because it was way too soon at first and then, once we grew closer, your life changed. How could I tell you that I'd hoped for and lost a chance at a family when you'd found yours? There was no way I wanted to be bitter or needy – and most of all, there was no way I was going to spoil the joy you have. Even if it doesn't feel like joy all the time.'

His expression held such an intense, heart-melting tenderness that her breath caught in her throat. 'I need you to know something. I was *never* going to get back with Imogen. You must have known that.'

'Maybe, but, again, I wasn't going to crash in if there was the slightest chance. I wouldn't ruin your chances and I certainly wasn't going to threaten Molly's plans, however misguided. She's a lovely girl who only wants what she thinks she's missed: her mum and dad together at last. She wants the fantasy of a perfect ending with a perfect family set-up that we both know almost never exists.'

'No, it doesn't. I realise that now. I pushed you away, thinking you couldn't deal with it – that you shouldn't have to. That you'd be better off without me than taking me with all this baggage.' He reached up and pressed his fingers to her cheek. 'Esme and Molly will always be part of my life. I thought that was too much of a burden for you – for anyone – to take on, especially as I knew your other workplace relationship had ended in disaster. I didn't realise quite how much he'd hurt you or why. And until the past

353

few days, I wasn't ready to accept how much pain I was causing by pushing you away.'

'It's OK. I understood.'

'You shouldn't have had to. I should have let you in . . .'

'You needed that space to process everything and I wanted to help. I was ready to help, and I want to, but only if you let me in and if you're truly ready, Flynn.'

'I am so ready for this, so let this be a new beginning for us. The *two* of us.'

She leaned in and kissed him. Any pain from his fall seemed to have melted away because he pulled her against his body, pressing molten kisses on her mouth and neck. There was a fresh intensity to their kisses, a sense of release and seizing the moment.

'Lara. Lara . . .' He kept saying her name as if she might vanish if he didn't. 'I want to give you the fairy tale, the happy ever after. I want to do all the romantic stuff people do when they get together, and have masses of hot sex – and I can't even do that.'

Lara raised her eyebrows. 'I thought it was only your knee that was broken?'

She gasped in delight as he pulled her on top of him. 'There's only one way to find out.'

Chapter Forty-nine

Flynn thought it fortunate that the delivery rider had been running late. He arrived as Lara was getting dressed in Flynn's bedroom and as Flynn himself had just put his T-shirt back on. They'd eaten the Greek meal by candlelight and retired early to bed, listening to the chimes from the tower clock and distant fireworks and rowdy choruses of Auld Lang Syne. All from the comfort of Flynn's divan.

Lara insisted she hadn't minded missing the party, and there had been enough fireworks in the bedroom to rival the ones that would have been lighting up the London sky by that point. Nothing could dampen the joy, the celebration, and the hope for the future in his heart – and in hers, if he'd read the signals right.

'Will people notice you weren't at the party?' he asked.

'Yes, but not until tomorrow – well, later today – after everyone has finally surfaced. I could say I got an early night,' she said, trailing her fingers over Flynn's bare thigh.

'Or you could be honest. You could say you spent a night with a handsome Harley rider who had to be very inventive given his damaged knee . . .'

'I could . . .' Lara's fingers rested at the very top of Flynn's thigh, creating a kick of desire that was almost impossible not to act on. 'But if we're truly being honest,' she went on. 'I ought to tell everyone the truth.'

On New Year's Day, Flynn insisted on making bacon sandwiches despite having to hold on to every available surface and swearing as he fried the bacon.

Over breakfast, Lara said, 'Do you think you'll make it to the ball?'

'I'm determined to. Are you looking forward to it?'

'I ought to be. I would have been . . . I mean, I am, but I'm going to have to confess about the chalice the next day. After Henry and Fiona have been so kind to me, I'm dreading telling them about it.'

'I can understand you being worried, but they don't seem like the kind of people to turn nasty. I'm sure they'll understand.'

'It's not a small thing, though. It's huge. It's the estate's biggest treasure. I'm going to have to pay for it.'

'It'll be insured.'

'It is, but there's sure to be an excess. Or a clause. Or something.'

'Don't think about it now. Let's enjoy the last few days of Christmas.' He raised his eyebrows and looked at her. 'That shirt suits you.'

'You think?' Lara had borrowed one of Flynn's dress shirts to have breakfast in.

'I do, but it would look even better . . .' He reached forward and undid one of the buttons. '*Off* you.'

'Surely you don't have the strength to do it again?' Lara

teased, and Flynn felt his desire flare into life again. 'An injured man?'

'Somehow I'll manage.'

The next few days whizzed by in a haze of sex and work for Lara, and sex and trying to rest – not very successfully – for Flynn. Gradually, word spread that he and Lara were an item, and Mrs Danvers, clearly blessed with telepathic powers, told Flynn she'd known all along.

Though still officially off sick, Flynn couldn't stay away from work completely. He hobbled into the office several times a day, often having to be shooed out by Carlos, but he was secretly pleased when his deputy asked for his advice on a number of things for the Spectacular and as well as regarding other maintenance issues.

The enforced rest was also a chance to spend time with Molly when she wasn't at the café. And with Esme. They called on him at the cottage and Lara gave him lifts to their house on her way to and from shopping.

If his colleagues wondered why he was spending so much time with the girl from the café, Flynn decided to let them. He wasn't ready to reveal everything about his private life yet.

He and Molly went for a walk one day – a shuffle in his case, though he was getting stronger – and stopped by the side of the lake to feed the ducks and swans.

'I'm sorry I set you up on New Year's Eve,' she said.

'It's OK.'

'That's not what Mum said.'

'We were both a bit shocked and confused.'

'I only wanted you and Mum to have a chance to spend some time together and work things out.'

'We will do. We have the rest of our lives for that, with you and Esme.' He rested his hand on Molly's. 'As friends.'

'I – I'm s-sorry. I'd hoped – I'd hoped you and Mum would get together.' Molly had tears in her eyes and Flynn felt a stab of guilt. But he knew he had to stand firm for everyone's sakes.

'I know that. I understand why, but we're not the right people for each other and your mum agrees. I don't think the trust would ever be there between us and no relationship can ever work without trust on both sides.'

Molly nodded. 'I realise that. Mum's admitted that, if she'd wanted to, she could have tried harder to find you.'

'She's admitted that to me too and, while we won't be partners, we do want to be friends, for all our sakes – and especially yours. I love you and Esme with a love I never thought I'd experience. I can't explain it. It's scary but wonderful too.'

'I do understand. I feel that way about Esme.'

'And I am your dad and Esme's grandad, but I'm also still *me*. You told me that you hadn't met the right person yet, that Esme's dad wasn't the one, and so you preferred to be on your own for now. I know you will meet someone special who'll worship you and adore Esme . . . and, you see, I think I already have. In fact, I know I have.'

'You mean Lara?'

'Yes. I do. She's the one. I want to spend the rest of my life with her and I'm hoping she feels the same too.'

'Have you told her that yet?'

'I've told her I want to be with her and that's enough for now. We've both had a lot to deal with lately. But I won't wait too long before I do say more. Shall we keep that our secret for now? You'll be the first to know.'

She squeaked in delight at being the guardian of such a confidence. 'I won't say, but can Esme be a bridesmaid?'

Flynn laughed. He hadn't actually thought about a wedding, only a commitment, albeit a very serious one. How quickly Molly made the leap, with all the romantic idealism of youth.

He shook his head in wonder. 'You'd make a great matchmaker.'

'I'd rather be a psychologist.'

'You'll be a great one. I already know that. Shall we go grab a coffee?'

'Yes, and I'll get them while you change Esme. I have a feeling she needs it.'

'Thanks a lot,' said Flynn, as Esme let out a gurgle that sounded very much like glee. 'I suppose I need the practice.'

Chapter Fifty

'My Lords, ladies and gentlemen! For tonight we are all lords, ladies and gentlemen. Tonight, we are all kings and queens. Tonight, the social norms are overturned and chaos reigns! For tonight is Twelfth Night, when anything and everything goes – so let the revelry and feasting begin!' The Lord of Misrule raised his tankard high and cheers rang to the rafters of the banqueting hall at Ravendale. He was actually one of the guides, dressed in a jester's outfit with a curly crown and strange beaked mask.

Lara had spent most of the day supervising the removal of the Christmas decorations from the castle, because centuries-old tradition had deemed it bad luck to leave them up – the irony. Although the rest of the rooms were back to their pre-festive Christmas state, the entrance hall and banqueting hall had been left with their greenery and Christmas tree intact.

There was no way that the decorations would be down by midnight but they'd just have to risk it. The thought reminded her of the next day, when she was planning to come clean about the chalice. She swiped a glass of mead from a tray and took a large gulp, pushing the inevitable aside and preparing to do as the Lord of Misrule had commanded: feast and revel.

She tried to work out who was behind the dazzling cast of characters packing into the great hall. There were jesters and harlequins, three Henry VIIIs, various cavaliers and Regency ladies, someone in a bear costume – they'd never keep that on all night. Lots of people complimented her on her costume, which had been delivered two days previously by Tessa. It had fitted her perfectly and she'd hardly been able to recognise herself in the mirror.

Jazz bounded up. 'You look gorgeous! Guinevere?'

'Close. The Lady of Shalott. You look amazing too.'

'Do you like it? Luke loves it too, but he feels OTT in his outfit, which is why he's gone to find a very large tankard of mead.'

'Nothing is OTT at a Twelfth Night Ball. OTT is the whole idea. Wow. Is that *Carlos*?'

Lara had to look hard at the man in a long curly wig who had just made an entrance into the banqueting hall on the arm of a tall character carrying a basket of oranges.

'I think Carlos has come as Charles II . . .' Lara said. 'And that must be his partner dressed as Nell Gwynne.'

'I'd no idea . . .' Jazz said.

'Nor me. I had no idea he was gay either.'

'I'd kill for his coat,' Jazz said, and both she and Lara gawped as Carlos strolled past them in his coral silk frock coat, breeches, and fancy shoes. He tipped his hat and Lara raised her glass. 'Bravo!'

PHILLIPA ASHLEY

'I love Nell's dress,' Jazz said, admiring the elaborate low-cut silk gown.

'I think that's actually *Neil* . . .' Jazz whispered. 'I recognise him now. He's a sous-chef in the kitchens.'

Feathers fluttered and tiaras shimmered as Carlos and Neil were soon lost in a sea of admirers.

'Where's Flynn?' Jazz asked.

'Getting into his costume. He didn't want me to help. Said he wanted to surprise me.'

'Can he manage – with his knee, I mean?'

'I've no idea . . . but I can't wait to find out.'

Luke returned, dressed as the Green Man. 'I feel like a right tit.'

Lara stifled a giggle. 'I think you look magnificent.'

Jazz snorted her drink.

They chatted for a few minutes – as much as you could chat amid the rising hubbub and the music from the medieval musicians – when Jazz pointed towards the door. 'Is that *Flynn*?'

Jazz stood on tiptoes, pointing in the direction of the rear of the banqueting hall, where Lara could just make out a tall figure in a tricorn. The inner fireworks exploded again. Flynn looked every inch the swaggering highwayman and she could hardly wait to explore what was under the top coat and breeches.

'Yes. I think it is . . .'

'See you later,' Jazz said, with a smirk. 'I want to join in the medieval dancing and I want you to show us how to do it.'

Lara made her way towards the corner of the hall, weaving past knights in armour, Elizabeth I, plus Robin Hood and Maid Marian. Flynn lingered in the archway, obviously struggling to hobble through the throngs with his crutches.

Finally, with many apologies for squeezing past people, Lara made it to the corner where Flynn waited at the rear of the hall – in the very spot where he'd made his dramatic entrance on a wild and stormy Halloween. She'd been lost for words then, and she was again now.

'Wow. Wow.' He blew out a breath. 'You look absolutely incredible. Like a princess.'

Lara was aware that the green velvet dress, fit for the medieval noblewoman she was, skimmed every curve of her body. She'd been taken aback when she'd first tried it on; it was so unlike her usual uniform of jeans and a fleece – but also stunned that she could look so regal. Flynn's reaction, his eyes practically devouring her, made her tingle all over.

'I'm meant to be the Lady of Shalott. She was in love with Sir Lancelot but it didn't end well.'

'Really?' He pulled her closer to him. 'Let's make sure *our* story does, then.' He kissed her.

'You don't look so bad yourself. Very rakish. Very disreputable.'

Flynn laughed. 'Two people have already asked if I've come as Long John Silver. All I need is a parrot on my shoulder. But, wow, I can't get over that dress on you – or you in the dress. I mean, I love everything you wear and everything you *don't* . . .'

Heat rushed to her cheeks and her décolletage – and

there was a lot of décolletage on show, thanks to the low-cut design of the dress. Her hand went to her breastbone, fingers touching the cool stones of the necklace Flynn had given her for Christmas.

'The necklace looks great, by the way. Is it OK?'

'It's perfect. The colours are beautiful, almost as if you knew what I was going to wear.'

'I didn't. You kept it a secret. I just got lucky.' His gaze raked over her again, seeming to leave a trail of heat. 'In every way.'

Lara thought of leaning in for another kiss when the clang of a gong interrupted them.

'My lords, ladies and gentlemen. May I have your attention as we welcome your hosts for the ball, Henry and Fiona, the Earl and Countess of Penhaligon.'

Leaning on Lara's arm, Flynn moved forward so they could see the arrival of Henry and Fiona. There were cheers and applause as they walked in dressed as characters that Lara and most of the staff would recognise instantly.

'Who are they?' Flynn whispered to Lara.

'The first earl and his lady.'

Behind them, a man dressed as a page carried a red tasselled cushion. Lara recognised him as one of the security team, although it was a stretch to see him in medieval livery in place of his high-vis and uniform.

Lara stifled a shriek of horror and squeezed Flynn's hand so tightly, he let out an 'Oof. What's the matter?'

'Th-that. That blue box on the cushion. It's the chalice!'

Chapter Fifty-one

It might have been the crowds or the heat in the banqueting hall, but Lara felt her legs weaken and a hot flush come over her.

Luckily Flynn was now holding *her* arm. 'Oh my God. They must know.'

'Maybe they haven't opened it yet,' he said.

'Then why have they brought it to the ball? Oh, no . . .'

The Lord of Misrule banged the gong again. 'Pray silence for His Lordship!'

'They're not – oh God, please no – going to open it here. I have to do something.'

'Hold on. Not now. You can tell them afterwards, but now would be the very worst time.' He squeezed her hand to prevent her from dashing forward. 'Trust me.'

'I *have* to tell them.'

'No. It's too late. They probably won't notice. Most people are pissed. Henry and Fiona won't look at it closely. They're too preoccupied.' She slipped from his grasp and made her way around the to the side of the room.

A hush descended that seemed even more portentous because of the revelry and noise that had come before it.

'As you all know, this is the anniversary of an important

event in the history of Ravendale. Many centuries ago, King Henry, bestowed this treasure on the castle.'

Lara longed for magic powers so she could melt into the flagstones. Instead, she had to watch in horror as Henry removed the chalice from the box.

'You could say that, throughout this time, our fortunes have depended on this small and rather humble looking piece of glass.'

She wondered if, at any moment, the chalice would spontaneously set itself on fire and start irradiating the people in the room like the Ark in *Indiana Jones and the Raiders of the Lost Ark*. Perhaps that would be preferable to Henry suddenly discovering the chip in front of a hundred people and having a heart attack. Why oh why hadn't she confessed before? All her reasons for keeping quiet now seemed ridiculous.

'Maybe that's true. Some of my ancestors certainly believed it, but, you know, while this chalice is precious – indeed priceless – to our family—'

'Don't . . .' Flynn warned, with a hand on her arm, having finally made it to her side.

Henry was on a roll. 'While it is very precious, I know our fortunes will never depend on it.' He held the chalice high like a tennis player who'd won Wimbledon. Convinced she could see the chip from metres away, Lara was sure it had grown bigger, possibly large enough to shatter in Henry's hands.

'Our future depends not on luck . . . but on you. You people here in this room and the many who have come before. The people who work here and volunteer here and love this place as we do. Tonight isn't about us, or the Penhaligons, or even Ravendale, but a celebration of your hard work and dedication and love for the place.

'We can never be the owners of Ravendale, we can only ever be custodians, along with you all. And on that note, I am delighted to announce that, over the Christmas break, our wonderful daughter Harriet, and her husband, Julian, have decided that the time is right for them to take over some of the reins. They will be moving to Ravendale this spring and jointly learning the ropes regarding running this property.' Henry still had the chalice in one hand, holding it by the stem.

Lara wasn't sure she'd breathed properly for the past half a minute.

Any impact and drama created by Henry's dramatic declaration that one of his children would be taking over was lost in Lara's terror of him noticing the damage to the base.

'I hope you will all give them the same unstinting support you have always shown us. Now, all that remains is me to urge to raise your glasses to the future of Ravendale and to yourselves!'

Clutching the chalice in one hand, Henry accepted a glass of champagne from a waiter and raised his fizz and the chalice high in the air.

Cheers erupted amid cries of 'hear, hear' and thunderous applause. Then, as Henry thrust the chalice even higher into the air, grinning like a World Cup-winning captain, several things happened at once.

The chalice slipped, Flynn let go of her hand, his crutch clattered to the flagstones, and he dived forward.

There was a collective gasp, a shriek from Fiona, a cry from Lara, and Flynn lay on the floor, the chalice clutched to his chest.

'Good God! How did that happen?' Henry declared.

'Because you're tiddly, that's why!' Fiona said, rushing to Flynn's aid.

Lara joined Fiona by Flynn's side. 'Are you OK?'

'You poor man!' Fiona said, taking the chalice from him and handing it to the page. 'What about your knee?'

'I – I think it's OK,' Flynn said, although Lara could see he was trying not to grimace in pain.

By this time, people were crowding around them, muttering and staring.

'Is anyone hurt?' Jazz asked, pushing her way to the front of the throng. 'I'm a trained first aider.'

'Are you hurt, Flynn?' Lara asked, worried about him far more than the chalice.

'Um. I – er . . .' He pushed himself up onto his elbows. 'I think I got away with it.'

Jazz and her husband helped him to his feet and Lara offered the crutch.

There was a sudden collective murmur of relief and then a round of applause.

'You should play for the village cricket team!' Henry said. 'What a catch.'

'Flynn's in no fit state to play any kind of game, Henry. He could have seriously injured himself!' Fiona said. 'Now, let's find you a seat while security put that bloody chalice back in the safe. Honestly, sometimes I think it's more trouble than it's worth.'

'You don't mean that, dear,' said Henry, shamefaced. 'But thank you for catching it, Flynn.'

'You're welcome,' he said, trying not to wince. 'And I'll be fine.'

A few minutes later, Flynn was sitting in a corner of the hall with a drink and Lara by his side.

'I don't know how you did that,' she said, her pulse rate gradually returning to normal.

'Nor me. Actually, I made the wrong decision, didn't I? If I hadn't been so stupid as to save it, and it was smashed to smithereens, no one would have ever known about the – you-know-what.'

Lara sighed and took his hand. 'I had thought of that, but I can't wish the thing to be destroyed, not even if it would save me. No, I think the time has come to face the music. The sooner the better.'

'Not until we have that dance,' Flynn said, cupping her cheek with a warm hand. 'I promised you that and nothing is going to ruin it. Even if I can only hold onto you and shuffle.'

Henry and Fiona left the ball at midnight, leaving most of the revellers still dancing.

'We should go to bed too,' Flynn said to Lara. 'We have a big day in the morning. We need our strength.'

Her heart sank at the thought of her confession, but she

was determined to do it. 'You go back to the cottage. I need to say some goodbyes and thank a few people for helping to organise the ball.'

'Promise you won't be long?' It was half plea, half threat.

'I promise,' said Lara. 'Can you make it back to the cottage without falling over?'

He rolled his eyes. 'I'll try.'

She watched him hobble across the hallway where people were collecting their coats and saying their rather drunken goodbyes.

Music was still pumping out of the very un-medieval disco and a couple of dozen hardy souls, including Carlos and Neil, were throwing shapes on the dance floor. Jazz and Luke had got a taxi home an hour ago.

Lara lingered in the hall a few moments longer, heaved a sigh, and headed for the family apartments.

Chapter Fifty-two

Fiona opened the door in her dressing gown. Her lips parted in surprise. 'Lara! Is everything all right? Is it Flynn? Don't say we've had another drama.'

Lara's stomach tightened. 'No, not tonight. I know it's late, but may I come in? There's something I have to say.'

Fiona frowned but gestured for her to come inside. 'Of course, but couldn't it wait until morning?'

'Not really.'

Henry emerged from the kitchen, wearing an old-fashioned smoking jacket that would have made Lara smile in other circumstances.

'Lara? Anything wrong? You look beautiful, by the way.'

'Thank you,' she said, touched by his gallantry while feeling incongruous in her own medieval gown. What she had to deliver wasn't fantasy: it was real-life bad news.

'Lara has something to tell us. Sit down, my dear.' Lara sat on the sofa while Henry took a chair and Fiona sat next to her. 'Go ahead. It can't be that bad, surely?'

'You're not leaving us, are you?' Henry asked, leaning forward in alarm. 'Not now Harriet and Julian are taking over. They'll need you!'

'I'm not leaving,' Lara said wearily. 'At least I hope I'm not . . .'

Fiona exchanged an anxious glance with Henry and murmured, 'This sounds serious. Go ahead, my dear.'

Lara dived in, reasoning it was best to simply get it over with, like ripping off a very large plaster from an unhealed wound. 'I have to tell you something that I should have said weeks ago and it's related to the chalice. I'm so sorry. You see, I – I – had a mishap with it the day that Flynn arrived. And I only mention him because that's how I remember the day it happened.'

Fiona raised her hand. 'Lara, take a breath, my dear. This can't be that bad.'

'I'm afraid it is, because I dropped the chalice onto the floorboards and I thought it was OK. But it wasn't, it *isn't*, and you must have noticed tonight, because there's a tiny chip in the base . . . and I'll hand my resignation in now.'

Henry's gaze slid from Lara to the chalice and back to Lara. 'Ah. I see.'

'Oh dear,' Fiona said, exchanging a tight-lipped glance with her husband. 'I can see why you've been so worried. Hmm.'

'I'll leave Ravendale, of course,' Lara said, feeling the disappointment in their voices crush her.

Henry made a harrumphing sound.

'Oh dear,' Fiona said again, glancing at the fireplace, as if she couldn't bear to look at Lara.

Lara glanced up miserably then jumped as the sitting room door flew open and Flynn hobbled into the room. 'Wait! I can explain!'

Everyone stared at him. He was breathing hard. Lara was dumbstruck. 'Please, don't blame Lara. It's my fault the chalice was damaged.'

'Your fault?' Fiona said.

'The day I arrived at the castle, I came across Lara in the tower. She was putting the chalice away and I burst into the room like a twa—idiot. She was startled and the chalice slipped out of her hands. So, I'm responsible and I'll resign.'

Henry raised his eyebrows and glanced from Lara and Flynn to his wife. 'My word, I don't think I've ever seen two people so eager to take the blame for something that wasn't really their fault.'

Lara found her voice. 'But it is *my* fault,' she insisted, glaring at Flynn looming over them all. 'Yes, it was an accident, but I ought to have told you immediately. I was . . . worried you'd had enough shocks, with Henry's illness, but that's still no excuse for deceiving you.'

'That's partly my doing too,' Flynn said, refusing to meet Lara's warning glower. 'I thought it was best if she – we – waited – until after Christmas. I kind of encouraged her to keep quiet.'

'Flynn. No. It was my decision. I wasn't influenced by him,' she said firmly.

'Can we all calm down, please?' Fiona held up her hands. 'And can we say something? Because we also have a confession to make.'

Lara's lips parted but she didn't say anything. Flynn also wisely kept his mouth shut. Even though the Penhaligons didn't seem unduly angry, Lara clenched her fists tightly because her fingers weren't steady and her stomach was churning.

'Please, sit down,' Henry ordered, with a steely glare at them both.

Flynn sat beside Lara, not daring to meet her eye.

Fiona took the armchair but Henry remained standing in front of the hearth, hands folded behind his back. It was all horribly like being summoned to the head teacher's office, only much worse, considering what was at stake.

'Now, I am a little disappointed that you didn't feel able to tell me at the time that you'd damaged the chalice,' Fiona began.

Lara closed her eyes briefly, longing to sink through the floor.

'However, I totally understand why you didn't want to risk upsetting us. That was kind of you, even if it was a little . . . misguided.'

Lara nodded.

'Mainly I'm disappointed because you could have saved yourselves a lot of worry if you had come to us immediately. Because I would have told you a secret that must not go further than these walls.'

Lara stared at Fiona. Henry was smirking.

'The chalice we used for the party is a twentieth-century replica. You don't think we'd risk a family heirloom at a drunken ball, do you?'

Flynn made a strangled sound that might have been a swear word that he'd managed to hold back.

'So it's not the *real* chalice?' Lara said.

Fiona was smiling. 'No, my dear.'

So, so . . . thought Lara, she'd confessed for no reason. She hadn't needed to blurt out the truth – not yet.

'And I know what you're thinking,' Henry cut in. 'That you could have waited a while longer to tell us the truth?'

Lara shook her head in shame. 'Yes, I could, but . . . I shouldn't have waited, so it's probably for the best.'

'Do you feel any better?' Fiona asked.

Lara realised she'd dug her fingers in the velvet sofa cushion. 'Not much, though I *am* terribly sorry.'

'Lara, this isn't just on you,' Flynn said, placing his hand over hers.

Lara didn't take her hand away. She needed the warmth and comfort for moral support.

'Well, this is very touching and chivalrous of you, Flynn, but we haven't finished telling you everything,' Henry said. 'My grandfather had the replica made in the 1920s.'

Lara was still struggling to process the series of revelations: hers and the Penhaligons.

'Oh. Oh, I see . . . I'd no idea, but I've still damaged the replica.'

'That one can easily be repaired,' Fiona said. 'The original is safely in a vault in London, and has been since Grandpapa had the replica made. We could never risk having such a precious object on display or even here at the castle.'

Flynn squeezed Lara's hand. 'So, Lara – we – haven't destroyed the Luck of Ravendale?'

'No one can do that,' Henry said, smiling. 'As any rational person must realise. I know you two youngsters don't believe in it.'

'I don't,' Lara said.

Lara thought of Belle, examining the chalice and giving it an odd look and refusing to repair it. Had she known it wasn't what it was purported to be, yet wouldn't admit her misgivings? She decided not to mention Belle's visit for now. It would only complicate things.

Flynn let out a sigh. 'Thank God for that. Does anyone else know about the replica?'

'No. No one outside the family and our current solicitors. And the truth must never ever get out,' Fiona said solemnly. 'People come to Ravendale to see the Lucky Chalice, sceptics and believers alike. Call it our version of a holy relic. It only has meaning if people believe – or if the rest of us keep its mystique intact. And that,' this Fiona directed at Lara, 'you haven't damaged in any way.'

'It only has meaning if people believe . . .' Flynn mused. 'Like Santa Claus.'

Henry chortled. 'Yes, I suppose so.'

'And, actually, I have a particular reason for keeping that magical secret,' Flynn said.

Lara glanced at him in surprise.

Fiona leaned forward with intrigue in her eyes. 'What's that?'

Flynn related, briefly, the story of Molly and Esme, much to the delight of the Penhaligons. 'I wanted you to be the first to know apart from Lara,' he said.

Lara thought she'd better keep quiet about Jazz knowing, but was relieved and happy that she no longer had to keep it all a secret. Flynn had sounded so proud, and she was delighted for him.

'Oh, how wonderful!' Henry declared. 'Embrace every moment. We only wish we saw more of our grandchildren, even though they're young adults now. We do remember those marvellous early days. Exhausting but so precious. You are a very lucky man, Flynn.'

Lara got to her feet, exhausted and light-headed with relief, yet still burdened with guilt. 'I still need to pay for the repair to the chalice. And my offer to resign still stands.'

'No. No to both,' Fiona said.

'We won't hear of it,' Henry declared. 'What would we do without you? The events programme and Spectacular have been a resounding success. We think it should become an annual event. The revenue will help to keep Ravendale going for years to come – you have helped maintain its fortunes. You could say you have saved us.'

'No. I can't take all the credit.'

'As for the replica, we can claim on the insurance,' Fiona said. 'You can help by finding an expert restorer to repair it. That way, no one will be any the wiser.'

'I – I might know someone,' Lara murmured. She noted Flynn was staring straight ahead with an expression of composed innocence on his face. 'Thank you.'

'How did you know I was going to confess?' Lara asked Flynn, as they descended the tower in the lift.

'I didn't. I was going to do the same myself, so I hung

around and then watched you go up to the tower. It took me ages to climb up, and I couldn't risk getting stuck in this bloody thing.'

'Oh, Flynn.' Lara put her arms around him. 'Thanks for trying to take the blame. Even though I told you not to.'

'I rarely do as I'm told,' he said.

She laughed. 'I've worked that out.'

'And is it a deal breaker?'

'I think . . . I think that, annoying and frustrating as it is that you do the exact opposite of what I ask you to, life would probably be a lot less exciting if you were predictable.'

Flynn heaved a happy sigh. 'Good. You mean everything to me. I'd rather get the sack than see you driven out of your beloved job and home because of something I had a hand in. I was worried I'd be too late. I was, but, in the end, it's all turned out OK.'

'I don't know whether we're lucky or it's all down to the Penhaligons' planning and cautiousness.'

'Who cares? All I know is that you're at the centre of my life and that I can't bear to be without you or to see you suffer. I need you more than I ever did. Along with Molly and Esme, you're my future, Lara.'

Lara leaned forward and kissed him, carrying on even when the lift gently touched down on the ground floor. Eventually, they broke apart and Lara's hand hovered over the button. 'What would we do if we got stuck? Everyone's drunk or asleep and no one could come to rescue us.'.

Flynn held her face in his hands. 'Do you know, I

don't think being trapped in a lift has ever sounding more appealing.'

'Agree . . .' She walked her fingers up his shirt, fireworks exploding all over her body. 'And I *still* haven't given you your present.'

'Don't worry. I've got all I want for Christmas.'

'Me too,' said Lara, toying with the button on his chest. 'But I have just thought of something that would be absolutely perfect . . .'

Epilogue

Eleven months later

'Three, two, one. Let there be light!' Hattie Penhaligon flicked the switch and the lights came on all over the park. Whoops and cheers rang out from the staff assembled around the courtyard.

'That went well,' Flynn said to Lara, holding her hand. 'Carlos did a good job on the coordination.'

Flynn and Carlos had timed the switch to the second, and it had all been coordinated by the control room. The final dress rehearsal of the Second Ravendale Winter Spectacular was complete and everyone could heave a huge sigh of relief – until opening night.

'He's been in a much better frame of mind since he and Neil moved off site and into their own cottage,' Flynn said. 'Though he still has his moments.'

'Don't we all?' Lara commented. 'It's not been plain sailing for Hattie. It was really brave of her to uproot her family and come up here.'

Flynn's gaze was fixed on Hattie hugging her parents, with her husband and kids standing around with huge grins on their faces. 'Well, she does have the compensation of inheriting a bloody great big castle . . .'

'True. I still wouldn't want the responsibility, though,' said Lara.

Hattie and her family had moved to Ravendale Lodge a few months previously. She had set up her sculpture studio in a folly in the grounds and was learning the ropes from Henry and Fiona. Her husband had left his job as a marketing manager and was going to work alongside her, running the castle and estate.

They seemed more than happy – grateful, even – for the advice and support of Lara, Flynn, Jazz, and the rest of the team. Hattie had even confided that the children adored living in the castle and were enjoying learning to kayak and sail on the rivers and lakes.

Lara went back to the cottage for a rest. It had been a tiring run-up to the second Spectacular and putting her feet up while Flynn and his team did their thing was very appealing. He came back at half-past nine, looking tired but as rakishly handsome as ever.

'Right,' he said, kissing her but not sitting down. 'I think a little glass of something fizzy is called for. Shall I fetch it from the fridge?'

Lara hesitated, the butterflies in her stomach taking flight again as they had several times that evening and over the past few days. 'Um. I think it will have to wait a while.'

'Are you not in the mood to celebrate, then?' asked a puzzled-looking Flynn.

'Oh, I definitely am in the mood to celebrate, just not with champagne or any form of alcohol. In fact, the booze is going to have to be put on ice for quite some time.'

He stared and then his jaw fell a little. 'Are you . . . are you trying to tell me something or am I way wide of the mark?'

'I am trying to tell you something.'

'You mean . . . you mean—'

'That it's time we also found our own place to live away from the castle. A one-bedroom cottage is never going to be big enough.'

He let out a whoop. 'Oh, Lara. Are you sure? Are you all right? How long have you known?' He raked his hands through his hair. 'Why didn't you tell me? I mean, how far along are you?'

She burst out laughing, so full of relief at his obvious happiness that she could have taken off. 'I'm pregnant, not ill, and I'm ten weeks-ish, according to the doctor. I didn't want to say until I was sure and I also wanted to wait a little while.'

He swept her into his arms and kissed her, murmuring 'Lara, Lara, Lara' over and over, as if he couldn't think of a single other thing to say.

'So, you're pleased? To be a dad – again?' she asked.

'Pleased? I'm bloody ecstatic and I'm going to wrap you in cotton wool until the baby is born. Oh my God, I can't believe it. A half-sister or brother for Molly. The baby will be Esme's uncle or auntie. Now that *is* weird.'

Lara laughed. 'One more thing to get used to but, after so many, I think we'll take it in our stride.'

Imogen had taken a job as manager of a holiday-lodge village up the coast so she could spend more time with Molly, Esme and Brenda. They'd extended Brenda's house, with Flynn doing the electrical work.

Molly was back at college, had passed two A levels, and was going to start her degree at the nearest university.

The chalice had been left as it was, with the agreement of Belle, Fiona, Henry and Hattie, because, as Fiona had pointed out, 'That flaw is part of its story now. Nothing stays the same. Nothing is ever perfect.'

Sitting with Flynn's arm around her, with a crackling fire warming her toes and the new life growing inside her, Lara was certain that her story was turning out to be as perfect as she could ever wish for.

Acknowledgements

Thank you so much for reading *All We Want For Christmas*. I do hope you've loved the story of Lara and Flynn as much as I enjoyed writing it. It was so much fun to live in a castle for a few months – even if Ravendale was only fictional.

My main source of information for this story – apart from visiting lots of castles – was my friend Moira Briggs, who has been a guide at several large historic properties. It amazed me to learn just how many people are needed to run such places and I loved hearing all the behind-the-scenes tales. Needless to say, all the incidents featured in this book are fictional, although there are a few she told me I wish I could have included . . .

I also want to give a big thank you to the members of my Facebook group, who, when I put out a plea to anyone who was a biker, responded magnificently. As avid readers, they are also great at coming up with scenarios. I'd like to give a particular mention to Sarah Hills, Tracy Burrington Brown and Susan Hodson.

While I have all the fun of writing my books, they wouldn't reach you without a brilliant team behind the scenes, including my editor, Claire Simmonds, who is a joy to work with and full of creative ideas. I also want to thank the brilliant production team of line editor, copy editor, production manager and proofreaders.

Then there are the vital people who make sure readers hear about my book and get it into the shops and onto your e-readers – which is no mean feat these days. Thank you so much to Lucy Hall, Hana Sparkes, Issie Levin and the indefatigable Century sales team.

This year, I will have been writing fiction for twenty years, and for almost all of them, I've been with my brilliant agent, Broo Doherty, who is also a very special friend.

I'd also like to thank the friends who help to cheer me on, commiserate when needed and are always ready to help: the Party People, the Coffee Crew and my lovely Friday Floras. And to my best mate, who I've known since I was eleven, Janice Hume – thank you for your friendship, cat memes and stocking my books.

When I started this story, I'd recently become a nanna for the first time and the topic of being a grandparent was very much on my mind. By the time you read this, my granddaughter will be over eighteen months old, but I had to have Esme stop growing at some point.

To my parents, my daughter, Charlotte, her partner, James, and little Romilly – thank you for bringing such joy and fun into our lives. And to John: you deserve a medal. ILY.

Don't miss the latest summer romance
from the million-copy *Sunday Times*
bestselling author Phillipa Ashley

A Wedding Under the Cornish Sky

Pre-order now!

Loved *All We Want for Christmas*?

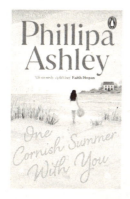

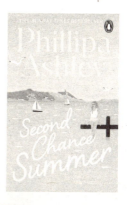

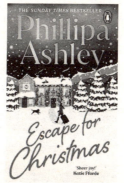

Discover more from the
million-copy *Sunday Times* bestselling author

Available in Paperback, eBook and Audio

Sign up to
Phillipa
Ashley's
newsletter for all the latest news, exclusives and giveaways!

www.penguin.co.uk/authors/298314/phillipa-ashley